KU-763-725

A FAR WILDER MAGIC

ALLISON SAFT

Orion

ORION CHILDREN'S BOOKS

First published in Great Britain in 2022 by Orion Children's Books
First published in the United States in 2022 by Wednesday Books,
an imprint of St. Martin's Publishing Group

1 3 5 7 9 10 8 6 4 2

Text copyright © Allison Saft, 2022
Cover illustration copyright © Em Allen, 2022
Map illustration © Rhys Davies, 2022

The moral right of the author has been asserted.

*All characters and events in this publication, other than those clearly
in the public domain, are fictitious and any resemblance to
real persons, living or dead, is purely coincidental.*

All rights reserved.
No part of this publication may be reproduced, stored in
a retrieval system, or transmitted, in any form or by any means, without
the prior permission in writing of the publisher, nor be otherwise circulated
in any form of binding or cover other than that in which it is published
and without a similar condition including this condition
being imposed on the subsequent purchaser.

A CIP catalogue record for this book
is available from the British Library.

ISBN 978 1 510 11075 5

Printed and bound in Great Britain by Clays Ltd, Elcograf S.p.A.

The paper and board used in this book
are made from wood from responsible sources.

Orion Children's Books
An imprint of
Hachette Children's Group
Part of Hodder & Stoughton Limited
Carmelite House
50 Victoria Embankment
London EC4Y 0DZ

An Hachette UK Company
www.hachette.co.uk

www.hachettechildrens.co.uk

C01 072 509X

A FAR

WILDER

MAGIC

ALSO BY
ALLISON SAFT

Down Comes the Night

For those with impossible dreams
and for those who feel dreaming is impossible.

There is so much waiting for you on the horizon.

DUNDEE CITY COUNCIL

LOCATION
CENTRAL CHILDREN'S

ACCESSION NUMBER
C01 072 509X

SUPPLIER	PRICE
aok	£7.99

CLASS No.	DATE
82391	4/6/22

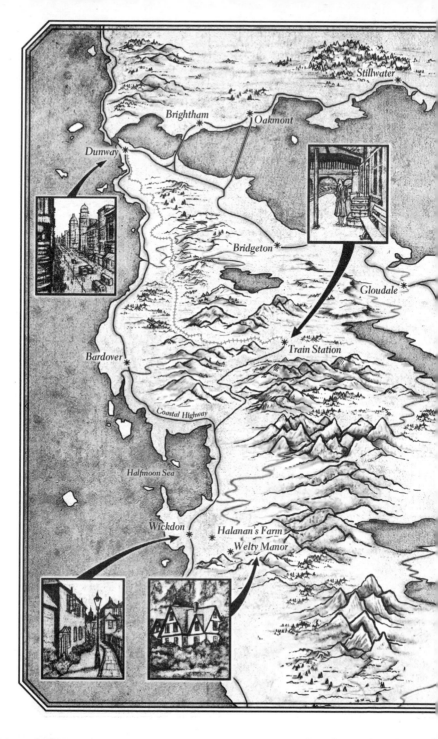

Stillwater

Brightham

Oakmont

Dunway

Bridgeton

Gloudale

Train Station

Bardover

Coastal Highway

Halfmoon Sea

Wickdon

Halanan's Farm

Welty Manor

Placerdale

to Dartmere

Rt. 88

DUNWAY BAY

Maywood

Riverside

Rt. 47

NEW ALBION

1

argaret shouldn't be outside tonight.

It's too cold for mid-autumn—the kind of cold that catches even the trees out. Just yesterday morning, the leaves outside her window burned in the sunlight, red as blood and gold as honey. Now, half of them have gone brittle and dropped like stones, and all she sees are the hours and hours of work ahead of her. A sea of dead things.

That's exactly the kind of thought Mrs. Wreford would scold her for. Margaret can almost hear her now: *You're only seventeen once, Maggie. There are far better ways to waste it than keeping that damn house, believe me.*

Fact is, not everybody can afford to fritter away seventeen. Not everybody *wants* to be like Jaime Harrington and his friends, cliff diving and drinking cheap moonshine after work. Margaret has too many responsibilities for nonsense like that—and more importantly, no firewood. Since it ran dry two days ago, the cold has made itself comfortable at Welty Manor. It waits for her out there in the night, and it waits for her inside, leering from a hearth full of white ashes. As much as she dreads splitting wood right now, she hasn't got any good prospects. It's freeze now, or freeze later.

The last of the day is bleeding out over the mountains, dribbling gutted-red light onto the yard. Once the sun sets completely, it'll only get colder. She shivered herself sleepless for hours last night, and now everything aches like she's been folded up in a shoebox. Procrastinating on her least favorite chore isn't worth feeling like this again tomorrow.

Freeze now it is.

Tugging her mother's old cloche hat over her ears, Margaret steps off the porch and trudges through the fallen leaves to the backyard, where the woodpile hunches beside a rusted wheelbarrow. The rainwater pooled in its basin is silvered with too-early frost and reflects a hazy glimmer of the bruised-dusk sky. As she reaches up to take a log from the pile, she catches a glimpse of her own drawn face. She looks as exhausted as she feels.

Margaret sets the log on the chopping block and grabs her maul. When she was young and wiry, she had to throw all her weight behind every downswing. Now, letting the blade fall is easy as breathing. It whistles through the air and sinks into the wood with a *crack* that sends a pair of crows fluttering from their perch. She adjusts her grip—then hisses through her teeth as a splinter digs into her hand.

She inspects the blood welling in the creases of her palm before licking it off. Cold settles into her wound, and the dull taste of copper coats her tongue. She knows she ought to sand the handle down before it takes another bite out of her, but there's no time. There's never enough time.

Normally she would've prepared better for the winter, but her mother's been gone for three months now and the chores have piled up. There are windows to caulk, shingles to replace, pelts to prepare. It'd be far easier if she learned alchemy like her mother always wanted, but no matter how hungry or desperate she gets, it will never come to that.

People say alchemy is many things. To the most pragmatic of scientists, it's the process of distilling matter into its essence, a means to understand the world. God-fearing Katharists claim it can purify anything, even men. But Margaret knows the truth. Alchemy is neither progress nor salvation. It's the stench of sulfur she can't scrub out of her hair. It's packed suitcases and locked doors. It's blood and ink on the floorboards.

She'll survive without it until her mother comes home—*if* she comes home. Margaret smothers that thought as quickly as it arises. Evelyn travels often for her research, and she's always returned. She's just taking a little longer than usual is all.

Where are you now?

Years ago, when she still had the heart for it, she'd climb to the roof and try to imagine she could see for a thousand miles, straight into all the fantastical places that called Evelyn away from her. But no matter how hard she tried, nothing ever materialized. All she ever saw was this: the worn, dirt road down the mountainside; the sleepy town glowing as faint as a firefly's belly in the distance; and past the golden fields of rye and bentgrass, the Halfmoon Sea that glitters black as a star-filled night. The gift of imagination skipped her over, and Wickdon is all she knows. She can't envision a world beyond it.

On a night like this, everyone will be huddled against the cold, simmering chowder and tearing open loaves of brown bread. The image stings, just barely. Being alone suits her fine—better than fine. It's only the grim prospect of boiled potatoes for dinner that invites jealousy. Her stomach rumbles just as the wind sighs against the back of her neck. The still living leaves sway overhead, hissing like the roll of the tide.

Hush, they seem to say. *Listen.*

The air goes terribly, eerily still. Gooseflesh ripples down her arms. Seventeen years in these woods, and they've never frightened her before, but right now, the dark sits thick and wrong on her skin like a sheen of cold sweat.

A branch snaps at the tree line, loud as gunfire. Margaret whirls toward the sound, maul raised and teeth bared.

But it's only Trouble, her coonhound, standing there. He looks both majestic and ridiculous with his oversized ears pricked and his fur shining copper-bright. Margaret lowers her weapon, the blade thudding against the frozen earth. He must've slipped out the front door when she wasn't paying attention.

"What're you doing out here?" she says, feeling foolish. "You scared me."

Trouble wags his tail absently, but he's still straining toward the woods and quivering with focus. He must feel it, too—the crackling in the air like a brewing storm. It makes her crave the weight of a rifle in her hands, not a maul.

"Leave it, Trouble."

He hardly spares her a second glance. Margaret sighs with exasperation, her breath steaming in the air. It figures she can't compete with a scent. Once he grabs ahold of one, he won't let it go for anything. He's as good a hunting dog as ever, even if he's stubborn as an ass half the time.

It strikes her then how out of practice they both are—and how much she misses the thrill of the hunt. Mrs. Wreford is right, in her way. There *is* more to life than preserving this crumbling manor, more to waste her seventeenth year on than surviving. But what Mrs. Wreford will never understand is that she's not keeping this house for herself; it's for Evelyn.

Before she leaves for a trip, she always says the same thing: *As soon as I get what I need for my research, we'll be a family again.* There's no sweeter promise in the world. Their family will never truly be whole again, but Margaret cherishes those memories from *before* more than anything. Before her brother died and her father left and alchemy burned up all her mother's tenderness. She holds them close like worry stones, turning them over and over in her mind until they're worn smooth and warm and familiar.

Every week, the four of them would go into Wickdon to buy their groceries, and without fail, Margaret would ask her mother to carry her home. Even when she'd grown too old for it to be reasonable, Evelyn would scoop her up and say, "Now who let you get so big, Miss Maggie," and kiss her until she shrieked with laughter. The world would go hazy and dappled with sunlight as she drowsed in her mother's arms, and although the walk home was five miles, Evelyn never once complained and never set her down.

Once Evelyn finishes her research, things will be different. They'll be together, and they'll be happy again. *That* is something worth putting her life on hold for. So she hefts her maul and splits the log again. As she bends over to collect the kindling, a chill slithers down her collar.

Look there, says the wind. *Look.*

Slowly, Margaret lifts her gaze to the woods. There's nothing but darkness past the windblown tangle of her hair. Nothing but the whispering of the leaves overhead, louder and louder.

And then she sees it.

At first, it's barely anything. A wisp, drifting boatlike through the underbrush. A trick of her addled mind. Then, a set of round, unblinking eyes shine out of the darkness. A tapered snout follows, the shadows sliding off it like water. Like the creep of fog over the sea, a white fox as big as Trouble stalks into the moonlight. Margaret has never seen a fox like this before, but she knows exactly what it is. An ancient being, far older than even the redwoods that tower above her.

The hala.

Every child in Wickdon is raised on legends of the hala, but the first time she heard one outside her home was the moment she realized her family was different. The Katharist church paints the hala and its kind—the demiurges—as demons. But her father told her that nothing God made could be evil. To the Yu'adir, the hala is sacred, a carrier of divine knowledge.

It won't hurt you if you show it respect. Margaret goes perfectly still.

The hala's gaze is solid white, pupilless, and she feels the weight of it like a blade at the back of her neck. Its jaw stretches open, a warning gape that makes something small and animal within Margaret cry out. Trouble's hackles rise and a snarl rumbles out of him.

If he attacks it, it will tear his throat out.

"Trouble, no!" Desperation roughens her voice, enough to break the spell on him. He rounds on her, ears flying and clearly bewildered.

And before she can process it, before she can even blink, the fox is gone.

Her breath shudders out of her. The wind echoes her as it combs through the leaves with a brittle, shimmering sound. Margaret staggers to Trouble, drops to her knees in front of him, and flings her arms around his neck. He smells disgusting—the yeasty stench of wet dog—but he's unhurt and that's all that matters. His heart beats in time with hers, the most beautiful thing she's ever heard.

"Good boy," she whispers, hating the hitch in her voice. "I'm sorry for yelling. I'm so sorry."

What just *happened*? As her thoughts clear, relief melts into a single, terrible realization. If that beast is here in Wickdon, the Halfmoon Hunt will soon follow.

Every autumn, the hala emerges somewhere in the coastal wood. And there it stays for five weeks, terrorizing its chosen territory until it vanishes again on the morning after the Cold Moon. No one knows exactly why it lingers, or where it goes, or why its power grows stronger with the waxing of the moon, but the wealthiest people of New Albion have made a national sport of its appearance.

Tourists pour in for the weeks of fanfare leading up to the hunt. Hunters register alongside alchemists in hopes of becoming the hero who slays the last living demiurge. And on the night of the Cold Moon, they set out on horseback to pursue the beast. There's alchemical power in circles, and legend has it that a demiurge can only be killed beneath the light of a full moon. Anticipation makes the hunt all the sweeter. Participants and spectators alike are more than willing to pay in blood for the honor of hunting the hala at its peak. The more destructive it is that season, the more thrilling the chase.

The hunt hasn't come to Wickdon in nearly twenty years, but Margaret has heard fragments of stories traded at the docks. The baying of hounds driven mad by its magic, the crack of gunfire, the scream of horses torn open but still alive. Since her childhood, the hunt has been nothing but a blood-soaked myth. The fare of true New Albian heroes, not country girls with Yu'adir fathers. It's never been *real*. But now it's here.

Close enough to register. Close enough to win.

The thought of disappointing her father pricks at her, but what does she owe him now? Being half-Yu'adir gives her no claim to kinship with the hala. Besides, maybe killing it for a noble cause is the most respect she could pay it. Margaret has no interest in hearing her name sung in pubs; she's never craved anyone's recognition but her mother's.

When she closes her eyes, an image of Evelyn silhouetted against the sun fills the darkness. Her back to the manor, suitcases in hand, her hair a golden ribbon unfurling in the breeze. Leaving. Always leaving.

But if Margaret wins, maybe it'll be enough to make her stay.

The grand prize is money, glory, and the hala's carcass. Most hunters would treat it as a trophy, a thing to be stuffed and mounted. But Evelyn needs it for her research on the alchemical magnum opus. According to her mother, long-dead mystics theorized that if alchemical fire were to incinerate a demiurge's bones, the prima materia—the base substance of all matter—would remain. From that divine ether, an alchemist could forge the philosopher's stone, which grants immortality and the ability to make matter from nothing.

The Katharist church considers any attempt to distill the prima materia heretical, so hardly any New Albian alchemists but Evelyn conduct research on it. Creating the stone is her singular, solitary ambition. She's spent years hunting down the few manuscripts that explain how to do it, and three months ago, she left the country to pursue another lead. But now the hala—one of the last missing pieces of her research—is here.

Trouble wrenches out of her grip, startling Margaret from her thoughts.

"Oh no you don't." She grabs greedy fistfuls of his ears, then places a kiss on the top of his head. He cringes. Margaret can't help smiling. Tormenting him is one of her few pleasures in life.

Trouble shakes his ears out indignantly when she finally releases him, then dances out of her reach. He stands there, regal head lifted, tongue lolling, one pink ear turned inside out. For the first time in days, she laughs. He does love her; he just hides it well, the proud, dramatic thing. But Margaret loves him plainly and far more than anything else in the world.

The thought sobers her. Trouble is a brilliant hunting dog, but he's not young anymore. Risking his safety for some foolish notion like joining the hunt isn't something she's willing to do. She's got no time to prepare, hardly enough money to pay the entry fee, and no connections to any alchemists she can trust, not that any of them can be trusted. Only two-person teams—one marksman and one alchemist—can participate.

Besides, there's only one surefire way to kill a demiurge that she knows of. The alchemy it requires . . . She'd sooner die than see someone try it again.

Even if there was another method, it wouldn't matter. If anyone found out a Yu'adir girl entered the hunt, they'd make her life a living nightmare. She's only survived this long by keeping her head down. *It's better this way,* she thinks. Better to quickly cut the throat of this fragile hope instead of letting it languish like a wolf in a snare. Margaret knows, deep as marrow, how this story ends. What happens to people who crave things beyond their reach. Maybe in another life, she could dream. But not this one.

Chasing after that fox will bring her nothing but ruin.

2

Wes awakens to the sharp pain of his forehead smacking into cold glass.

As the taxi lurches out of a divot in the road, the sputter of its engine sounds suspiciously like laughter. He swears under his breath, rubbing away the ache blooming in his skull—and then, with the very edge of his sleeve, dabs gingerly at the drool gathered in the corner of his mouth.

It's not as though the pothole-ridden streets of the Fifth Ward are any better maintained, but this is absurd. He was told it takes an hour and a half to reach Wickdon from the train station, and at this rate, he'll consider himself lucky if he's not concussed by the time he arrives on Evelyn Welty's doorstep.

"You awake back there?" Hohn, his driver, grins at Wes in the rearview mirror.

Hohn is a middle-aged man with a kind, wind-chapped face and a blond mustache that spirals neatly at its ends. It cost Wes nearly everything he'd saved to pay him for the ride. If all goes to plan, his return trip to the city won't be for a good long while.

"Yeah," Wes says with forced cheer. "It's rustic out here, huh?"

Hohn laughs. "You won't find many cars or paved roads outside Wickdon, I'm afraid. I hope you know how to ride."

He does not. The only horses he's ever even seen are enormous, plodding beasts that pull carriages full of rich people through the park. Besides, he's pretty sure taking riding lessons would earn you an ass-kicking if anyone found out. Kids from the Fifth Ward don't *ride*.

This apprenticeship is already testing him, and it hasn't even started.

No complaints, he reminds himself. Winding up in the middle of nowhere is his own damn fault. Mostly. Partly. Slightly.

In the past two years, Wes has burned through more alchemy teachers than he can count. The first time he was expelled, Mam was outraged on his behalf. The second time, outraged *at* him. The third, dismayed into silence. And so it continued in a cycle of anger and bewilderment, until last week. When he told her he was leaving for Wickdon, she sat him down at the dinner table and clasped his hands so tenderly, it took a second for him to remember to be annoyed. "I love you, a thaisce. You know I do. But have you considered maybe you're not cut out to be an alchemist?"

Of course he'd considered it before then. The world is determined to remind him that the son of Banvish immigrants will never be a real alchemist. But he'd never considered it more than in that moment, when he could see all the new gray shot through his mother's hair.

Sometimes, he thinks it'd be easier to take a job anywhere, doing anything, so that his family wouldn't have to suffer anymore. Ever since Dad's accident, Wes has watched Mam come home from her extra shifts and soak her hands in hot paraffin wax every night. He's watched his youngest sister, Edie, get thinner and his oldest sister, Mad, grow harder. Most nights, he lies awake wondering what's *wrong* with him: why he can't retain more than half of what he reads, why he can't seem to translate unfamiliar words on the page into meaning, why no amount of natural talent or passion can compensate for his "limitations" in his teachers' eyes. It all makes him sick with anger and worry and self-loathing.

Wes knows he possesses some innate magic, a type of enchantment more banal than alchemy. When he speaks, people listen. And while that gift has landed him all his apprenticeships, it's done nothing to help him keep them. Once he fails a single written exam, he can see the vindication in his instructors' eyes, like they've been waiting for him to confirm their suspicions. They always say the same thing: *I should've known better than to take a chance on you.* It's obvious what they mean by that gritted-out "you," even if they never come out and say it. *Banvishman.*

There are no more well-connected alchemists left in the Dunway metropolitan area whose apprenticeships he hasn't already flunked out of—or else advertise NO BANVISH NEED APPLY. None except for Evelyn Welty, who makes her home in a town so small, it isn't even on the map.

Nerves and car sickness send his stomach roiling. He rolls down the window and tips his face toward the wind. Overhead, the sky sprawls so blue and wide open, he thinks it may drown him if he breathes in too deep. In the city, everything is solid gray: smog and concrete and the flat slate of the bay. But here, the landscape changes quicker than he can track it. Along the coast, jagged bluffs wear coats of prickly scrubs and blue wildflowers. Just beyond it, evergreen trees bleed into towering redwoods. Wes can't help thinking the firs' upturned branches look like middle fingers.

When he told the neighbors where he was going, they offered the same brand of platitudes. *Small town! Not much going on there!* or *Well, at least the air will be clean.* Of all the well-intentioned comments he got, the promise of clean air is definitely the biggest lie. There's no pollution, sure, but it tastes like salt—and worse, with the hundreds of seals lounging on the sand, it reeks of sunbaked seaweed and rotting fish.

So much for provincial charm.

It occurs to him that the wind may ruin his hair, which he carefully slicked back this morning with the patient coaching of his sisters. He closes the window again and checks his reflection. Still intact, mercifully. Christine and Colleen practically welded it into place with God knows how many dollops of gel. Nothing, not even a single misplaced hair, can ruin his shot at a perfect first impression.

"So, Hohn," Wes says, "do you find yourself out this way often?"

"When I was a younger man, I did. They've got the best foxhunting in the country. In fact, if rumor holds true, Wickdon's hosting *the* hunt in the next few weeks. It'll be first time that's happened since I was your age."

Most of the country goes wild for *the* hunt, as Hohn put it. Wes doesn't consider himself a particularly devout practitioner of the Sumic faith, but the whole concept of the Halfmoon Hunt is a little sacrilegious even for his loose morals.

In Sumic tradition, it's said that God carved demiurges from his own flesh. They're his divinity incarnate and, as such, deserve both fear and respect. Mam buries their statues in potted plants and lovingly mounts their icons on the walls. Sometimes, she'll mutter a prayer to them if she's lost something, or ask them to put in a good word with God since he's apparently too busy to field requests himself. Katharists would call that kind of reverence idolatry at best and heresy at worst. It's the same scorn that draws them to immigrant neighborhoods to throw stones through Sumic churches' stained-glass windows.

Wes can't be sure what Hohn thinks or which version of God, if any, he worships. He doesn't want to be thrown out of the cab yet, so he says, "Is that right?"

"There's not much other reason to come here, if I'm honest." In the mirror, Wes catches Hohn's appraising look. "I don't mean any offense, son, but you don't look like the foxhunting type. What brings you here?"

"None taken. I'm an alchemist." Hohn makes an appreciative noise. "Evelyn Welty's apprentice, actually," Wes adds.

It's only a lie by omission. Master Welty never exactly responded to his letter, but he knows she's a busy woman. Every apprenticeship he's landed, he's landed by pleading his case in person. Even though he's terrified his charm has run dry, he thinks he can manage it one last time.

"Evelyn Welty, eh? Best of luck to you."

From his understanding, he'll need it. "Thanks."

He's heard all the rumors by now. None of her students make it longer than two weeks. Ghosts prowl the halls of Welty Manor at night. Evelyn subsists on nothing but photosynthesis. Etcetera. In his experience, all alchemists are a little odd. Technically, anyone can perform alchemy, but it takes an obsessive kind of person to *want* to. They spend years dissecting arcane texts and cramming their heads full of the chemical composition of thousands of objects. To take something apart, you have to know exactly how it's made. Or maybe it's the sulfuric fumes that eventually drive all of them mad.

In any case, it's nothing he can't handle. If it must be, it will be a war of attrition. Wes has never lost a battle of wills.

At last, they arrive in civilization. Nestled in the curve of a valley, Wickdon is just as quaint as promised. Light from jewel-cased streetlamps glazes the cobblestones, and colorful cottage homes and storefronts line every block. Shop windows strung with lights glow softly through the mist, illuminating tempting displays of baked goods, produce, and more taxidermy and ammunition than a war museum. What strikes him most is the complete lack of alchemy labs. In Dunway, you can find at least two per block: jewelers peddling enchanted rings, restaurants serving food that promises a variety of psychological effects, workshops filled with metalworkers who produce the strong, lightweight steel that makes New Albion's military so formidable.

As the car rumbles through the town center, people crack open their front doors and draw back their curtains to watch it pass. A pretty young woman sweeping the street in front of her shop meets his eyes. On reflex, he breaks into a wide, easy grin. She turns away from him as if she didn't see him at all. Wes presses his face miserably to the glass, which stings with a cold as bitter as the rejection.

It unsettles him more than he cares to admit. Back home, people know him. They like him. *Everybody* likes him.

At least they did before this streak of failures.

Although he keeps expecting to stop at one of the charming, brightly painted homes along the way, they continue down the main drag toward the edge of town. The warm lamplight grows sparser, and the wheels jolt sharply as the car rattles onto a dirt road. Wes looks out the back window, where Wickdon glimmers through the exhaust.

"Say, where are we going?"

"Welty Manor. Evelyn lives a bit out of the way."

They follow the switchbacking road into the mountains, the engine whining in protest as they ascend. Wes finds the courage to look out over the town in the distance and the endless expanse of the ocean beyond it. The water has darkened to a steely gray, streaked with sunlight the color of rust. The redwoods soon blot out the view, and after driving a few nauseatingly winding miles beneath their looming height, the car creaks to a halt in front of a lonely redbrick house.

Thick sheets of ivy climb the siding, and flowering weeds spill from the garden beds like beer overflowing from a tap. The splintered wooden gate lists on its hinges, less a welcome than a plea for help. Welty Manor looks like the kind of place people weren't meant to live—the kind of place nature clearly wants back.

Wes climbs out of the cab and peers up at the lamp burning in the second-story window. It's far colder than it was when he left Dunway this morning—way too cold for it to be natural, even with the sea air and the altitude. And it's too still, too quiet. Already, he misses the noise of Dunway. The constant drone of traffic and the soft tread of their upstairs neighbors' footsteps. His mother puttering in the kitchen and his sisters bickering in their room. Here, the only sound is the distant cawing of some bird he can't name.

Before he lets himself get too despondent over his new home, Wes helps Hohn unload his things from the trunk. All his worldly possessions fit into three scuffed suitcases and a satchel with a frayed strap.

"Need help getting inside?" Hohn asks.

"Oh, no. Don't trouble yourself. I'll be just fine on my own."

Hohn fixes him with a skeptical look, then fishes a card from his breast pocket and hands it to him. Hohn's name and telephone number are printed on the front in faded ink, as if it's been in his jacket for years. "If you need a ride again . . ."

"I know who to call. Thank you, sir."

Hohn claps him on the shoulder and squeezes. It's so fatherly, Wes has to swallow a sudden pang of grief. "Alright, then. Good luck."

With a tip of his hat, Hohn climbs back into the cab and backs it out of the driveway. Darkness slithers into the empty space left by the headlights, and as it enfolds him, Wes feels as though someone is watching him. His gaze anxiously drifts toward the upstairs window, where a ghostly silhouette flickers in what looks to be firelight.

Get yourself together, Winters.

He climbs the groaning porch stairs until he is face-to-face with the red front door. He's never been so nervous in his entire life—but then, he's never had so much to lose. For good measure, he smooths back his hair and smiles at his reflection in the window until the sweaty look of desperation slides off his face. Everything is in place. He's rehearsed his speech a thousand times. He's ready. He broadens his chest, raps on the door, and waits.

And waits.

And *waits.*

Wind gusts through the veranda and shreds through his threadbare coat like it's nothing. It's cold as hell out here, and the longer he stands here shivering, the more convinced he is that there's something lurking at the tree line. The way the dead leaves rattle in the yard sounds too much like whispering for his taste. He hears his name, hissed over and over again.

Weston, Weston, Weston.

"Please answer," he mutters. "Please, please, please."

But no one is coming. Maybe Evelyn isn't home. No, that can't be right. The upstairs light is on. Maybe she didn't hear him. Yes, that must be it. She didn't hear him.

He knocks again, and again, the seconds stretch eternal. What if she never answers the door? What if she moved? What if she's *dead,* rotting beside that dully burning lamp? He's been so single-mindedly determined, it never occurred to him that he could fail. This scheme was always a gamble—one he now realizes may leave him stranded and alone. The thought is so upsetting, so humiliating, he pounds more urgently on the door. This time, he hears footsteps on the staircase.

Finally.

The door swings open, and his breath leaves him in a rush. There is a girl standing in the threshold. In the dim porchlight, she looks like something out of a poem he read in school before he dropped out—or like one of the aos sí from his mother's stories. As his eyes adjust, her face comes into view blink by blink. Her hair, unbound and golden. Her skin, white as cream. Wes braces himself for the inevitable ache of love.

But nothing comes. On closer inspection, the girl is far less beautiful and far more severe than he expected. Not to mention incredibly unfashionable with her long hair and longer hemline, if his sisters' catalogs are to be believed. She regards him with thin, downturned lips and heavy eyelids, like he is the most loathsome, unimpressive thing to ever crawl onto her property.

"Can I help you?" Her voice is as flat and cold as her stare.

"Are you . . . Are *you* Evelyn Welty?"

"No." The word plunks mortifyingly between them.

Of course she isn't Evelyn Welty. She looks no older than him. He barrels onward. "Is she at home? My name is Weston Winters, and—"

"I know what you're here for, Mr. Winters." Judging by her tone, she must assume he's here to sell her snake oil. "My mother is away on a research trip. I'm sorry to have wasted your time."

It's so final, so bleak, he's still reeling by the time she begins to close the door. "Wait!"

She leaves the door cracked open barely an inch, and even from here, he can see the tension coiling in her shoulders. He still hasn't overcome his panic, but he can make this work. While Evelyn's absence is a setback he didn't anticipate, he can figure it out once he's settled. His very last shot at an apprenticeship rests in her daughter's hands, and by the look of her, she doesn't care a whit what he wants or what happens to him. She gives him nothing to work with. No smile, no warmth. She only stares at him blankly with eyes the color of whiskey. They snatch every coherent thought from his mind.

"So." He grasps for something, anything, to keep her talking. "What *do* you think I'm here for?"

"You're here to ask for an apprenticeship."

"Well, uh . . . Yes, actually. I wrote to her a few weeks ago, but she never responded."

"Then maybe you should learn to read between the lines."

"If you'd just let me explain—"

"I understand the situation already. You think you're deserving enough that your own lack of planning is no barrier to you getting what you want."

"That's not . . . !" Wes takes a deep breath. No good will come of losing his composure. "I think I've given you entirely the wrong impression. Let me start over."

She says nothing but doesn't move, which he decides to take as encouragement.

"I want to be a senator." He pauses, trying to gauge her response. She is, however, still disconcertingly stoic. "My best shot of making it is through an apprenticeship. My family doesn't have any money, and I had to drop out of school, so there's no way I'm getting into a university unless it's with a letter of recommendation."

Only alchemists can become politicians. It's not a law, really, but it may as well be. Although New Albion fought for its independence as a democratic nation almost 150 years ago, the aristocracy lives on in disguise. He can't think of a single politician elected in the last ten years who isn't a university-minted alchemist with a Katharist pedigree and a network of other wealthy, overeducated people. As a Banvishman, he'll never have the pedigree, even if he converts, but he can claw his way to electability otherwise.

"There are plenty of alchemists in the city," she says. "You didn't need to come so far."

There's no point in asking how she knows he's from the city. His accent always gives him away. "Every alchemist in the city has turned me down." It hurts to admit it, but he does. "Your mother is my last chance. I don't have anywhere else to go."

"If you've already failed out of another apprenticeship, you won't survive this one. My mother won't tolerate mediocrity."

"I'll work harder than any student she's ever had. I swear it."

"Mr. Winters." Her voice is a closing door.

Think, Winters. Damn it, think. This is his chance. His *only* chance. Since this girl clearly doesn't go in for pity, he doubts it'll do him any good to give her the sob story about wanting to fight the injustice and corruption in their government. So he'll do what he does best. Not even she can be immune to charm.

He leans against the doorframe, and in his most seductive voice, he says, "Maybe we could talk more inside? You must be lonely out here by yourself, and I've come an awfully long way . . ."

The door slams inches from his nose.

"What the hell? You can't just . . . !"

But she did. Wes threads his hands into his hair and pulls until it all comes loose from the gel. What does his appearance matter now? Everything he owns is scattered in the driveway. His savings are running thin, and while Mam gave him some money as a goodbye present, he can't bring himself to touch it. She's sacrificed too much already—and all for him to find out Evelyn Welty isn't even here.

No, he can't go home. He'll die of shame.

Mustering up the very last of his dignity, Wes stalks off the porch to collect his things. Three suitcases. One satchel. Two hands. Five miles back to town. No matter how he does the math, it's not looking good. As thunder rolls in the distance, he searches deep inside himself for the optimism his oldest sister, Mad, often mocks him for.

Spoiled, she calls him. *Idealistic.* Like that's a *bad* thing.

For a moment, he's not in the middle of nowhere, shaking with cold and frustration. He's back in Dunway, sitting with Mad on the fire escape while she burns through her third cigarette.

Last night, they said their grim goodbyes. He remembers thinking he didn't really recognize her anymore. She sheared all her hair off a few weeks ago, trying too hard to turn herself into one of those fashionable girls with their bobbed hair and drop-waist dresses. She smelled like smoke and liquor from her late shift at the bar, and she was obviously pissed off at him again, even if she wouldn't admit it. The little things tipped him off. The boxer's hunch of her shoulders, the chain smoking, the mean glint in her eyes when she finally deigned to look at him.

He hates it—hates that his own sister thinks he's selfish, that this apprenticeship will end up like all the others, that he's doing this only to avoid his responsibilities. But ever since Dad died, it's been like this. Resenting each other more than they love each other. He doesn't know how they got here. All he knows is that they were talking, and then they were yelling—as much as you can yell in whispers, anyway. Edie was asleep on the other side of the wall, and neither of them wanted to go through the whole bedtime ritual again.

You're such an asshole, Wes, she finally snapped. *You're not entitled to everything you want just because you want it.*

Mad can misread his intentions all she wants, but alchemy has never been a dream he's pursued at his family's expense. It's to give them a way out—to give every family like theirs a better life. Now more than ever, Wes wants to prove her wrong. He'll march the five miles back to town if it kills him. And if he has to, he'll come back here day after day until he cracks Evelyn Welty's daughter.

3

By morning, Wes has inured himself to the sting of rejection and prepared himself for the misery of trudging five miles through the cold *again*. He's come too far to let a girl like Evelyn Welty's daughter stop him. Once she lets him eke out more than three words about his family's situation, she won't turn him away. That is the only kind of alchemy he has mastered: spinning words into gold. Turning girls' hearts soft.

He combs his hair into submission again, scraping it back from his face with a coat of gel, and buttons himself into the shirt Christine ironed for him. Apart from his tidied hair, he looks like himself in the mirror. But he doesn't want to look like himself. He wants to look like an alchemist—someone who gets taken seriously.

He loosens the tie knotted at his throat and fastens it again, tighter, crisper. When he's suitably armored, he meets his own reflected gaze. "You can do this. You have to do this. If you have to tell Mam you got sent home again . . ."

He can't even finish the sentence. If he sees his sweet mother's disappointed face even one more time, he'll die. Instead, Wes imagines himself as Evelyn's beloved apprentice—how her face will glow with admiration when he demonstrates his competence. He imagines reading her gushing letter of recommendation, one that will launch his long and storied political career. He imagines himself in an expensive tailored suit—not some ready-made one Mad ordered him—and a blue satin tie, standing behind a podium draped with New Albion's flag. From there, he will give a moving speech, and press cameras will pop until all the world sparkles. He will smile at blushing, beautiful women, and everyone who doubted him, every person who called him a slacker or a drunk or an illiterate Banvishman, will line up to shake his hand. Then, he will work to dismantle their nationalistic government from the inside out.

When he lets himself dream, the future is rosy.

The cold reality of the present, however, crashes down on him as soon as he steps out of the Wallace Inn. A fat water droplet slides off the eaves and spatters on the top of his head. Shuddering, he tugs on a flat wool cap and drags his suitcases into the street.

It rained overnight, and the cobblestones are glazed like cakes, shining and silver in the early morning light. The air has frothed into a mist as fine and shimmering as crinoline, veiling the cheerfully bright buildings that line the square. At his back, a brittle wind rises off the ocean and carries with it the taste of salt. Wes slips into the gathering crowds and dodges slow-moving cars as their wheels churn puddles into muck. People step out of cabs with suitcases and pour in from the docks alongside carts full of gleaming silver fish.

So Hohn's information was good. The hunt has arrived.

Sumic guilt has kept him from ever thinking too hard about entering, but it's impossible to avoid completely given the sheer amount of magazine articles and radio programs it inspires. It's practically the national pastime, at least for people classy enough to care about things like foxhunting—or "patriotic" enough to take pride in New Albion's settler-colonial history. Over the next five weeks, rich people across the country will come by the thousands to participate in all the dog shows, horse races, and galas that lead up to the hunt. By the end of it, the spectators will have exhausted themselves between emptying their wallets and slavering for the death of the hala. Only the most dedicated of them will follow the hounds on horseback instead of nursing their hangovers. At least a few of them will die for getting too close.

It's quite a spectacle, from what he hears. The excitement already buzzing in the air is intoxicating—the fame that winning promises even more so—but throwing away his morals to join the hunt isn't what he came here to do.

Wes keeps his pace brisk as he breaks onto a sleepy side street. People in thick coats stand outside their houses, raking the leaves knocked loose by the storm. Their gazes follow him as he passes, and he can only assume it's because he looks ridiculous dragging around his luggage like a pack mule. At the end of the block, a man surrounded by burlap sacks stuffed with tree litter waves him over.

He leans on the handle of his rake. "You lost? You won't find any hotels this way."

"No, sir. Not lost, sir." Not exactly, anyway. Wes prays he doesn't try to give him directions. They'll inevitably slip through his mind like water through a sieve. The difference between right and left often escapes him. "Just on my way to my teacher's house."

"Going to Welty Manor, then? You've got a ways to go."

Wes tips his face to the rain-swollen sky. "It's a beautiful day for a walk."

The man smiles good-naturedly, but Wes sees the pity behind it clearly. "Tell you what. I'm only here this morning to help Mrs. Adley with her raking, but home's the same direction you're headed. Wait here a minute."

This is how Wes finds himself in the back of Mark Halanan's cart, perched on a seat made of luggage and empty grain sacks. A chicken sits in his lap, clucking contentedly, while Halanan guides his pony along the road to Welty Manor. Wes tries his hardest not to look ill from the jittering lurch of the wheels on the unpaved road.

"Been a while since we had a student of Evelyn's in town," Halanan says. "They come and they go."

"So I've heard." It comes out grimmer than he means it to. The

fragile confidence he mustered earlier already feels as though it's splintering.

Halanan must sense his souring mood because he changes the topic. "You timed your arrival well. Registration for the hunt starts soon. You planning on entering?"

"Me? Oh, I don't know."

"Opening ceremony'll be in two days. After that, you've got another two weeks to decide."

"Honestly, I don't think I'm cut out for it."

"You're sensible. That's good."

Wes doesn't think anyone has ever called him "sensible" before. He likes the sound of it. "Thank you. I try to be."

"In any case, I'm glad there're folks out there who'll do it for God and country or what have you. Someone has to kill it. The damn thing's a menace."

Wes braces himself for a sermon. "What do you mean?"

"Take a look for yourself."

As they crest a hill, Halanan gestures toward a field. It's a stretch of tall, golden rye that feathers into grass so noxiously green it's the color of absinthe. A church in the plain Katharist style and a mansion rest side by side on a bluff, and it takes all his self-control to bite his tongue. Wes has never seen anything so extravagant.

There's an impressive orchard of apple trees on the manicured grounds—but the air itself seems to hang wrong off their boughs. Blackened, curled leaves wave like tattered flags on their branches. As the cart rolls past, he smells rotting fruit and sulfur. Nearly all of the apples have dropped from the trees, swelling and oozing like boils. The sight strikes Wes cold. He's always known the hala is fearsome, but it's only ever been a bedtime story Mam would tell them in her darker moods, mostly to scare them into saying their prayers.

It's here to remind us that God is always with us. She would pause for dramatic effect and then add, pointedly: *Always watching.*

Sumic doctrine claims that the demiurges taught humans alchemy. He's never fully believed it. But the telltale smell of sulfur in the air and the dusting of black powder on the grass are both by-products of an alchemical reaction. He still isn't convinced the hala is God made flesh, but now he knows that anyone who signs up for the Halfmoon Hunt is at least halfway mad.

"You're telling me a fox did *that*?"

"No ordinary fox for no ordinary foxhunt." Halanan pauses. "The kids are excited. This is probably the most action Wickdon's seen in their lifetimes. All they're thinking about is running hunt-paces and shooting their guns, but they haven't seen what I have. It's a field that's been destroyed today, but it'll only get worse as the hunt draws nearer."

"It'd be easier to shoot it now," Wes mutters. But even if it were possible to kill it before the Cold Moon, victory means nothing if it isn't hard-won. The more dangerous the monster, the more glorious the hero who slays it.

"Where's the fun in that?" Halanan asks wryly. "Outrage lets them feel good about what they're doing. The organizers compensate us for the trouble of letting it run amok, but some losses you can't fix with money. When I was your age, a baby got snatched from its crib. Nobody wanted to win it more than the father that year, but it always gets away in the end."

"Oh." He cannot think of anything to say in light of something so awful.

"Anyway, if you ask me, the Harringtons can afford a bad harvest this year. A little tragedy is good for the constitution."

Wes isn't entirely sure he agrees, although he doesn't know a thing about the Harringtons other than their apparent wealth. But he's endured enough lectures to know when to keep his mouth shut.

They ride in comfortable silence until the manor and its low wooden fence appear. It looks even gloomier and lonelier in the day-light, swathed in the silvery fog rolling down the mountainside. Halanan clucks at the pony and stops her in front of the gate.

Wes hops out of the cart and begins to collect his things. Once he's sure he hasn't forgotten anything, he extends his hand to Halanan, which he takes with a solemn nod. "Thanks for the ride."

"Good luck to you, Mr. Winters. Say hello to Maggie for me, would you? Tell her to come by if she needs anything."

Maggie. That must be the girl he saw last night—Evelyn's daughter. Dread coils within him. "Will do, sir."

"And a word, son? Don't try anything funny. That girl has enough troubles as it is."

It's an odd, ominous warning. But despite his kind face, Mark Halanan is a large man and he's looking at Wes as if he expects an answer. "Y-yes, sir."

Apparently satisfied, he grunts and prods his pony into motion. She sighs, her hooves squelching in the mud as she trots resignedly back toward Wickdon.

Once again, Wes is left alone.

The manor leers down at him, but he won't be daunted. In the cold light of day, there is nothing that can reasonably drive him away. He has the advantage of time and renewed desperation.

Wes unhitches the gate and makes his way through the overgrown yard, the sweet scent of decay curling up from the fallen leaves. Ten paces away from the wraparound porch, a guttural yowl shatters the silence. He freezes, and just then, a red dog rounds the side of the house and charges straight for him. Beneath his fear, there's a glimmer of relieved acceptance. Mauling, he thinks, is a preferable death to shame.

Purely on instinct, he drops his bags and throws up his arms. The next thing he knows, he's sprawled out on his back with the air whooshing out of his lungs. Cold mud seeps into his shirt. The dog pins him to the ground, dribbling thick threads of saliva onto his face. The stench is ripe, but before he can wipe it off, the beast leans down and licks him square on the mouth.

"Okay," he growls. "Get off me."

He shoves the dog off, which does nothing to deter it. It circles him, tail wagging, and snuffles at his hair with the investigative fervor of a radio-program detective. Slowly, Wes sits up and takes stock of his shirt. Twin paw prints are stamped in mud on his chest. He groans. There goes his good second impression.

"Trouble!" It's a girl's voice, one the dog responds to immediately. They both turn toward the sound.

And there, only a few yards away, is Evelyn's daughter—Maggie—with a hunting rifle in her hands. As his blood thickens with dread under her cold assessment, Wes suddenly isn't confident that death by Maggie Welty's hand would be any easier to bear than his mother's disappointment.

After an agonizing moment, she flips the safety catch on her gun and props it against the side of the house. She's wearing wide-legged overalls stuffed into work boots and a thick denim jacket rolled up to her elbows. When she peels off her gardening gloves, Wes notices the ring of dirt around each bare forearm, like bracelets of burnished gold. The sudden dip in his stomach puzzles him. Even with the hazy sunlight drenching her hair and pooling in her eyes, she still isn't beautiful.

Maggie offers her hand to him. He doesn't want to smear mud all over her, but judging by her impatient expression, she doesn't mind. He clasps her wrist and allows her to pull him up. They're the same height, nearly nose to nose. Wes decides this means she is tall rather than the alternative. Their breath mists in the air between them.

"You came back," she says.

"Yes, I did. I'm . . . Well, you know who I am. You must be—"

"As I said last night, my mother isn't here. I'm sorry about your shirt." With that, she turns on her heel.

"Hey, wait a minute!" He trots after her and catches her by the elbow. She whirls around so quickly and with such accusation in her eyes, he stumbles a step backward. "Sorry."

Her silence is answer enough. Maggie clutches her arm like he's burned her. Mud streaks her from elbow to wrist, and a lock of her hair has escaped the severe hold her tortoiseshell clip has on it. All her soldierly composure from before has vanished. Like this, she looks hollowed out and wild.

"Please, Miss Welty. I need this apprenticeship."

"Do you?" He hears the same disdain that dripped from Mad's voice when she said, *You're not entitled to everything you want just because you want it.*

Frustration wells up within him. Is everyone so determined to think the worst of him? "Look, I'll go stand on the other side of the fence if it makes you feel better. Can we talk for a minute?"

Maggie purses her lips like she's measuring the worth of every inch of space that arrangement would put between them. "Fine."

Thank God. Wes blows out a sigh. "I know you don't owe me anything and you have every reason to doubt me, but I swear I can handle it. I won't screw this up. Please let me stay here until your mom comes back. If she's going to turn me away, I need to hear that from her myself." The silence stretches out until he can't bear it any longer. "I can't pay you rent, but I can help around the house. Chores, errands—anything. I'll do anything. *Please.*"

"Go home, Mr. Winters."

But he *can't.* How can he possibly make her understand?

Fine. If she wants a reason, the one behind his ambitions, he'll bare his soul to her. Covered in mud and dog saliva, he has no dignity left to lose. Wes pulls his wallet from his pocket. Inside, there's painfully little money and a picture of his family, back from when Dad was still alive. Even now, it twists his guts to see them together, all of them pulling ridiculous faces. In the center, Dad and Mam look as smitten with each other as they do in their wedding photos. Wes is smiling so wide it's a grimace, balancing Edie on his hip. Christine's planting a kiss on his cheek, Colleen's in the middle of shouting something, and Mad is, well, Mad. She's standing off to the side, looking deliberately miserable, but the fond glimmer in her eyes betrays her.

They all look so happy.

Wes swallows the sudden flood of grief and shoves the photograph toward Maggie. "This is my family. My dad's gone, and . . ." And what? There are no words sufficient to finish that sentence. *Now we have no money. Now we're barely making it. Now the whole world is duller, and I don't think I'll ever be as good a man as he was.* "My sisters who are old enough work. So does my mom. I don't have the education or connections right now to get a job that'll support them, so I just need a chance. A real chance. I'm trying to do right by them."

Maggie stares at the photo for a long time with a beetle-browed expression. When she looks up at him again, her stare is hard, assessing, like she's trying to boil him down to his very soul. It makes him feel like a curiosity at a curbside menagerie. For the first time, he notices how big her eyes are. She looks like a very serious owl.

"Fine." She hands the photograph back to him. "Come in."

"Really?" He can't help it. He's grinning like a fool. Even the humiliation of trying to collect all his bags can't dampen his mood. "You have no idea how much this means."

Maggie snatches a suitcase out of his hand, and Wes understands that's about as much reciprocity on his enthusiasm as he can hope for.

He follows her into the house and almost gasps at the size of it. He's greeted by a double staircase that arcs elegantly upward to a central landing. A chandelier hangs above it, weighed down with more crystals than a rich lady out to the opera. On one side of the foyer is a carpeted room filled with plush chairs and lined from floor to ceiling with bookcases. On the other is the kitchen, where worn copper pots and pans hang from the ceiling above an island countertop.

Although Welty Manor is grander than anything he's ever seen, it's still as sad inside as it looked on the outside. The dirt streaking the bay windows lets in enough sunlight to illuminate the dust motes swirling around them. The wooden banisters are scratched and dull, dog hair covers the dark upholstery, and dishes loom in unstable towers on the countertops. A few small slivers of the house have been scraped clean. The floor looks freshly swept, and the sink has been recently caulked. Clearly the mess isn't for a lack of trying.

Maggie is already hauling one of his suitcases up the stairs. He trails after her as close as he dares, down a narrow hallway lined with cobwebbed sconces. She opens the last door on the right and ushers him through.

Wes stifles an embarrassing cry of excitement. The bedroom is *huge*. He's never had so much space to himself, since he's always shared a room with his sisters. It smells musty, but he can work with musty. As he drops his suitcases at the foot of the bed, the floorboards cough up a cloud of dust. He sneezes so loudly, Maggie flinches.

"Excuse me," he says, sniffling.

She goes to the window and struggles with the latch. It cracks open a few inches, showering flecks of crumbly paint onto the sill. Fresh air sighs in through the gap. It seems like no one's been in here in years, but Wes can see this room hasn't been unoccupied forever. A few alchemy textbooks lie forgotten on the floating shelf above the writing desk. There's even a pleated skirt hanging in the open closet. His stomach twists into knots. How many others have come before him?

How many have actually made it?

"You can stay here until she comes back," Maggie says, "but I wouldn't bother unpacking unless you want to leave something behind when she throws you out."

"O ye of little faith. I can be very convincing." There's something endearing about her skeptical expression that makes him feel like it's worth pushing his luck. "You let me in here after all, didn't you?"

"I did." She frowns at him. He can't tell if she's more bothered by him existing in her space or by his once-white shirt, which looks like he's dunked it in coffee. He feels clammy with it clinging to his back. "Give me your shirt. I'll wash it."

Heat floods his face. "What? Right now?"

Part of him isn't shy at all. It's hard to be when he grew up with four sisters. He was still young and impressionable when he would fall asleep to the lullaby of Christine and Mad gossiping over their latest conquests. But the other part of him—the part that has fum-blingly half-undressed for only a handful of girls in the dark—wants to shrivel up on the spot. Maggie Welty looks like the kind of girl who would sooner kill a man than admire one.

She slices through his mortifying fantasy with her curt reply: "Of course not. I'll wait in the hall."

"Right. Of course not."

God, he's such an idiot.

As soon as she slips into the hallway, he makes quick work of unfastening his tie and stripping off his sopping shirt. The door hangs open a sliver, and he catches a glimpse of Maggie in profile. Wes is startled by the anxious, almost guilty look on her face. As if she feels his eyes on her, she glances over. Her lips part, and pink spreads across the bridge of her nose. Her gaze flickers from his bare chest to his face, and they sustain eye contact for one excruciatingly long second. The tips of his ears burn with embarrassment. On a normal day, he'd feel rather pleased with himself, but her owlish eyes strip him even more naked than he already is. Maggie breaks first, turning her head to bore holes into the wall instead of his bones. It's a greater relief than it should be.

Wes clears his throat and passes his shirt through the crack in the door. "Thanks."

She snatches it from him and folds it over her arm. "The bath-room is just across from you."

As she stalks down the hall, Wes has the sinking feeling he'll never get that shirt back. Christine's going to be so mad at him for losing it.

The amenities of Welty Manor are not at all what he expected. For a renowned alchemist's home, it has surprisingly few alchemical modifications. Wes finds not even a single shower tile infused with magic, not a stitch of alchemized thread on the bedclothes. Appar-ently neither Evelyn nor Maggie values home improvement much.

Only the wealthiest people can afford alchemized goods if they aren't alchemists themselves. With the knowledge he's cobbled together from his apprenticeships, Wes performs transmutations to make his family's life easier: simple things, like imbuing Mam's favorite knife with essence of quartz to keep it sharp, or enchanting Edie's blanket with pepper seeds so that it's always warm. Maybe he can convince Maggie of his usefulness if he tinkers with a few things around the house.

After he showers off his failures and puts on an unstained shirt, Wes goes to find Maggie. The air in the hallway is like honey, thick and golden in the afternoon sunlight. He pauses in front of a wall filled with framed photographs, each one covered in a film of dust. An older, colorized one strikes him first. In it, a blond woman sits beside a wooden boat on the shoreline, grinning back at the photographer. Evelyn, he assumes. With her thin lips and wide brown eyes, she looks so much like Maggie it's uncanny. But where Maggie is dour, Evelyn is positively radiant.

A few frames over, there's Evelyn again, beaming at a tall, bearded man. Each of them carries a yellow-haired toddler on their hip. His favorite of the bunch is one of Maggie. She's maybe seven years old, glaring at the camera with a toy gun slung across her shoulder and a puppy with overlarge ears curled up at her feet. Evidently, she's always looked like a tiny adult.

Guilt sours his stomach. Even though these photos are displayed here, it feels like an intrusion to examine them. Wes can't reconcile these happy moments with what he knows of Welty Manor and its inhabitants. This place has the same solemnity as a closed-down fair. To him, home is a loud, cramped place, warm with bodies and stove heat and love. But Welty Manor is none of those things.

Ghosts, not people, live here.

As he makes his way downstairs, he sees Maggie in the kitchen with her back to him. Her long, golden hair is swept up on top of her head with a tortoiseshell pin. A silver necklace chain glimmers against her pale skin, and beneath her wispy baby hairs, a line of black dirt encircles her neck like a collar. It oddly fascinates him. Maggie's shoulders bunch around her ears, and Wes darts his eyes away just as she tilts her head to look at him.

She's holding a knife in one hand and a whole chicken in the other. Tufty white feathers are scattered on the countertop like snowdrifts. He cringes but keeps his smile easy. Things are *different* in rural New Albion, after all, and he's determined to not ruin things with her this time. Third time's the charm.

Wes pulls out a chair at the counter and sinks into it. Like everything else in this house, it whines in protest. "Thanks for letting me stay."

"Sure." She doesn't look at his face but at the ends of his hair audibly dripping onto the countertop. Self-consciously, he leans back and smooths his hair out of his face. Water runs down his neck, as cold as ice in the chill of the house.

He clears his throat. "Can I do anything to help?"

"No."

It's becoming increasingly obvious that Maggie doesn't like him very much. It's unfair since *he's* the one who should be disinclined to speak to *her* after the dog incident. Yet here she is, acting like he's an imposition. He resists the urge to remind her that she's the one who invited him in.

"I'll keep you company, then," he says brightly. When he receives no response, he asks, "Do you know when your mom will be back?"

For a moment, she looks flustered. Then, she separates the chicken's head from its body with a crack of her knife, and it's as if he imagined that her face changed at all. "Two weeks."

Two weeks. It's certainly not ideal, but he can manage that. He'll just have to find a way to fill the time until then—and keep his family from finding out that he hasn't exactly secured the apprenticeship he assured them he already had.

"Where is she?"

"On a research trip."

The way she clips her words indicates that's all she has to say on the matter. He fishes for another topic. "I was looking at the portraits on the wall upstairs. Was that your brother I saw?"

"Yes."

"And where is he? With your mom?"

Maggie freezes. Sunlight winks off the blade of her knife. When he meets her eyes, they're empty. "He's dead."

"Oh. I'm so sorry."

What is *wrong* with him? Will he ever say the right thing to her? He flounders hopelessly for a few moments before she says, "Do you have any other invasive questions you'd like to ask, Mr. Winters?"

"No," he says quietly.

"Then dinner will be ready at six."

Wes knows a dismissal when he hears one. The steady *thunk, thunk, thunk* of her knife pursues him up the creaking stairs.

Shut into the spare bedroom, he searches for something, anything, to keep his thoughts from spiraling into humiliated despair. It only takes a minute to find an alchemy textbook on a shelf, one he's been assigned so many times, he has the first chapters memorized. At the end of chapter two, there's an exercise—still incomplete, which says a lot about how long its previous owner lasted here—that explains how to disintegrate paper with alchemy.

Tear out the sheet on the next page and follow these simple steps!

Next to the condescending instructions, there's a meticulously annotated transmutation circle. It's a basic formula for nigredo, the process of decomposition—the first of three types of spells alchemists can perform, along with purification and reconstitution. Transmutation circles trap the energy used in an alchemical reaction inside their borders, and while the runes inscribed within them are more idiosyncratic, broadly, they allow an alchemist to bend that energy to their will.

Maybe it's boredom, or maybe it's nostalgia, but Wes finds himself tearing out the sheet along its perforated edge and rummaging for chalk in the writing desk's drawer. The first time he tried this spell, it took him twenty minutes to replicate the transmutation circle. Now he's done it so many times, he has the entire array sketched on the floor in five. He places the paper in the center and focuses his attention inward.

Any alchemist worth their salt considers themselves a scientist, but there's something inexplicable about alchemy, too. Something magical. *At the core of each of us,* one of his first teachers said, *there is a spark of divine fire.*

As Wes imagines cupping that flame in his hands, his palms grow warm and his mind goes perfectly still. He presses them to the floor, and as his energy flows into the circle, the paper ignites with white fire. It blisters and curls in on itself until all that remains is the lingering smell of sulfur and a pile of black ash. Alchemists call it caput mortuum: dead head, the worthless remains of an object. But the essence of that paper lies buried within the ashes, waiting for him to distill it and harness it for an enchantment.

A successful transmutation usually leaves him flushed with awe, but right now, staring down at the caput mortuum, all he feels is bitterness. All he sees is Maggie's infuriatingly blank face when she told him, *My mother won't tolerate mediocrity.*

Wes slams the textbook shut, his face burning with shame. What does Maggie Welty know about him, anyway? He's not a mediocre alchemist; he's only undereducated. If someone measures his progress with *anything* other than how well he performs on a written test or regurgitates alchemical theorems, he'll thrive. He just needs someone to believe in him.

Hours later, he lies awake, shivering and restless. Nights in Dunway are hot, sometimes unbearably so, but here, the draft slipping through the windows is bitter cold. The shadows sharpen against the ceiling, and bare branches scrape against the window like nails. At home, he'd fall asleep to the sound of his mother snoring. To the couple downstairs arguing. To Colleen singing along with the sputtering old radio in the kitchen. But here, the silence is too loud without anything to dampen it, and the swatch of sky outside his window presses too close without skyscrapers to hold it back. The new moon leaves the night dark and full of stars he's never seen before.

He's homesick, and it's only been a day. How pathetic can he be?

Wes doesn't think he's cried in years. Not since Dad's funeral. Not since Mad told him to suck it up for the younger ones. He feels frustratingly, tantalizingly, close to it right now. But as he blinks through the burning behind his eyes, he wonders if he's even capable anymore. Maybe he's finally succeeded in hollowing himself out.

If he can't grieve his father or his impossible dreams without hurting his family or himself, what other choice does he have but to keep things light? To dazzle people so they can't look for the cracks? He's survived this long by letting everyone believe he's selfish and shallow. It's better that way. No one knows how to hurt you if you always play the fool. No one can truly be disappointed in you if they don't expect any better.

4

It takes fewer than forty-eight hours to regret her decision.

Weston Winters is a nightmare. He is everywhere, even when he isn't in her line of sight. Margaret finds him in his muddy shoes in the foyer; in all her mother's textbooks strewn across the kitchen table; in the strange, incomprehensible notes he leaves himself scattered around the house. It's maddening. Margaret keeps her world simple, small, orderly. She likes her solitude and the mindless, soothing rhythm of her chores. She likes Trouble's silent, easy companionship. She likes going about her life uninterrogated. Weston, apparently, enjoys nothing more than noise and chaos. Or perhaps it's her distress he relishes. She can't be certain. All she *can* be certain of is how misplaced her sympathy was.

Misplaced enough to lie to him.

Although it wasn't a lie, exactly—just a hunch. In truth, she has no idea if her mother will be back in two weeks or two years. But soon enough, Evelyn will catch wind that the hunt has come to Wickdon, and she will return. Margaret wants to believe that. She *has* to believe that, even though belief has never served her before.

But now she's paying the price for dragging Weston into this fantasy and shackling him to this house alongside her. Time has eroded the memories of her mother's former apprentices. Now, she remembers everything all too well. How shaven hairs always sullied the pristine white of her bathroom sink, how she'd have to take all her showers cold, how her mother's shouts would echo through the house. *How can you be so idiotic,* she'd say, *so useless, so—*

No, she hasn't missed sharing her space. Although she was alone before Weston arrived, at least she was comfortable. She was safe. Nothing about him is safe. If he has one redeeming quality, it's that he has the courtesy to sleep until noon. She has a precious few hours of solitude before he emerges from the guest room like a bear from its winter slumber, which means she can make breakfast in peace. Margaret stands in the kitchen, wrapped in a knit shawl, and sets oats and coffee on the stovetop to boil.

"Good morning, Miss Welty."

Margaret startles, and the spoon flies from her hand. It lands in the pot with a dull squelch, spattering oats all over her—and more dismayingly, the stovetop, which she just scrubbed clean last night. Blinking her tacky eyelashes, she heaves a thin sigh through her teeth. "Good morning."

"Oh, sorry! I didn't mean to scare you."

Margaret turns around, and there he is, languid and bright as a summer afternoon. He's got his blade of a grin turned on her, and his black, bed-mussed hair sticks up in every direction, the shape of a wildfire. In all her life, she's never known anyone to be so constantly underfoot. Trouble often deploys a similar tactic, and really, that's only when he's attention starved or she's a few minutes late serving his dinner. Weston Winters is as good as having a second, less well-behaved dog.

Determined to ignore him, she focuses more intently on the bubbling porridge. His looming presence rolls over her back like the tide, carrying with it the smell of his aftershave. It reeks of citrus and bay leaves and rum. *He probably doesn't even have to shave,* she thinks dourly, if only to stave off the image of him half-naked in the doorframe—and the strange kinship that came with it. Despite the boyish roundness of his face, the hard lines of his body clearly demonstrate that he knows hunger like her. The impression of his hand on her arm is like a burn she's still nursing.

He peers over her shoulder. "Smells good."

The prospect of sharing a meal with him, of enduring another round of his badgering about where her mother might be or which of her relatives is tragically gone, is enough to make her skin crawl.

"You think so?" She pours the porridge into a chipped white bowl, then shoves it into his hands. "It's all yours."

"Oh. Thank— Wait a minute. Don't you want this?"

"I'm not hungry." She brushes past him, grabbing her rifle off the kitchen table.

He follows her to the front door. "Will you be back late? I heard the opening ceremony is today."

Margaret's blood runs cold. "Opening ceremony?"

"Yeah, Halanan told me about it the other day. The opening ceremony for the Halfmoon Hunt?"

She knew it was coming; the first sighting of the hala signals the beginning of the season. She hoped there'd be more time until someone else saw it—or maybe, foolishly, that it'd leave and make her decision to avoid the hunt less painful. But knowing the hunt has officially arrived worsens the unease she hasn't been able to shake since she looked into that beast's horrible eyes. She's felt fear like that only once before, but the memory of it lies in shards on the floor of her mind, too sharp to pick up and handle. The sulfuric smell of alchemy, her mother's blond hair puddled in blood, the sob she loosed when Margaret dragged her from the lab, and . . .

"Miss Welty?" Weston's voice sounds garbled. "Are you alright?"

Her vision goes hazy, like she's looking at him from the bottom of a frozen pond. *God,* she thinks, *please don't let this happen now.*

She curls her fist into the coat on the rack, focusing on the weave of the cotton to steady herself. She is here, *here,* and Weston is staring at her as though she's about to take flight. She can see the pale thumbprint of her face reflected in his gaze, the way her eyes flash like a cornered animal's. It's almost too humiliating to bear.

Margaret snatches her coat and shrugs it on. "I'm fine. I have to go."

Wes looks puzzled, if not somewhat relieved. "To the ceremony?"

"Sure." She needs air, not crowds and fanfare, but it's easier to agree with him. Margaret has lived with her fear long enough to know how to cope with reminders of it. She's learned how to abandon herself, to let numbness slip in and possess her like a ghost. *It's nothing,* she told Mrs. Wreford the first time she witnessed it. *Just a little episode.*

It's been so long since anyone else has watched her do it.

"Can I come with you?" he asks.

"Do what you like, but I'm not waiting for you."

"Fine." He glumly spoons porridge into his mouth. "I'll catch up with you later."

As soon as she makes it out the front door, the crisp autumn air washes over her and the panic coiled in her chest loosens. Alone, she can breathe easier. Sometimes it's hard to believe this house ever held more than one person.

After her father left but before the walls began rotting around them, her mother started taking students. Margaret had no love for them or their pleading, expectant gazes. It's almost laughable to think about how they would wheedle her for information. She held no secret key to her mother's favor. Nothing but alchemy holds any sway over Evelyn Welty anymore. Stranger or daughter, they occupy equal importance in the narrow breadth of her mother's world.

They came. They tormented her. But they never stayed long.

Weston, with his foppish hair and calculating smile, wouldn't last two minutes against her mother. He's lucky that she's gone. It's better to have his hopes quietly extinguished rather than thoroughly eviscerated. She thinks of him lingering in the doorway like an anxious hound, the spoon still hanging from his mouth. He looks kicked when disappointed.

Margaret sighs. Maybe she's been too impolite to him. It's not that she dislikes him. It's that she resents him for thinking he's immune to the corruption of alchemy. He seems kind enough now, but as soon as he tastes what it's like to pull at the very fabric of the universe, he will change. They all do in the end.

Margaret combs her fingers through the waist-high grass that lines the road to Wickdon. There are still deep, wet trenches from the car Weston arrived in. She toes the edges of them carefully, like she's hugging a cliffside, and the mud sucks eagerly at her boots with every step. As dense forest gives way to open hills, she can see cars zipping along the coastal highway and the boats docking in the harbor. Soon, they'll be overrun with tourists from around the country.

"Maggie."

She startles, her hand flying to her rifle strap. But it's only Mark Halanan leaning against his cart, which is half full of jars and crates of apricots. She'd been so trapped in her own head, she didn't realize she'd already reached the Halanans' farm. Sugarlump, his white pony, is already harnessed and looking incredibly put out over it. She does hate to work. She and Shimmer, Margaret's gray gelding, have that in common.

"Good morning," Margaret says, hating the quiet tremor in her voice.

She's still on edge, but if Halanan notices, he doesn't comment. Instead, he asks, "Want to give me a hand? I need to get my stall set up in town. I'll pay you handsomely in jams."

The Halanans have always been too generous to her, but it's easier to bear when they disguise their charity as payment. It stings, even after all this time, to know that he thinks of her as someone to take care of. *If there's one thing you have to learn,* her mother told her, *it's how to take care of yourself.* And she has learned that well. Wickdon is an effective teacher. Besides Mrs. Wreford, the Halanans are among the only people in town she can count on consistently for kindness. They've never hated her or her father for their Yu'adir blood.

Margaret manages to smile. "Alright."

They work in companionate silence while Sugarlump lashes her tail impatiently. Just as Margaret hauls the last of the crates into the cart, Halanan fixes her with a stern look. "So, is Winters behaving himself?"

"Well enough. He mentioned you'd met."

"We did, and I told him to watch himself. If he pulls anything funny—if he so much as lifts a finger to you—you say the word. I'll be up there faster than you can blink."

This time, her smile comes easy. "If he pulls anything funny, I'll shoot him myself."

Halanan shakes his head fondly as he helps her into the back of the cart. Margaret leans over the side as they rattle down the road, squinting against the wind as Wickdon comes into sharper focus. By the time they reach the town center, the streets are bustling with more people than she's seen in her entire life. The air thrums with the same energy as the night she saw the hala.

Anticipation.

For the first time, she feels lost in her own home—and this is only the beginning. By the day of the hunt, thousands more people will be packed into Wickdon's narrow streets. Along the main drag, everyone has pushed their storefronts from their shops to their porches. Mr. Lawrence has hauled his daily catch from the docks and laid out rows of silver-scaled fish and shining black mussels on a bed of ice. Mrs. Elling, surrounded by wooden carts full of apples, is spooning steaming spiced cider into paper cups.

People walk shoulder to shoulder, carrying woven baskets full of grapes and greens. They haggle and gossip as they buy wildflower bouquets and candies, each one bright as a polished stone. Although she hasn't indulged in years, the sweet, buttery smell of caramel stirs up memories. On festival days like this, her mother would give her brother, David, a handful of pennies and turn him loose. But she'd let Margaret guide her through the maze of market stalls by the hand, bending down so that Margaret could whisper what she wanted into her ear. That quiet kind of happiness feels so impossible now. Even if Evelyn were here, Margaret doubts she could've persuaded her to leave the manor.

When they finish setting up Halanan's stand, Margaret cranes her neck to see where the current of people leads. They eddy around the doors to the Blind Fox Pub. A cream-colored banner above the sign reads REGISTER HERE in bold, black letters. A pang of longing knocks her breathless, and she almost laughs at herself. Against all her better judgment, a small part of her still wants to register for the hunt. But *wanting* is exactly the problem. It's only ever hurt her.

Halanan follows her gaze. "You sure that's a good idea?"

"I'm only looking."

"Youth is wasted on the young," he mutters. "Go on and look if you must. I'll bring the jams by later."

The words "thank you" are barely out of her mouth before she shoulders her way into the crowds. She ducks inside the pub, inhaling the familiar scent of baking bread and bubbling chowder. The Blind Fox is cozy on a normal day, drowsily warm from the fire and filled with locals who come looking for a drink after work. But today, it's a more sophisticated crowd. Women in pearls and wide-legged pantsuits. Men in herringbone suits and two-toned oxfords.

She supposes she shouldn't be surprised to see them. Avid hunters breed expensive hounds and buy expensive guns and keep stables full of expensive horses. Foxhunting is a display of both wealth and sportsmanship, which makes it the national pastime for the New Albian elite. And only the best of the best would travel this far to stake their lives on *the* foxhunt of the year. She's more than once heard Jaime Harrington, the mayor's son, boasting about long, arduous days of joyriding his mare through open fields and drinking sherry at nine in the morning.

Margaret makes her way to the corner of the bar and takes a seat. From her vantage point, she has a clear view of the entire place. Although it makes her feel small and foolish for hoping, she searches for her mother's golden hair among the crowd.

"You going to order anything, or are you just going to sit there?" Reginald, the bartender, glares at her as he dries a pint glass.

"Depends on how much you feel like charging me today." He always inflates the prices for her. Before he can bluster his way through a response, a voice cuts through the din of the crowd.

"In the beginning, there was the One."

A woman stands at the back of the bar, her gray curls wreathing her face like smoke. It takes her a moment to recognize Mrs. Wreford, the owner of the bar, when she looks like something ethereal and ancient in the sputtering firelight.

"The One was All, and All was the One, and All was within the One," she continues. "In his infinite light and love, he emanated the prima materia. It was chaos. It was everything and nothing, perfection and quintessence, an expanse of nothingness like dark water. But when God breathed over it, he created life.

"The first beings to emerge from that chaos were the demiurges. The first to awaken was named Yal. He knew nothing of God or where his power came from. He only knew that when he lifted his hand, the prima materia answered his call. As his siblings stirred, he said to them, *It is only us alone here, gods of this chaos. Shall we shape it as we see fit?*"

It never fails to strike Margaret how similar and how different this version of the creation myth is from her father's. The demiurges, so the Katharist story goes, fashioned the material world and ruled over it as tyrants. They imprisoned God's divine spark within matter and created humans, a pale mockery of him and a mirror of his own imperfections. When God realized what they had done, he punished them by trapping their souls in bestial forms. But the Yu'adir bible says that God created the material world with the loving attention of a sculptor. When he finished, he wanted to share his divine knowledge—the secret of the making of the universe—with his chosen people. So he scooped up of a handful of prima materia, poured it inside the hearts of ten pure-white beasts, and set them loose.

Whether they are a gift or a scourge, the demiurges have wrought destruction, and humans have slaughtered them for it throughout recorded history. Now all that remains is the most cunning of them: a fox that still prowls the western coast of New Albion.

"You like this story, don't you?"

Margaret stiffens at the sound of Jaime Harrington's voice. She turns to see him looming over her with one elbow braced against the back of her chair. He looks, as he always does, radiant in a tailored blue suit and a derby hat. He wears his father's money well. His coppery-blond hair is gelled flat against his head like a gleaming helmet, and his eyes are the clear blue of a wave shot through with sunlight. The cherubic red of his face, however, is marred by the cruelty of his smile.

"How do you figure?" she asks.

"Don't play dumb." A familiar, pious hatred burns in his eyes. "I know your twisted god is proud of making the world. Explains why your people are so materialistic, anyway."

Anger stirs within her, but she's practiced the art of non-reaction for too long to let Jaime rankle her. He's hated her for years. Once, she believed it was for something concrete and petty. Maybe the time she'd bitten him for stepping on Trouble's tail when they were children, or because he thought her strange for her silences. Now, she knows better. She's guilty of the crime of having a Yu'adir father.

If she scrapes at the bottom of her memories, she can conjure the rough shape of a chanted melody, the taste of bitter herbs and apple chutney, his simplified explanations of a bible written in a script she will never be able to read. It's hard to know if those fragments make up enough of her to give her the right to feel wounded by Jaime's barbs. But knowing little of her father's faith doesn't matter to people like Jaime; it matters only that her blood is "sullied." New Albion doesn't expel or massacre its Yu'adir like they do across the sea, but Wickdon has done its worst within the confines of the law.

"I'm the one who saw it first, you know," he continues. "Two nights ago, I saw it as it was destroying our fields."

If he truly saw it two nights ago, then *she* was the first to see it—and came away unscathed. Although he can't possibly know that, she scrambles to keep her face blank. Three years ago, there was a particularly violent hunt in Bardover, a town about fifty miles north of here. Over its five-week stay, the hala destroyed almost every acre of farmland, except for the orchard of the one Yu'adir family in town. The last she heard, the property's now unoccupied.

"What do you want, Jaime?"

"I'm just making conversation. The real question is what do *you* want? You've crawled out of your cave."

"I'm here to listen to the opening remarks, same as anyone else."

"Hello, Miss Welty—oh, am I interrupting something?"

Weston leans against the bar with affected nonchalance. He's wearing that old trench coat of his again. The fabric is faded and tattered, and careful stitches have preserved its life far longer than is kind. Worst of all, he insists on slinging it over his shoulders like a cape. It irritates her more than is probably reasonable. He looks ridiculous.

He's standing near enough to the open window that a soft breeze cards through his unruly hair, which drips from its ends with golden light. Margaret can't read his grave expression, but as he regards her from beneath his eyelashes, she notices for the first time that his eyes are a striking shade of brown, as rich and dark as the earth after it rains. Her heart gives an answering stutter.

"Mr. Winters," she says, "I see you found your way here well enough."

"I did. The people here are friendly." He lifts a bottle of wine in her direction, as if toasting her. She doesn't want to guess how he came upon that. "Are you going to introduce me to your friend?"

He sounds pleasant enough, but the cold glint in his eyes makes the unspoken meaning behind his question clear: *Is this guy bothering you?* Of course he'd have a hero complex. Margaret considers remaining silent just to spite him for his unwelcome intervention, but she can feel the malevolent glee practically radiating from Jaime.

Who is she to keep them from each other's throats? Reluctantly, she says, "This is Jaime Harrington."

Weston extends his hand toward him. "Weston Winters."

Jaime stares imperiously down the bridge of his nose until Weston, with a strained smile, tucks his hand back into his pocket.

"Wait a minute," Jaime says. "I think I see what's going on here. You two aren't entering the hunt together, are you?"

"Wha—"

"And if we were?" Margaret cuts in.

Weston gapes at her. She knows it's unwise to lose her composure like this, but she warns him to be silent with a sharp look.

Jaime's face grows splotchy with anger. "I'd say it's none of your business to be interested in and a dangerous thing besides. You've got nothing but that old gun and that old hound. You'd get torn to bits."

She itches to challenge him, but as much as it burns on the way down, Margaret forces herself to swallow her pride. What good would it do to fight him now? Why make herself a target for his amusement? "Thank you for your concern."

She relishes the look of disappointment on his face. Jaime will never win this game against her.

But then Weston smothers a laugh. He doesn't, however, manage to keep the insufferable smirk off his face—or out of his voice. "I'd be shocked if you fared much better. What, you're so afraid, you have to bully her out of competing?"

Margaret is going to kill him. Must he always *speak*?

The dangerous look in Jaime's eyes sharpens, but before he can get in another word, Mrs. Wreford's voice cuts through the silence. "For generations, the hala has destroyed our crops. Slaughtered our livestock. Killed our spouses and children. With the death of the hala comes the end of an era. One of you could be the last hero of humanity—and the first of New Albion—to slay a mythical beast."

The last word hovers in the air, ominous, before a grin brightens her face. "And, of course, a lifetime guest of honor here in Wickdon.

Not to mention the prize money—seventy-five dollars this year, thanks to our generous donors—and the hala itself. We're honored be hosting the 147th annual Halfmoon Hunt. Registration opens two weeks from today, and then the fun really begins. Thank you, everyone. Enjoy your stay!"

As conversations resume and beer sloshes out of taps, Jaime leans in until Margaret can feel his breath hot against her ear. "You hear that? A hero."

She hears his meaning plainly. *This isn't your heritage to claim.* True New Albian heroes are Katharists with neat family trees, only a few generations separated from the first colonists. The hunt isn't *for* a half-Yu'adir girl. It's for him.

Jaime unfolds to his full imposing height. "As for you, Winters, we treat people with respect in this town, so if you don't want trouble, I'd watch your mouth."

With that, he turns on his heel and disappears into the crowd. Margaret lets out a shaky breath. More than anything, she wants to pry out this anger from where it sits like a lit coal in her gut, to regain the control rapidly slipping through her fingers. But Jaime is *wrong.* An old gun and an old hound are all she needs to outshoot him. She's seen him time and time again at the range with his sloppy technique, made sloppier with alcohol. He's far too smug for his own good, and someone ought to take him down a peg. It ought to be her who does it.

But she can't.

Margaret craves certainty, safety. And with hunters traveling from all over the country, all of them with more time and money and gear than she could ever dream of, there are no certainties in this game. Even with the perfect dog and the perfect shot, she can't stake everything on some foolhardy dream. Especially not when she'd have to depend on an alchemist. No matter how much she misses Evelyn, that is the one thing she can't do.

"*As for you, Winters, we treat people with respect in this town,*" Weston says in a nasally voice. It doesn't sound much like Jaime, but if she weren't so annoyed with him, she might've found it amusing. "God, what's his problem?"

"That's how he always is, although he tends to be more pleasant if you don't provoke him."

Weston huffs. "I didn't provoke him. If anything, he provoked *me*."

"I don't need your gallantry."

"It's not about being gallant," he says defensively. "It's about having a spine. You were seriously going to let him talk to you like that?"

"Yes, I was. You can run your life how you'd like, but stay out of mine."

"Alright. Sorry." He has the good sense to look chastened. Slowly, he sinks into the barstool beside her. "What did he mean when he said, 'It's none of your business to be interested in,' anyway?"

Of course he'd pick at the one thing she wishes he'd forget. "Exactly what he said. Why? Are you interested in foxhunting?"

"What do you mean by interested?" he counters.

"Interested." She sighs when he gives her an agonized look. "You came to watch the opening remarks, didn't you?"

"I went where the people were." He pauses. "I couldn't participate even if I wanted to. My mom would kill me."

"Why?"

Guardedly, he says, "She thinks it's barbaric."

"And what do you think?"

"I don't know. Barbaric, maybe. High class, definitely. Sure, I want to be the guy who can afford to dress like Harrington does. I want to take a five-week-long vacation to hobnob with all the famous alchemists and show off in front of the whole country. But I guess it's none of my business to be interested in all that, either."

The bitterness and longing in his voice call to her. Is he saying that because he's poor or because he's an outsider like her? For a moment, she forgets to hold him at a distance. "What did you make of the story, Mr. Winters?"

"Huh? The one the old woman told? What's there to make of it?

It's the same story everyone tells. I saw what the hala did to the Har-ringtons' orchard, though, so it's alright in my book. Seems like a shame to punish it for that."

Although it's a more evasive answer than she hoped for, she finds herself smiling. "We may be in agreement."

"We are? Oh." Weston glances away sheepishly. "Anyway, are you going to register?"

"You heard Jaime."

A wolfish grin steals over his face. "But isn't it more fun to do the things people don't want you to?"

"Maybe."

"Maybe," he repeats skeptically.

"It's impossible. I don't have a partner, and I can't afford the entry fee. If my mother were home, I'd have more free time to earn some money, but . . ."

He makes a sympathetic noise. "Would you, though, otherwise?"

It's a stupid question if she's ever heard one. There is no world in which it is *otherwise.* But she can't deny such a way of thinking about the world is tempting. Margaret lets herself consider it. If her victory would make her mother stay? If it would make Jaime angry? If her fear wouldn't paralyze her? Yes. She would enter right now if she could.

Maybe it's not so stupid a question, after all.

"Yes, I would. Would you?"

Weston whistles. "I mean, can you even *imagine* what you could do with seventy-five dollars? I'd kill for that. Hell, I'd kill for the recognition. But I'll be plenty busy as soon as your mom gets back, and like I said, entering the hunt isn't really something someone like me . . ." He trails off, frowning. "Why?"

Margaret hadn't realized the implication of her question until now. She can't trust alchemists as a rule, but an alchemist she has under her thumb . . . Maybe, just maybe, Weston is the answer to her problems. He defended her from Jaime. He was desperate enough to promise her *anything* in exchange for staying at Welty Manor.

And if the photograph he showed her is any indication, he has a heart—at least for now.

Ask him. If she does, maybe his reservations will crumble. Although he's playing coy, he all but told her how badly he wants to win. *Why should we let people like Jaime say what is and isn't for us?*

But her tongue sits thick and useless in her mouth. She hardly knows him or if he's got any alchemical talent at all, and there's no guarantee he wouldn't take the fox from her the moment he got the chance. Even if no alchemists but Evelyn believe there's any use for the hala beyond killing it to test their skill, it's a trophy few would easily surrender. Besides, Margaret has only survived this long by making herself small, by needing nothing and no one. Wanting something for herself is bad enough, but the very thought of admitting she *needs* Weston feels like cutting her own throat. If he denied her now, it'd crush her.

"No reason," she says.

"Right." He leans back in his chair, as though he's searching for some intervention in the ceiling. "Well, I'm sure there are plenty of alchemists who'd register with you. So if it's only the money for the entry fee holding you back, why don't you give me some chores so you can free up your time? I did promise you I'd earn my keep."

Her stomach twists as a thousand different feelings seize on her. Mostly guilt that she's keeping Weston's hopes up—and fear that he's offering her the means to register. Can she actually go through with this? Thinking about entering is one thing. Committing is another entirely. She has everything to lose if she fails. The hala could kill her and Trouble both. She could spend all of her savings for nothing but disappointment. But if she does nothing, she doesn't think she can live with herself. She can't wait like a forlorn hound for Evelyn to return anymore. She can't keep making coals of her anger and swallowing them whole.

Girls like her don't get to dream. Girls like her get to survive. Most days, that's enough. Today, she doesn't think it is.

"Alright," she says.

"Alright?"

"I'll let you help around the house."

"Great." He pauses, and his smile turns wary, as if he's already bracing himself for her rebuttal. "If I'm really good, will you stop avoiding me?"

She grimaces—and her face must be bright red because he laughs. It's a strangely pleasant sound, unguarded and warm, when so many of his smiles are wicked and calculated. When was the last time someone laughed because of her?

"I'll consider it." With those words, some of the tension between them thaws.

Somewhere behind this slick act of his, Weston has a good heart. But that isn't enough for her to feel safe yet. She's been burned by "kind" people enough times to know hatred of the Yu'adir is a powerful poison. Still, registration doesn't open for two weeks. That gives her two weeks to determine if she can trust him and gather up the nerve to ask him. Two weeks to get together the entry fee. Two weeks until every eye in Wickdon will be on her. As purpose crystalizes within her, she feels more grounded, more solid, than she has in years.

Maybe she really has put her life on hold for too long.

5

Wes hisses as the splintered maul handle jabs him. Again. He's beginning to regret that he wasn't more discerning with the terms of this bargain. Four days ago, he was foolish enough to offer Maggie *anything* in exchange for room and board. Now, as the branches of the redwoods clatter like chimes in the wind, he thinks he'd do things differently. Everything about these woods gives him the creeps, from the silhouettes of the trees' broken arms to the insistent whisper of his name in the dying leaves.

The canopy's so dense he can scarcely see the flushed face of the sky, and the redwoods' trunks are so tall and straight they cage him in like prison bars. The darkness that unfurls between them is thick as fog and—he's convinced—full of watchful eyes. He can't shake the idea that the hala is out there, waiting to sink its teeth into him. Mam would tell him it's a ridiculous fear as long as his soul is right with God, but he's not so sure it is anymore.

When Maggie asked him if he was interested in the hunt, he couldn't deny the temptation. It's more than the money. Maybe if he won, people would squint less at his Banvish-Sumic background when he runs for office; it'd be as good as being a war hero in the public's eyes. But it's as unlikely as any of his other dreams. Nobody in their right mind would sign up with an unlicensed alchemist who hasn't completed an apprenticeship. Or a Banvishman, for that matter.

Maggie can do better than him—both for her reputation and her chances at victory. It's for the best. If entire orchards decay beneath the hala's paws, what could it do to something as fragile as him?

Wes sets the maul down to inspect the damage. What the splinters haven't flayed of his skin is raw, rubbed into peaks and valleys with water blisters. At the center of his palm is a gash of shining red, a chunk of flesh shorn away in his downswing. Blood wells from it and fills the creases of his hand.

"Damn it." His breath rises around him like smoke.

As much as he hates to admit it, the sight of blood sets him on edge. His mother has told him enough stories to instill a healthy fear of God and the aos sí in him. Enough to know that bleeding alone in the woods at dusk is as good as asking for the undead king Avartach or some wicked fairy girl to spirit him away—or worse. Even if it's just superstition, he's not about to tempt fate when it comes to something as wily and unpredictable as fey magic.

Wes glances toward the house. Through the cracked window, he sees Maggie standing at the counter, chopping carrots with such solemnity it must be an act of devotion to some vegetal god. With the setting sun stooping down to peer inside and the copper pans glinting over the range, the kitchen is bathed in a polleny glow. In the golden-hour light, she's almost pretty. Almost. He tears his eyes away from her.

He can't help feeling a little bitter as he remembers the cold precision with which she butchered that chicken, or the dirt braceleting her muscled forearms. She could probably cut them a whole mountain of firewood in half the time it'd take him. In the city, he doesn't have to endure this sort of indignity, mostly because his apartment is sweltering year-round. But even if it wasn't, modern technology and alchemy—

Realization dawns on him. He *does* need to practice alchemy before Evelyn returns. With no equipment, he's limited, but he only needs the most basic of transmutations to make woodcutting easier. Maggie will be so pleased.

Wes sits on the chopping block and finds a stone and a stick on the ground. Once he distills the stone's coincidentia oppositorum—the liquid essence of an object—he can use it to enchant the maul. In theory, it will be sharper, more durable, and more efficient.

On one hand, he etches the alchemical formula for nigredo, carefully inscribing the perimeter with symbols for the chemical composition of stone. Silica and oxygen—simple enough. It's more of an educated guess than anything, but he figures he can get close enough for it to decompose the bulk of it into something useful. Destroying things has always come easy to him.

Once he's finished, he clutches the stone in his fist and channels the magic within him. White flame knifes between the grooves of his fingers, and sulfuric smoke weaves around his hand like a cat. When he opens his hand, he's holding a charred pile of caput mortuum. It bubbles and breathes uneasily like bog water. Since his calculations were imprecise, it's less stable than he'd like, but it'll get the job done.

Next comes albedo, purification and the second step in the alchemical process. It requires a certain finesse—and a good deal of trial and error—to burn off everything that doesn't comprise the essence of an object. While nigredo is pure chemistry, albedo is intuition. Mastery of it separates competent alchemists from exceptional ones. His stomach churns with dread.

Relax, he tells himself. He's seen albedo done countless times. Just as many teachers have attempted to drill it into him.

Useless. Uneducated. Lazy. Someday, he'll prove they were wrong about him.

Once he draws and activates the formula, fire leaps up from his palm. He uncurls his fist and watches the caput mortuum blanch like a bone left in the sun. Slowly, it melts into a liquid as white and brilliant as diamond. The coincidentia oppositorum.

Some of it dribbles through his fingers and sinks into the half-frozen earth. Before he loses it all, he pours it onto the maul's head and carves the formula for rubedo—the final step, the process of reconstitution—in the dirt beneath it. With this, he'll finish imbuing the maul head with the essential properties of the stone. The metal glows red with the light of rubedo, then dulls to gray like cooling steel. His life is about to get so much easier.

When he attempts to heft the maul, however, it's impossibly heavy. He only manages to lift it an inch off the ground before he has to drop it.

"Shit," he mutters.

This is *not* what he wanted to happen, although he supposes he can understand why his transmutation might've had some unintended side effects. Certain stones might distill down into pure sturdiness. Others, into sharpness . . . No, this is no time for troubleshooting. Maggie is going to kill him when she realizes what he's done. He needs to hide the evidence, or at least pretend that nothing is amiss, until he can figure out how to reverse the enchantment.

"What are you doing?"

Maggie's voice cuts through his panic. She's standing on the porch, dressed in a thick knit cardigan and untied leather boots, but somehow, she's still imposing.

"Nothing! I was just finishing up out here."

She must smell his fear or read it in the way he fumbles to pick up the kindling because she's making her way over to him with a frown notched into her brow. Every crunch of the leaves beneath her boots sends his blood pressure rocketing higher.

He's so doomed.

She makes it within five feet of him before she stops dead, her nostrils flaring. A strange, sickly light fills her eyes. He recognizes this look on her now. It's the same one she got before she left for the opening ceremony. Haunted, like she's suddenly a thousand miles away.

"Um, Miss Welty?"

Maggie startles, then blinks at him dazedly. She sounds as though she's waking from a dream when she says, "It smells like alchemy."

"Oh, does it?"

"Yes." Her gaze lands pointedly on the mud-drawn symbols on his hands. He shoves them into his pockets, but her expression softens with curiosity. "You already know how to perform alchemy?"

"Of course I do." It comes out more peevishly than he means to.

"You said you failed out of your other apprenticeships."

"I never said that. You assumed that. You assumed correctly, but that's beside the point." He slumps onto the chopping block, groaning. "I'm not a bad alchemist, I swear. I just . . . don't test well."

"Then let's see it."

"Well, uh . . ."

It takes her all of one second to sniff out what he wanted to hide. She stoops to retrieve the maul, then swears under her breath when it refuses to budge. Her face contorts into some mixture of befuddlement and irritation. "It's dense as an anvil. What did you do to it?"

"I was trying to be resourceful! It's only that I kind of fudged the chemistry."

She glowers at him. "You shouldn't try transmutations you don't know how to do. It's dangerous."

"Who says? I had a theory, and I tested it. That's science."

"This isn't science. It's property damage."

"I'll fix it, I swear!"

Maggie shakes her head as though she's talking herself out of saying what she really wants to say. Then, she primly dusts her hands off on her skirt. "Do what you like. It's your prerogative if you want to play with fire."

She sounds so disappointed Wes feels as though he failed a test he didn't know he was taking. Desperate to salvage at least some scrap of his pride, he says, "If it's any consolation, I did cut some firewood."

Her gaze drops to the paltry bundle of kindling at his feet. "It's too thick."

"I can cut it smaller," he says miserably. His hands throb in protest.

"No. Just . . . leave it." She sounds exhausted, as if he's the most useless person she's had the misfortune of speaking to. "I'll deal with it later. Come inside before you catch cold."

Wes tries not to dwell on it as he follows her back inside. It's hardly any warmer in here. Trouble, curled up near the door, heaves a long, dramatic sigh as they enter. Wes nudges him with the toe of his shoe. Trouble grunts at the effort of rolling onto his side, one paw curled and limp. Wes kneels beside him and pats his side obligingly. The sound resonates in the grim silence of the kitchen. A moment later, there comes the answering *thunk, thunk, thunk* of Maggie's kitchen knife.

All at once, it strikes him how depressing this scene is. This is her *life*.

He can't stop thinking about how Jaime treated her at the pub, or about the rumors he heard before he left Dunway—that Evelyn Welty is a monster and a recluse. Even though he's never met her, he can't help wondering if there's some truth to them. What kind of mother leaves her daughter to fend for herself for months?

Although Maggie's probably had about enough of him for to-night, he thinks his company is probably better than none at all. Sometimes he catches her looking at him like she's about to ask him something. Besides, he likes the way annoyed looks on her. Her eyes are so much brighter when she's trying not to scold him.

"The dog says he likes me better," Wes says slyly.

"He's a hound, not a dog."

"Fine. The *hound* says he likes me better."

Maggie does not dignify him with a response.

He deflates. That's the kind of inconsequential comment that would have started a war in his household. One thought of his sisters turns his heart as heavy as his alchemized maul. He's homesick again. Worse, he's lonely. No one ever comes to visit here. Everyone promised him that rural New Albion would be as cozy as a knit blanket, the people warmer than in the city and their bonds thicker. Like it was in Banva before the crops blighted and famine emptied out the countryside. Clearly none of them have been to Wickdon.

The weeks after his father died, his family's apartment was never empty. How many hugs had he been crushed into? How many home-cooked meals had they crammed into their icebox? How many mourning songs had been played? It felt stifling at the time, but now he yearns for nothing more than that kind of love. Does Maggie even know what she's missing?

Wes tries not to feel sorry for her. She's not interested in any of his white flags of friendship, and he can't easily forget the look in her eyes when she growled, *I have to go,* after he asked if she was alright. Whatever fragile comradery they found yesterday has crumbled, and Wes feels as alone as he did on his first day here.

"Hey," he says, more somberly than he intended. "Do you have a phone?"

"There's a phone booth in town."

Of course the nearest phone is five miles away. Nothing surprises him less.

Without responding, he stands and whistles for the dog. He doesn't miss Maggie's sour look as Trouble stretches, shakes out his ears, and obediently trots after him. Maybe he isn't the only one eager for some fresh air.

"Put him on a leash," she calls after him. "He won't cross the property line with you otherwise."

He hears the unspoken warning in her voice: *I don't trust you not to lose him.*

"Yeah, yeah." Wes grabs the leash from where it's draped over the coatrack and clips it to Trouble's collar.

As they walk down the mountain road, he tries to convince himself he's doing the right thing by being here. All his life, Mad and his teachers have called him a layabout, a slacker, a procrastinator. The kind of guy who skirts by on superficial charm. It stings, but it's not as though he's given them a reason to think otherwise. It's not his fault he was born friendly, but it *is* his fault for turning that into a shield against his own despair. What difference would it make if Mad knew the weight of his failures would crush him if he let them?

She wouldn't resent him any less. But now, here he is, playing lumberjack and idling away his life. Maybe he deserves her scorn.

God, he needs to talk to Mam before his guilt consumes him entirely.

By the time he reaches the lonely phone booth standing watch over town, he's shivering and breathless. He'll never get used to scaling these inclines. Inside, it's bitter cold and hazy, the glass frosted and veined silver with moonlight. As Trouble plops down on his feet, Wes feeds the meter and dials his home number.

It rings twice before someone answers. "Hello?"

For perhaps the first time in his life, the sound of Christine's voice fills him with something like happiness. "Hey. It's me." There's silence on the line. "Christine?"

"Me? Who's me?"

Wes pinches the bridge of his nose. "Wes."

"Wes . . . Hmm. I don't know a Wes . . ."

"Very funny. Can you put Mam on the phone?"

"Oh, Wes!" He hears her snap her fingers as fake realization sweetens her voice. "My sweet only brother, Weston. It's been so long since you called, I forgot what you sounded like. You said wanted to talk to Mad?"

He grimaces. "No. I said Mam."

"Oh! Colleen?"

"No." If she puts Colleen on the phone, he'll never be free. He is far too broke for a conversation with her. "God, no. I'm on a pay phone. Put Mam on."

"Okay." He dreads the smile in her voice. "Colleen! Wes wants to talk to you."

Damn it all.

As he listens to their faint chatter, he imagines himself there. They'd be gathered in the living room with the radio playing. Christine would be lounging on the couch with the phone tucked against her chin. Edie would be clambering onto his knee and demanding he play with her. Colleen would be yammering on about baseball or chemistry or whatever topic interested her that week. And Mad would be leaning out the open window with a lacquered cigarette holder between her fingers.

God, he wants to be there. He wants it so badly he feels heat build behind his eyes. He snaps himself out of it when Colleen, his fourteen-year-old sister, picks up the phone. "Wes!"

"Hey, Bean! Listen. I've only got about five minutes before the call cuts out. Can you please put Mam on?

"Yeah!" He hears a chair slide across the floor. He can all too easily imagine her sinking into it as she tangles her fingers into the phone cord. "I miss you already. How's Wickdon? When are you coming home? Do you have any friends? Do you have a *girlfriend*? How's your apprenticeship? How's—"

"It's great! Everything is so great."

"Not failing out yet?"

"Not yet!" If his smile stays bright enough, it may carry over to his voice. "Amazing, right?"

"Aw, that's good. Hey! Mrs. O'Connor was asking about you this morning. Since you haven't stopped by in a while, she was getting worried. Her daughter was there, too, and she's *gutted* you left. Gutted."

"Which one? Jane? The one with the bird?" He hates that bird. He still has a scar from when it bit his ear.

"That's the one."

Wes puzzles over that. He and Jane haven't spoken more than a few words to each other, but he considers any attachment she feels may be his fault since he calls her beautiful every time he sees her. As much as he wants to gossip about the butcher's oldest daughter, the clock is ticking. His empty wallet burns in his pocket. "Tell her . . . that's very kind of her to ask after me. Also, can you get Mam?"

The sound on the other end is muffled—as if she's covering the receiver with her palm. Anxiously, he fishes another coin out of his pocket and drops it into the slot with a *clink*. The bickering he hears does not fill him with confidence, but eventually, the phone is wrested away.

This time, his mother speaks. "Wes, is that you?"

Her voice fills him with warm relief. It sounds like home. "Hi, Mam."

"Oh, a leanbh. It's so good to hear your voice. How are you? Is it freezing out there? You brought your coat, didn't you? You're warm enough?"

"I'm warm enough, Mam. Quit worrying."

"Don't *worry*? You've known me for eighteen years. I'm going to worry."

"I know. I'm sorry. I know I've been . . ." Wes draws in a steadying breath. Putting on his best adult voice, he says, "I don't want you to worry. You don't need to worry about me anymore, okay?"

"You got the apprenticeship?"

"Yeah." He cringes at the blatant lie. "I sure did."

"You did? Oh, that's fantastic news! I'm so proud of you."

You wouldn't be if you could see me. At what point in his life has lying become second nature to him? But what other choice does he have? He can't break her heart again. What kind of son would that make him when he promised his father he'd take care of them all? "Thanks."

"Out with it! Tell me all about it."

"Oh, it's great. It's only been a few days now. Master Welty is, uh . . . She gives me a lot of independence to study."

"Don't work too hard. I don't want you to shut yourself away. Have you made any friends?"

"She has a daughter my age. She's very . . ." There isn't really a word to settle on for Maggie. ". . . nice."

"Are they treating you well there?"

"They are. Everything's grand, honest. How are you?"

"They're talking about raising the rent again, but what can we do? We're all healthy, and we're happy. That's all that matters. God will provide the rest."

The phone line buzzes, a warning he has only seconds. "Hey, I'm about to run out of time on this pay phone. The Weltys don't have a phone, so if you need me, they can take calls at the Wallace Inn. I'll call again soon, alright? I love you."

"Oh! I'll let you go. I love y—"

The line goes dead, and he lets out a shaky breath. How can he be so selfish, to put all his faith in Maggie when the noose draws tighter around his family? But it's only another week and a half until Evelyn returns.

He sets the receiver back on the hook and shoves his hands in his pockets. It is so damn cold, and he has another five miles to walk back to Welty Manor. Or he could turn around and walk until the sea swallows him whole. That would be an easy solution to his problems.

But it's not a solution to give up. It won't change his family's situation if he goes back and takes a job at the docks or a factory—assuming he can find one that will hire him. The rent will still climb higher. The immigration laws will still grow more restrictive. Everything is riding on him becoming Evelyn Welty's student. Everything. He just has to hope he's persuasive enough when she finally returns.

6

As they follow the road home from Wickdon, Margaret watches Weston and Trouble trot ahead of her, vanishing and reappearing in the fog slowly rolling down the mountainside. Although it's cold and gray, the leaves underfoot blaze bright with autumn colors and she feels lighter than she has in weeks. After hunting all week, she traded in a handful of pelts, and now she has enough saved for the registration fee and another week's worth of food. This freedom is a strange thing, bought with suffering through Weston's company.

Weston. She holds the shape of his name in her mouth.

The sound of his laughter as he chases Trouble strikes her with *fondness* of all things, even though she has half a mind to snap at him to stop jostling the groceries he's carrying. But maybe she's been too hard on him. Thanks to him, she has the time to train uninterrupted. It's been years since she could measure the dreamlike monotony of her days with anything but chores. Lazy late afternoons like this remind her of how she once had nothing to do but run wild with Trouble in the woods. For the first time since she lost her family, she can almost believe she is happy.

Registration for the Halfmoon Hunt opens in two days, but Margaret still hasn't summoned the courage to ask him to enter with her. Every time she imagines telling him she's Yu'adir, she freezes.

But perhaps what stills her the most is that she will have no choice but to confess why she wants to join the hunt—and why they have to win. Both of their dreams rest on this. Margaret isn't ready to tie her fate to his yet, but she can't afford to let fear hold her back much longer.

"Come on, Miss Welty," he calls over his shoulder. "You're wasting daylight."

It's times like this that she feels vindicated in her reticence. If they work together, he won't survive the month of preparation. She'll wring his neck long before the starting gun goes off.

As they head deeper into the woods, a chill settles over her. The madrone trees are all half-naked now, their bark peeling away in long, papery strips, and the redwoods loom above her, solid and steady as they have been for thousands of years. The ancientness of this forest has always grounded her. It has watched her grow up, and it will watch her die. There should be comfort in that certainty, in that familiarity. But today, it feels menacing. The shadows grin in the corner of her vision, and the hissing of the leaves sounds so much like her name.

Margaret, Margaret, Margaret.

It raises the hairs on the back of her neck. Trouble circles back to her and tilts his head, his tail wagging uncertainly. She touches the tips of her fingers to his head to steady herself.

"Did you hear something?" Weston asks.

"Just the wind."

He gives her a skeptical look. "I—"

A *crack* echoes through the woods, and the flock of crows roosting overhead rise like a cloud of smoke.

Gunfire.

The silence that follows smothers her beneath its weight. Everything's gone too still, like the whole world is holding its breath. She shouldn't be surprised that other hunters are out practicing their shot and whetting their hounds, but they're a little too close to her home for comfort. Curiosity gets the better of her, and soon, she's pushing through the underbrush with Trouble on her heels.

"Uh, Miss Welty? Where are you going?" She ignores him, but after a moment, he comes crashing after her, still carrying their groceries at his hip. "Is it a good idea to run *toward* the gunfire?"

"If you're so worried, you can go home and put the food away yourself."

"I don't know where anything goes, and you'll fuss at me again if I guess wrong."

"Then come along and don't complain."

Weston heaves a long-suffering sigh, then follows her along the deer trail. The thickets give way to a grove, where clusters of redwoods lean against each other like old friends. As soon as she sees who's there, she regrets coming at all.

Jaime Harrington and his best friend, Zach Mattis.

Mattis, tall and lumbering, looks like a bear wearing a vest. He's holding a still-smoking rifle, and even through the acrid bite of gunpowder, she can smell the oil he's slathered on its tortoise-shell paneling. It's a beautiful machine—one he doesn't deserve. For as long as she's known him, he couldn't hit a wall two feet in front of him. If Jaime's snickering is anything to go off, today is no exception.

If she's completely silent, she can slip away unnoticed. But as she takes a step backward, she bumps into Weston, who leaps away from her like she's electrocuted him.

Jaime turns toward them as if he's caught their scent on the wind. His smile spreads slowly, then catches at the corner. "Creeping around in the woods, Maggie?"

"Shooting air?"

Mattis scowls at her. "Shut your mouth."

"Ignore her." Jaime spits on the ground.

Mattis takes his advice and busies himself loading another magazine, which suits her fine. Jaime, however, prowls toward them, his pale eyes gleaming like a predator's. "Well, aren't you two a fetching couple?"

"I don't know what you're talking about," Margaret says.

"Oh, come on. I've never seen you keep company with somebody willingly—twice, no less. Did you take in another mutt?"

Weston bristles beside her. "Who're you calling—"

Margaret shoots him a glare. "We were just leaving. Sorry to disturb you."

"What? No, stay a while." Jaime's gaze lands on the rifle strapped to her back. "You came out here to practice, right?"

Margaret doesn't reply. If Jaime doesn't know she plans to register, she'll have at least another few days of peace.

"Oh, that's right. You can't afford it, since your witch of a mother's gone and abandoned you again. Unless you've finally put that capitalistic mind of yours to use."

Margaret's face heats under the barb. Mattis guffaws, which earns him an irritated look from Jaime.

Weston wedges himself in front of her like he means to shield her. "Do you honestly have nothing better to do with your time? Lay off her, alright?"

"Are you desperate enough that you think you're going to get somewhere with this act, Winters?" Jaime pauses, and his whole face lights up as if he's been struck with a brilliant idea. "Or is it that you don't know what she is?"

Margaret sucks in a sharp breath. "Jaime, *don't.*"

His smile turns vicious. "So he doesn't know."

In the distance, someone screams.

It's terror and grief wrapped into one. For a moment, she hears Evelyn's voice echoed over it. Memories surge in the corners of her vision. Her chest tightens, and the smell of sulfur claws its way up her throat. Trouble presses into her leg, an anchor against the tide of her fear.

You're here, she reminds herself sharply.

"Where did that come from?" Mattis asks.

"The only thing in that direction for miles is the Halanans' farm." Jaime's face slackens with concern. It wounds her more than she wants to admit. It's evidence that he's not always awful—not to everyone. "Come on, Mattis."

The boys tear off through the clearing. As soon as they're alone again, Weston rests an uncertain hand on her shoulder. "Hey, are you alright?"

She flinches away from him, hating how guilty he looks as his arm drops to his side. It'd be far easier for them both if he stopped noticing when she isn't alright. "We have to go."

"What? *Why?* You can't seriously want to go after them."

Mark Halanan has been nothing but kind to her over the years, and she's wrangled many a chicken and calf over the fence for him when he was too exhausted to do it himself. As much as she dreads the thought of spending another second willingly with Jaime, she has to go. "Like I said, you can go home if you want."

"No. I'm not leaving you alone with them." He hesitates. "Listen, I don't know what he was talking about, and you don't have to tell me if you don't want to. But there's nothing anyone could say that'd make me treat someone the way he treats you. Believe me, I've been on the receiving end of it enough times."

Margaret's breath catches. For over a week, she hasn't been able to find the words to get the information she needs from him, and here he is, offering it to her freely. She searches his face for any hint of deception, but his expression is as unbearably earnest as ever. It feels like safety—and something like kinship. If she thanks him, if she acknowledges it at all, she worries she won't be able to maintain her composure. Instead, she says, "Fine. Don't slow me down."

"I won't."

Side by side, they tear off after Jaime and Mattis. To her shock, neither of them protests when they fall into stride alongside them. Branches snap beneath her boots, and brambles tear at the bare sliver of ankle below her overalls. By the time they stumble onto the Halanans' yard, the sky is stained an angry, dying red. The farmhouse is silhouetted starkly against it. The wind shivers along the wild rye. They wade through it until it thins out and gives way to pasture.

The fence is broken, char-licked and splintered, and the air around them reeks of sulfur. Caput mortuum dusts the ground like blackened snow, coating the bottom of her shoes.

An alchemical reaction.

The smell of it untethers her mind from her body, and the world ripples dreamlike around her. Margaret feels as though she's watching herself through the hungry eyes of the woods as she slips through the jagged gap in the fence. Beside her, Trouble quivers like he's readying himself for the chase. A bay rumbles in his chest.

"Hush," she says.

As they make their way through the pasture, the building stench of rot makes bile rise at the back of her throat. Beneath the sound of her shallow panting, she hears the drone of flies. Jaime shoves past her, then lets out a sound of disgust. When he lifts up his foot, Margaret sees red streaking the sole of his boot. It catches the light like garnet.

"What the . . . ?" he mutters. "Is this blood?"

Gouts of it spatter the grass, forming a grisly path to the house. They round the stable and stop dead. Out in the field lie at least five cows, their bodies shrouded by fog. But right at their feet is Halanan's white pony. Margaret's breath hisses out through her clenched teeth.

Sugarlump's throat is torn open, her fur matted down with blood and ash. Blackened streaks of decay snake around her neck, weeping coincidentia oppositorum and sebum. But it's the flies swarming the body that turn Margaret's stomach. It reminds her of the smallest, sourest apples that no one picks. By the end of the season, they drop off the boughs and litter the ground, burst open and covered in a jacket of bees.

The farmhouse door swings open, and Halanan staggers onto the porch, shotgun in hand. "What are you kids doing out here?"

"We heard someone scream," Jaime says.

"That'd be my husband." Halanan drags a hand through his hair.

"I appreciate you checking in, but you need to get home. It's getting dark."

"What the hell happened here?"

"The hala," Halanan says gravely.

It's hardly been two weeks, and already, it's killing livestock. Margaret dreads what it'll do by the time the full moon rises.

"We can run it off for you," Jaime says.

"Absolutely not. What would your father say if he knew I let you go gallivanting through the woods with that *thing* on the loose?"

Jaime scuffs his boot on the ground. "He wouldn't care."

"Oh, no? And what about you, Zachary?" Halanan scowls. "You think your mother will appreciate me delivering the news that you've had an arm taken off? Or worse?"

"No, sir," Mattis murmurs.

Before Halanan can turn his attention to Margaret, the air thickens around them. It's still and frigid as the moment before the first snow falls. Then, the wind comes hissing through the grass. It carries the stench of death—and the sound of a brittle, many-faceted voice.

Margaret.

She whirls around, and there, standing at the edge of the fence, is the hala. There's a terrible moment of anticipation before its unblinking white gaze locks onto hers. It feels like plunging into cold water. Its eyes glow, eerily bright in the foggy gloom.

"Why isn't it moving?" Weston asks quietly.

"Jaime," Mattis whines. "What do we do?"

Sometimes, Margaret feels sorry for him; Jaime has made a pet of him. He's no better than a puppy, dependent on his favor and guidance.

"We're going after it." Jaime's pale hair ruffles in the wind, a mirror of the rye over his shoulder. It's moments like this where Margaret thinks he could almost be gallant if he wanted. She hates that he has the choice and she doesn't. Even if this town holds no love for her, it's still her home, and she's so tired of letting Jaime make her feel otherwise. Like she doesn't have a right to protect it, too.

Mattis clutches his gun closer to his chest. "I don't know about this."

"Man up," Jaime snaps, already stalking toward the fence. "We're going."

Margaret trails a few steps behind him. "I'm coming, too."

"Like hell you are."

Trouble lets out a low, impatient whine.

"Track, Trouble." It's all the encouragement he needs. Trouble tears through the field, yowling, just as the fox turns tail and slips beneath the pasture fence. "That's my hound. Good luck finding it without him."

With a growl of frustration, Jaime says, "Fine. Come on."

Margaret glances at Weston. There's something about him that steals her breath away. He looks wild, from his wind-tossed black hair to the mingled fear and excitement sparkling in his eyes. In this light, they're the color of the heart of a damp redwood. He *is* wild, but in the same familiar, steady way these woods are. He licks his lips and says, "I'm still with you."

"Then let's go."

Halanan throws up his hands in defeat. "Be careful, will you?"

They take off after Trouble, past the fence and back into the woods, beneath snaring branches and over fern-bearded embankments. With the blood rushing in her ears, this is more alive than she's felt in years. As the sun sinks lower and the moon begins to rise, the light dribbling through the trees runs red as blood. Ahead of her, the boys whoop and shout, dark slashes against the wildfire sky. Trouble bays, and the sound tears through the brush like an angry sow.

They run until they break into a clearing, and there it is, pale as the moon and perched on a branch. Trouble circles the base of the tree, baying his triumph. There's something uncannily *aware* about the way the hala looks at her. But before she can process it, Mattis is raising his gun. He takes aim and blows a branch clean off the tree. It shudders and groans before crashing to the ground.

"You idiot!" Jaime barks. "You'll have a mob after you if you kill it before the hunt."

"You see a full moon?" Mattis glares back at him. "It's not even alchemized! I'm just trying to scare it off."

"Move." Margaret elbows her way between them and unstraps the gun from her back. It feels like possibility in her hands. She draws in a breath and raises the rifle, its weight bearing into her collarbone. In her crosshairs, she sees the gore mottling the hala's snout and its solid white eyes. Hatred sets her heart to racing.

Demiurges have ruined her.

Seven years ago, her mother tried to distill the prima materia with the antlers of another demiurge—a fragment of a relic she stole from a Sumic church in Umbria. It was the worst night of her life. Margaret can't remember most of it, but she remembers this. As she tucked her mother into bed, combing the flakes of dried blood from her hair, all she whispered was, *It's not over.*

If Margaret wins, it finally will be.

Her hands tremble. The hala isn't natural. Any other fox would fight for its life, but the hala sits there with its tail folded neatly over its paws. As if it knows they're only playing a game. As if it knows *her.* At her side, Weston stares at it like he's seen the face of God. His lips move in a silent prayer.

Margaret fires, and the shot ringing in her ears drowns out the sound of Jaime's shouting. Smoke rises up around her. When it clears, the hala is gone, but where its head was, the tree bark splinters like a shattered bone. Sap oozes out, as thick and dark as heartblood.

"See?" Mattis says, clearly vindicated. "It's gone."

"No thanks to you." Jaime rounds on Margaret. "Lucky shot."

"You should hope my luck runs out soon, then. I'm registering."

She's painted a target on her back, but the satisfaction of seeing

Jaime's mouth hinge open in outrage makes it all worth it. Margaret turns on her heel and calls for Trouble. His disappointment is written in the droop of his tail; it's rare he loses his mark.

But soon enough, Trouble will get his chance, and she'll get hers.

Weston trots after her. As they slip back into the woods, the red glow of the sunset softens as if it's been poured through a colander. "How do you think you can possibly kill something like that?" She's never heard him so rattled—not even on the day she met him. "It's . . ."

She thinks of the way he prayed when he saw it. Not like he was asking God for protection. Like he was awestruck. "Divine?"

"What does it matter if it is? It looked like it was toying with us, and it's still early in the month. It'll kill you before you kill it."

"You're afraid."

"Of course I am! Aren't you?"

Margaret adjusts her rifle's strap. "I think it's wise to be afraid of something like the hala."

"Then why? Glory can't be worth your life."

"What if it's not for glory?"

"Then what? Money? A dead fox?"

Margaret scoffs. A dead fox. As if that's all it is to him. By now, she knows his thoughts are more complicated than that.

There's nothing anyone could say that'd make me treat someone the way he treats you, he told her. *Believe me, I've been on the receiving end of it enough times.*

She's almost positive now that Weston isn't Katharist, which explains his reticence to join the hunt—and his bullheaded insistence on protecting her from Jaime. Unless his research interests are as arcane and heretical as her mother's, he probably doesn't even want the hala dead, much less boiled down to create the prima materia.

Which means he'd be the perfect partner for the hunt.

Hope blooms within her. "The fox wouldn't be worth it to you?"

"No." He looks dumbfounded. "I'm not dying for some trophy or to do God a favor or whatever it is that lady in the pub said. Even

I'm not that vain, and I'm sure as hell not that pious. What use could you possibly have for it?"

"It's not the hala I want—not for its own sake." When she closes her eyes, she tries to imagine how Evelyn will look at her when she places the hala in her hands. She can't picture her joy clearly, but the idea of it turns her stomach with longing. "Wouldn't you say it's worth risking your life for the people you love?"

"Of course." His expression softens. "That's worth risking everything."

If there's one thing to admire about Weston Winters, it's his conviction. He told her that he'd do anything for a chance at his dreams, and now she believes him. She's never been certain of much in her life, but she's certain of this. Her mother will never give him an apprenticeship unless he uses the hala as his bargaining chip. And once Margaret tells him the hunt is his only way forward, he won't abandon her or take the fox for himself.

By tomorrow night, she'll find the words to break the news to him. Then, she'll ask him to hunt alongside her.

7

After nearly two weeks in Wickdon, Wes has come to understand its sunsets. They are normally slow, preening things, like a woman shrugging off her shawl. But tonight, darkness falls like a stage curtain. Fat rain clouds pour off the mountains and clot over the sea until there's nothing but gray past the window.

A fire sputters in the library's grate, sap and damp crackling in the heat. He sits bent over an alchemy textbook, threading his fingers into his hair. He's not sure if he's been here for ten minutes or ten hours, but by the time he blinks, the fire gone to ashes, he's retained hardly anything of this chapter, and there's a pile of shredded notebook paper beside him. He mutters to himself as he sweeps the scraps into his hand.

Before he dropped out of school—back when Sumic parochial schools weren't under attack for allegedly promoting sedition—he used to get in trouble constantly for fidgeting. Between that and the public humiliation he endured every time his teachers made him read aloud, the prospect of going to class made him nauseous. He learned to hide it better during his apprenticeships, tearing apart whatever he got his hands on to help himself focus. Paper, the laces on his shoes, the buttons off his jacket, which Christine always begrudgingly sewed back on.

Wes shuts the book and lays his head on top of it. Maggie hasn't been home in hours, and she took Trouble with her. He still hasn't grown fully accustomed to the loneliness here. Every sound is too loud. The creaking of the floorboards, the drumming of the rain on the roof, and the moan of the frame as it shifts and swells in the storm.

How does she bear it out here? Five miles from civilization. A dead brother, a missing father, and a mother who may as well be either. Once, he dreamed of something like this: a mother who didn't care and a house he could run wild in. His days of slinking around like an alley cat, kissing girls out on the fire escape or in the park, hungrily swallowing every sound, would be over. But now that he's seen the reality of it, it makes him a little sick to his stomach that he'd ever envied this kind of life.

Here he goes again, feeling sorry for Maggie Welty. She'd probably gut him alive if she could guess at what he was thinking.

Someone pounds on the front door.

Wes jerks upright as a roll of thunder shakes the house to its foundations and a flash of white lightning splits open the night. He probably shouldn't answer the door, considering this isn't his house, but when the knock comes again, sharp and urgent, he reluctantly creeps into the foyer. Through the eyehole, he sees Halanan on the porch, drenched with rainwater and panting.

Startled, he opens the door. "Halanan. Do you want to come in?"

"No time. I came by to tell you that they've got a call for you down at the inn. Says she's your sister. Madeline?"

Shit. A call from Mad is never good. "What about?"

"I'm sorry to be the one to tell you this, but she said your mother's been in an accident."

The Wallace Inn's lobby is as he remembers it from the other night, charmingly fashioned after some of the glitzier hotels in the city. A chandelier sparkles overhead, bright and fizzling as champagne, and over the muffled chatter of the people at the restaurant, someone plays a shimmering piano melody to a syncopated beat that's grown popular in Dunway.

A girl around his age leans against the check-in counter, half hidden by the fronds of an oversized plant. On any other day, he's sure he'd flirt with her, but right now, he can't seem to notice a single thing about her. All he can focus on is what Halanan said, the word "accident" playing in his mind over and over again. Mam can't be dead. Halanan would've told him. And deep down, Wes thinks he would know. There'd be some shift in the polarity of the earth, or the snap of something vital within him.

He pulls off his cap and speaks in a rush. "Good evening, miss. My name is Weston Winters. I hear there was a call for me?"

"Oh." Her lips press into a thin, sympathetic line. "You can return the call back here, Mr. Winters. Can I get you some coffee?"

"Yeah, actually. That'd be great."

She leads him behind the counter and into a cozily cluttered office with a plush carpet and a solid wood desk. He sinks into a chair and waits for the girl to return. It only takes a minute for her to reappear and place a mug in his hands. The heat soaking into his skin soothes his cold-stiffened joints.

Steeling himself, he dials his home number on the rotary. The surface of the coffee quivers, shattering his reflection over and over again while the phone rings in his ear. It sounds only once before the line goes quiet. No one says anything, but by the tense buzzing on the other end, he can tell someone's there.

"Mad?"

"Weston," Mad replies sharply.

He sucks in a breath as soon as he hears the fury barely restrained in her voice. "What's going on?"

"Mam needs surgery. She fell asleep at work and took a needle through her hand."

Wes flinches. "Is she alright?"

"Did you hear what I just said?"

He bites down on his tongue to keep himself from saying something regrettable. Mad isn't often the most reasonable person, and she's far more attached to being right than he is. "Yes. I heard you."

She sighs heavily. He can imagine the smoke curling from the end of her cigarette as she leans out the window. He can almost hear the rush of traffic outside and the clatter of the rain on the fire escape. "Technically, yes, she's fine. But she can't work anymore—not like this. If she doesn't get the surgery, she won't be able to use her hand again."

"Oh. Shit."

"Yeah."

The line crackles under the weight of their silence.

"It's been a good run," she continues, more gently this time, "but you have to come home."

It's a sucker punch to the gut. A good run? Like he's been putting on some low-budget stage production? His thoughts scramble and the only thing that comes out of his mouth is "No."

"No? Our mother is almost fifty years old! If it's not glaringly obvious to you at this point, she can't go on like this anymore. Have you even noticed?"

"Of course I've noticed." He fights to keep his voice even. He doesn't want to yell right now. He doesn't want to alert anyone outside this room that anything is wrong. "God, Mad. What do you take me for?"

"Then you know what I'm getting at. Christine and I sure as hell don't make enough to afford surgery, much less to keep us clothed and fed. I need help, Wes."

"I know. I know she can't do this anymore. I know you can't do this alone. But if you give me some time, you won't have to think about working ever again, and—"

"You keep saying that. You keep making promises and asking for time and second chances. And I've let you go on like this for *years* because I thought you'd learn your lesson on your own. It's time to grow up."

"So what do you want me to do? You want me to come back and

find some awful, dead-end job without hiring restrictions? You want us to keep scraping by for the rest of our lives? I can't do this. I'm tired of surviving; I want to live."

"I don't care what you want."

"I'm *trying*, Mad. I'm trying to give us a way out of this."

"Trying isn't good enough anymore."

His breath shudders out of him. He can't say anything because she's right. Goddamn her, she's right.

"Say something, Weston."

"What do you want me to say?" he asks hoarsely.

"Anything. Anything at all that's not about *you*."

It's pointless to argue. All his life, he's wanted nothing more than to be an alchemist despite the odds. To believe that a Banvish-Sumic kid from the Fifth Ward could measure up to the Katharist politicians whose families have been here for generations. To believe that someone like him could make a difference. But how can he ever hope to protect the downtrodden of this country when he can't even protect the people he loves?

Hell, he can't even protect Maggie from the likes of Jaime Harrington, not that she's ever wanted him to. Although neither of them has admitted it, he can't shake the suspicion that she, too, has faced the kind of prejudice he has. He can't help feeling protective of her for that.

All is One and One is All is the fundamental tenet of alchemy. It's always been an ethical code for him. To help one person is to help better the entire world. But right now, it's not so cut and dry. If he stays, he hurts his family. If he leaves, he's throwing Maggie to the wolves. No matter what he does, he loses. But if he's forced to make a decision, he'll make the same one every time: his family. If pursuing his dreams mean abandoning them, they're not dreams worth pursuing. What would be the point? He'd be no better than what Mad says he is. Selfish, baselessly optimistic, childish.

Maybe he's been naive all along if all his ideals crumble so easily.

This dream isn't for him. Alchemists are the kind of people who grew up rich and will always be rich. So he says, "Okay."

"Okay?"

"I'll come home." Wes clutches the phone tighter. "I mean it. I'll get on the next train."

Mad doesn't say anything at first. All of the fight seems to have gone out of her. "Good."

"Want a souvenir? The hunt's here this year."

"No." She doesn't laugh, but her voice is gentler. "I'll see you tonight."

The line goes dead, then buzzes in his ear.

It's the right decision. He knows it is. But it still feels awful.

If he lets himself, he can remember how it was *before,* when things between him and Mad were good and she was his entire world. He wanted nothing more than to be with her—to be like her. When they were kids, he'd slip into her room at night, pulling all the blankets off her until she relented and let him sleep in her bed. As they got older, he'd chatter at her while she got ready for her shift at the bar. She was working even when Dad was alive because money was always a little tight, and even back then she must've been suffocating.

He'd say something like, "When you get home, do you wanna see a movie?"

Sometimes she'd throw things at him until he left. Sometimes, she'd keep applying pencil to her plucked-thin eyebrows and say, "I've got better things to do today than hanging out with you."

"Tomorrow?"

"Tomorrow."

Tomorrow and tomorrow and tomorrow, and here they are. Miles between them and an ocean of resentment to fill them.

By the time he hangs up, his coffee has gone lukewarm. It'd be rude not to drink it after he asked for it, so he throws it back—which proves to be a terrible mistake. It's bitter as sin and feels like mud going down, but it gives him enough of a jolt to stand. Wes makes his way back into the lobby and groans at the sight of rainwater beading on the windows. Somehow, he'd forgotten that God hates him, which means he still has to suffer the miles-long walk to Welty Manor in a storm. He pulls the back of his father's trench coat over his head like a hood.

"Hey."

He turns over his shoulder to see the girl from behind the counter. Wes forces himself to smile. He's long since mastered the art of smothering his feelings. If he doesn't let it, despair won't drown him. "Thanks again for the coffee."

She rests a hand on his shoulder. "Come on. Let me drive you home."

"You don't have to do that."

"Yes, I do. It's pouring."

He tilts his head up to the sky. "So it is."

She takes him out back, where her car is parked in a rapidly flooding field. It's a new model, gleaming black and chrome. "Had to make room for all the people coming in. Watch your step."

He climbs into the passenger seat, sighing at the pleasant new-leather smell of the interior. She slips in beside him, bringing with her the scent of roses and rainwater. He fastens his seat belt as the engine revs to life. He doesn't even need to tell her where she's going. She pulls onto the main road and turns out of town, straight toward Welty Manor.

The girl doesn't say anything or ask him what happened or how he's doing, and Wes could weep from relief. She turns the volume up on the radio until he can hear the music dimly over the patter of rain on the roof. He leans his head against the window and closes his eyes when he recognizes a tune Colleen likes to hum when she's doing the dishes. His heart squeezes with longing, but there's no point being homesick anymore. Soon enough, he'll be with her again.

The girl parks the car in the Weltys' driveway. Out in the distance, he thinks he sees two white circles that look like unblinking eyes.

"Hey," she says. "I know it's not my place, but I'm really sorry to hear about your mom."

Of course he wouldn't be lucky enough to avoid this topic completely. "Thanks. I appreciate it."

"Are you going back home?"

"Unfortunately."

That seems to puzzle her. "Really? Why do you say that?"

"There's nothing for me in Dunway."

"Compared to here? I find that hard to believe."

He turns to look at her. Although he can't make out her features clearly in the dark, he can see the bright red of her lipstick when she smiles. "Have you been before?"

"No," she says, almost dreamily. "I'd love to, though. All the lights and music and people . . . It sounds magical. I feel like you could be anyone and anything you wanted."

How sweet. He wishes he could live in her romantic vision of his home.

But as long as he's in this car, why can't he? If this girl wants to fancy him a worldly city boy, he can be that for her. He can keep his life light and uncomplicated and charmed. He's always liked to surround himself with people who let him pretend, who let him talk enough to drown out the noise of his own feelings.

"And what would you be?" he asks.

"An actress." She sounds almost embarrassed by it.

"I can see it. The city's the place to go if you want to make it big. How about you come with me?"

"Oh, Mr. Winters—"

He winks. "I'm only kidding."

"How cruel to play with a girl's heart," she says archly. "I was going to say I'd consider it."

"Were you really? Well, the last train leaves in a few hours. It's now or never."

Maybe she *would* make it big in the city; she really does look like she's considering his offer. Dropping the mask, she laughs. "I wish I could. But if you need anything else before you leave, let me know."

"You've done more than enough. Thanks again for the ride."

"Sure. Take care, Mr. Winters."

He gets out of the car and makes his way to the front door by the headlights' glow, shot through with needle-fine streaks of rain. As soon as he's inside, all the mirth drains out of him. Exhaustion is all that remains, and not even seeing Trouble run down the stairs to greet him can cheer him up. He closes the door behind him, shucks off his jacket, and heads upstairs to pack his things.

8

Through her lace curtains, the glow of the fire is dampened. Here, safely swaddled in blankets and tucked away on the sill of her bay window, nothing can reach her. Not the cold pressed eagerly against the rain-streaked glass. Not the hala prowling the woods outside her house. Not Jaime and his barbs. Right now, all that matters is that she's drenched in heat and light—and that she's finally, completely alone.

It should be more of a comfort than it is. But Weston is out in this storm.

Every time she imagines him walking through the door, her stomach clenches as tight as a fist. But she's run out of time. Tomorrow is registration day, and she can't let the fear of letting him into her life, of handing him the means to hurt her, stop her. It's now or never.

As a chain of lightning cleaves open the sky, Margaret turns anxiously back to the book in her lap. It's a comfort read, one of the beaten-up romance paperbacks her father used to read when he thought nobody was looking. Margaret trails her fingers over the torn, faded cover before she cracks it open like a holy tome. The first time her mother caught her with one of these, she stood stock still in the doorframe. Slack-jawed and pale, she looked as if she'd seen a ghost. Then, with a curl of her lip, she said, "Don't waste your time on that drivel."

Margaret sometimes wishes that her sentimentality didn't survive her upbringing, but it did. She started reading "drivel" because she was beginning to forget what kind of man her father was, beyond the kind that leaves. Every day, the image of his face grows foggier, the exact tenor of his voice more imprecise. But in these books is a piece of him that she can't lose—not like the words of his songs or the meaning of the letters in his bible or the recipe for the spiced honey cake he'd make every fall.

As soon as she begins to settle into the familiar story, there comes the growl of an engine. Trouble, who's been drowsing on the carpet near her fireplace, lifts his head from his elegantly crossed paws. Bright headlights pare twin slivers out of the darkness, illuminating the swirling storm clouds that drift down from the mountains. Margaret presses her forehead against the window and squints against the flood of light. Fog blooms across the glass as she watches a sleek black car rattle its way up the driveway. At this hour, it looks like dread itself. Hardly anybody in Wickdon drives a car when half of them can't even afford to keep a horse. And car or not, nobody in Wickdon ever comes to visit Welty Manor.

The passenger door flies open, and a man—no, it's Weston—steps out. She can spot him by his overlong hair and the beaten-up trench coat draped over his shoulders. Now that she's looking closely, she recognizes the car, too.

It's just her luck that Weston has decided to affiliate himself with Annette Wallace, a friend of Jaime's and one of the darlings of Wickdon. The Wallace family is old money, grown rich on panned gold, and now they own several properties in town. No doubt they're a huge source of funding for the hunt this year.

When the key twists in the front door's lock, Trouble leaps to his feet and dashes down the stairs. Betrayed by her own hound. With the door open, Margaret can hear the full force of the storm. It rattles all the trees, and the rain beating down on the earth churns all the hard-frozen dirt to mud. It'll be a nightmare getting into town now, and for a moment, she worries Annette may get stuck. But mercifully, her engine revs, and the car surges out of the muck and toward the foothills.

As Weston's footsteps plod steadily up the staircase, Margaret's heart kicks into a gallop. The door to his room slams shut. She turns back to her book, desperate to calm her nerves before she talks to him, but she can't quite focus. The sound of him rummaging and slamming drawers is maddening. What could he possibly be doing?

With a huff, she rests her book facedown and stalks down the hallway. She flings open his door to find him in the process of emptying all his belongings onto the floor. Her stomach bottoms out when she sees his half-packed suitcases.

"What are you doing?"

Wes jumps as he wheels around to face her. Margaret nearly staggers back a step herself at the sight of him. He's ghostly pale, and with his hair flattened to his head with rainwater, he looks like a wet dog, shivering and too small with its fur matted down. Worst of all, though, are his eyes. There's no mischief that lights them, no humor. Just a hollowed-out exhaustion she recognizes from her own face.

He clutches a string of rosary beads, which he quickly shoves into his pocket as though she's caught him with something unseemly. Margaret had her suspicions, but this confirms them. Weston is Sumic. But it brings her no relief or vindication when he's clearly in the middle of leaving.

"Have you heard of knocking?" he splutters.

"Where are you going?"

He regains his composure enough to smile at her. It sits crookedly on his face, an ill-fitting mask. "Home."

"What?" She can't keep her voice even. "Why?"

"I wasn't cut out for country living," he says breezily, looking up at her through his eyelashes. With raindrops pearled on their ends, they glitter in the light. "You sound distressed. Are you going to miss me?"

A spark of annoyance lights within her. From someone she thought was so dedicated to a dream, she can't abide flippancy. Not now. Not when she *needs* him to stay. Not when she has finally worked up the courage . . . "You can't go home."

"What are you talking about?"

"You'd give up on your dream so easily? Was it worth begging like a dog to stay here, only for you to get homesick after two weeks? Do you value your pride so little?"

His smile falters. "It's not like that."

"Then what is it like?"

He rakes his hand through his hair. Beads of water trickle down his jaw and neck. She finds herself tracing their path to where they slip beneath his collar. "It's a long story. Let's just say my sisters need me at home and leave it at that."

"But I need you here," she says before she can think better of it. She was so cautious, so prepared. How can everything be going so wrong?

"I thought you had enough for the entry fee."

"I don't have a partner."

Wes's face goes slack with confusion. "What does that have to do with me?"

"I need you to be my alchemist. My mother doesn't take students anymore, but she wants the hala more than anything on this earth. You're the only one I can trust to give it to her when the hunt is over because if you do, she won't have any choice but to give you the apprenticeship."

Wes looks entirely overwhelmed. "But . . . But I'm not an alchemist. Not officially."

"Don't be so modest." Margaret sits gingerly on the edge of his bed, which seems to placate him some. "If you can perform a transmutation, you're an alchemist. There's nothing in the rules about being licensed."

"I appreciate your vote of confidence, but there's no way I could give you any kind of competitive advantage."

"All you need to do is enchant something that can kill the hala and show up. That's it."

It's a simplified version of an alchemist's duty during the hunt, but it's the truth. In practice, the Halfmoon Hunt is like any of the other foxhunts that fill this stretch of autumn. Hunting clubs set a pack of scent hounds loose in the woods and follow them on horseback. It ends only when their quarry has gone to ground, gets torn to shreds, or is shot dead. The only difference is that *the* hunt's quarry can only die by an alchemist's hand on the night of the Cold Moon—or so the spotty historical records claim. Despite their best efforts, no alchemist has killed a demiurge in the last two hundred years. Now, the only one who knows for sure how to do it is Evelyn.

No, there has to be another way. She has to believe that.

"But that's not it!" Weston protests. "Look, I've heard of the kinds of stunts alchemists pull during the hunt. Alchemical traps? Sabotage? We both know I'm not subtle or experienced enough. Besides, I don't know anything about hunting." He holds up his fingers and begins ticking them off. "I don't know what kind of equipment you'd need beyond a weapon. I wouldn't know how to anticipate what other competitors are planning. I don't know how to shoot a gun. I've never even ridden a horse!"

"I can tell you what equipment I need, and I can teach you to ride a horse. As for the rest, you won't need to do any of that. I don't need you for cheap tricks. I just need you to exist. Why are you arguing with me?"

"I'm not arguing with you. I'm trying to make you understand that me leaving isn't anything to be disappointed about. I'm sorry. I really am. But you'll have to find someone else."

"You would honestly give up this chance for your family's sake?"

"Every time."

What would it be like if people would come home when *she* asked them to? If love always outweighed ambition? "I see."

"Miss Welty, I . . . I see you're upset, but I don't understand. If your mother's coming back tomorrow, you can enter with her, can't you?" When she says nothing, realization slowly darkens his expression. "But you don't actually know if she's coming back, do you?"

"No." The knife twists in her secret shame. "Not for certain."

It wasn't a lie. It was a truth she wanted to believe.

She's braces herself for his anger, but when she meets his eyes again, he smiles at her ruefully. "I guess you were right to tell me to go home from the beginning, then. Why did you change your mind?"

"Because I felt sorry for you."

She expects him to chafe at her, but what flickers across his face is worse than anger. It's pity. "You feel sorry for *me* and your mom's been gone for three months? Mag—Miss Welty. I know I'm overstepping my bounds here, but that's not normal. You know that, right?"

This is exactly what she was hoping to avoid. She doesn't need any more of his overbearing outrage on her behalf, and she won't endure his judgment. "She's not a bad person."

"I didn't say that." He hesitates. "Wouldn't it be better to go somewhere you're not alone all the time?"

"I don't mind being alone. She trusts me to keep things in order while she's gone."

"*Trusts* you? Really, being trapped in this godforsaken house is some kind of honor?" As his words ring in the tense silence, his eyes widen. He clearly didn't mean to say it like that, but it's too late now.

It *is* an honor, though. Evelyn's love is subtle and hard-won, and Margaret has learned how to see it in every small kindness, every rare gentle word. Her face burns with humiliation. "I don't expect you to understand."

Weston drags a hand down his face. "I'm sorry. You're right. But I'm trying to."

If he can't understand her situation, maybe he can understand her devotion. "My mother researches demiurges. That's why she travels so much. But if I win and give the hala to her, she'll stay. I know it. So I'm . . ." She pauses, drawing in a shaky breath when her throat begins to burn. She will not cry—not in front of him. "I'm asking you again, Mr. Winters. I won't ask again after this. Please stay. There's no one else I can ask."

"God," he says softly. "Please don't look at me like that."

It's as good as a rejection.

Muttering under his breath, Weston rummages through his belongings until he finds a notebook. He tears out a page, scrawls something on it, and hands it to her. "Here. My phone number and address. Just in case you need something or your mom changes her mind about wanting students."

"Thank you." Although there's nothing else she could need from him, Margaret folds it and tucks it into her pocket. "Are you sure you don't want to stay until morning?"

"I'm sure. I said I'd be on the next train." He frowns. "I hate to leave you like this."

"I understand." And she does. His choice is unsurprising, and she can't resent him for it. Margaret counted four siblings in that photo, and he mentioned his father passing. She considers telling him that she's sorry he had to make this decision in the first place, but it's better to leave it at this, to let the cut be clean.

She grabs one of his bags and helps him down the stairs. Trouble prances excitedly around them, as if he thinks he's going somewhere with Weston. It guts her to see how her hound has taken to him.

"Well. I wish I could say it's been a pleasure." He tips his cap to her. "Take care, Miss Welty."

He says it so earnestly, as if he wants to press those words into her hands like a gift. He smiles at her, but all she can see is the worry in his eyes. Rain sparkles off the garden stones, so loud she can scarcely hear her own breathing. "Goodbye, Mr. Winters."

As she watches him walk away, the answering squeeze of her heart is as distressing as it is painfully familiar. How many times will she watch someone leave this place and never look back, while she is left here like a ghost to haunt it?

When her mother left her alone for the first time, she didn't know what to do with herself. At first, she tried to enjoy her freedom. She put on the record player and let the music fill the emptiness. She ate all the sweets in the house and poured herself a glass of her father's expensive scotch. But come morning, her head ached and her stomach churned and she was still completely, crushingly alone. As hours became days became weeks, she realized that if her mind could protect her from remembering Evelyn's failed experiment, it could protect her from this pain, too. She could learn how to make the sting of abandonment fade into numbness. She could learn to detach until it felt like she wasn't real at all.

But as she shuts the rain-swollen door, Margaret feels Weston's rejection like a blade wedged into an old wound. It's a sharp, sudden reminder of being wretchedly lonely in the wake of her mother's grief. Here in the echoing dark of the manor, there are ghosts all around her, ones she can only half see. Being left alone with them again is more than she can bear right now.

Everything she wants and all the tenuous happiness she claimed is slipping through her fingers. She can't believe she made herself vulnerable to this pain *again*. She can't believe she was so stupid as to wait until the last minute. If only she'd been braver . . .

No, she can still do this. If she must choose between giving up and working with someone else—anyone else—then she will have to compromise. Tomorrow, she will go to Wickdon and find herself an alchemist.

The very thought makes her feel ill, and her hands itch for something to do. Something mindless and safe and useful. *Laundry,* she thinks. That, at least, she can do.

In a daze, Margaret goes to Weston's bedroom and strips the bed. As she folds a pillowcase over her arm, a cryptic note comes tumbling out—a twice-underlined exhortation to *remember carbin necks week,* whatever that means. The sheets smell like him. Cloying aftershave and a touch of sulfur. It almost hurts to breathe it in.

I don't mind being alone, she told him.

How has she managed to convince herself of that lie for so long?

The next morning is bitter cold, the sky roiling and black as the sea.

The windows of the Blind Fox are streaked with water and lamplight, and when Margaret pushes open the doors, the noise of the pub spills onto the street like ale. Panic constricts her chest as she takes in the crowd. It's just past nine in the morning, way too early to be drinking. But judging by the laughter and flushed faces all around her, she wonders if any of these people went home at all. Everyone wants to see who is brave—or foolish—enough to sign up for the hunt.

Never has she wanted to be seen less.

Margaret keeps her hood raised as she takes her place in line. Few eyes find her in the early-morning dark, and the ones that do slide off her like water on butcher paper. It only takes a few minutes to reach the front of the line, where Mrs. Wreford sits behind a table with a pen ready in her hand. Beside her, a radio crackles out a tune too jaunty for the occasion.

Margaret slides the hood back from her face and shakes her damp hair loose. As soon as they make eye contact, Mrs. Wreford rears back. "Maggie? What're *you* doing here?"

Her reaction draws some attention. Margaret sinks deeper into her jacket. "I'm here to register for the hunt."

"And does your mother know about this very dangerous thing you plan to do?"

"My mother isn't here to have an opinion one way or another."

She heaves a resigned sigh. "Well. I guess that's all we can say about that."

Mrs. Wreford has never cared much for her mother.

Margaret places her entry fee on the table, and it aches to see all those bills laid flat on the stained tabletop. Mrs. Wreford scrapes the money off the table. "And the alchemist accompanying you?"

"I haven't decided. I was hoping there would be someone who hasn't found a partner yet."

Mrs. Wreford gestures at the full bar behind them. "I'm sure you could have your pick of them."

As Margaret looks out at all the beer-ruddy faces, all of the people in their pearls and fine clothing, she realizes exactly how out of her league she is. Some of these people drove that Yu'adir family out of Bardover. Some of them subscribe to the conspiracy that the Yu'adir are involved in manipulating global financial markets, or that they use Katharist children's blood in dark rituals. How can she possibly know which one of them won't see her hang for daring to enter as soon as they find out what she is? How can she know which of them won't steal the fox from her?

The only one she could depend upon on either count was Weston.

She feels so foolish and cold now for dancing around the topic for two weeks. He is Sumic, and she is Yu'adir. What judgment could they have passed on one another? If anything, he may have understood her better than anyone else in Wickdon.

As if sensing her despair, Mrs. Wreford says, "You have until midnight. Come back and get your money if you don't find someone by then."

Margaret turns to leave just as Mrs. Wreford cinches her fingers around Margaret's upper arm. *The claw.* Everyone in Wickdon knows this move well. It can stretch a fifteen-minute errand into an hours-long interrogation. It says, *You won't be leaving until you've answered my questions.* She applies just enough pressure to lock Margaret in that flailing space between flight and freezing. "You know you don't *have* to do this, don't you?"

"I know."

"And you understand what people will say if you go through with this? You're aware of what they might do?"

"Of course I am."

Mrs. Wreford looks like she wants to say something else, but her grip goes slack. "Then I suppose there's no talking you out of this."

"I'll be alright. I promise."

Mrs. Wreford's look of concern follows her all the way to the door. She can feel the rainwater and sweat drying stiff beneath her collar. She can feel a hundred eyes on her, cutting her down to the bone. She shoves her way into the bitter cold. She's already shaking before the wind gusts through her loose hair. It's plastered to the back of her neck, slick as kelp. She rakes it out of her face, then shoves her hands into her pockets to warm them. Her fingers brush against the wadded-up paper Weston gave her before he left.

My phone number and address. Just in case you need anything, he told her. The city is only about a three-hour train ride from here. It's not too late for him to come back before registration closes. Assuming, of course, he *wants* to come back.

Ambition wasn't enough to tether him here, but family still grounds him. If he's serious about providing them a better life, maybe she can tempt him with more than his own dreams. Money is tight these days, but Margaret doesn't need seventy-five dollars.

All she needs is Evelyn.

Margaret jogs across the street and into the Wallace Inn. Annette leans over the counter with her chin in her hands and a dreamy, far-off expression. When her gaze lands on Margaret, she goes rigid and glances away as though the very sight of her is catching. It's long since ceased to surprise or bother Margaret.

"Good morning, Maggie." At least Annette manages to sound pleasant.

"Can I use your phone, please?"

"Oh, um. Sure?"

Margaret ducks underneath the counter and into the back office. She unfolds the paper as carefully as she can, but her wet hands are trembling with cold and nerves. When she finally manages to peel it open, what she sees dismays her. Moisture has smudged the ink, and even if she could read it clearly, his handwriting is abysmal. Is that a nine or a six? A one or a seven?

Why did she expect he'd make this easy on her? With a groan of frustration, she dials what she thinks is the correct number. It rings and rings before someone picks up. "Hello?"

"Is this the Winters residence?"

"Sorry, sweetheart," he says blearily. "You've got the wrong number."

She hangs up and swears softly, resting her head in her hands. If she dials every possible permutation, she might land on the right one eventually. But she doesn't exactly have the patience or the time for *might*.

Margaret stares at the paper again. Although her damp eyelashes make the words hazy, his address is mostly intact. Enough for her to read: 7302 Slate Avenue, Apartment 804.

Registration closes tonight. If she leaves now, she can make it to Dunway and back before midnight. It's the most reckless, harebrained scheme she's ever concocted. It may be the *only* reckless, harebrained scheme she's ever concocted. But Weston is her only chance, and competing is the only way she can survive.

If she wins, her mother will return, and Margaret will forge her victory into armor. No one like Jaime could hurt her again. No one would dare if she makes herself into the New Albian hero they've been waiting for. She has to do this. If she wants anything to change, she will have to find Weston—and convince him to come back.

9

It's been twelve hours since Wes returned home, and already, he longs for Wickdon. He misses the privacy of his bedroom in Welty Manor, dust and all. He misses the perfect silence of the mountains before daybreak and the way the mist glitters on the firs. He even misses the ghost of Maggie's presence, her silent judgments and her full-moon eyes. Life had a simple, comfortable rhythm in Wickdon. Better yet, it held promise. Maybe in a few days or weeks, the dream he's clung to all these years will seem as childish and impossible as Mad thinks it is. But for the time being, he feels completely wretched.

The afternoon sun filters through the window and dapples the floor with dust-swirled tiles of light. That's always been a small joy for him—living here, where the windows open to the city down below. Some of his friends still live in tenements built before the reform some twenty years ago. Their rooms face dumbbell-shaped air shafts, where the stench of bilge water and garbage rises like wildfire smoke. But Wes can hardly take comfort in this view when all he can think of is how Welty Manor overlooked miles and miles of redwoods and the perfect blue of the sea.

He sits on the threadbare couch in their living room, watching a cup of coffee go cold on the table. His youngest sister, Edie, is draped over him like a drowsing cat. Normally, he'd think it's sweet if not horribly irritating, but he can't muster much else but dismay at the moment. He wants be alone, but he doesn't have the energy to tell her off—or to deal with her inevitable crocodile tears if he tries.

Her arms have been locked around him since the moment he came home. Last night, he sneaked through the door with the precision of a thief. But when the lock *snick*ed shut behind him, a blanket-swaddled figure appeared in the hallway. He lifted a finger to his lips, but as soon as Edie locked eyes with him, she gasped and came careening toward him. Her every step shook the photos of their long-dead relatives and the statues of the entire communion of saints.

It's always been Edie he sees first. It's always been her waiting by the door when he slunk back from another failed apprenticeship or a night out. Those were his favorite nights. Most of the time, he was merry with drink and would carry her around the apartment, singing until Christine yelled at them to go to sleep.

Edie touches a sticky hand to his face, startling him so badly he nearly conks their heads together. "What's wrong? You look so sad."

"I'm tired. That's all."

She looks at him skeptically. "You slept all morning."

Ah, yes. Now *there's* a touch of what he was used to in Wickdon. It only adds insult to injury that it's a six-year-old giving him attitude. "Well, that's because I need my beauty sleep. It takes a lot of work to look like this, you know."

"Yeah, right."

"He's just feeling sorry for himself," Christine calls from the kitchen.

"I am not!"

"Did you get kicked out again?" Edie asks.

"No, actually. For your information, I came back because I missed you too much, but if you're going to be unappreciative, I guess I'll toss you out the window. Or maybe right into the garbage. What do you think about that?" He throws her over his shoulder, and Edie shrieks in delight.

"Can you not?" Christine says. "Mam's sleeping."

His stomach pangs with guilt. "Sorry."

Edie huffs her disappointment. As they sink back onto the cushions, the apartment falls eerily quiet—as quiet as it can be, anyway. The cuckoo clock ticks and traffic whirs seven stories below them, and somewhere down the hall, the McAlees are shouting at each other over the radio.

Then, of all things, there's a knock on the door.

"Can you get that?" Christine asks.

"Move, Edie." She clings to his neck as stubbornly as a barnacle to the hull of a ship, giggling wickedly as he staggers to his feet. With a groan, he extricates himself and sets her onto the floor. "Go help your sister with dinner. Maybe she'll give you a treat if you're good."

It's enough to convince her to leave him alone. She scampers into the kitchen with such enthusiasm, he hears Christine swear in surprise. He sorely hopes he hasn't doomed dinner. Christine insisted on making something overcomplicated in honor of his return.

Now there's the matter of their visitor.

There's no one else it could be other than another well-meaning neighbor here to offer another casserole or ask after his mother. The prospect of making small talk or fielding questions about his future makes him want to perish on the spot, but he'll have to perform, just as he always has. Drawing in his breath, he slips on a smile and opens the door.

It's Maggie.

Even in the dim light of the hallway, her hair shines like poured gold. But her face is drawn and her eyes are wide mirrors, reflecting his own haggard bewilderment. For a moment, he can do nothing but stare. Then, realizing he has to say *something,* he stammers, "M-Miss Welty? What are you doing here?"

"I couldn't read the phone number you gave me."

"That . . . still doesn't answer my question."

Her eyes skirt away from him. "I need to talk to you."

Wes leans his hip against the doorway. "You really must've missed me if you came all this way. A letter would've sufficed."

"I don't have time or interest in writing you love letters." Her sharp tone sends his stomach plummeting with a feeling he doesn't fully understand. "I'm being serious."

Gently, he says, "So talk to me."

"I know I said I wouldn't ask again, but I am. I have to. I need you to come back to Wickdon with me."

Of all the things to come out of her mouth, this is the last he expected. Wes casts a furtive look over his shoulder. "Look, I meant what I told you last night. I can't abandon them. They need me. It would've saved you a lot of trouble if you'd—"

"It'd benefit you, too." Frustration edges into her voice. "The prize money is all yours."

All yours.

His mind short-circuits at the thought of seventy-five dollars. He should not entertain this. He *knows* he should tell her no. But last night, he asked every saint in heaven to put in a good word with God, and they have delivered. This opportunity would keep his family afloat *and* let him pursue his dream.

He only wishes they'd found something a little more . . . certain. This plan depends entirely on her winning—and riskier still, his ability to be of any use to her. "I need to think about it."

"There's no time to think about it." Her ferocity startles him. "You wanted a chance to be an alchemist and help your family. This is it."

"Oh! And who is this?"

Christine rests her elbow against his shoulder and smiles so deviously at Maggie, he feels himself blush with embarrassment. She's wearing his hand-me-downs again: a crisp shirt that is whiter than when he owned it, loose trousers over her oxford heels, and a pair of suspenders. Her voice is playful, her eyelashes drawn flirtatiously low, and it takes everything in Wes's power not to scream. She's just doing this to annoy him—not that either of them has any genuine interest in Maggie, of course, but still. It's a sore subject.

Once, when he was sixteen, he tried to woo a girl named Hedy Baker who worked at some swanky downtown theater. He waited for her every day after her shift so that he could walk her home, even though coming home late irritated his alchemy teacher to no end. The way the lobby lights twinkled on Hedy's dress made every verbal lashing worth it. One night, he invited her to come by his apartment before dinner, and right as he opened the door, Christine swaggered out with one of Wes's old bow ties loose around her neck.

I'm ready for our date, she announced, and the moment he saw Hedy's starry expression, he knew he didn't stand a chance.

It wasn't the first time Christine poached one of his dates, but at least it was the last. They've been together for two years now, and while a petty part of him still hasn't forgiven his sister, he can't blame her. They're both their father's children, charmers to their last.

"Christine," Wes says, a stiff grin fixed in place, "this is Miss Welty. Miss Welty, this is my sister Christine."

"A pleasure." Christine shoulders past him and extends her hand. Maggie shakes it uncertainly.

"Wes," she says primly, "were you going to leave poor Miss Welty standing in the *freezing cold hallway*? Or are you going to invite her inside?"

"Well—"

"Excuse my brother. He's a bit dense sometimes. Please come inside. I'll make you some coffee."

By the time Maggie crosses the threshold, looking like a dog ready to bite, Christine is already halfway to the kitchen. It's almost unbearable, having her *here* in this cramped foyer. She looks so painfully out of place in his home, like she's been cut out of Wickdon and pasted here. A sloppy collage of two lives he can't fit together.

He watches her examine the mountain of shoes at their feet, then the cheerfully painted statue of the Holy Mother veiled in blue. He wants to tear down every incriminating Sumic relic and throw sheets over all the dust-caked furniture. But it's too late. She can see it all, the pieces of his soul, just as he saw hers. There's no hiding the realities of their lives from each other. He remembers the way her lip curled when he told her he felt sorry for her. Now, ashamed of how small and cluttered his home is, he understands how alike they are. Misfortune has hardened them both. It's roughened her, but it's polished him to a sheen. If he lets the world believe he is all surface, then there is nothing to expose. Beneath her implacable stare, however, he is utterly naked.

"Can I have your coat?" he mumbles.

"If you're not coming with me, I really should go."

"Have some coffee at least. My sister will be offended if you don't."

"Fine." Maggie shrugs out of her jacket and hands it to him. It's warm and covered in dog hair, but it smells like Wickdon—like her. The brine of the sea and the richness of the earth after a storm. "But I can't stay long."

She tries to slip past him, but he catches her by the elbow. While she looks affronted, she doesn't scowl or flinch like he's struck her this time. "I know you want your mom to come back, but there has to be some other way. Joining the hunt is as good as a death wish."

"It's not only about my mother," she bites out. "I want to win. I want Jaime Harrington to leave me alone. I want to show everyone I'm not afraid to do this, because I'm not. I'm not afraid of dying."

"Well, I am."

She meets his eyes steadily. "I wouldn't let you."

"Oh, no? And how many people are participating, hundreds? I can't believe it's me of all people telling you this, but you have to think this through. Do you really think there's a remote chance of you winning, even if we don't die?"

"There's more than a chance. I won't lose. I swear it."

"How can you be sure?"

"I haven't met a better shot than me, a better hound than Trouble, or anyone playing for a higher stake than ours." The conviction burning in her eyes makes his mouth go dry. Here in the hazy sunlight, they are the intoxicating color of honey, of whiskey, of—

Edie clears her throat.

They whirl around to face her. While she doesn't say a word, her gaze is locked pointedly on Wes's fingers curled around Maggie's elbow. She smiles angelically. "Christine says the coffee is ready."

With that, she turns and sashays back to the kitchen. Where the hell is she learning these things? How much of her life has he missed while he was away?

"She's cute," Maggie offers.

"Don't let her hear you say that." Wes grimaces and lets go of her arm. "Alright. I've thought about your proposal."

Her face goes soft with surprise. "You have?"

Not well enough to be sensible, but enough to make up his mind. If only for a few weeks, he'll be a real alchemist. He won't have to surrender his dream. As long as there's a glimmer of hope, he must seize it. Even if his family will hate him for it. Telling Mam he's joining the hunt will be as good as slapping her in the face.

A part of him has always known it would come to this: choosing between his heritage and his ambitions. Devout Sumics don't become politicians in this country. If he doesn't assimilate, he'll be unelectable, since most people believe that Sumics pledge their loyalty to the pope rather than the president. Elections have been won on a simple platform of *New Albion for New Albians*. A few years ago, it was hard to go a day without hearing some Katharist minister on the radio decrying Sumicism as "the ally of tyranny and the enemy of prosperity." But what better way to swear fealty to New Albion than to kill the hala, a creature Sumics hold sacred? Assuming, of course, they don't run him out of Wickdon the moment they find out what he is.

"I'm in," he says with more confidence than he feels. "I have to figure out how to break it to my family."

He thinks he sees the entire spectrum of human emotion pass

over her face in the blink of an eye. It settles on guilt. "You'd best do it quickly. We have to register before midnight."

"Before *midnight*? It takes at least three hours to get back to Wickdon from here." He groans. "God, they're going to kill me for leaving on such short notice."

"I did try to call."

"Well, that would've saved us both a lot of grief," he mutters. The cuckoo clock on the wall chimes. "The rest of my sisters will be home for dinner soon. I'll tell them then."

"Where should I wait for you?"

"Wait for me? Oh, no, you're staying right here. You need to drink your coffee. Besides, my mom will wring my neck if she finds out I had a guest over without feeding them."

Her face pales. "You want me to stay for dinner?"

"Yes." He tosses her coat onto the overflowing rack. "I know it'll be a little different than you're used to, but my family is a friendly bunch. Maybe a little too friendly, but hey, at least it'll be interesting."

"Interesting," she repeats flatly. "I can't wait."

Wes grins at her. Then, his cheer fades as he realizes what he finally has to confess. "I'm sure you've already figured it out by now, but . . . When I tell them what I'm doing, things could get awkward, so I guess I should mention that my family is Sumic. *I'm* Sumic. Just in case that bothers you."

He braces himself for her judgment, but she only tips her head to the side and blinks those doe eyes of hers. For the first time, he thinks he understands why people say dogs resemble their owners. Trouble has given him the same look before. "Why would that bother me?"

"I . . ." He fumbles for words, embarrassed of his own fear. "I don't know."

Maggie watches him like she wants to tell him a secret. Like she's weighing his trustworthiness. In the end, he must come up short. "What you think of the hala doesn't matter to me. Only that you're prepared to kill it."

"I am." At least he certainly hopes so. To stave off his grim mood, he adds, "I promise there aren't any pagan rites or ritual cannibalism or anything like that. That's only during Mass."

"That's a little disappointing."

Never has he tasted a relief so sweet in his life. He laughs breathlessly. "Why don't you come sit down?"

10

Margaret has never seen a home like the Winterses'. Although night has swept through the city like the tide, it's warm and bursting with life. Pans hang above the range alongside thick, twine-tied clusters of herbs, and all sorts of strange objects fill their shelves. There are small statues of haloed saints, candles burning inside painted glass jars, and a particularly disturbing collection of icons: the demiurges, drenched in silvergilt blood, looking beatific even as they're struck down by hunters. Margaret can almost understand Weston's propensity for dramatics when confronted with these images. The only church in Wickdon is a plain, dignified Katharist building with clear windows and white walls. The Sumic one she passed on the way here, however, glimmered like it was inlaid with jewels.

Outside the window, clotheslines web across the alley and a gray tabby cat meows impatiently from its perch on the sill. Weston unlatches the casement and scoops it into his arms like a baby. The cat looks indignant, slowly blinking its yellow eyes at her, but it remains docile as he carries it to the table and slides onto the chair beside her.

Elbow-to-elbow, the seven of them crowd around a table meant for four, and they're all shouting over each other, nearly hysterical with laughter. Margaret tries her best to look attentive, although all she'd like to do is lock herself in the bathroom until the noise dies down. Weston was right in saying that she'd be out of her element here.

She wasn't made for the city. Everything about it was tailor-made to overwhelm her. Cars blaring their horns at traffic stops. Zeppelins advertising brand names dragging their bellies low across the sky. And the people—all the people. People in drop-waist gowns, people dripping with pearls, people pouring out of blindingly bright shopping malls. Even now, her hands tremble with the dregs of her adrenaline.

The Winterses' home doesn't provide her much more security. She hasn't eaten dinner with her mother in years, and seeing the easy companionship Weston's family shares is almost painful. It reminds her of happier days, when her mother would set her and David on the countertop to "supervise" while she cooked. These days, Evelyn takes her meals in her lab if she remembers to eat at all. Dinner here, meanwhile, is a production. With all the glasses, dishware, and food piled high on the table, the wood groans under its weight. The smell of browned beef and simmered bay bubbles thick from a cauldron in the center, and a loaf of bread still steams with oven warmth. Margaret is about to tear into it when Weston's mother says, "Who wants to say grace?"

Everyone falls silent, as though she's asked which one of them shattered her favorite vase. Aoife Winters sits at the head of the table, surveying her children with a graveness belied by the mirth sparkling in her eyes. Her hair is near-black and streaked with stately gray, as if she'd woven a silver ribbon through her braid.

"No one? Really?"

She speaks with a lilting Banvish accent Margaret doesn't hear often in Wickdon. Only from the sailors and dockworkers on shipment days. When they leave in the morning from the inn, she's heard people mutter, *The whole place'll reek of ale for weeks.* Margaret still aches from the earlier worry in Weston's eyes when he confessed that his family was Sumic. Now, she regrets her response. Maybe she should have reassured him more earnestly. Maybe she should have told him her own secret, assuming he hasn't already figured it out himself.

"Miss Welty should do it," Edie says solemnly. "She's our guest."

Weston smothers a laugh in his sleeve. Colleen elbows him hard enough that he hisses something under his breath. The cat in his arms wriggles free and lands with a dull *thud* of its paws against the floorboards.

"I'll do it," Christine cuts in.

"Thank you," Aoife says.

In eerie unison, they steeple their hands and bow their heads. Margaret imitates them as best she can, watching from beneath her hair as she slumps lower in her chair. Sumic tradition is unfamiliar to her, but these small rituals comfort her. They remind her of the prayers her father used to say over their Shabbos meals.

"Bless us, O Lord, and these thy gifts which we are about to receive," Christine begins. The rest rushes by in a practiced monotone, so quickly Margaret can't make sense of the words. When she finishes, the rest of them intone, "Amen."

Then, the room bursts into chaos.

Weston dives for the ladle, only for Mad to swat his hand away. "Wait your turn, Weston. Your *mother* and your *guest* may want to eat something, don't you think?"

"Yeah, yeah."

While Mad isn't looking, Colleen tears off a hunk of bread and stuffs it into her cheeks like a squirrel. She gives Margaret a conspiratorial wink. The finer details of their faces differ, but the Winters children all have various shades of their mother's dark hair—and the same spark of mischief in their eyes. Colleen, however, is the only one of them with eyes as pale as frost.

The oldest girls are beautiful in very different ways. Mad, with her bobbed hair and red-painted lips, is glamorous and stark in the way women in the fashion magazines are. Christine wears her hair even shorter—and certainly more well-groomed—than even Weston does, and her nose is dusted with freckles.

"Here, let me get you a plate, Margaret," Aoife says. "They're sharks, the whole lot of them. Especially my son."

"You don't have to do that." Guilt curdles her stomach as her gaze lands on Aoife's bandaged hand.

"No complaints." Aoife ladles a heaping portion of stew with her good hand and places it in front of Margaret. "What else can I get you?"

Christine spears a piece of meat on her plate. "Mam, let the poor thing breathe."

A strange emotion grabs hold of her heart and squeezes. She feels suddenly like a spider in its web, watching herself from the darkest corner of the room. From here, Margaret sees herself for what she is. A dour, inkblot stain on the brightness of this home. She doesn't belong with these people. She doesn't deserve their kindness or their attempts to fold her into their easy rapport with one another. No, it's more than rapport. They love each other. It suffuses every kind gesture and sharp word.

I know I'm overstepping my bounds here, but that's not normal, Weston told her before he left. *You know that, don't you?*

She wonders if *this* is what normal is to him. Once, her family was like his. If she closes her eyes, she can imagine the four of them safely tucked inside the manor, gathered around the fireplace. Margaret's throat tightens against the sudden wave of homesickness. That version of Welty Manor is irrecoverable, which makes her feel all the more desolate.

Weston nudges her knee with his and leans in close enough to murmur, "Hanging in there?"

It feels as though he's pulled a sheet over their heads; her world narrows to the electric sensation of his leg against hers and the attentive, concerned glow in his eyes. She nods. He frowns skeptically but doesn't press. As soon as he glances away, the fluttering in her stomach stops. All she has to do is finish dinner, and they'll be on their way to Wickdon again.

Margaret reaches for the bread at the exact moment Weston does. Their hands brush, and both of them jerk away like they've been singed. Her stomach twists itself into another impressive knot. If she doesn't collect herself quickly, one of his sisters will notice. Margaret has endured mockery all her life, but somehow, the embarrassment of being teased about *this* would destroy her. It's not as though she can tell them she finds him repulsive.

"Sorry," he mutters. "After you."

Heat still tingles up her arm as she tears off a piece of bread for herself. She dips it into the stew and takes a bite. It's heartier and far better than anything she's had in months, rich with salt and a pungent touch of fresh oregano. She stops only when the table goes quiet. The tips of her fingers sting with heat from where she's submerged them to the knuckle in broth.

Sheepishly, she says, "It's good."

Aoife smiles radiantly. "Have as much as you want."

"So," Christine says. "Tell us about yourself, Margaret."

Margaret swallows thickly. The half-chewed bread slithers down her throat and rakes against her sternum like nails. She's suddenly aware of Weston's leg brushing hers again. It makes her skin itch.

"Don't interrogate her," he says. "She's had a long day."

Christine folds her hands beneath her chin. "Interrogate her? Such an accusation. Forgive me if I want to get to know our guest better."

"I'm curious, too." Mad's every word is knife-point sharp. "What brings you here, anyway? You're awfully far from home."

"Behave." Aoife is slathering butter on a slice of bread with surprising dexterity. Weston opens his mouth, ready to fire off a retort, but snaps it shut when his mother shoves the bread into his hand.

"Mam, honestly," he says at the same time Mad hisses, "Stop babying him."

They glare at each other across the table.

Aoife busies herself with buttering another slice of bread. "Stop bickering and eat your dinner. It's only going to get cold. Margaret is the only one of you with any sense."

Mad takes a long sip of her drink. Her eyes meet Margaret's over the rim of her glass. It's immediately clear that Mad doesn't like her, but Margaret can't be certain if it's something she's done or if it's because Mad doesn't like anyone.

"Well." Christine claps. "Shall we break the ice some other way? Maybe some fun facts. Madeline, why don't you start us off?"

"I'm holding a very sharp knife." Mad waves it for emphasis. "As a reminder to all of you."

"That's not *fun.* Oh!" Colleen slams her hands on the table, rattling all the cutlery. "How about this one? Did you know that we have ten times as many bacterial cells as our own—"

"Gross!" Edie cries.

Colleen looks dejected. "Clearly we all have our own ideas of fun here."

"Miss Welty, please, save us from ourselves," Christine presses. "Tell us how you met our darling brother."

Six sets of eyes lock onto her. Weston's burn with a pleading intensity, the meaning of which she can't discern. "Evelyn Welty is my mother. Mr. Winters is—was planning to stay at our house until she returned from her trip. She's conducting research elsewhere, but I suspect she'll be back soon enough once she hears about the hunt. Demiurges are a particular interest of hers."

"I see." Aoife's withering gaze falls on her son. "I was under the impression that she'd been instructing him."

Weston goes as pale as sun-bleached sand.

Colleen prods intently at a potato in her bowl, but she smirks at him and mouths, *"You are in so much trouble."*

"I *did* say she gave me a lot of independence," he says weakly.

"I can't believe this." Mad's chair scrapes the floorboards as she stands.

What have I done? Margaret thinks.

As Christine and Colleen dissolve into hushed chattering,

Margaret helplessly watches Mad stalk toward the window. She throws it open and lights a cigarette, and the rainwater beaded on the glass glimmers beneath the flame dancing on her lighter. The gray tabby hops onto a stool beside her and butts her hand until she relents and strokes its head.

"Wes, why did you lie to me?" Aoife asks.

"Why *didn't* he lie to you?" Mad snaps. The end of her cigarette smokes like a just-fired gun. "He's a selfish child who's never thought about anyone but himself."

"Madeline, enough. Our guest—"

"I don't care! I don't care about her." She rounds on Margaret. "Why are you even here?"

"Because I need his help," Margaret says as evenly as she can. "I intend to register for the hunt, but I need an alchemist to do it. If we win, my mother will give him the apprenticeship and the prize money will be enough to pay for your mother's surgery."

"A charity case, then. We're not interested in your pity or your blood money."

"You don't get to make that decision!" Weston flushes. "This is my choice, and I'm going."

Colleen chokes on a nervous laugh.

"Mamaí," Edie whines.

"Colleen, take your sister to her room."

"But—"

"Now."

Colleen dips her head deferentially and grabs Edie by the hand. "Yes, ma'am."

"As for you two," Aoife says, rounding on Weston and Mad, "if you two want to brawl like drunks, then do it outside. But as long as you're in my kitchen, you will talk to each other like reasonable adults."

"I don't have anything else to say to him," Mad says. "He's already turned his back on this family."

Tension sits between them like an unwelcome guest. Margaret

spoons another bite of stew into her mouth and tries not to wince when it burns her throat. Her eyes water.

Aoife rests her head in her hand. "It's too dangerous for a girl your age. What would your mother say if she knew what you were doing? You'll get yourself killed."

"Mam, please," Weston protests. "No one is getting killed."

"But if Wes dies," Christine says brightly, "it's one less mouth to feed."

"She's got a point," he says.

"Don't even joke about that!" Aoife cries. "That hunt is wrong, Wes. You know it is. I worry about you too much already. I can't worry about your soul on top of it."

"He won't have to kill it himself," Margaret says. "I'll handle it."

"I don't think the bible says accessory to murder is a mortal sin," Christine offers. "The Lord forgives and all that, right?"

"Exactly!" Weston slides out of his chair to kneel at his mother's side. He takes her good hand in both of his. Like this, he's the image of a perfect, devoted son. "I know it's wrong, but what other choice do we have? Miss Welty needs me, and we need the money. This is my last chance. The last time I'll ever take this risk. I swear, after this, I'll come home if I fail. I'll find a job. You won't have to worry about me anymore."

"And if you succeed?" Aoife asks.

"Then I'll devote my life to making up for what I've done." He pauses, then continues with redoubled solemnity: "To both you and God."

When was the last time Evelyn had looked at her so tenderly? Aoife's love is a knot of concern and anger and affection. If she were to tug at Evelyn's until it all came apart, she isn't sure what she would find at the center.

"I can't let you do this in good conscience," Aoife says, "but I can't stop you, either. All I can make you promise is that you'll come back to me in one piece."

"I will. I promise."

When Aoife cups his cheek and kisses the top of his head, Christine and Mad exchange exasperated looks. There is a secret language of sisters, Margaret thinks. One that she will never understand.

Mad stiffens, as if sensing Margaret's gaze, and turns sharply toward her. It's hard to read her through the swirling gray of her cigarette's smoke, but her eyes look solid black. Her voice is all venom when she says, "I hope you're pleased with yourself."

The worst part is, she's not. For so long, she tended only to herself and Trouble. But now if they fail, it's not just her life on the line. It's not just her who suffers. It's all the Winters girls—and their hopeless brother, too.

Weston is suspiciously quiet.

He didn't speak during their grim walk to the station, and he doesn't speak now on the empty southbound train. The air crackles around him with a manic buoyancy that Margaret doesn't care for. He's got one foot kicked up on the seat across from them, and with the other, he chisels away at her patience with its ceaseless *tap-tap-tapping* against the floor.

He probably doesn't even realize what he's doing. As much as it irritates her, she bites her tongue. She'll give him leniency for now, considering he's earned the bitter resentment of his entire family in only one evening. Especially considering it's her fault for dragging him back into this scheme. Margaret tries not to coddle her guilt too much, but it's tenacious and doesn't need much to survive. Remembering the hatred in Mad's voice will feed it for days.

Outside her window, the New Albian countryside unspools into threads of night-dulled green and gold. She can see little through the darkness or the reflection of the snack cart as it trundles down the aisle. When it stops in front of them, Weston buys a cup of coffee.

"Do you really need caffeine?" she asks.

He pauses mid-sip, his expression sour. "Yes. Why?"

Tap-tap-tap.

Margaret jabs a finger into his bobbing knee and pushes until his foot rests flat on the ground. He *harrumph*s and takes another agitated sip.

"You're anxious," she says.

"I need to stay awake. Besides, coffee calms me down."

"Maybe you should take a nap instead. You're in a foul mood."

"A foul mood?" She swears she hears something within him crack when he smiles. "No, I could never be in a foul mood in a situation like this."

"And what kind of situation is that?"

"One where I'm alone with a beautiful woman."

Her face burns. Once, this kind of behavior might have annoyed her, even flustered her. But right now, all she feels is anger at how empty and calculating those words are. And maybe a little hurt that he would lie so plainly to her. As if he would find a girl as rough as her beautiful.

You can't hide from me, she thinks. *I've seen you.*

She realizes now that Weston Winters is very good at only letting people see what he wants them to. Golden-boy polish. Reckless confidence. Honeyed words. But he's nothing but a liar, his pieces held together with cheap gilt. As she stares at him, unblinking, his smile withers. Half of her wants the satisfaction of flaying him to the bone, but the stronger, kinder half pities him.

And you've seen me. As much as she wanted to, she couldn't shut him out, either. That is the chain that binds them together. They've seen each other at their most vulnerable, and now they must bear each other's burdens.

"Does this act usually work for you?" Margaret asks.

"Excuse me?"

"Talk to me honestly, or don't talk at all." The tips of his ears go red. *Good.* If he's angry, he'll be easier to crack. She's seen his temper flare enough now to know it's his most easily exploited weakness. "You're acting like nothing is wrong."

"And what would you rather I do? Would it make you happy if I cried?"

"No." She can't keep the edge out of her voice. "I want to understand why you're so determined to be cavalier when we stand to lose everything. I want to understand why you're shutting me out when we need to trust each other. Your sister called you a liar, and she clearly thinks you're selfish. I don't think either of those things is entirely true."

"Who, Mad? Of course she thinks that. She always will. It doesn't matter what I do."

"You make it easy for her."

"It keeps her expectations low."

"Mine are high."

They glare at each other, swaying with the motion of the train on its tracks. At last, Weston lets out a defeated, frustrated sound.

"I have to be cavalier, or I'll lose my mind. You saw what they think of what I'm doing. All I am is a disappointment, and if I acknowledged it, I'd . . ." He runs a hand through his already tousled hair. "It's not like I can stay in Dunway, anyway. The only job prospects I have are the factory or the docks, and where will that leave everyone? Then maybe someday I'll get married and have kids, then I'll drop dead young and leave my family to scramble, just like my dad. Unless I become an alchemist, nothing is ever going to change."

"What difference does it make if you're an alchemist?"

"I meant what I told you when we met. I want to run for senate. Only alchemists are electable, and only politicians can make any real change in this country."

"They don't, though."

"Exactly! Alchemy is supposed to be about change and progress, but everyone in power has forgotten that. None of them will change a damn thing as long as they benefit from how things are." Bitterness coats his every word. "With real progressive policies, no six-year-old would go to bed hungry. No one would lose a parent to unsafe working conditions. No one would have to fit six people into a two-bedroom apartment. So there. Are you happy now?"

She is, and she isn't. It's a noble dream. If it weren't for the earnest *want* smoldering in his eyes, she may not have believed him. It makes her think of her father. Once, he told her that all people have a holy duty: tikkun olam, the repair of the world.

For Yu'adir, alchemy is a science as well as a spiritual practice. Even Katharists believe that much. But where Katharists see the alchemical fire as a symbol of God's divine judgment—the means to separate spirit from matter as God will someday separate the wheat from the chaff—Yu'adir see alchemy as a gentler thing. Only by understanding the physical world can they understand the divine, and that in itself is a means of tikkun olam. But wisdom is only one path of many. Her father also spoke of good deeds and acts of justice. Margaret thinks he would admire Weston for wanting to use alchemy to create systemic change, but she doesn't know if she can be so idealistic.

She's read almost every alchemical text in her mother's library, and despite what the early philosophers believed, no matter what the bible says, alchemy isn't a process of purification. It's a process of corruption. It has a way of making even pure-intentioned men like Weston Winters hard and distant.

"All alchemists say they want to make the world a better place," she says quietly. "I don't think any one of them has succeeded."

"Because all of them molder in their labs and spend more time theorizing about the world than living in it. They're all cynical and shortsighted."

Margaret can't help smiling. "It's true that most of them are nothing like you."

"I can't tell if you're making fun of me or not."

"I'm not." It surprises her to find she actually means it.

Weston drapes an arm over the back of her seat. "Alright, then. It's your turn to bare your soul. Did your mom not teach you alchemy?"

"She tried."

"And?"

"What are you asking me exactly?"

"I'm just curious why someone who's related to one of the most famous alchemists in the country isn't much of an alchemist herself."

Before *everything,* her mother told her she would teach her alchemy. Alchemy—real magic. Any child would light up. But once Margaret saw what it was capable of, it lost its luster. When it was time for the lessons her mother promised, Margaret seized up. She couldn't do it. The disappointment on Evelyn's face still torments her.

"I don't care for alchemy. That's all."

"Why not?"

There are many ways she could answer that question. *Because alchemy makes monsters of men. Because what good is alchemy if it can't bring her back?* "It can be used for horrible things."

"Sure." It's an uncontroversial statement. Although they're too young to have lived through the war, every New Albian citizen knows the damage alchemically enhanced weapons can do. They've all heard horror stories of military alchemists who tamper with their own bodies—or those of unwilling test subjects. "But so can anything. It's about how you apply it."

Margaret shrugs. "Then maybe not all of us have big dreams."

He grins at her humorlessly. "Now you *are* making fun of me."

"I'm not. It's the truth."

"That's depressing. You can't mean that."

He'll see soon enough. Just like all the others, he'll come to see Wickdon and the manor as a prison, small and boring and provincial. Something to overcome or step over on his illustrious path to success. But while this is nothing but a blip on the map for him, Wickdon is her whole world. Surviving it every day leaves no space for dreams. "I do, Mr. Winters."

Weston frowns. He's clearly not satisfied with her answer, but he lets the subject drop. "You can call me Wes, you know."

Her hands suddenly feel empty and unoccupied. She tucks a loose strand of hair behind her ear. "Okay."

As the silence settles over them, he rubs the back of his neck self-consciously. It isn't entirely uncomfortable. She's used to silence, cherishes it as her only friend besides Trouble. But Weston—Wes—is like a woodland creature, suspicious and edgy in the face of it.

Then, she watches an idea strike him. His eyebrows rise, and a sly smile curls on his lips. He leans closer, and she becomes acutely aware of how he's nearly slung his arm over her shoulders. Margaret fights the urge to pull away. The phantom sensation of his hand on her skin returns like a slow-blossoming bruise. It's an ache she craves and hates in equal measure.

"So," he says. "You realize you've never *actually* told me your name? It's Margaret, right? That's how you introduced yourself to my family."

Margaret. She likes the sound of her name in his mouth: the deliberate way he holds it between his teeth and how his city accent softens all the *r*s. Nobody calls her Margaret, even though she's asked them to. She nods, finding herself suddenly at a loss for words. How has he managed to fluster her so easily?

Determined to dissect whatever charm he's put on her, she drinks in his features up close. His unkempt hair is the same glossy black as gunpowder, and his eyes are narrow and fringed with dark, thick lashes. When he smiles, she can see the thin gap between his front teeth. He *is* handsome—not that he needs the validation—a fact that kills her a little to admit.

Lowering his voice, he says. "So what can I call you? Peggy?"

The spell instantaneously breaks, and Weston Winters is once again the obnoxious *child* who has taken up residence in her mother's spare room. "No."

"Marge?"

"Absolutely not."

He laughs "Alright, alright. Margaret, then. So you don't want to be an alchemist. What *do* you want to be?"

"A sharpshooter." She doesn't know what possessed her to say it, but she regrets it immediately. There's nothing Margaret hates more than being *seen*. If there is one thing she's learned in life, it is how to make herself invisible to survive.

"A sharpshooter, huh? You going to join the military?"

"No. Not exactly." She'd considered it briefly, but she isn't willing to sign her life away to a country that holds no love for her.

What *does* she want? Margaret imagines breathing in the damp earth and pine scent of the woods. The wind fondly ruffling her hair and mist beading on her eyelashes. The crack of a gun and the baying of a hound. If she could be selfish, if she could have anything, let it look like this. Her, in a red hunting jacket with a crown of bay laurel and a fistful of white fur, high enough on that winner's stand to step on Jaime Harrington's sneering face.

"I think winning will be enough," she says.

"And then what?"

"I don't know. I haven't thought about it beyond that."

"That's so . . . practical."

"Is it? It feels ridiculous to me."

"It's not. It's not ridiculous." He's trying for a serious expression, but the earnest, determined fire in his eyes makes him look younger, almost sweet. "Besides, dreams don't always have to be practical. That's why they're *dreams*. And now ours live and die together."

"Together." It's such a foreign concept.

He grins at her. "It's you and me against the world, Margaret."

She doesn't like the way that pronouncement makes her chest ache. Their fates are bound, but what frightens her more are the feelings he instills in her—this tentative hope and horrible yearning. It's too much like standing with the toes of her boots off the edge of a cliff. What lies beneath her is as dark and inconstant as the sea, and if she lets herself surrender, Margaret doesn't know if anyone will be there to catch her.

Wes and his dreaming, she decides, are dangerous things indeed.

11

Margaret is making him nervous.

Wes watches her from the behind the fogged glass of a phone booth while he waits for Hohn to pick up his call. She's sitting on a bench that faces a stretch of rolling hills, where a small army of goats grazes behind low stone fences. Her expression is as unreadable as alchemic research and her stare as glassy as a doll's, but he's slowly learning her language. The tension in her shoulders. The dart of her eyes at every sudden noise. The way she keeps pinning and unpinning her hair.

Even when she's restless, everything she does is precise and mechanized—and oddly hypnotizing. She's gathering up her hair in one hand and brandishing her tortoiseshell clip like a weapon in the other when Hohn finally answers.

Once Wes secures their ride and hangs up the phone, he drags his suitcase to Margaret's uneasy perch. He supposes he ought to feel more anxious than he does considering his future is riding on registering for the hunt on time. But his sense of time has always run a little differently from most people's, and besides, it won't do much good to worry about something he can't control.

"Relax." He jerks his chin toward the clock tower. Its face glows like a full moon in the starless sky. "It's only eight thirty. We're going to make it."

The last train of the night awakens from its slumber, wheezing, and swallows up her reply. As it heaves itself out of the station, it coughs up a trail of smoke and drags the wet, still air behind it. His coattails whip around his knees from the gust, and a few strands of her hair come loose from her bun. They cling to her lips, which are pursed at him with typical dispassion. He considers brushing them away—and whether she will bite if he lets the pad of his thumb linger. He recoils from the impulse. Never has anything as banal as *hair* made him feel so depraved.

When the wind dies down and the train's whistle fades to a distant whine, she says, "It'll take at least an hour and a half for him to get here."

"And an hour and a half to get back." He waves dismissively. "Which means we'll still have thirty minutes to spare."

She is, apparently, neither impressed nor assuaged by his calculations, so they wait in grim silence as the cold thickens around them. A raven lands on a nearby fence post and lets out a scream that almost severs his soul from his body. Margaret doesn't even flinch.

Just as he thinks he'll go mad, the clock gongs ten. Moments later, he hears the rumble of an engine and nearly weeps from relief. The headlights come next, blinking out of the darkness like the wide yellow eyes of a cat. As Hohn's sleek black cab pulls up to the curb, Wes grabs his bag. "See? He's here right on time. Nothing to worry about."

Margaret glares at him witheringly as Hohn climbs out of the car. "Mr. Winters, good to see you again! And is that— Maggie Welty, what in God's name are *you* doing out here?"

"I went sightseeing."

"Mind giving us a ride to the Blind Fox?" Wes adds.

Hohn looks befuddled but says, "Alright, then," before taking Wes's suitcase and loading it into the trunk.

Wes and Margaret clamber into the back seat, separated by bare inches of space and the solid wall of her frustration. He makes a few passing attempts at conversation as they pull onto the coastal highway—about how the weather has turned and the traffic has worsened—but neither Hohn nor Margaret pay him any mind beyond the occasional monosyllabic response. Margaret's reticence is unsurprising. Between surfeiting on his company today and her generally sour disposition, he expects she'll ignore him for the next three days. Hohn's silence, however, unnerves him. It's not until he catches a glimpse of his eyes, thinned like a serpent's, in the rearview mirror that he begins to understand.

Wes can all too easily imagine the steady diet of cautionary tales Wickdon girls are raised on. The kinds where city boys like him come to ferry away sheltered, lonely girls like her, only to drink them dry and leave them husks. But Margaret is no blushing maiden, and she'd shove the barrel of her gun down his throat before he could even hatch a single thought of pulling anything untoward.

He remembers how she stared down the hala, wild and determined in the bloody sunset. In that moment, all he could think to do was pray; all he could feel was his pulse in the hollow of his throat. But she looked so poised, so . . . terrifying.

Really, she's not his type. Not that Hohn knows that.

Wes wonders what exactly Hohn suspects. Maybe that he's after her estate, especially now that her mother isn't around to protect her from opportunistic snakes like him. It depresses him how plausible it sounds, so he tries to distract himself with the scenery. Nothing but featureless darkness whirs past his window. Even the sea is near-invisible tonight, rippling black and indigo behind the reflection of Margaret's face. His breath condenses on the window and blots her out.

He suffers for what feels like an eternity before they make it to Wickdon. When he arrived last time, it was a quaint little village—but now it's as rowdy as the Fifth Ward on Lá Fhéile Pádraig. They drift down the street, parting the crowds like water beneath a prow. Eventually, they're hemmed in on all sides and the cab eases to a stop about a block away from the Blind Fox.

"I think this is as far as I go," Hohn says. "It's a damn zoo tonight."

Wes goes to fetch his suitcase. He can barely hear his own thoughts over the shouted conversations around him, and it sends a shiver of exhilaration through him. As he slams the trunk closed, he sees Margaret counting out the fare while Hohn, with a pointed glance in his direction, whispers something in her ear. Her face flushes red as autumn.

It'd be endearing if it wasn't plain confirmation that Hohn thinks he's nothing but a scoundrel. Sometimes, he wonders why he bothers denying it. Maybe that's the only thing he'll ever amount to.

One moment he's brooding, and the next, Margaret is seizing him by the elbow. She yanks him backward just as a man stumbles over a loose cobblestone. Beer sloshes out of his cup, narrowly missing Wes's shoes as it spatters onto the street.

"No," the man whispers. "Damn it."

It's almost heartbreaking.

"You just saved my life," Wes says wryly.

"Thank me later." Margaret gives his arm another impatient tug. "Come on. It's almost midnight."

She steers them through the crowd with all the grace and purpose of a bulldozer. All around him, he catches fragments of city accents and glimmers of city fashion. Broad vowels and sequins. Too-loud laughter and lacquered cigarette holders capped with brightly burning cherries.

Once they're inside the pub, the clamor reaches a fever pitch. There's scarcely enough air to breathe; it's all tobacco smoke and sulfuric fumes and the bitter-anise smell of absinthe. Fire leaps in the hearth, throwing its light against the walls. It paints Margaret in stark gold; she looks like one of his mother's saintly icons. He can't tear his gaze away from her. She sets her jaw in fierce determination, and the glint in her eyes is far brighter than flame.

She hasn't let go of his arm, but he finds he doesn't want her to. The pressure of her hand anchors him in the chaos. Together, they shove their way through the crowd until they find a clump of people that somewhat resembles a line. He can't see what's at the front of it, even standing on his toes.

"Maggie Welty!" It takes Wes a moment to recognize Halanan's warm voice and kind blue eyes. "And Winters. What are you two doing out tonight?"

"We're here to register for the hunt," Margaret says.

"I'll be damned." He doesn't look thrilled, but he claps another man beside him on the back. "Clear way. We've got one more."

"Clear way!"

It passes from mouth to mouth, building into a rallying cry that spreads through the bar like brushfire. Space clears for them, and with a hand at his back, he's shoved into the crowd. As they're shuffled from person to person, Wes can see little but the warm glitter of sequins and the bright red of fox-fur stoles. Finally, they're thrust in front of a counter manned by the same woman who told the legend at the opening ceremony.

Her mouth falls open when she sees them. "*This* is your alchemist? Where did you find him?"

"Dunway."

The woman sighs, as though she's received a non-answer like this from Margaret a thousand times before. Her gaze locks on to him with an intensity that nearly bowls him over. "What's your name?"

"Weston Winters, ma'am." He flashes her what he hopes is a ten-kilowatt smile. "A pleasure to meet you."

"Weston Winters, huh? You're sure you didn't find him in a children's book?"

"I'm sure."

The woman gasps, startling him so badly he almost jumps. She jabs an accusatory finger at him. "Wait a minute! Winters. I knew I recognized that name. The other day, Mark Halanan came by and told me the strangest story. Do you know what he said?"

Neither of them speaks.

"He said that Evelyn had a new apprentice, a young man named

Winters. I told him he was full of shit. But here you are." The woman folds her hands neatly on the table. "Why do I get the feeling that you two are up to something smart?"

"Smart?" Wes sputters. "No! I mean, no, *ma'am*. I would never presume to do anything smart."

"He *is* her apprentice," Margaret cuts in. "She gave him permission to move in early. His lessons will start as soon as she returns."

"Is that so? You're not lying to me?"

"Of course not."

The woman's shrewd gaze darts back and forth between them. Wes keeps his smile firmly in place. She doesn't look at all reassured, but she throws up her hands. "Alright, then. You know what happens next, city boy? You make a sacrifice."

He must be gawping at her because she barks out a laugh and taps the countertop. Carved in its surface is the basic formula for nigredo. Orange firelight pools in the grooves of the transmutation circle. "Nothing too precious. A drop of blood or a lock of hair."

It strikes him as unusual that a Katharist tradition like this would remind him so much of a Sumic wedding. Traditionally, the priest will perform an alchemic ritual, usually on the wedding bands, to symbolize the joining of bodies and souls. It's quintessentially, morbidly Sumic to walk around wearing a ring enchanted with the essence of your spouse's baby teeth or fingernails. They're always cutting pieces of themselves off for God's amusement. Apparently, the church down the street from his building has the littlest toe of the martyr Saint Cecelia perfectly preserved beneath the altar.

The woman watches him expectantly. He really doesn't want to think about marrying Margaret Welty, even metaphorically, but he nods anyway. Satisfied, she places a glass bowl, a piece of chalk, and a knife on the table. Wes feels a little ill as he takes the knife. The idea of parting with any of his hair disturbs him more than the alternative, so blood it is. As he presses the blade against his palm, the crowd quiets. His heart thuds against his eardrums.

Then someone shouts, "Wait!"

Jaime Harrington strides toward them with a self-important look on his face. He's got a cap pulled over his sandy hair, and his shirt is pristine white against his suspenders and cuffed at the elbows. Hatred coils in Wes's gut. Margaret bristles beside him.

His pet of a friend—Mattis, if memory serves—trails a few uncertain steps behind him, along with a young woman with auburn hair and a crow-feather headpiece. Judging by the bloodied cloth around her hand, a twin to Jaime's, they must be partners in the hunt. Poor Mattis, meanwhile, has an impressive bald spot shorn into his temple, and Wes feels vindicated in his vanity.

"The rules say registration has to be *final* by midnight." Jaime taps his wristwatch. "It's five past."

"What the hell is he doing?" Wes mutters under his breath.

"Meddling." The venom in Margaret's voice surprises him.

"The hunt is our oldest tradition. Our heritage as true-blooded New Albians," Jaime continues. "We've always followed the rules the first settlers laid out. I know I speak for everyone when I say nothing should ruin the sanctity of this event."

A lopsided silence falls over the bar. Then, a few mutters of agreement rise from the crowd.

"He can't be serious," Wes hisses. "What does it matter if we're five minutes late?"

"It's not about the time."

His gaze slides uneasily to Margaret. She holds herself around her middle, staring out at the crowd like a cornered animal. What is she not telling him? Either way, if they enforce this rule, it's over for them. His family will be in a stranglehold, and both his and Margaret's dreams will be shattered.

From the very back of the bar, someone shouts, "Oh, mind your business, Harrington."

The delight on Jaime's face sours. The woman behind the counter makes a show of checking her watch. Wes's breath catches when the minute hand slots into place beneath the five. They're doomed.

"Well," the woman says, "it's a moot point. *My* watch says exactly midnight."

"But—"

"My bar, my time." She turns her attention back to Wes. "If you would, Mr. Winters, before we have any other hecklers come out of the woodwork?"

Firelight slicks the edge of the knife in his hands. The very thought of making a sacrifice for Margaret petrifies him. How much of himself has he really given to anyone? But if she's already seen all of his wounds, how much more will it hurt to spill a little more blood for her?

This is nothing more than they've already exchanged. A sacrifice for a sacrifice, a dream for a dream. Their bargain is its own kind of alchemy. With the sharp point of the blade, he reopens the half-healed cut on his palm. A few red drops fall and burst in the glass.

As delicately as he can, he passes it to Margaret. She doesn't hesitate before pulling the clip from her hair. It spills over her shoulders like a river of shining gold. His mouth goes dry as she slips the knife along the delicate skin at the base of her skull and cuts off a lock of hair at the root. She lets it fall into the bowl. The strands scatter, fine and pale as corn silk, and redden with his blood.

Wes wonders what the two of them would boil down to—what *he* would boil down to—if alchemy could go deep enough. Maybe then he could see what he's made of and what kind of man he really is. But there's nothing in the flesh that can get at the soul. It's nothing but a prison of oxygen and carbon.

Wes chalks in the runes for the reaction, then lays his hands against the counter. As he pours his energy into the array, a tongue of white fire leaps from the bowl, charring its contents into caput mortuum within seconds. The pieces of them crumble into each other, becoming one, and the scent of sulfur fills the air. Heat shimmers around the woman's face like a veil.

"The last of our entrants, Margaret Welty and Weston Winters. Let the hunt begin!"

The bar explodes with noise.

It gives him a thrill unlike any he's ever known. Jaime scowls at them, a look of pure disgust, and slips into the crowd with the rest of his posse. But as he scans the room, his gaze keeps catching on that same expression, over and over again.

Through the fire-cast shadows, he can pick out a few people from town—people who know Margaret—looking at her with hatred burning hideously in their eyes. The man who sells oysters along the main drag. The baker who gave him an apple tart for complimenting her hair last week. One of the bartenders overfilling a pint glass.

He knows those looks well. They spark something dark and protective within him. The week after his father died, he'd nearly gotten himself killed for trying to fight a pack of kids who'd followed Colleen home from school. His knuckles still pop out of place if he squeezes his hand just right. He wishes he'd known alchemy back then.

In this world, a Katharist pedigree is power. Money is power. But so is alchemy. He feels the hot glow of its potential burning at the center of his chest.

"Wes?" Margaret lowers her head until her hair curtains her face. "Can we leave? Please?"

The edge of fear in her voice sobers him. "Yeah. Let's get you home."

"Take her out the back," the woman says. "They're wolves out there tonight."

"I will. Thanks."

Without thinking, he wraps an arm around Margaret's shoulder— then immediately realizes the grave mistake he's made. He expects her to wrench away from him, but instead, she nestles closer until her forehead is tucked against his neck. Her eyelashes flutter against his racing pulse. Docile as a lamb, she lets him shield her and whisk her out the back door and into the waiting night.

12

Late-morning sunlight washes over Margaret like a wave. As she stirs awake, nestling deeper into her blankets, she relishes its warm, drowsy caress against her face. It's been so many years since she's slept in past dawn.

Then, like she's been doused in cold water, the haziness of her thoughts sharpens into a bitter realization. She's wasted the first morning of the hunting season.

Swearing, she clambers out of bed and winces as the chill of the floorboards seeps into her bare feet. The stress and exhaustion of the last twenty-four hours haven't abated, but she can't coddle herself today—and not for the next three weeks. Until the hala is slain, she can't relax. The packed hunting-season schedule will see to that.

To keep the tourists entertained, each week promises another competitive spectacle. First, an alchemy exposition and then a shooting contest. Poor performance doesn't disqualify anyone, but winning offers crucial advantages. Foxhunting is a traditional, hierarchical sport with so many rules both unspoken and formalized, Margaret can hardly keep track of them. But chief among them is observing the proper arrangement of people on the field. A regular hunting club divides its members into four groups based on their skill level and seniority: first flight, second flight, third flight, and hilltoppers. The

Halfmoon Hunt officials, however, place each team in a flight according to how well they score in the weekly competitions.

The first flight rides closest to the hounds, and while it's the most dangerous place to be, it's also where they'll have the best shot of cornering the hala before anyone else. Unofficially, anyone who winds up in second or third flight has no chance of winning. Only the strongest riders with the best-trained hounds could hope to make up for such a setback.

Last night was nothing but fanfare. Today, everything truly begins.

Margaret rushes through her morning routine, and as she finishes braiding her still-wet hair, she hears the sounds of skittering claws and footsteps coming from downstairs. She tries to remind herself of how lonely she was only the day before and how fortunate she is that Wes decided to register with her. It's hard to cling to gratitude, however, when she knows he's doing something foolish. She doesn't need to have him in her eyeline to be sure of it.

Sighing, Margaret goes to investigate the commotion. She drapes herself over the second-floor banister just in time to see Trouble come tearing around the corner with a shoe dangling from his mouth by the laces. He drops into a play bow with the enthusiasm of a dog five years younger. A moment later, Wes skids across the floor with a wicked gleam in his eye.

"Caught you, you bastard. Give it up."

Trouble growls, his tail wagging with anticipation.

Margaret watches the scene unfold with growing irritation. It's less that they're bonding without her—although it does sting—and more that Wes is encouraging terrible behavior. She needs Trouble in prime shape, ruthless and focused, not bounding through the house like an ill-trained puppy.

"What are you doing?" she asks.

Wes nearly stumbles backward in surprise. "Ah, Miss Wel— Mag—Margaret! I didn't see you there! I'm trying to get my shoe back."

"Trouble, drop it."

Without a moment's hesitation, he does. It clatters to the floor, shining with leather polish and saliva. As she descends the stairs, both hound and boy gaze up at her with something like reverence.

"How did you do that?"

"He knows you're playing." She crouches to retrieve his errant shoe and scratch behind Trouble's ears. "Hounds will only listen to you if they respect you."

"And how do you go about getting a hound's respect?"

"By being more respectable." She hands the shoe back to him. "Maybe you can start by doing something better with your time. The alchemy exposition is at the end of the week."

"I'm aware," he says sourly. "You're the one who decided to sleep all morning. I wanted to talk to you before I started on anything."

Her ears burn, but she chooses not to take the bait. "Do you really need my consultation? You ruined my maul well enough on your own."

"Hardy-har-har," he mutters. "I'd rather not waste time making something you won't use. It'd also be helpful if I had some equipment. As you might've noticed, estimating the mass and composition of things doesn't exactly get the best results."

She supposes he's right. Alchemy isn't a science of guesswork, and they'll never stand a chance if she forces him to treat it like one. Even though dread knots tight within her, she knows what she has to do. "You can use my mother's lab."

His entire face lights up. "Really?"

She nods, even as her stomach corkscrews anxiously at the feverish, overbright shine in his eyes. "Come on."

Margaret leads him upstairs and hesitates in front of her bedroom door. Standing here, with Wes lingering barely a step behind her, makes her feel vulnerable, like a crab tipped onto its back. No real harm can come of letting him inside when he's already rummaged through the broken pieces of her life. But this is the one place still left untouched, still hers. If she can refuse him the most tender, silliest parts of herself, she will.

"Wait here."

She catches him craning his neck as she slips through the door, and she shoots him a glare as she shuts it behind her. At the very back of her desk drawer, she finds an old iron key, mottled green beneath a fine layer of gritty film. As Margaret rubs it clean, the engraved scales of an ouroboros chafe against the pad of her thumb.

Under no circumstances was Margaret allowed into her mother's lab uninvited once she began her work on the philosopher's stone, but Evelyn entrusted her a set of spare keys in her absence. The one to the lab, Margaret keeps here in her room. The other, which opens the hidden drawer in Evelyn's desk, hangs safely around her neck. It goes against her every instinct, her every lesson, to let someone else inside. But what other choice does she have? She can't have him making any more unmovable mauls with only six days to spare.

Outside her room, Wes waits by the window with his arms crossed behind his back. Last night's rain streaks the glass and shimmers faintly in the sunlight, casting watercolor shadows across his face.

"Ready?" she asks quietly.

"Yeah."

Every step down this stretch of the hallway fills her with a terror half-remembered. How many times has she traced this path, bedroom to lab, in her nightmares? How many times has she jerked awake to her mother's imagined scream still ringing in her ears? The key twists in the lock. The cold of the doorknob knifes into her palm. Then, the door swings open with a tired whine.

Sunlight floods the room and blinds her. Blinking away the spots in her vision, she drinks in the hazy churn of dust in the air. Nothing about this place has changed. Once, she and David would sprawl on the floor and watch as their mother enchanted silly baubles for them to play with. Floating, featherlight toys and stuffed animals with noses that glowed like fireflies. The summer breeze would sigh through the open windows and chase away the smell of alchemy.

But that reverie burns up when her gaze lands on the jagged stain on the floorboards, as dark as rust. Another memory pulls her under, quicker than she can stop it.

With everything swimming and sparkling around her, Margaret feels as though she has sunk to the bottom of the sea. Her throat thickens and her ears roar with blood, and she is both here and a thousand miles away, choking on the stench of sulfur, shivering as the water sluices over the floor and seeps into the hem of her nightgown—

"Margaret?"

It's her mother calling for her again. It's the hala, speaking her name in the hiss of the fallen leaves.

"Margaret, can you hear me?"

No. It's a man's voice, saying her name over and over again like an incantation.

Margaret, Margaret, Margaret.

Her breath shudders out of her. As if waking from a dream, she finds herself staring into Wes's redwood eyes as the film over her vision recedes.

The confusion and concern she sees there humiliates her. At first, she can't remember where they are or what they were doing. Then, bit by bit, sensation returns. His hands firm and steadying on her shoulders. The solidity of the chair beneath her. The cold sweat beaded at her temples and the sandpapery dryness of her eyes.

"Hey," he says, almost tenderly. "I think you went somewhere else for a minute. Is everything alright?"

It's too painful to suffer his kindness again, when only last night she was heedless enough to wrap herself in his protection. She can still recall the exact rhythm of his pulse against the bridge of her nose and the way he didn't let her go until they cleared the edge of town. He didn't ask her about it, and she can't be sure what she would've told him if he had. But this—these episodes—are hers alone to bear. Wanting comfort is a weakness she can't afford to coddle.

"Yes." She shrugs off the weight of his hands and rises unsteadily to her feet. "Everything's fine."

Wes shoves them into his pockets, looking for all the world like he's about to argue with her. "Right. Okay."

Margaret knows he wants to understand, but how can she explain the ways her mind protects her from things no one else can see? How can someone with a family like his ever truly understand hers?

In the months after David died, her father used to tell her that there were two Evelyns who lived in the manor. She isn't sure if she resents him for it or appreciates what he was trying to shield her from. In a way, he never lied to her. Not really. If she unravels her memories like a skein of yarn, she sees them both clearly. There is the first Evelyn, woven in rich, bright colors like a sunset—the one who's easy to love. And there is the second Evelyn, faded and gray, who makes you wonder why you try.

The first Evelyn is quick to laugh. The Evelyn who shouts, ecstatic, *hurry, hurry, hurry,* to show you a meteor shower in her telescope. The Evelyn who kneels beside you in the mud to dig up banana slugs and red-bellied salamanders from the loam. The second Evelyn is as cold and remote as a far-off planet. The Evelyn who doesn't eat for days, whose silent anger fills up the house like smoke. The Evelyn who doesn't look back when she leaves.

Remember her on her good days, her father would say. *That's who she really is.*

Eventually, she was the only one left remembering, and now there are no Evelyns at all.

Margaret rattles the casement of the window until it opens. She likes the sting of the cold against her sweat-dampened face, and the faint breeze that flutters the curtains sweeps the staleness out of the air. It's not enough to feel grounded or even remotely normal. If Wes wasn't here, she would lie in bed and curl around Trouble until she remembered how to settle back into her own skin. But she doesn't want him to handle her carefully like Halanan and Mrs. Wreford. She doesn't want him to know.

Wes watches her cautiously as she approaches him, but he accepts the key when she presses it into his palm. "It's a little messy," she says, "but consider it yours for now."

"It's fitting, I think. Thank you."

Wes tucks the key into his pocket before turning his attention to the lab. It's cluttered with glass beakers and mortars, scales and alembics with a coiling network of tubes. Shelves teeming with books line the walls, which are papered with hastily scrawled notes. He trails his fingers along them, mouthing words as he attempts to read the formulas. So much good it'll do him, considering her mother wrote everything down in code. Eventually, Wes abandons his translation efforts and sinks into the chair behind the desk.

He folds his hands beneath his chin and lowers his eyelashes at her. "Well? Do I look like a real alchemist?"

"Don't let it go to your head."

"Too late." Wes turns an hourglass on its head. "So. What do I need to get ready for you?"

"We can only bring four alchemized items with us on the hunt, and since you can't ride on your own, we'll want something for the horse to ease the strain on him. Beyond that, all we need is a weapon that can kill the hala. Anything else will be a convenience, since we'll be outside for twelve hours in the cold."

"Then what do you want me to work on for the exposition?"

A good question. While Margaret knows she can perform well in the shooting contest, their scores will be averaged. Whether she likes it or not, she's still yoked to him. Ambition is rewarded in the exposition, but based on what she's seen of his skills so far, she doubts he can execute anything more than a simple transmutation.

Clearly sensing her worry, Wes says, "Listen, I know you haven't seen anything inspiring yet, but I swear I can pull this off."

"I believe you." She doesn't entirely mean it, but it does make her feel like they're living in a world where it's at all possible they'll win. "The safest option is to work on something you know you can actually do."

"But if I want to guarantee we make first flight?"

"Then you'll need to dazzle them."

"Right. No pressure."

"The only thing we absolutely need is a bullet that can kill the hala, so focus on that." Margaret prays he can uncover a method other than the one she already knows. Unconsciously, she lays her hand flat over her collarbones, where her mother's key sits hot against her skin.

"I can do that."

His throat bobs above his unbuttoned collar, and his pale skin goes even sallower. She remembers Mad and his mother's outrage at the idea of him joining the hunt. While she doesn't know the intricacies of the Sumic faith, she can understand the complicated feelings that come from forsaking your heritage.

"Are you sure about this?"

"Weren't you the one who said we had to trust each other? I know you're still mad about the maul, but—"

"That's not what I mean."

"Oh, *that*." He rests his chin on his fists. "Don't tell me you're worried about the fate of my immortal soul, too."

"I'm not. Only your mortal self."

"I'm fine. Honest. I won't let you down. I know how to live with guilt at this point."

Margaret hesitates, partly because she doesn't want to offend, partly because she doesn't want to pry. But it's been so long since she's had anyone to talk to. "Why is your mother so worried? Is the hala a Sumic saint?"

"Demiurges aren't really saints. Some people pray to them as intercessors, but they're more like extensions of God himself. They *are* God but separate from God, too, because they all have the same divine essence."

He stops there, as though he has sufficiently explained the concept. Margaret stares at him uncomprehendingly.

Wes flushes, then barrels on. "I mean, that's the official statement from the pope. It's a whole thing. All of the bishops have been arguing about it for centuries, and I don't think anyone really understands it anyway. God in his infinite mystery and all that."

"I see." She doesn't think her father would be content with a god who enjoys his own remoteness. And he certainly wouldn't be content accepting another man's account of the nature of the divine without testing it himself. But if Aoife truly believes her son is killing a piece of God—or God himself as it were—Margaret can understand her concern. "Do you worship saints, too?"

Wes looks only slightly exasperated. "Not really. We do venerate them, though. Pray to them and take their names when we come of age. Things like that."

"Which did you take?"

"Francis Xavier. Which makes me Weston Carroll Francis Xavier Winters."

"Carroll," she repeats.

"It's a family name," he says defensively. "Anyway! The point is, saints are regular people who've done something impressive enough to be canonized. Usually that means dying in some dramatic, grisly way when someone tries to get you to convert. Although I hear there's a dog saint that has a cult following."

Now that is the first thing he's said that makes sense. All dogs deserve veneration, maybe even canonization. "And is that . . . the goal?"

"Not for me. If you want to be a saint, you have to suffer and be celibate on top of that, which is why I fully intend to go to hell." He traces the shape of a circle on his forehead with the back of his thumb, then again on his lips and chest.

Margaret rolls her eyes. Every time she starts to believe he has even an ounce of maturity in him, he proves her wrong. "I suppose we'll both be well on our way there when we have the hala's blood on our hands."

Margaret waits for him to ask the question burning in his eyes: *Why would you be going to hell for a thing like that?* This is another thing she's learned about him. It's not only his pain he hides behind that too-slick smile. It's his wits, too. He notices far more than he lets on. There are plenty of tolerant Katharists in the world, if Mrs. Wreford and Halanan are any proof. But Wes has seen enough of her life and the way this town treats her to know she's not just a tolerant Katharist.

Surely, he must know.

If he does, he doesn't push her. Instead, he leans so far back in his chair until she fears, maybe hopes, that he will topple over. "Well, if I'm going to pull this off in the next six days, I'm going to need some supplies. Which means . . ." The chair's legs drop back onto the ground with a loud *bang*. "You'll have no way to weasel your way out of showing me around town this time."

"Fine." Margaret dreads the triumphant grin that steals across his face. "When do you want to go?"

"I could use some fresh air. How about now?"

13

The most beautiful girl Wes has ever seen stands on the other side of the general store's fence. She's waiting in line with her friends outside one of the red-roofed market stalls that sprang up overnight like the tents of a traveling circus. People bustle by with cups full of steaming drinks and candy-glossed apples, but all he can focus on is her.

She wears an oversized knit sweater pulled over a pleated green skirt. The hemline flows down to her calves, sinuous as water, and the aching stretch of skin between fabric and her heeled oxfords nearly drives him mad. Her hair tumbles from beneath her cloche hat in curls, as rich and round as chestnuts, and pearls drip from her ears like raindrops from the lip of a petal. There's something familiar about her. Not only in the trappings of city fashion, but her face . . .

They must've met before. But no, he'd remember a face like hers.

Wes considers abandoning his post to say hello, but Margaret left him with the stern command to behave. Frankly, he expected this trip to be about buying alchemy supplies, but she wanted to check off everything on her miles-long errand list. The thought of glumly trudging behind her through the market sounded about as good as peeling his own skin off.

He's done it before—the trudging—and it's mind-boggling how long she can spend measuring the worth of a single apple. Instead, he opted for people watching and skimming gossip off the ambient chatter. Rumor has it that last night, the hala desiccated a hundred-year-old vineyard's entire harvest, which is apparently as tragic as it is exciting.

Another sign it'll be a sporting chase.

While he waits for Margaret to finish up her shopping, he sees no harm in occupying himself with flirting. If he does nothing, then he'll have to confront his fear that he will fail, that three weeks isn't enough time to prepare for the hunt, that the hala will tear them apart. If he stops moving, he'll sink.

One of the girl's friends casts a furtive look in his direction, and she turns over her shoulder to look at him. Wes smiles. It's one he's practiced many times in the mirror, the same as he practices the speech patterns of all the best orators in the country. It's a careful calculus. Too wide makes it look like a grimace, too loose and it devolves into slack-jawed staring. But this one lands just right, because when he waves, they reward him by conferring among themselves.

He pretends not to notice it, but he does. He thrives on attention, a fact he is unashamed to admit. Anyone would after growing up in a house like his, where attention is a commodity as precious as gold. As a kid, he wielded every advantage he had over his sisters as the only boy, the only one with a penchant for alchemy, and the only one who could reliably sweet-talk their mother into forgiving his many sins.

When they finish their conference, the girl's friends shove her in his direction. She navigates through the crowd, then folds her arms neatly over the posts of the fence. This close, he can see every shade of green in her eyes, how her pupils are ringed with catlike yellow. He thinks he's forgotten how to breathe.

"Hi," she says. "Can I help you? You've been staring for ten minutes."

"Oh, was I staring? I'm so sorry. I was on my way to do some shopping, but then . . . Well, I got horribly distracted and couldn't work up the nerve to say hello."

"Ah, Mr. Winters, playing coy doesn't suit you."

"You . . . You know my name?"

She smiles deviously. "Of course I do. We met the other day. How quickly you've forgotten *me,* though."

His mind goes blank with terror. "You're joking."

"I'm very serious."

He's not usually so terrible with faces. He's especially not so terrible with faces that are as beautiful as hers. Where could they have possibly met?

"You must offer elopement to many girls if it's not noteworthy enough to remember."

Oh. *Oh.* The girl from the inn—the one who drove him home. He was so locked in his own head that night, but now he remembers her silhouetted in the car window, limned in silver rainwater. He remembers the dreaminess of her voice when she spoke of Dunway.

Heat spreads across the back of his neck. "I think this might be the most embarrassing thing that's ever happened to me."

She throws back her head and laughs, a sound as sparkling as champagne. "Don't worry about it. I think your mind was elsewhere that night."

"Still. I'm ashamed of myself."

"Don't be." She rests her hand on his forearm reassuringly. "Besides, I never properly introduced myself. I'm Annette Wallace."

"A pleasure to meet you again, Miss Wallace."

"Call me Annette."

"Annette, then." The words are halfway out of his mouth when he catches a flicker of movement over her shoulder—then, the spine-tingling sensation of eyes raking across his face. Two people are glaring at him. The first, of course, is Margaret. The second is Jaime Harrington, who stops dead in the street when he sees him.

Wes wonders how thin his luck will run before it snaps altogether.

Margaret's ire, he can deal with. Even though he's not sure where they stand lately, he's accepted that he will annoy her no matter what he does. Jaime, though . . . That sniveling protest he raised at the pub last night still rankles him. Although they've hardly exchanged more than five words, Wes already has him pinned. Big ego, all bluster. Wes would love nothing more than to take him to task for it, and—

No, he can't actually entertain the thought of fighting Jaime. For Margaret's sake, he will take the high road.

Annette follows his gaze. "Oh, are you here with Maggie?"

"Huh?"

"Maggie Welty." She doesn't say it *unkindly,* but Wes detects her meaning. From what he understands, Evelyn isn't well-liked in town, and her daughter . . .

Her daughter. He quashes any thought of Margaret before it can blossom into something more distracting. But it's hard to ignore her when she's driving needles into him with her eyes. They say, *Let's go. Now.*

Just one minute, he wants to say. *Don't ruin this for me.*

"Not exactly. I mean, yes, I'm here with her, but only in the sense that we both happen to be here at the same time." He clears his throat. "I don't think Miss Welty likes me very much."

"Don't take it personally. She doesn't like anyone very much."

"Neither does Jaime Harrington, apparently."

"Jaime? Oh, don't pay him any mind. He's wary of outsiders, but he's harmless."

Wes very much doubts that, but he responds with a noncommittal sound.

"In any case, I'm glad you decided to stay after all. I heard a rumor that you've entered the hunt. What do they know about foxes in the city, Mr. Winters?"

"Please." Offering her his most winning smile, he takes off his hat. Static prickles along the shells of his ears, so he knows his hair has to be reaching to high heaven at this point. "Call me Wes."

"Alright, Wes. The question stands."

"Nothing, honestly. But if I'm going to be living here for a while, I figured I should live as the locals do. I hear it's going to be an especially good chase this year. Did you hear about the vineyard?"

"By 'good,' they mean dangerous, you know."

"I know." Wes laughs thinly. "The truth is Miss Welty asked me to join her, and I can't say no to a woman in need."

"How gallant of you. Now I know for sure whatever's between us is meaningless," she says with an overwrought, teasing sigh.

He's relieved to put the subject of Margaret—and the hunt—to rest. "That's not true. Let me prove it. I've hardly gotten to see the sights, so . . ."

"I'm terribly sorry to disappoint you, but there aren't any sights. We've got salt water and trees and fish."

"Oh, come on. Surely there's some hidden gems in Wickdon. You've lived here your whole life. I'd bet you could show me a thing or two."

Annette laughs. "I don't think there's anything a girl like me could show you."

"Well," he says, lowering his voice. "I don't know about that."

A shadow falls over him. A heavy hand clamps down on his shoulder. "Is this guy bothering you?"

"Jaime," Annette squeaks. "Hi."

Wes shrugs him off as he whirls around—only to find himself eye level with Jaime's sneering mouth. He has to crane his neck to meet his eyes, a fact he tries not to resent. "We're just talking."

"We're just talking." Jaime imitates him in way that makes it clear he finds the way he talks ridiculous. All exaggeratedly broad vowels and dropped consonants. "I didn't realize Maggie Welty let her dogs slink around unattended."

"Always a pleasure, Harrington."

"A pleasure." Jaime shakes his head, like he's enjoying some private joke. "I can't get over that accent. You know he's from Dunway, Annie?"

Annette lowers her eyes. "I know."

"She's always wanted to go," Jaime says offhandedly. "Can't imagine why."

"You've been, I take it." Wes fights to keep the irritation out of his voice.

"God, no. My parents were born there, but they moved when it started getting too crowded. Banvish immigrants breed like rabbits, and more of them pour off the boat every day. I don't know how you live with it." Jaime pauses, as though he's waiting for Wes's reaction. When he gives him nothing, he shrugs. "Besides, you can't compete with the Yu'adir if you want to maintain any kind of integrity. They cheapen their goods so they can make more money."

"A very impressive account," Wes says, "for someone who's never removed his head from his own ass."

Annette claps her hand over her mouth, smothering a laugh.

Jaime's stunned expression sours. "You think you're real smart, don't you? Let me make this clear. If you want to stay out of trouble, keep your mouth shut and your hands to yourself. There are a lot of people angry you two registered, and it'd be a shame if anything happened to you because of that. Do we understand each other?"

Any sane person staring down the raw hatred in Jaime's eyes would apologize. But Wes only feels his ego rise up to meet it. Especially because Annette is watching him with a mixture of horror and fascination.

"Leave him alone, Jaime," Annette says. "He's not hurting anybody."

"Who said anything about hurting anybody? We're just having a conversation, aren't we, Winters?"

"That's right."

"That's right," Jaime echoes, clapping Wes on the back. "In fact, I'm giving him some helpful advice. Getting to know the competition is part of preparing for the hunt. See, Winters here is an alchemist. How about you show Annie a magic trick, since you're so eager to impress her?"

Anger burns hot as a forge within him. A thousand retorts

bubble up at the back of his throat, only some of them even halfway coherent. A week ago, Wes would have clocked him here and now, no questions asked. But there's too much on the line for him to be anything but Margaret's leashed dog. That doesn't mean he can't remind them he's got teeth.

"Honestly, I can't tell if you're stupid or you've got guts." It's the same tone of voice he uses when he wants to make Mad's vision swim red with fury. A little impertinent, a little cocky. "You know I'm an alchemist, and here you are, threatening me openly."

Jaime tilts his head. "What, planning on setting me on fire or something? Do it. I dare you."

The air feels hot and ready to spark.

"You know what I think?" Jaime continues. "I don't think you could do a damn thing, even if you wanted to. As a matter of fact, I know you came here to learn from Evelyn. Don't you think you're a little old for that? The last apprentice she took on was ten."

To hell with respectability. This son of a bitch is going down.

"Mr. Winters."

Margaret. Wes bites back a groan as he turns reluctantly toward her. A cold wind tears through the street, billowing her skirt around her and loosening some of her hair from its severe bun. Clouds pass over the sun the moment she meets his gaze, the gold draining from her eyes as they narrow. Like this, she looks more wolf than girl— like some magic far wilder than alchemy runs through her. The sight of it stills him. Wes lets his hands relax. The tendons in his right knuckles crackle and slip back into place.

"We should go," she says. "We need to get your supplies."

Jaime jerks his chin toward Margaret. "Go on. Be a good boy now."

Margaret's lips thin, but she's as unreadable as ever.

How can she tolerate this? Or maybe it's that she's tolerated it so long, it's gotten easier. He balances on a knife's edge of pity and anger at her passivity. Cruelty has worn her down, but he can't let himself slink away without spilling a little blood.

"It was good to see you again, Annette. I'll see you around."

Wes sees the exact moment Jaime registers her answering smile and the deliberate choice of the word "again." His face twists with impotent anger, and Wes knows the first victory is his.

14

They walk side by side through town, and although Margaret knows she shouldn't be, she's annoyed with Wes. Rationally, she knows she's only irritable and tired, as she always is after one of her episodes, but rationalizing it does nothing to improve her mood. She can't stop thinking about him preening like some exotic bird for Annette Wallace. She can't stop seeing him in the corner of her eye, smirking to himself like a fool. In thirty minutes, he's managed to enrage Jaime even more than they already have. He can't be left alone—not even for a second. He's no better than a teething puppy.

"You've made friends, I see," she says.

"Maybe I have." His grin turns obsequious. "Are you jealous?"

"No."

"Hmm." It's a skeptical, teasing sound, one she's not exactly accustomed to.

The sleeves of his trench coat trail limply behind him like a second set of arms. He looks like himself again—absurd—but she can't easily forget the sight of him with his teeth bared and his eyes dark with anger. Another moment without intervention, and he would've fought Jaime. She's sure of it. Maybe she should have let him.

"I've told you before that Jaime isn't the kind of person you want to make an enemy of."

"I'm not afraid of him," he says tartly. "He started it, anyway. I was minding my own business."

"Flirting outrageously with Annette Wallace is hardly minding your own business."

"I was not flirting *outrageously*."

"He's in love with her."

"So am I."

Margaret rolls her eyes. Everyone knows that Jaime has been completely besotted with her since they were kids, not that she's ever given him a glimmer of reciprocity. Once, he made Sam Plummer cry because she had the gall to ask Annette out for coffee. "You're painting an even bigger target on your back. If you stay out of his way—and hers—he'll leave you alone."

"And have you been cavorting about town with Annette, too? He hasn't exactly been leaving you alone."

Margaret doesn't like the probing look he's giving her. It would be so easy to tell him, but her tongue feels thick every time she even thinks of saying it: *It's because I'm Yu'adir.* She's still infuriatingly afraid of what he would say. Pity would be as bad as disgust.

"He's angry. And threatened."

"Obviously. I'm only wondering why he's chosen you of all people to be threatened by."

"You haven't seen me shoot to kill," she says curtly. "Maybe you'd like a demonstration."

He throws up his hands. "No, that's alright. I have a vivid imagination. Besides, what would you do without me here to bother you?"

Judging by the scheming glint in his eye, Margaret knows he has no intention of listening to her counsel, and she has a feeling pushing the matter will only make Annette more appealing. If he wants to embroil himself in this avoidable mess, it's his prerogative.

As the afternoon light fades, the shops begin to turn on their lights. Wes peers into every storefront they pass, but he lingers at the tailor's. He stares so intently and longingly at the suit in the window that she's sure he'll leave an imprint of his face behind. The fine embroidery on the sleeves—stitched in every color of the ocean at daybreak—is almost certainly worth more than both their lives combined.

"Come on," she says. "They should have what you need at the Morgans'."

They trudge up the walkway to V. K. Morgan's, and the cheerful jingle of the overhead bell announces them. It's a cramped little closet of a store, part apothecary, part grocers, part cigar shop, which means it always smells something like a burnt-out candle. Sun-blanched antlers hang like a grim chandelier overhead, twinkling with pendant lights.

The tourists have left it nearly empty, like an animal butchered and cleaned. Nothing but bones remain. Everybody in Wickdon does their shopping here, and while the Morgans break even on visits from regulars, the real money comes from selling furs to alchemists in Dunway. Fashion catalogs advertise all sorts of alchemized clothing: stoles of mink imbued with the luminescence of diamond, fur-lined capes threaded with essence of pepper for warmth, sleek rabbit-skin coats infused with the rain-wicking properties of petroleum.

The Morgan twins sit side by side behind the counter like two grizzled crows on a telephone wire. They wear their red hair in loose, long waves beneath wide-brimmed hats.

"Oh dear, Katherine." Vivienne leans forward in her seat. Shards of bone adorn each of her golden rings, which clatter like rain as she spreads her hands on the glass countertop. "It seems Maggie Welty has come to visit us again."

"So it is. It has been so very long since we've seen her last."

"No, not so long. Have you already forgotten? I do believe it was two weeks ago."

"Surely not, Vivienne. It has been months."

They speak with a strange, halting lilt that is, as far as anyone knows, no accent but their own since they were born and raised in Wickdon. Wes stares at Margaret in wide-eyed confusion as they bicker.

It's just as well the shop's named after their first initials, considering Margaret can't shake the suspicion formed in childhood that they are, in fact, the same person. They look identical. They sound identical. They often speak in the royal we and converse as if they can read each other's mind. While they tend to unsettle most people, Margaret is used to them by now. She has to be, considering they're among the only ones in town who'll give her a fair price for what she sells.

"Ignore them," she tells Wes. "Let's get what you need and go."

Just as he opens his mouth to reply, their eyes land on him.

"And who is this?" Katherine asks.

That's all it takes for him to undergo a radiant transformation. Wes sidles up to the counter and braces his elbow against it. His voice is slick as oil, his smile bright as sunlight. "Weston Winters, ma'am. It's a pleasure to meet you."

"Oh." It's a bare exhalation. "How very nice to meet you, too, Mr. Winters."

"Very nice, indeed," Vivienne says.

He's insatiable. First Annette Wallace, and now the Morgan twins. How does everyone keep falling for this act? How is everyone so oblivious? Every single thing he says and does is calibrated to get people to like him. It's embarrassing, how transparently he craves acceptance.

As he chatters on, Margaret slips away to browse the aisles for what Wes asked her to get for his experiments. She watches him from behind a small tower of osmium, just as the magic-hour light comes in through the window and paints him warm and golden. He's talking animatedly to Vivienne, and if the lowered pitch of his voice and the looseness of his body against the counter tell her anything, it's that he is flirting with her. It should be ridiculous, but she's never seen the Morgans look so . . . captivated.

Have I been the oblivious one?

His appeal is more than the easy smile and earnest eyes, more than his uncomplicated, almost overwhelming friendliness. He's magnetic because he looks utterly in love with whoever and whatever is in front of him. She realizes, too late, that she is staring at him. As if he senses it, Wes cuts Margaret a sly look from the corner of his eye. It gleams like polished jet in the sunlight, and a smirk curls catlike on his lips. He winks at her. Actually *winks.*

God, she despises him sometimes. He exists purely to annoy her. To remind her that everything comes easy to him and not to her.

"Are you Evelyn's new apprentice?" Katherine asks.

"Not exactly," he says. "At least not until she comes back. But I am Miss Welty's alchemist for the hunt. I wanted to help with her errands—and meet the neighbors, of course."

"How kind of you. It's been a long time since we've had an alchemist of our own. A very, *very* long time. No one takes interest in our town."

"How could I not take an interest? Charming businesses, gorgeous scenery, beautiful women . . ."

The twins cackle, and Margaret holds onto some private hope that they will rebuke him at last. But Vivienne only says, "You won't get anywhere with flattery."

The fondness in her voice betrays her. He will get plenty far.

Margaret shoves a hunk of osmium into her bag and begins rummaging through a particularly nightmarish shelf crammed full of inconsistently labeled glass bottles. Once she finds the camphor oil he wanted, she approaches the counter and lays her items on the table. Wes looks at her with laughter sparkling in his eyes. She wants to douse it.

"I have something to show you," she tells the twins, managing to keep herself composed.

She finds the fox pelt in her bag and unfurls it on the countertop, as delicately as a wedding gown's train. The twins hem and haw as they pick it up, snatching it from one another and holding it to the sunlight as though they're looking for a counterfeit bill. The fur ripples like wind-stirred wheat beneath their eager fingers and blazes with brilliant shades of red and white. It's fetching, she knows. Most foxes in Wickdon are dull, almost brown. This one, however, belongs around a wealthy woman's neck.

Without consulting, without even looking at one another, they deliver their sentence in unison. "Three dollars."

"Six."

"Oh dear," Vivienne whispers in dismay. "Four."

"I can sell it to any one of the tourists outside for double that. This is a favor."

Margaret watches them weigh their pride against the beauty of the coat the fox will become. Katherine says, "Five. I am afraid that is the highest we will go."

"Done. Give me the difference." Each crisp bill gives a papery *snick* as Katherine counts it out into Margaret's palm. It'll be enough to get them through the next few weeks.

"Ready to go?" Wes asks.

"Yes. I'm very ready to go."

The moment they step into the cold, all of her irritation sparks hot again. Very quietly, very evenly, she says, "You shouldn't get used to this. We'll lose if you spend all your time socializing."

"Oh, lighten up. That was five minutes, not 'all my time.' It's called being polite. Maybe you should try it sometime."

She means to hold his gaze, to make him realize that he's missing the point. But as her eyes sting with an emotion she'd rather not name, she turns sharply away from him and storms toward the edge of town.

Wes trots to keep pace with her. "Hey. What's wrong?"

"I can't figure out how you've managed to put a spell on everyone."

"It's because I'm charming."

"Hardly."

"You really ought to be nicer to me," he says sullenly. "I've put a lot on the line for you."

"And what would Annette think if I were suddenly nice to you?"

His face crumples. She can see endless, disastrous possibilities flicker behind his eyes. All the dreams of their blissful future, dashed. For once, it seems he has nothing to say. Satisfied, she turns on her heel—only for him to reach out and catch her by the strap of her shopping bag. "Wait a minute. You *are* jealous."

That's just the thing. She is.

She isn't jealous of Annette exactly. The only thing enviable about her position is that Wes will soon grow bored of her and Margaret will never be free of him. No, it isn't Wes's attention that she wants. Not attention *from* him, anyway. She's lived here her entire life, but few in Wickdon look at her like they look at Wes. Those who don't hate her for her sullied blood only pity her. She resents him, unfair as it may be. Even though she knows she never will be, she wants to be something more than her grief and fear. But she won't admit that to him.

Margaret wriggles free of his grasp and shoves past him. She only makes it a few paces more before he cuts in front of her. "Would you stop for a minute?"

Usually, his eyes shimmer with mischief or a newly hatched scheme. But right now, they are filled with a somberness that looks entirely out of place on him. "I can't read your mind, you know. We can keep playing this game, or you could talk to me."

She bristles at the presumption that he could understand anything about her life, even something as small as this. But can't he? In this one regard, they are painfully alike, although Margaret can't convince herself that it matters. Even if he's experienced the same kind of rejection she has, even if she wanted to confide in him, what would she say? She has hidden behind too many locked doors to know how to open them anymore.

"There's nothing to tell. Gravity doesn't suit you, Wes."

For a moment, he looks wounded. Then, as though she'd imagined it altogether, his usual carefree expression slots into place, and he is invulnerable once again.

15

W es reaches for his mug and takes a long sip of coffee. Almost immediately, he spits the cold sludge back into the cup. He's amassed such a collection over the past two days, he's entirely forgotten which ones are still potable. Groaning, he rubs his bleary eyes and tries to piece together what time it is.

The sliver of sky he can see out the window has darkened to a rich amethyst purple. Inside Evelyn's lab, the only light comes from the glass alembics shimmering with the pale silver light of coincidentia oppositorum, the liquid byproduct of albedo. The last time he checked, it was early afternoon, and he swears he only blinked since then. Time is slipping away from him, as it always does.

The alchemy exposition is only four days away, and he's spent every waking moment calculating molar masses, experimenting with rune placement, and distilling batch after batch of coincidentia oppositorum. The entire lab reeks of sulfur and brine, but at least he's managed to develop a few viable prototypes. Margaret wanted ammunition, so he's done his best to give himself a crash course in ballistic science. Three shining bullets stand like toy soldiers on the edge of his desk.

What matters is stopping power, the likeliness to debilitate a target. By itself, a bullet is a harmless object; it's the transfer of energy from bullet to body that's deadly. To maximize stopping power, maximize the amount of energy stored within it. From what he's cobbled together from the chemistry and physics he's learned over the years, there are a few ways to accomplish that. The first bullet, he's enchanted to decrease its density. The second, to increase friction. The third, to raise its heat capacity. He still needs to ask Margaret to test them. It's impossible to pin her down lately. He only catches glimpses of her through the window as she comes and goes, riding her horse, Shimmer, at a thundering gallop with Trouble bounding behind them.

Wes pushes over one of the bullets and watches it roll across the desk. Although he's confident one of them will technically work, he's dissatisfied. An alchemist's purpose is to seek the truth, and he can't help feeling that everyone is missing something crucial.

Ever since the global war ended some fifteen years ago, the military has generously funded its alchemists. No doubt they've already developed far more advanced firearms than Wes—or any other civilian alchemist—could ever dream of producing. If that knowledge is available, why has the hala eluded New Albian hunters for almost 150 years? The most recently recorded death of a demiurge was 1718, nearly two centuries ago. What did they know that he doesn't?

Every Katharist legend about the slaying of a demiurge has the same three elements: a hero with a divine weapon, a full moon, and a beast who bleeds silver. Silver blood sounds like coincidentia oppositorum, and since alchemy is always the path to divinity regardless of which god you worship, he has to believe the common wisdom extracted from those stories. You kill a demiurge with alchemy on the full moon, when its light falls over the earth like a transmutation circle. The question is *how*. Alchemy is nothing more than breaking matter down to its essence. But if the demiurges boil down to the very ether of the universe, what are their bodies made of? If they're truly divine, how can you decompose God himself?

Once, Margaret said that her mother wants nothing more than the hala, so surely Evelyn knows how it's done. Maybe she recorded it somewhere.

Wes forces himself out of his seat and examines the shelves by the ghostly, pulsing light of the alembics. Old tomes collect dust an inch thick, the gilt rubbed off their spines with use. A few on the lowest shelf catch his eye. *The Matter of All Forms. The Soul of the Elements. The Chrysopoeia of Malachi.* The last is a thin, yellowing document that looks like it'll crumble to ash if he looks at it funny. With painstaking care, he pulls it from the shelf and carries it to the writing desk.

The Chrysopoeia contains nothing but illustrations, more a journal than a textbook. There's an alembic annotated with letters in a language he can't read, a double-ringed transmutation circle without any runes, and on the last page, one of the eeriest drawings he has ever seen. A fox swallowing its own tail. Its eyes are enormous and solid white, outlined in frantic black strokes.

Feeling oddly ill at ease, he closes the book and pushes it to the edge of the desk. If there's some secret about the hala contained in *The Chrysopoeia,* he can't translate it himself. Wes tamps down his frustration as best he can. Maybe when he has his apprenticeship, Evelyn will teach him whatever the hell *that* is.

Assuming, of course, he can alchemize something that will kill it.

No, he can't despair yet. He can work out the kinks of his design and test his theories over the next few weeks. For the purposes of the showcase, he only needs to demonstrate competency—and dazzle the judges enough to land them in the first flight. *Easier said than done.* Failing won't doom them on paper, but it will in practice. Nobody in the second or third flights will ever catch up to the hounds.

Wes pillows his head on his forearms. He's tired and restless, and he's got a tension headache that feels like someone's driven a pickaxe into his skull. If he doesn't get air, he'll fall asleep here and now.

He makes his way downstairs and drinks in the complete stillness of the manor. Margaret returned from training a while ago, so she's probably in her room, avoiding him as usual. He considers asking her if she wants to go for a walk but thinks better of it. He's not in the mood for rejection or bickering tonight. Snatching his coat from the rack, Wes throws it over his shoulders and heads out into the night.

It's cold as hell outside. He cups his hands over his mouth and exhales to warm them. Behind him, the manor hunches in the darkness. Only a single light burns in Margaret's room, tracing the shape of her curled up in the windowsill. The sight of her stirs more feelings than he cares to interrogate, none of them good. He turns sharply on his heel and continues along the worn dirt road through the forest. Although he's come to appreciate Wickdon's fierce beauty, the redwoods are no less unsettling than when he first arrived. Impossibly tall, with bark like the skin of some weathered reptile. Some two miles out, there's a break in the trees that overlooks a view of the ocean. Wes cuts his way through the underbrush and perches on a rock.

Far below him, the fields of rye shiver and shift in the wind. Something about being this high up makes it easier to sift through the churn of his thoughts. Even days later, he hasn't quite finished letting his bitterness toward Margaret fester. It's ridiculous, he knows, to feel so underappreciated—or at least so misunderstood. But as much as he hates to admit it, her words still sting.

Gravity doesn't suit you, Wes.

He thought they were beyond these games. He's bared himself to her in more ways than one at this point, yet she's pretending like she's never seen it—seen *him*. She said it to hurt him, and he can't figure out why.

Like every other girl he's met, Margaret is a mystery. Deep down, he still feels fourteen years old, as confused as he was when Erica Antonello ignored him for a whole week and wore cherry-red lipstick to school. She'd never done *that* before, and he didn't know what he'd done to earn it apart from walk Gail Kelly home instead of her. When he complained about it to Colleen, who was ten at the time, she rolled her eyes and said, "What's there to get? Girls are *people,* just like you."

Colleen has always been old for her age. He still hasn't plumbed the depths of that wisdom. Of course girls are people. People far beyond his understanding.

When the damp cold of the wind knifes into his jacket, he shudders. It smells faintly of an alchemical reaction, and as it whistles past him, he swears he hears his name in a sibilant voice. This place is clearly determined to drive him mad.

That's about enough brooding for one night.

He carefully navigates through the tangle of ferns that separates him from the road. His sense of direction has always been terrible, but he's walked this route countless times already—so often he thinks he could find the way back to the manor blindfolded. But as he approaches the path, he swears the trees have uprooted themselves into some new formation. Everything looks unfamiliar, and the redwoods towering above him regard him hostilely from on high.

Wes takes another tentative step and stops dead when something squelches beneath his shoe. Whatever it is reeks like sulfur and rancid meat. Like death.

He forces himself to look down.

The mangled thing at his feet might've once been a rabbit, but he can't tell anymore. Blood and silvery liquid ooze from the gash in its stomach, and the ropy coil of its insides slumps into the earth. His stomach twists painfully in revulsion. He hurries past it and spits out the saliva that floods his mouth. He can only think of one thing that'd make a toy of its food like this.

The hala.

Overhead, the half-full moon shines dully through the thickening clouds. There's still another two weeks before the hala reaches the height of its power. It wouldn't come after a human so early in the season—at least he doesn't think so. But he can't shake the skin-crawling feeling of eyes on him.

When he peers into the woods again, there's nothing. The night is still and placid as pond water. No snapping twigs. No rustle of the underbrush. He's alone.

Then the wind hisses, *Weston,* in its thin, ghostly voice.

He blinks, and there—deep in the fronds—he sees something. Pupilless white eyes, boring into him. They're bright as a pool of star-light. At first, he thinks he must be hallucinating, that maybe the alchemic fumes have gotten to him at last, but no.

There's a fox there, white as bone.

Wes staggers backward. The hala regards him with an almost hu-man intensity. His blood runs cold. He's seen it surrounded by other people, but it's a different thing entirely seeing it alone at night. With Margaret and her gun between them, it struck him with won-der. But right now, it fills him with animal terror. There's nowhere to hide and only ten feet between them.

His mother taught him the two things he is supposed to do in the face of a demiurge. As a good, faithful Sumic boy, he should beg forgiveness for his every sinful thought and deed. Banvish su-perstition calls for something more tangible—an offering of blood or cream or a slice of bread drizzled with honey—but that ship has sailed.

All he can do is pray.

Wes drops to his knees. The hala must take a step forward, but he doesn't see it move. It's there, then it's closer. The wind wails louder. He holds his breath, and his heart thuds against his eardrums.

God, protect me. Guide me.

It's close enough now that he can smell it. Salt and sulfur and iron. Its bottomless eyes seem to pull him in until his mind hums with fear. As it stretches its jaw wide like a snake, he sees the blood glinting on its teeth. He feels the chill of its breath on his face.

He's going to die.

Run, says the frantic whisper of the wind. *Run, run, run.*

As it lunges, Wes scrambles to his feet again and breaks into a sprint. He doesn't stop for anything. Not the branches and leaves that tear into his skin, not the painful jolt in his knees when he stum-bles over an upturned root, not the shred of his lungs with every brittle gulp of air. He doesn't know how far he runs before he sees the manor gate, rocking back and forth on its hinges.

Wes clears it, then leaps up the porch steps. His hands are shaking so hard, it takes a few tries to fit the key in the lock. When he finally shoves through the door, he bolts it behind him and slides down to the floor in a heap.

Everything aches. His legs throb, his ankle twinges from where he twisted it, and a swatch of skin above his socks stings with open wounds. But he is alive. *Alive.*

"Fuck." He laughs breathlessly, hysterically, until tears roll down his face.

"What are you doing?"

"Margaret," he wheezes.

She looms over him with a hand on her hip. Her hair hangs loose around her face, and he's so relieved to see her, all he can think about is grabbing fistfuls of it and kissing her square on the mouth. Although he's horrified by the very idea, he gasps through his fit until he finds his voice again. "I saw it. God, I saw it."

"You did?" She drops to the ground beside him. As her worried eyes rove over his face, she reaches out to touch his cheek. He flinches, and her fingers come away smeared with red. "You're bleeding."

Wes takes her by the wrist, and this time she doesn't pull away. "We can't do this."

All her edges harden again. "What are you talking about?"

"It's *out there,* waiting. It was . . ." He rakes a hand through his already wind-torn hair. "I was . . . How can we possibly . . . ?"

"Wes, slow down."

"Have you looked into its eyes?" He can't articulate the horror of it. Like he might've lost himself if he didn't look away. For the first time, he truly understands why Sumics worship it. "It was terrible."

"I know." She is silent for a long while. "Do you want to quit?"

Yes.

God, yes. If it means he never has to face that thing again, then of course he does. Especially when it's only going to get more aggressive as the month wears on. But it's not an option to quit, just as much as it's not an option to abandon his family. It's his life against a life worth living. His life against his sisters'. He would sooner die than disappoint them again.

"No," he rasps. "I made a promise to them—and to you. I'm not backing out of it now."

Her lips part. From the surprise on her face, it's clear she expected him to give a different answer. "I see. That's noble of you."

"I know gravity doesn't suit me—"

"No. I'm sorry. That was unkind to say, and I didn't mean it. I was upset, so I . . ."

"It's alright." He can't bear it if she confides in him out of guilt. "I was egging you on all day. I deserved it."

"Why are you always so stubborn?" Frustration breaks her voice. "It's not alright."

"I said it was," he mutters. "Let me at least decide that for myself, would you?"

"Fine. Where were you?"

Wes scowls. How quickly she returns to criticism. "I went for a walk. I needed to clear my head for a minute."

"A minute? You were gone for over an hour without telling me where you went or how long you'd be, and when I looked out the window and saw you running, I thought . . ."

"Aw, Maggie. Don't go crying over me yet."

"Don't. Don't make this into a joke." She clenches her fists in her lap. "I don't intend to cry over you. Certainly not if you got yourself killed in some careless way, like wandering around after dark by yourself. That thing is on the loose, and you've already made enemies, so I can't fathom what you were thinking. If you'd died, what would I have done? What would your family have done? Everything you've ever dreamed and worked toward would be for nothing!"

"Alright, *alright*," he cuts in. "I get it. I'm a selfish idiot. Is that what you want?"

"No, that's not what I'm saying." Her voice wobbles. It's enough to undo him. "I'm saying I was worried about you."

"Margaret . . ." His heart lurches. "I'm sorry."

He goes deathly still when she places her hand on top of his. It's warm and callused, but her touch is surprisingly gentle. "You have to be more careful. Wickdon is more dangerous than you know."

He thinks he has some idea, though. The danger of Wickdon runs deeper than just the hala or Jaime or the restless sea. It's here, within him and right in front of him. Maybe it's a trick of the light, or maybe it's the adrenaline. But right now, he swears that her hair is spun from moonlight and her skin is dusted with silver. Try as he may, he can't exactly recall what it was he once found so repulsive about her.

16

Wes is sitting in her mother's lab, bent over an alchemy textbook and clutching a steaming cup of coffee. Margaret wonders when it won't strike her as uncanny to catch a glimpse of him through the invitingly cracked-open door, slumped over his work in the same way her mother often was. It reminds her of a happier time, when the lab was safe and not haunted. When her mother worked late nights, she and David used to peer forlornly into the lab until Evelyn noticed them and her bleary expression melted into a smile.

Alchemy-warm air comes sighing out of the open door. The entire house breathes with the change in temperature, deep and slow, as if it's waking from a long slumber. It has missed its alchemist.

Three days ago, she tested his prototypes. At the time, she was admittedly impressed with his vague answers about the density of metals and the expenditure of kinetic energy. She was less impressed with the results. The less dense bullet pinged off the target, as harmful as a raindrop. The one with higher heat capacity was too hot to even touch. The higher-friction model didn't seem to do anything at all, but Wes muttered to himself, snapping his fingers, as though seeing something anew.

The showcase is tomorrow. It will kick off the event season—and for many entrants, it will make or break their chances of winning.

If he doesn't come up with *something* that works, they'll be relegated to third flight, and she won't be able to kill the hala even if they manage by some miracle to pin it down.

Still, it'll do him no good to exhaust himself. It's almost five in the morning, and he's wasting electricity and clearly fighting sleep. His eyelids droop, and one hand fists in his hair. With the other, he stabs the book with his index finger and drags it like a yad across the page. He reads laboriously, his brow furrowed and his mouth forming the shape of each word. Gradually, line by line, he slumps over until he pillows his face on the book.

He'll spend all morning on page one at this rate.

The lamp casts his face in a warm, steady glow. The shadows of his thick eyelashes feather across his cheekbones. This light softens him, and she's not sure if she likes it. Normally, Wes is a wildfire with his untamed hair and his loud voice. And like this, he is so . . .

She shakes herself out of it, clutching her book closer to her chest. It isn't that she intended to watch him, exactly. She wanted a cup of tea while she read—a small respite before she sets out to train—but he distracted her with memories and his irritatingly endearing face. Her frustration sits on her tongue like a rusted coin, something to worry. Wes has potential enough. He's intelligent and determined and kind, but he is so . . .

The word continues to elude her. All she knows is that it won't do. She needs him to be *more* to justify her attachment.

Wes begins to snore. Margaret sighs and reaches into her pocket, where she finds an old shopping list. Crumpling it in her fist, she closes one eye and takes aim. There is a moment, like the moment before a gunshot, where everything goes perfectly still and clear. She lines him up in her imaginary sights, then lobs the paper at him. It tumbles through the open air until it bounces off his temple with a quiet *smack*.

He shoots upright, arms flailing as though trying to throw off a spiderweb. Then, his gaze finds her through the darkness. "What was that for?"

"To keep you on track. You have until tomorrow."

He grumbles and rubs his eyes.

Hesitating, Margaret crosses the threshold of the lab. She waits for the reflexive terror to root her in place, for fog to crowd out her vision. But the gentle light of the lamp and his bleary presence smooth over the jagged edges of her memories. The burnt transmutation circle lies dormant in the recesses of shadow. Emboldened, she pads over to the desk and takes a seat beside him. She considers placing her book on the desk, but she knows he'll mock her relentlessly for it. As discreetly as she can, she slips it beneath her chair and assesses his workspace.

Wes's notes are scrawled in tottering handwriting without any semblance of order, slanting and sideways and starred at random. His thoughts seem to launch off like a hound unleashed for the chase. The chaos makes her skin crawl. Her world is governed by method and pattern—how to disassemble and clean a gun, how to skin a deer, how to train a hound—not this madness.

"What are you doing up so early?" she asks.

"So late," he amends. "I've been at it all night."

She taps the open page of his book. "You're not even a quarter of the way through."

Any remnant of politeness falls from his face. He slides the book closer toward himself and curls around it protectively. "I know."

"Do you have a new version of the bullet?"

"Not yet."

"Do you expect to find something in this book?" He pointedly ignores her in favor of writing letter by haphazard letter in his notebook. Margaret feels no guilt for needling him. No one ever granted her the luxury of preserving her feelings. "The exposition is tomorrow."

"Yeah. You just said that."

"So why are you slacking off?"

Irritation flashes in his eyes. "I'm not."

She reaches toward his notes.

"Hey!"

Margaret spreads them out on the table like a hand of playing cards. Apart from being messy, the notes are riddled with errors: letters mirrored, whole words indecipherably misspelled. But most striking are the marginalia. Doodles of strange little monsters smile jaggedly at her. There's even a man being crushed by a book entitled *The Alchemical Properties of Metal*. He's labeled with the name of the author.

Wes gathers up his papers up so quickly, they crumple. "I know what it looks like, but this is how I focus, alright?"

Margaret has already said what she thinks, so she doesn't see much point in pressing the matter further. He huffs out a breath that ruffles the too-long hair in his eyes. Then, he picks up his fountain pen and makes a show of intently reading the book. He holds his pen like a hammer and applies so much pressure to the point, the metal tip bleeds ink across the page.

A thought occurs to her, and the shame that blooms within her is enough to sour her stomach. "Can I ask you something?"

"Sure," he says with exaggerated enthusiasm. "Why not?"

"You have a hard time reading, don't you?"

He smiles at her broadly, but the glint in his eyes is nothing like mirth. "Is that a joke? You, of all people?"

"I'm not joking."

Wes sighs, turning his pen through his fingers. "I get headaches if I read for too long, and seeing words I don't recognize . . . It's like an interrupted radio signal." Then, quickly: "It's not a big deal."

Margaret doesn't fully understand what he means, but the worried frown notched in his brow indicates he isn't as lazy as she initially suspected. He's trying his best. "What are you trying to do?"

"The last few transmutations I've done haven't worked how I wanted them to, and no one's ever technically taught me how to do albedo. So I'm trying to see if there's something I'm missing. I need to figure out how to distill a more concentrated coincidentia oppositorum."

Margaret pulls the book he's reading toward her. From memory, she leafs through the pages, through chapters and chapters of introductory and historical material, until she arrives at the section that discusses albedo, the process of purification, in depth.

"Thanks," he says glumly.

"If it would save you time, I can read it to you."

She surprises them both—herself most of all. She's considered it in an abstract sense: that if they succeed, he will become her mother's apprentice. That he is, already, an alchemist. But it's different to place the gun in his hand herself. Despite her misgivings, she wants to believe in him and his dream. She wants to believe that his goodness can survive his training.

He takes a sip of coffee. "That'd be helpful."

So Margaret begins to read.

He listens with his eyes closed and his brows pinched together, occasionally scrawling a note on a torn sheet of paper. By the time she finishes the chapter, excitement fills him to bursting.

"Don't go anywhere." He buttons his sleeves at his elbows and springs from his seat. "I don't want you to miss this when it works."

Margaret leaves him to fuss with the transmutation circle he's drawing on the desk. He scrubs away runes and redraws them until a fine mist of chalk residue swirls in the lamp-golden air around him. She retrieves her book from beneath her chair and settles onto the sill of the bay window, one that overlooks the sea. The sun is beginning to breach the water and stain it a brilliant red.

Wes lays his hands over the chalk circle and begins to burn a dish full of sand. Like this, alchemy seems so simple. Sometimes, Margaret wonders what she would boil down to, or if she could even bear to look at the loneliness at the heart of her.

Soon, the smell of sulfur drowns out everything else. She cracks open the window to let in a rush of fresh air. The early-morning chill feels nice against her skin. Wrapped in the warmth of her wool socks and alchemy, it's oddly . . . cozy.

When she's certain he's thoroughly engrossed in his work, Margaret draws the curtains over herself and opens her book, the latest from her favorite novelist, M. G. Huffman. She's been anticipating the next scene far more than she'd care to admit. Although Margaret has been reading romances for years, she's rarely rooted for a couple this desperately. After nearly two hundred pages, she will be rewarded for her patience, her worry, her yearning. As she reads, the world around her slips away. All that exists are the characters, the paper between her fingertips, and the familiar, aching heat steadily pooling within her.

"Margaret?"

She bites down on a swear as the sound of Wes's voice shatters the spell. He's a hazy smear behind the cream-white of the curtain. Maybe he'll get the hint if she ignores him.

"Oh, Margaret," he drawls. "I know you can hear me."

The floorboards creak under his footsteps. A flutter of panic seizes her; she shoves the book underneath the pillow behind her. The curtains part, and in flows the scents of alchemy and his rum-and-bay aftershave.

"Hey. What are you doing back here?"

She is acutely aware of the emptiness of her hands and the flush on her cheeks. "Reading."

"Oh, well, I need your help with something, and . . . Hey! Liar. You're not reading anything."

The corner of her book presses into her back. "I *was* before you interrupted me."

"Well, then. What was it that you were reading? Hieroglyphics on the wall?"

"No."

Wes braces his hands on either side of the window and looms over her with a wicked look. "I know you're hiding something. You're bright red."

Her heart leaps into her throat. "No, I'm not."

"I knew it! I knew you weren't perfect. What is it?"

"It's none of your business."

Wes reaches toward the pillow, and she grabs his forearm. It only fuels him; he twists out of her grip and shoulders her aside until he manages to snatch her book from beneath her. Weightless with delight, he springs back a few paces and drinks in the cover.

Death would be a mercy over this mortification. She buries her face in her hands. In her mind's eye, she can see the scandalous triangle of skin exposed by the hero's unbuttoned shirt and the look of pure rapture on the heroine's face. She can see him bearing her down onto the desk alongside all the alembics and books, and oh *God,* why did she think she could get away reading this unbothered with Wes in the same room?

She peers up at him through her fingers. A huge, self-satisfied grin spreads across his face. "*Taming the Alchemist.* Ha!"

"Don't you have your own books to read? Give it back."

Wes ignores her. He's practically giddy as he flips through the pages. In only a matter of seconds, he finds what he's looking for—there, marked with an accusatory index finger. Margaret watches him scan the text with mounting dread, made all the worse by him mouthing along with each word in his slow, deliberate way. His eyebrows rise until they disappear into the disheveled mop of his hair. When his gaze flickers back to hers, his eyes are glittering with mischief and his teeth are bared in a smile that glints like a blade catching the sunlight.

This man is a demon, she decides. There are no two ways about it.

"Why, Miss Welty. How *improper.*"

"Give it back, Wes," she snaps—and regrets it immediately. She has made the fatal mistake of letting her humiliation creep into her voice. It only makes him more impish.

He sits beside her on the windowsill, snickering. "I gotta hand it to you. Never in a million years would I have taken you as the type to read trash."

"It's not trash."

"No? Then what's this?" He clears his throat and slips into the most exaggeratedly debauched tone she has ever heard. "'As he hooked her knee over his shoulder and kissed his way up the inside of her thigh . . .'"

Her every rational thought dulls until the only noise in her head is a sustained scream. An impulse to claw and bite seizes her then, one she hasn't had since she was a child and one of her mother's apprentices chipped one of her model guns. She becomes that woods-raised child again, feral to her core, and dives for the book.

Wes holds her at arm's length. "'. . . she let out a moan of—'"

"Stop!" she hisses.

Margaret grabs his wrist with one hand and the book with the other. As she tries to wrench it from him, she throws them both off-balance.

Wes strangles a curse as they tumble to the floor together. She hits the ground first in a heap. His elbow cracks against the hardwood bare inches away from her head. Every glass instrument rattles on the shelves, but neither that nor Trouble's alarmed barking from downstairs can muffle Wes's pained moan. The sound reverberates against her ear, sending a wave of chills down her spine.

He braces himself above her. Both of them breathe heavily, their lips inches apart. Wes's eyes are as dark and wild as the sea. He looks utterly stunned, like *she's* the one who wronged *him,* and his ears begin to turn a ripe shade of crimson. When Margaret shifts against him, she feels his heart pounding against hers and—

Is that . . . ?

Her mind goes blank, and she lands a knee in his ribs. He rolls off her and doubles over with a wheeze, at last relinquishing his hold on her book. Margaret snatches it from the ground and scrabbles to her feet. If she stays near him another moment, she'll catch fire. She'll do or say something regrettable, and it'll jeopardize all the tentative trust they have built together. She cannot, will not, risk that when the exposition is tomorrow.

Wes props himself up on his elbows and gives her a look that makes her feel oddly powerful. It's not a weapon she wants or one she knows exactly how to wield. "Alright, alright. I yield."

A bright silver light sparks in the corner of her eye. Unease crosses Wes's face. Then, the array he's drawn on the desk begins to smolder—not with the telltale smell of alchemy but with ignition.

"Um." He coughs. "I need to check on that."

She nods mutely, too afraid of what her voice may betray if she speaks.

For the rest of the day, as Margaret practices her shot, as she runs Shimmer and drills Trouble's commands, a slick, horrible knot of tension sits in her gut. Between Wes and the looming exposition, she's wound tight and ready to snap. But when night enfolds the manor and she's alone and safe in her bed, she succumbs to the desire to relieve it. Normally, when she lets her hands slide between her thighs, she thinks of nothing and no one in particular.

Tonight, she thinks of Wes.

She thinks of what might have happened if she had canted her hips against his instead of shutting down. She thinks of his tousled hair and bared forearms and their hands rough on each other. She thinks of the expression he wore when they lay tangled together. He looked the same as he did when she fired that dud prototype bullet. Like realization dawned on him, and he could see everything clearly for the first time. Hidden beneath the confusion was something else, burning hotter than an alchemical reaction. Hunger.

17

The exposition arrives the next day, whether Wes is ready or not.

It's another typical Wickdon afternoon, cold and thick with the promise of rain. Silvery mist wends through the base of the redwoods and veils the forest in swirling gray. Wes keeps his gaze fixed straight ahead as he walks toward town, breathing steadily through his growing unease. Everywhere he turns, he swears he sees the hala's blank white eyes boring into him.

He woke at dawn and spent the morning watching Margaret test his new designs. He lurked bleary-eyed on the porch with his coffee, pointedly trying not to make eye contact or notice the way the early morning light burnished her hair. Each bullet she fired embedded itself soundly in a felled tree. The trunk shattered on impact, spewing sap and wood splinters like a lanced boil. It worked more or less as he hoped, but it lacked pyrotechnics. He alchemized a perfectly deadly bullet but not a dazzling one.

"I know it's not enough to get first flight," he told her. "I know. I'll figure it out."

Margaret didn't answer him. At least her defeated expression made it easier not to look at her. He can't bear the combined weight of their anxieties any more than he can bear the siren wail of his thoughts whenever she's near him—which is exactly why he left for Wickdon without her.

God, he needs to clear his head. He's anxious and miserable and sexually frustrated, which is the exact cocktail of emotions that usually lands him in trouble. How did she catch him so off guard yesterday?

When he had her pinned beneath him, he couldn't think of a single thing to say. He *always* has something to say. But in that moment, his wit abandoned him; all his mind could hold were the words in that infernal book and the warmth of her breath against his lips and that furious glint in her eyes before she kneed him in the ribs. Thank God she did. It worked as well as dousing him with cold water. He prays she didn't get the wrong idea about where his head was at. Maybe she'll assume it was nothing deeper than their proximity.

What does any of this matter? He doesn't have time to deal with his confused feelings or fantasize about—no, simply *consider* the abstract concept of kissing Margaret Welty senseless on the floor of her mother's lab. He needs to focus on alchemy, on winning, on figuring out what the hell keeps going wrong in his transmutation.

Everything depends on that. His future. His mother's health. His family's security. He can't afford to blow this chance like all the others.

The thing is, his transmutation works. If it did that much damage to a tree, he dreads to imagine what it'd do to a fox. But it's too simple, too obvious, and he doesn't see a point in trying to do something showy if he can't go full-out. He wants more than shattering; he wants *sparks*. Fire requires a combination of heat, fuel, and oxygen. Oxygen and fuel, he has plenty of. Which means he still hasn't generated the eight hundred degrees he needs to kindle a flame.

As towering trees give way to golden hills, he runs through his formulas again. Margaret's preferred rifle bullet weighs approximately ten grams, which means he can enchant it with ten grams of coincidentia oppositorum. He's calculated the mass of each substance involved in this alchemic reaction a thousand times over and tried nearly every combination of them. His most successful brew is composed of six grams of sand, two grams of osmium, and two grams of camphor. It results in a bullet that's lightweight enough to increase the total momentum in the system but dense enough to retain the heat from the camphor essence and the gunpowder's ignition. While he could have tried distilling something different, he doubts it would make a considerable difference when he's working with such small quantities . . .

He's startled from his thoughts when a group of hunters on horseback nearly trample him. Wes lets out a shout of surprise that's swallowed up by the thunderous four-count beat of their hooves. In their wake, the ground is torn up and muddied, and on the other side of a pasture fence, he can see the telltale blackening on yet another field of crops.

It's getting worse, as promised. It's only a matter of time before it moves onto something more substantive than horses and vineyards.

By the time he reaches Wickdon proper, he's nearly drowning in people. The streets are lined with market stalls, where vendors hawk gun polish and hunting jackets in a hundred gem-bright colors. Wes wields his carrying case like a battering ram to maneuver through the crowds. They cram into the perimeter of the town square and throng on balconies, straining to peer over each other and into the center, where the hunt officials have arranged tables in efficient, geometric lines like an alchemical array. The wind cutting through the alleyways smells of tobacco and sweat and liquor. Between his own dread and the heady charge in the air, he can't help feeling he's about to attend a public execution.

When he at last stumbles into the square, a man in a scarlet coat directs him to his workstation. Wes sets his carrying case on the table, and as he carefully unloads his instruments, he watches the other alchemists filter in. They move in packs like well-dressed wolves, all of them self-assured and easy, like they've done this many times before. Some of them stop to chat and shake hands with the judges. Their wristwatches and cuff links glitter gold beneath the streetlamps, and Wes is struck with a pang of bitter longing. Who is he kidding by being here? Even if he wins, even if he gets accepted to the finest university in the country, he'll never truly be like them.

"You nervous, kid?"

Wes startles. A short, stocky woman in her midtwenties stands at the work station beside his. Her accent is from Dunway—subtle but distinct—and so is her gown, a ruffled knee-length number stitched with sparkling glass beads. The ends of her ash-brown hair escape from her felt hat and curl gently against her jawline.

Wes offers her the most genuine smile he can muster. He feels it wobble. "Nervous? No, not at all."

"It's alright. I was nervous for my first hunt, too. Judith Harlan."

Deflated, he says, "Weston Winters."

Harlan scans him from head to toe, and he's painfully aware of his father's worn jacket draped over his shoulders. It detracts from the overall effect of his suit, but the overlong sleeves would look worse than the alternative. Besides, it's cold—and the familiar weight of it soothes him. He resists the urge to fidget with the knot on his tie. "Fifth Ward, huh?"

"Yeah. That's right."

"Thought so," she says wistfully. "Anyway, what's eating you? You look like you're about to faint."

Wes isn't naive enough to trust her, even if she seems well-meaning. Fumbling to recover his cool, he drawls, "Nothing. Beautiful women frazzle me, is all."

"Lord." She wheezes a laugh. "I think you're a little young for me. What are you, seventeen?"

He feels the tips of his ears burn with humiliation, but he manages to keep the defensive edge out of his voice when he says, "Eighteen, actually."

"All the same. I'm not trying to trick you."

"I . . ." He rakes his hands through his hair and immediately regrets it. A few stubborn strands escape from the gel he slicked on this morning and fall into his face. There's nothing to be done for it now. "I can't seem to get enough energy in the system. I don't know what's wrong."

Harlan hums sympathetically. "Have you checked your math?"

"Of course I have."

"Have you tested the transmutation more than once?" She throws up her hands when he scowls. "Alright, alright, enough with the scary look. I'm just asking. Listen, if the system is alchemically sound, the problem's you."

"Me?" he sputters. "What's that supposed to mean?"

"You can be a brilliant chemist but a mediocre alchemist, and—well, are you a good chemist?"

"Passable."

"Good. If we were brilliant chemists, we'd be in a pharmaceutical lab somewhere. But alchemy is about intuition, too, right? It's not hard science. It's . . . well, it's magic. You're the one channeling and controlling the energy circulating in the reaction. It's not only the laws of matter governing what happens—it's you." Harlan taps the center of her chest, exactly where he feels the spark within him when he transmutes. "Maybe you're holding back, or maybe you're thinking too much. Either way, somewhere down the line, you're losing too much energy to entropy. So relax. You know it works in theory, so why shouldn't it in practice?"

Relax. If only it were that simple.

Once, before all of the rejections and disappointment, Wes believed in himself. He believed that determination and good intentions and natural aptitude could carry him through. But when he's staring down the gulf between him and all these other alchemists, it's hard to stay positive. "I appreciate the pep talk and all, but why are you telling me this? Isn't this a competition?"

She winks. "Just some advice from one Fifth Ward kid to another."

Before he can reply, a voice on a microphone cuts through the din of conversation. "Good afternoon, everyone."

Standing at a podium draped in New Albion's red-and-gold flag is a man who looks disconcertingly like Jaime, blond and sharp-smiled and decidedly evil. "As the mayor of Wickdon, I want to welcome each of you to the one hundred and seventy-fourth annual alchemy exposition, one of our most cherished traditions in the lead-up to the hunt. This event is a cornerstone of New Albian culture, a monument to our country's imagination and industry. Alchemy is God's gift to mankind, and it continues to pave the way to a brighter, more equitable future."

Wes swallows down his bitterness at those empty words. One day, if he survives this, he'll stand on a podium exactly like that one and mean every word.

"I'm pleased to introduce our panel of judges this year, all of whom are renowned scholars in their fields."

Beside him are three middle-aged folks whose faces he can't make out from a distance. The first, whom the mayor introduces as Abigail Crain, wears a fur coat and jewels that glister cold as stars around her neck. The second, Oliver Kent, is a man so tall and thin it looks as though he's been stretched like saltwater taffy. The third, Elizabeth Law, has a feather headpiece nestled into her fair ringlets.

"Our judges will assess each competitor on technique and innovation," the mayor continues. "After a short recess, they will test each design and score them on both showmanship and functionality. It's my honor to declare this alchemy exposition—Wickdon's first since 1898—open!"

With a smattering of applause and cheers, it begins.

Wes does his best to watch the first two competitors with a queasy, masochistic fascination. From here, there's not much to look at but the silver flash of alchemic fire and the twist of smoke as it rises into the darkening sky. Maybe it's the thickening smell of sulfur or maybe it's his nerves, but he thinks he's going to be sick.

As the judges make their way down the line, the sound of chalk scratching against wood grows louder and the drone of conversations duller. Wes can't be sure if he's been waiting for seconds or hours when the panel finally stops in front of his table.

Crain speaks first. "Name?"

He's transfixed by the string of diamonds resting above her collarbones; they must be alchemically modified to have that kind of brilliance. "Uh, Winters. Weston Winters, ma'am."

She purses her lips but scribbles something on her notepad. "Very well, Mr. Winters. You may proceed."

Wes fishes the chalk he's brought out of his pocket. Although his hand is trembling, he draws the transmutation circle for nigredo with the ease of having done it literally hundreds of times this week. He arranges the components of the reaction in the center, then places his hands over the array to activate the magic circulating within it. It ignites, and as it burns the sand and osmium to blackened caput mortuum, Wes watches the judges take notes and confer from beneath his eyelashes. One step down. Two to go.

"When you're ready," Crain says.

His confidence wavers.

It's not only the laws of matter governing what happens. It's you.

Alchemy is a science far stranger and less precise than any other he knows. Maybe what fuels it is the divine or chaos or magic, but whatever it is, the missing piece in this reaction is within him. It *is* him. Maybe all he needs to do is concentrate harder. To bend the universe with the force of his will.

But as he puzzles over heat and friction, his thoughts go slack—and then, as panic sets in, they carry him soundly back to Margaret. God, no, he can't think about her right now. It will derail him entirely when every thought of her forces him to confront an emotion he can't bear to look at head-on. He focuses more intently on drawing the alchemic array. He corrals his mind by concentrating on the facts of what he is doing, on infusing each stroke with purpose. A circle to embody the unity of all things and the cyclical flow of energy. Runes to harness that energy and shape it to his own ends. Heat and friction. The heat of Margaret's mouth if he kissed her, the friction he desperately wanted between them, and good *Lord,* he is going to lose his mind if he can't rein himself in.

Maybe you're holding back. Or maybe you're thinking too much.

Maybe Harlan's right. Maybe he has been holding back. For so long, he's been terrified of what would happen if he sat quietly with himself for too long, if he let himself grieve, if he let his family see that he was hurting. But Margaret has a way of finding every crack in his armor. As he holds onto the thought of her, he feels the spark of divine magic at the core of him leap.

Wes activates the array.

The coincidentia oppositorum condenses in the alembic drop by drop. It shines as bright as the diamonds on Crain's neck and illuminates the table with a glow like moonlight. Although he can't know if it worked until they fire that bullet, his heart races at the sight of it. He knows, deep down, it's the best work he's done. Once he binds the essence to the bullet with rubedo, he places it into Crain's waiting hand.

"Thank you, Mr. Winters."

"Oh, no. Thank *you*."

As soon as the judges move on, Wes slumps over until he can rest his elbows on the table and his head in his hands. Through the wayward strands of his hair, he sees Harlan smiling at him slyly. "Now that's how it's done."

"Th-thanks."

He thinks he needs a shower.

As the technical evaluation winds down, the sun dips into the sea and afternoon melts into evening. In thirty minutes, the second round of judging will begin. It's a brief respite while the judges and spectators move from the town square to the field outside Wickdon. No one wants to risk a misfire in the crowds—or accidentally blow one of the darling storefronts sky high.

Technically, now that he's done his job for the night, Wes is free. He entertains the idea of slinking back to the manor or persuading someone to buy him a drink, but he supposes he ought to soberly bear witness to it if his career ends tonight. Stronger than any other temptation, however, is finding Margaret. It buzzes insistently in the back of his skull and makes his skin crawl with a restless energy he doesn't care for.

But assuming she's even here, he's not sure he can face her. Wanting her, even her company, makes him feel small and pathetic and vulnerable. Now that the rush of alchemy and adrenaline has drained from him, he's painfully aware of just how raw he is. Performing that transmutation opened a floodgate within him—one he's all too eager to slam shut again. He doesn't *want* to want Margaret. He doesn't want to want someone who consumes his thoughts this way, who expects anything of him, who would wound him if she denied him.

He wants something easier. Someone who doesn't make him pine or reconsider his worldview or *feel*. He wants . . .

"Wes!"

Never has Annette Wallace's voice sounded sweeter.

Wes turns on his heel to face her. Her hair is carefully gelled in spirals around her temples, so crisp and glossy it's all he can do to not tug one loose. "Fancy meeting you here. You off work?"

"I wish. I'm on break, but I wanted to say hi."

"Hi," he says. "Let me take you out."

"Well, I . . ." She looks flustered for a moment before she composes herself. "Aren't you supposed to be at the exposition?"

"I finished the technical portion. They're not judging the execution for another thirty minutes, so I'm free and bored. So what do you say? Don't make me beg."

"You want to take me out for thirty minutes?"

"It'll be the best thirty minutes you've ever had. Or maybe we can watch the evaluation together. I may need comfort depending on how it goes."

She cracks a smile she clearly doesn't want to. "I can't. My dad will be furious if I don't come back on time."

"All the better. Come on. The night is young and so are we."

"Alright, fine." She points a finger at him. "But only until I see what you've wrought. Then I really have to go."

That suits him fine. Just enough time to drown out all the noise in his head. "You've made me the happiest man alive."

Annette snorts before sliding her hand into his. "You're ridiculous."

Wes nearly dies then and there, but he holds it together enough to say, "Am I?"

"Yes." A cold breeze whips through the street, full of salt and promise, and tangles in her curls. She looks painfully lovely like this. "I can't believe I let you talk me into this."

"You're telling me you've never been late to work before? You have such a long way to fall. Have you even snuck out?"

"Of course I have!" She rests a hand on her chest, feigning outrage.

"Ah, then you have ideas. Where should we go?"

"There's not much of anywhere *to* go."

Wes nudges her shoulder with his. "What do you usually get up to?"

"A lot of us will drink by the pier sometimes. Sometimes we'll go cliff diving."

"Cliff diving, huh?"

"It's hardly as exciting as you're imagining. Not like all the dancing and high-society mingling I'm sure you get up to in the city."

Wes considers telling her that he and his friends have no money to do anything of the sort. He considers telling her that he's likely something out of her father's worst nightmare, a Banvishman with no formal education and no prospects. He considers telling her he lives in a tenement home in the Fifth Ward and nowhere near the ritzy clubs she dreams of. But that'd put a damper on the mood. He's only just gotten her out, and their time is limited. It's better if she believes he's the kind of worldly, well-to-do man she imagines him to be. "Humor me. I'm very easily impressed."

She sighs. "Have you ever had Wickdon ice cream?"

"I can't say that I have."

"It's good." She says it like it's a painful admission. "Let's go."

They wait in an interminably long line for ice cream, then follow the rest of the hunt-season crowds toward the field. Hand in hand, they wade through the knee-high grass until they find a clear spot near a cliff that overlooks the ocean. Moonlight shivers on the water, and sea-foam laces the near-black sand. They settle onto the grass, and Wes watches Annette from the corner of his eye as her ice cream melts on her plastic spoon. He finishes his in barely a minute, the taste of peppermint still bright on his tongue.

"It's weird to have so many people here," she says.

"I bet. The population's about quintupled."

"It's not that. I like to come out here alone sometimes." He gets the impression she's trying to tell him something weighty, but he can't discern the meaning of the sad look she's giving him. "Sometimes I sit here and wonder what's on the other side of all that water."

"The Rebun Islands."

She swats him. "You know what I mean."

He grins apologetically. "Have you really never left Wickdon?"

"No. Never. I want to, though, more than anything. It feels like this place is squeezing the life out of me. Everything about it. The inn. My parents. Even my friends. I don't think any of them really understand when I try to tell them. They were born here, and they'll die here. That's just how it is."

"Why don't you leave, then?"

"It'd break my father's heart. Or maybe it's that I'm a coward. Imagining going all the way to the city by myself . . . I don't think I could bear it."

"It's not cowardly." Out in the distance, a lighthouse blinks in the gloom. "Loneliness is a terrible thing. Maybe the most terrible thing."

"And you've chosen the loneliest corner of Wickdon." She gives him a sympathetic look. "How are you managing?"

The very last thing he wants to think about is Margaret. And yet, perversely, she's all he wants to think about. "Oh, you know. I make my own fun."

He hesitates. Annette is perhaps the only person in town who might talk to him honestly about Margaret and her mother. It feels like a betrayal to even think it. Margaret hasn't exactly been forthcoming about anything in her life, but if she is so determined to shut him out, what other option does he have to sate his curiosity?

"Although if you don't mind my asking . . . It doesn't really seem like the Weltys are part of the community. Why is that?"

"Oh." Discomfort twists her mouth. "Well, Evelyn is a recluse. When Maggie's brother died, she stopped leaving the house. And then after her husband left, she kind of lost it. I feel sorry for Maggie, honestly. She's had a tough life."

That, he already knew—apart from her father's leaving. But it still explains nothing, unless people in Wickdon think grief is a disease. "If you feel so sorry for her, why aren't you friends with her?"

He surprises himself with the edge in his voice. It surprises Annette, too, because she's blinking at him with genuine, wide-eyed concern. "You said it yourself the other day. She's not the most pleasant person to be around. She doesn't want friends."

"Bullshit." All of it, bullshit. Everybody wants friends, even Margaret. Even if she won't admit it. "You're telling me that's why Harrington has it out for her? Because she's unpleasant?"

"No," she says, a little defensively. "Jaime has it out for her because he's a bigot."

"Obviously," Wes mutters. "What does that have to do with Margaret?"

"I guess you wouldn't know. Her father was Yu'adir. Not that it matters to *me,* but people here can be so backward, and . . ." Annette's voice swirls together with the steady *shhh* of the waves and the chatter of the crowd.

Margaret is Yu'adir.

So much clicks into place, and Wes is left feeling like a fool for not figuring it out sooner and horribly sorry he asked. But Margaret never told him. Why didn't she tell him? Even after she met his family. Even after he asked why Jaime was so hell-bent on torment-ing her.

Not many Yu'adir live in the Fifth Ward. While his parents fled famine in Banva before Mad was born, most Yu'adir immigrants came to New Albion's shores a few decades earlier, seeking refuge from pogroms in their home countries. But even though they've been here longer than the Banvish, he's seen how much they're hated. Their businesses and temples burned. The inventor of the automobile pub-lishing articles about how they manipulate the global economy and have funded every war for centuries.

It turns his stomach to realize why all these people despise Mar-garet so much, to think she's endured it alone for all these years. If he'd known, he would have . . . would have what, exactly? There's nothing he can do to protect her from these people when he can hardly protect himself. But still, it rattles him. Why is she so con-vinced she has to bear everything alone? Was she afraid of what he would think, or—

"Hey." Annette rests a hand on his arm. "Are you alright?"

"You said it doesn't matter to you, but it clearly does."

"What?"

Wes draws in his breath, determined to keep his voice even. "If you cared, why didn't you stand up to him? You were right there when Harrington started mouthing off about immigrants and the Yu'adir, and you didn't say a word. If you cared, shouldn't that bother you?"

Annette flushes. "You saw what happens when you stand up to him."

"Nothing," he says sharply. "Nothing happens. All he did was spout more hateful nonsense. The only difference is that it'd be di-rected at you instead."

"And what should I have done? He's my friend."

He can see she's upset, but he can't stop himself from pushing. "Maybe you should get better friends."

"I *can't,* Wes." Her voice breaks. "I can't. I can't be better than him."

"What are you talking about? Of course you can."

"What would you know?" She takes a deep breath. "Jaime is the mayor's son. All of my friends worship him, probably because they're afraid of him, and for good reason. You haven't seen the worst of how cruel he can be—not even close. I'm sorry I'm not as cosmopolitan as you, but you don't get to sit on your high horse and judge me or tell me how I feel. What this town has done to Maggie is a sin. But I can't end up like her. As long as I'm stuck here, silence is my only option. My friends are all I have."

"You know, my parents are Banvish immigrants. They were poor farmers in Banva, and we're still poor here. I've dealt with people like Harrington all my life, so yeah, forgive me if I judge you for worrying about what your stupid friends would think of you. The world's bigger than this town." He waits for her response, but she gives him nothing. Anger and disappointment sit bitterly on his tongue. "So that's it, then."

Annette blinks hard and shakes her head, as though rousing herself from a dream. Even in the darkness, he can see tears glimmering in her eyes. "I have to go."

"God," he mutters. Guilt sours his stomach; he hates making women cry. "I'm sorry. I didn't mean to . . . At least let me walk you back."

"No." She stands and dusts off her skirt. "I'll be fine on my own. Good night."

Wes watches her until she disappears into the crowd, then flops back into the grass with a groan. He's been on his share of disastrous dates, but this is one for the books. Now he's back to feeling just as terrible as he did before. Maybe worse.

His stomach churns with anger. Maybe he shouldn't have told her he was Banvish. Maybe he should've laughed it off or changed the topic. But he's laughed off too many jokes at the Banvish's expense over the years, and tonight, he couldn't abide either of them pretending to be something they weren't.

His unbroken view of the sky is suddenly eclipsed by the pale moon of Margaret's face. "Annette looked upset."

"M-Margaret!" Wes chokes out. He scrabbles to sit upright. "You came."

"Of course I did." She crosses her arms. "What did you say to her?"

What can he possibly tell her? *We were talking about you, and one thing led to another . . .* No, he can't tell her the truth. He feels too wretched for what he knows without her consent. Carefully arranging his features into nonchalance, he shrugs. "I think I got too fresh with her. Would you believe it?"

Margaret frowns. "Right."

"Next up," a voice crackles over a microphone, "is Weston Winters."

"Shit." Wes hauls himself to his feet. Since his decision to lie down and die here, it seems the crowds have grown even thicker. "There's no way we're getting much closer than this."

"So let's get farther away." Before he can ask what the wisdom behind that paradox is, she starts running. Exasperated, he trails after her as quickly as he can.

The tall grass shivers around them as Margaret leads him up to a hilltop. The vantage point is better—enough to see someone break away from the crowd. They lift their rifle, take aim at a target rigged from the branch of a gnarled cypress, and fire. The sound echoes across the field, and then, as they wait for the smoke to clear, there is a breathless silence.

The wooden target kindles. Sparks rain down from the target and glimmer like fireflies. A beleaguered hunt official runs toward it, shouting and brandishing a fire extinguisher.

"Yes!" Wes claps his hands together. "Yes! It worked! Did you see that?"

The burning target is a smear of orange against the night, but even up here, he can see its glow reflected in Margaret's eyes. There's quiet reverence in her voice when she says, "I saw."

"How many points do I need again?"

"One hundred fifteen," she answers without hesitation. She's run every possible scenario a thousand times by now.

Together, they watch the judges confer and the fire die. Wes twists his fingers around the long blades of grass, and he swears Margaret stops breathing. After a few minutes, the announcer says, "The panel has awarded one hundred seventeen points to Weston Winters. Next up, we have—"

"Margaret," Wes breathes.

She sits perfectly still, as though she hasn't heard correctly.

"Margaret!" He throws his arm around her neck and crushes her into his side so hard, they nearly tumble into the grass in a heap. It's only when she lets out a strangled noise of protest that he comes to his senses—that he registers he is *hugging* her—but even then, he's too giddy to care or let her go. "We did it!"

Margaret squirms until he loosens his grip. Her cheeks are dusted with red, a warm, rosy color that makes him think of a summer afternoon. "*You* did it. I'm sorry for doubting you."

He grins at her. She smiles back softly, and it nearly knocks the wind out of him. For the first time, he thinks maybe, just maybe, they have a shot at pulling this off.

18

By the time afternoon fills the manor with drowsy golden sunlight, Wes is still sleeping. Margaret can't blame him, considering they got home at almost midnight and he's kept himself awake for almost a week straight. Besides, after his performance last night, he deserves to stay in bed all day.

She can hardly believe he actually pulled it off. After fighting her way through the exposition crowds, she saw the moment alchemical light illuminated his face, as radiant as a grounded star. For the first time in years, it struck her that alchemy can be eerily beautiful. That maybe it can do more than hurt.

And now, if she places well in the shooting contest this week, they'll make first flight. They'll have a real chance at winning.

In her room, Margaret finds Trouble curled up on her bed and napping in a pool of milky sunlight. She has half a mind to kick him off, but she can't bring herself to do it. Thanks to Wes, she feels tender and hopeful today—and strange for it. It makes her crave his company, which won't at all do.

It's bad enough that she's done something that she can't undo: allowed herself to acknowledge, even once, the pull between them. She can endure her idle imaginings of what use they could make of this empty house, with its hidden alcoves and sun-warmed nooks. She can live with the knowledge of what he looks like unarmored and braced on his knees over her. But what feels dangerous is the way her stomach flutters when she remembers how he hugged her last night as though it were the most natural thing in the world. His smile was so wide and guileless. Joyful. His free and easy affection reminds her too much of what she's lost—and what she can lose again.

Margaret unlatches the window and tips her face into the cool caress of the wind. It's too late to train again unless she wants to be caught out after dark, but she may as well make use of all this restless energy. It'd be a shame if Wes upstaged her.

She fetches her tool kit from the closet, pulls her rifle from its mount on the wall, and settles onto the floor. Disassembling and cleaning her gun is her own kind of worship, a task she could do blindfolded. By the time she finishes lubricating the metal and polishing the stock finish to gleaming, she's light-headed with the smell of kerosene and lead. The wood gleams in the sunlight, gold and warm as honey.

"Trouble."

He jolts upright. One ear folds in on itself.

"Trouble," she drawls, more playfully this time.

He watches her from his spot on the bed, his tail thumping softly against her sheets. He knows he's not supposed to be up there, but he also knows she's gone soft today. A better trainer would set him straight, but she's never minded a little precociousness now and again.

Margaret slings her rifle over her shoulder. "Want to go outside?"

His ears perk.

"Come on. Let's go."

He springs off the bed and races downstairs. Margaret can't help laughing as she follows him. Outside, the shadows are deepening as the sun sets. In the distance, pine and fir spill over the mountains and toward the ocean like the slow dribble of syrup.

She goes to the paddock fence out back and calls for Shimmer, her gray gelding. He comes running, only to look betrayed when he sees her carrying the halter. Once she ties him to the post, she brushes the dirt off his back and tacks him up. Her thighs ache from days of riding, but she forces herself to climb up onto his back and nudge him into a trot.

As they make their way toward the tree line, Margaret dares to cast a glance back over her shoulder. She should start bringing Wes out so he can get a taste for hunting, but she needs to focus today. Besides, he'll scare away all the quarry in a five-mile radius as soon as he opens his mouth.

"Trouble," she says, "track."

He pauses, nose lifted to the sky, then takes off into the underbrush like a fired bullet. The silence that settles over the woods in his absence is eerily complete. There's no sound but the steady drum of Shimmer's hooves. She pats his neck as he snorts uneasily.

They come to a stretch of woods she doesn't recognize. Ferns grow thick and too green on the embankment of the trail. Patches of flowers grow wild, choking one another, and overhead, new growth bursts from the trees and oozes sap, too tender to survive the sudden cold. Everything here is too alive; it's starving itself, and the air reeks of decay.

She knows this is the hala's doing. Whole orchards rotting. Whole swaths of the forest falling on the blade of its own growth. It reminds her of a sketch in her mother's notebook, one she locked away a long time ago, of a serpent devouring its own tail. Margaret clutches the key around her neck.

The Halanans and the Harringtons have already been victim to the hala's blight. How many more of them will suffer before the Cold Moon rises? How much suffering is worth the promise of glory?

The sound of her name hisses through the leaves. She goes rigid in her seat.

She doesn't like the shift in these woods—*her* woods. Once, nothing about them bothered her. Not the croak of a raven or the trilling of jays. Not the unblinking gleam of a jackrabbit's eyes in the dark. But right now, she's watching for a smear of white against the trees.

Her breath plumes in the cold.

Trouble bays.

He's found something. Margaret kicks Shimmer into a canter. Cold wind buffets her face and rocks clatter down the slope as they ride toward the sound of his call.

Margaret leans forward, her legs burning, as Shimmer leaps over a felled redwood in the path and breaks into an even clearing. Trouble stands on his hind legs with his front paws against the trunk of a massive redwood, tail whipping. He tosses his head back and bays again. Spittle flies from his jowls in thick strings.

He's so pleased with himself, the show-off.

"Alright, I hear you."

She slides off Shimmer's back. Ten feet overhead, she spots her target. A plain red fox, pressing itself flat against a lichen-covered branch. Margaret unstraps her rifle and raises the scope to her eye. Its wood-paneled body is smooth and cold against her cheek. It still smells like wood polish and oil.

Although she despises alchemy, one of its core tenets has always resonated with her. Everything—from humans to foxes—is composed of the same primordial stuff. All is One and One is All. At their core, they are all the same, all of them trying to survive.

Her mother would call that kind of ethical application misguided or sentimental. But Margaret is nothing if not her mother's daughter, and she is far from sentimental. The truth is simple and amoral. She will live because the fox will die.

In her crosshairs, the fox pins its ears back and lashes its tail. It's relieving to see an ordinary fox, one full of mortal fight and not eerie detachment. Over the pounding of her heart in her ears, all Margaret hears is *shhhh* as the wind rattles the leaves. It sounds like hushed anticipation rippling through a crowd. Margaret draws in her breath and holds it deep in her gut.

There.

She pulls the trigger. The resounding crack sends birds fluttering from the treetops. A small, red body strikes the earth with a dull *thud.* The forest sighs along with her, sweeping hair into her eyes.

Margaret approaches the crumpled shape in the leaves. They're rusted brown, like dried blood. The fox lies in a circle at the toe of her boots, tail to open mouth. The image of the ouroboros startles her. It must be some kind of message, or warning, or—

No, the hala is nothing but an animal.

It's not watching her, much less trying to tell her something. The pressure of the hunt and her own confused feelings for Wes must be making her paranoid.

Margaret lifts the fox by its bushy tail, and the weight of its body hangs from her fist like a purse full of coins. Its golden eyes are just as fierce in death, still full of fire. As the forest forgets the gunshot, life returns in trickles. A raven croaks. A hare rustles the underbrush. Even Trouble dares to move now. He trots to her side and leans his full weight against her, nearly toppling her off-balance. When she thumps his flank, the sound is pleasingly resonant, like patting a ripe gourd.

"Good boy. We can do this." Another two weeks to train a mostly retired hound and horse to be the best in the country. More outlandish things have been done.

But the rattling in the trees still makes her feel uneasy. The longer she stands here, the more convinced she becomes that the wind really is speaking. That it's imparting some wisdom or warning to her that she can't possibly understand.

By the time they arrive in Wickdon, tonight's fanfare is in full swing.

The sun scatters coins of light over the sea and drapes all the trees with a shawl of red. Over the years, the ones along the coast have been wind-whipped so thoroughly, they lie with their bellies flat to the earth like cringing dogs. Margaret knows the curve of this shore as well as the grooves between her fingers, but the coastline is the only thing familiar about Wickdon tonight.

It's as startling as the first time she saw her mother emerge from her office after David died. The same bones, the same skin stretched over them, but something dark and changed behind the eyes.

Crowds sweep through the streets like water sloshed from a laundry basin. They bubble out alleyways and eddy over the cobblestones, which are streaked with the glow of torches burning on nearly every corner. Children dart beneath legs, their cheeks gashed black with painted whiskers and fox tails swaying from their belt loops. Adults wear eyeliner elongated to vicious points, dressed in fox-fur stoles and coats. Overhead, strings of lights twinkle and the colorful fabric knotted on telephone wires flutters in the wind. It's a razor's edge at her throat, sharp and cold with salt.

Somewhere on the other side of all these people is where she needs to be: the rock-lined path that leads to the shore, where she will shoot to secure their place in the first flight.

Wes rests a hand on the small of her back. It's an innocent enough gesture, only to get her attention, but his every touch electrifies her. He seems oblivious to it, at least, or maybe he's pretending not to notice. Either way, she's grateful for the casual way he keeps close to her side, solid and safe amid the chaos.

"How are you holding up?" he asks.

"I'm fine." She tucks a wayward strand of hair behind her ear. Warm orange light from the fires and streetlamps spills over his shoulders. "You should go on ahead. Enjoy your night."

"Sick of me already, Margaret? Without you, I'll just spend it pining—for you and all the things I can't buy."

He is so full of shit sometimes. "Would you like a quarter?"

His devious expression slackens into surprise. "Are you serious?"

"Very." Margaret fishes her purse from her jacket pocket and rummages until she finds one. Taking his wrist gently in hand, she turns it over and presses the coin into his palm. "Go wild."

Little of the ambient light reaches his eyes, but Margaret can still see them shining in the darkness. He looks wistful, almost sad, before he remembers himself and shakes his head. "I'll pay you back."

"With what money?"

"Mm. Good point." He doesn't *say* anything, but that languorous smile and the way he examines her from beneath his eyelashes speaks volumes. Margaret hates that her face warms under his attention, even when he is insincere. It makes a fool of her. "Surely there's something else I can do . . . ?"

"No. Just leave."

He laughs good-naturedly, letting his hand drop to his side and into his pocket. The memory of his touch still burns against her back. "Fine, fine. Are you *sure* I can't do anything for you? I can at least stay to throw some elbows for you."

"I'm sure." He's already done his part. Tonight is for her to worry about, and Margaret knows she can win.

"What time does it start? I want to see you shoot."

"Six thirty. I'm not sure it'll be worth the wait, though. It's tournament style. Each round is over in seconds."

"Of course it'll be worth it," he protests. "You did promise me a demonstration. Besides, how else am I supposed to know if I've made a terrible mistake throwing my lot in with you?"

She doesn't resist the tug of the smile on her lips. "I'll try not to embarrass you."

"You won't." He grins back at her, one of his rare, earnest ones that warms her from the inside out. "Well, good luck. I'll find you later."

When he slips into the current of people, she feels more alone than she did in the woods, even surrounded by crowds and a hundred shouted conversations. Margaret braces herself and shoulders her way through.

The air smells like woodsmoke and salt, mouthwatering with baking breads and roasting meats. Market stalls line the streets, selling wide-brimmed hats woven with intricate felt flowers, riding chaps and leather boots, and all sorts of alchemical goods. Artisanal alembics blown plump and shiny as periwinkle shells, hand-shaped glass in every color of seaside pebbles. In the square, show dogs and their handlers preen in front of a panel of stern-faced judges.

A few people glare at her as she passes. The sound of her name dogs her every step, as low and hissed as the wind through the rye.

Her chest tightens with fear. All her life, surviving has meant making herself small and unseen. But tonight, she will be in the limelight, and that is as terrifying as any demiurge.

When the cobblestones stop at the bluff overlooking the ocean, she breathes easier. Margaret slides as gracefully as she can down the rocky embankment and wades through the yellowing beach grass until she hits the shoreline. The water is rough tonight, frothing itself into a mist so thick she can scarcely see the moon beyond a veil of silver. Bonfires burn every few yards and spatter the sand with orange light. The largest one silhouettes her fellow competitors, who're hunched against the autumn chill. And far above them on the edge of the cliffs, spectators begin to gather and filter down to the beach.

Margaret approaches the other sharpshooters until she can see their features outlined in firelight. She recognizes almost none of them. Many are older than her, dressed in regal hunting jackets in gemstone shades and carrying rifles embossed with gold. She can only imagine what their hounds will look like. Sleek and powerful as bullets.

A shiver of unease runs through her. She can feel someone glaring at her.

As she turns toward the cove, she meets Jaime's eyes through the darkness. She's accustomed to his indifference, his distaste, but she's not prepared for the unbridled hatred in his gaze. It makes her belly swoop low with fear.

Composing his face into some illusion of cool, he breaks away from the group and swaggers toward her. Mattis, as fawning as an anxious hound, trails a few steps behind him.

Instinct tells her to shy away, to hide. But the anger she usually swallows bubbles up within her, too hot to tamp down. Maybe she's been spending too much time with Wes, or maybe she's had enough, but shrinking has never given Jaime any less of her to despise. He hates her. He has always hated her, and he always will.

If she must be seen tonight, she will be incandescent.

When they stop in front of her, Margaret says, "Jaime."

"Maggie." Jaime's breath reeks of whiskey and chewing tobacco. "Where are your mongrels tonight?"

She doesn't answer.

He and Mattis laugh, as though she's delighted them with her silence. "You know, I heard an interesting story about Winters. It turns out he's actually made quite a name for himself in the city. Did you know he's failed out of every single apprenticeship he's ever gotten?"

"I didn't take you as the type to listen to idle gossip."

"It's not gossip," Mattis snaps. "It's the truth."

Jaime shoots him a glare, as though he's interrupted something important. Mattis falls obediently quiet. Shaking his head, Jaime continues, "I thought it was strange that someone could be that much of a loser. But I've finally gotten to the bottom of it. He's a Banvishman."

"What does that matter?" Her voice sounds smaller and more uncertain than she intended it to. Where could he have heard such a thing?

"Because he's Sumic! They're practically animals. Aren't you afraid, all alone in the house with him?"

Margaret has heard a whole host of things about Sumics. That they worship idols. That they carve unborn Katharist children from their mothers' wombs and devour them raw. That they're here to establish the capital of a new Sumic empire on New Albian shores and pledge their allegiance to the foreign nation of Umbria, where the pope sits on his holy throne. But all she saw from the Winters family was kindness.

"No," she says. "I'm not."

"Ah, I see now. I should've guessed that you'd like to warm your bed with beasts. You deserve each other: the Sumic usurper and the Yu'adir conspirator." He sneers. "It'll be a pleasure beating you tonight. My friends and I are going to ensure you don't stand a goddamn chance, Maggie. I warned you."

A blast of a horn silences the crowd. When it fades, all she can hear is the hiss of the waves. As she trembles with fury and shame,

Jaime turns on his heel and stalks back to the shield of his friends. Mattis lumbers behind him, casting an uneasy look at her over his shoulder. *Coward.* Margaret knows Jaime meant to rattle her, which makes it sting all the more that it worked.

His voice echoes through her skull, over and over again. *I warned you.*

All around her, the crowd looks hungry and wild and wicked. What was she thinking? Against them—against Jaime—she is powerless and alone, just as she's always been. Her mother isn't here to protect her, and maybe she won't ever be again. Maybe she has doomed Wes along with her.

Her heartbeat thuds against her eardrums and a cold sweat breaks out on her temples. Through the thickening haze of dread, she thinks she hears the emcee's voice crackling through a microphone and the answering roar of the crowd. But everything around her feels surreal and distant, as if she's submerged herself in the autumn sea, and she knows she's teetering on the brink of another episode.

The feeling bursts along with the peal of gunfire. Margaret startles back into herself with a strangled gasp. The competition has begun without her noticing.

You're here, she tells herself. *Focus.*

If not for her own sake, then for Wes's.

Smoke wafts up from the shore, and when it clears, she sees two men standing at the edge of the water. One turns to the crowd with a grin on his face, his features stark and warped in firelight. The other casts his rifle into the sand and stalks off.

Already, the first of them has fallen.

While the alchemy exposition is judged on multiple criteria, the rules of this game are simple. Fifty points for each victory, zero points—and the end of the line—for anyone who loses a matchup. Wes scored in the top third of alchemists, enough to position them well for the point threshold for first flight. With roughly a hundred teams in the hunt, Margaret will need to win at least five of seven rounds. One imperfect shot will cost them everything.

She steadies herself by focusing on the rhythm of the event. The emcee calls a pair of names. There's the glint of firelight on rifle barrels, the *crack* of a fired bullet, the exhilarating smell of gunpowder in the air. As her heart kicks up in anticipation, she wipes her sweaty palms on her thighs.

"Margaret Welty and Kate Duncan."

It's finally time.

Nerves sour her stomach, and she feels woozy from the heat of the fire as she approaches the shooting range. A few meters in front of her, a small island breaches the waves. Torches guide a flickering path across the water to a rickety wooden structure, where a target sways on rattling chains. The ocean hisses at the toe of her boots, and a particularly rowdy wave surges up and soaks her to the knees. Cold seeps into her bones, but she concentrates on the firelight running into the water like blood. Out in the distance, moonlight dances and sparkles, iridescent like silver scales against solid black waves.

Margaret raises her rifle and lines up the target in her sights. She draws in a breath and holds it. Two more thuds of her heart, and the world goes perfectly still. Her mind goes blank. Her stomach settles. Her finger curls around the trigger with the familiarity of a lover's touch.

Then, she fires.

Smoke drifts over the ocean like mist. It slowly dissipates, unveiling the hole blasted clean through the target's center. The crowd erupts in cheers, and she finds Halanan's familiar face among them, broken out in a wide, triumphant grin. Margaret slips away before she can let her gaze settle on her opponent's gutted expression. There's no satisfaction to be had there—none at all until she hears her name called with the rest of the first flight.

As she slips back into the crowd, she hears *Jaime Harrington* enunciated clearly over the ruckus. He clips her shoulder as he strides past, then takes his place at the edge of the beach.

Margaret has been watching Jaime fire a gun for as long as she can remember. He always fidgets before he takes a shot, rolling his shoulders and cracking his neck like it'll make a difference. But tonight, he goes through none of his ritual. He simply lifts the sight to his eye and fires, a thing done without fanfare or relish. Like he doesn't care at all—or has nothing to lose. The target rattles on its chains, and her stomach drops at the sight of the neat entry hole in its center, a twin to hers.

A perfect shot.

Jaime turns to the crowd, smiling beatifically. It rankles her, but her unease runs deeper than that. Has he practiced that much since she last saw him fire a gun? He's gotten astoundingly better.

Or maybe he hit on a vein of luck this time around. That has to be it.

But the next round, he does it again. And the one after, too, matching her shot for shot. He moves with unnatural grace, with a precision that's almost otherworldly. Margaret can't figure out how he's doing this. She can't figure out how he has come to match her in skill so quickly. The light of the bonfire paints the steel of his gun with an eerie red that reminds her too much of rubedo.

When she's called up for her fourth round and raises her rifle, she feels precarious, as though she's clinging to one of those rocks jutting out from the waves. *Two more rounds,* she tells herself. Two more rounds, and she'll lock them into the first flight.

Margaret aims, but she squeezes the trigger too hard. The gun shifts, just barely, and the bullet strikes the target left of center. She sucks in a breath through her teeth.

Careless. That was a careless beginner's mistake, and it could cost them everything. Her stomach doesn't stop churning until her opponent's bullet pings off the chain.

God, she needs to hold it together. What does it matter if Jaime's doing well? What peace will it give her if she dissects his technique? The only thing that matters is this: if she goes head-to-head with him and can't keep her nerves in check, she will lose.

Margaret clears out of the range and sinks heavily onto a rock to collect herself. She closes her eyes and tries to anchor herself to the earth, cataloging the rush of the waves and the salt on her lips and the cold against her cheeks. Only one more round, and they're safe.

She can do this.

"For our next round, we have Jaime Harrington," the emcee calls in his brassy radio voice, "and Margaret Welty."

Margaret's eyes snap open. Across the beach, their gazes lock. In the firelight, Jaime's hair shines like beaten copper, and his smile is that of a man who knows he's already won.

19

Wes thinks he may rattle out of his skin from the excitement of it all. With so many people, all unrecognizable and smiling and dressed to be seen, it feels like being back in Dunway. His heart thuds to the beat of a song playing somewhere in the distance.

He wanders the festival, jostled by the crowds, until he is more or less thrown into the side of a red-painted stall selling apples dipped in caramel and candy glaze. They gleam like pendants in a jeweler's case, resplendent in shades of amber and garnet. He tightens his fist around the coin Margaret gave him.

Her unexpected kindness makes him feel off-kilter. It reminds him of how his father used to give him and his sisters a single nickel, as precious as gold, and turn them loose in the candy shop. The memory hits him harder than he expects; he breathes through the sting of tears at the back of his throat and tries to focus on something, anything, else.

Like the charming shade of red Margaret turned when he teased her.

Wes bites back a groan. No matter where he turns or what he does, everything leads back to her. He hates it. He hates how he admires her, how imagining her reading those books in her room at night has become his new favorite method of self-immolation, how vulnerable and desperate she makes him feel. For so long, he's kept himself whole by refusing to examine himself too closely, by never letting anyone sink their claws into him too deep. But of all the women in the entire world, Margaret—severe, taciturn Margaret— has reduced him to this.

Christine used to tease him for falling in love with every woman he met, but it's never been serious. It's never been *real*. Once he falls, he'll fall hard because he's never let himself do a thing halfway. But he can't afford to place his heart in anyone's hands until he makes it to the top. He can't afford to have a weakness yet.

"You want something, kid, or are you just going to stand there collecting flies all night?" The vendor looks at him impatiently, gesturing to the line that has begun to form behind him.

"Yeah, sorry. I'll have one—"

Someone across the street waves to get his attention. There, only a few yards away, is Annette Wallace with a dead fox draped around her neck. Its jaw hangs open, revealing pearl-white teeth that gleam wetly in the torchlight. Her hair is loosely curled, and her lips are painted the exact shade of blood. When she meets his eyes, his stomach sinks with dread.

But the anger he expects never comes. Annette smiles at him radiantly.

His thoughts short-circuit as she begins weaving her way toward him. Last week, he made her cry. Apparently, he's now forgiven. There's no way it could be that easy, but the prospect of having company beats out his wariness. Talking to Annette will provide a much-needed distraction from his own wallowing. Before he can question the ethics of using Margaret's money to buy something for another girl, he says, much to the vendor's relief, "Make that two caramel apples."

As soon as he's made his purchase, he ducks out of line and Annette seizes him by the elbow. "Wes! I was looking everywhere for you."

"Were you now?" His voice sounds higher and more alarmed than he'd prefer. He clears his throat. "How convenient. I happened to end up with two of these, so maybe you could take one off my hands."

"How funny. Me, too." Before he can blink, she swaps one of his apples with a steaming, overfull mug of something that smells sweet and cinnamon spiced. For a few moments, they stare at each other in silence. Then, she says, "Truce?"

"Truce."

"I'm so sorry about the other day. I shouldn't have melted down like that. You were right, and I realize now I must've sounded so—"

"Annette," he cuts in. "It's alright."

"Really? Are you sure?"

Wes feels suddenly exhausted. Absolving her would mean finding out what exactly she's sorry for, but that would require having a serious, potentially difficult conversation. He doesn't think she's a bad person—not really. At the same time, if he's being honest with himself, he's not sure everything is *alright* or whether her silence means she's complicit in Margaret's suffering. Fortunately for Annette, he doesn't have much interest in being honest or alone with himself at the moment. For his sanity's sake, he can keep things light. He can swallow his own misgivings. "Really."

"Okay." Her relief is a tangible thing. "Well, thanks for the apple."

"Thanks for the . . . what is this exactly?"

"Cider," she says, so angelically he can't help being suspicious.

She slides her hand into the crook of his elbow and leans her head against his shoulder. Drunk, if the affection and the flush on her cheeks is any indication. He feels absolutely nothing, which disturbs him. Some magic has drained from the world if a beautiful woman on his arm does *nothing* for him. When he peers into the copper mug she's given him, he finds that the liquid inside is the same color as Margaret's eyes. It makes him a little queasy, but he won't let it put a damper on his mood.

Enjoy your night, Margaret told him. He intends to, one way or another. He takes a swig, then nearly chokes. Alcohol rakes its way down his throat and resolves in a sparkly burn of clove and apples.

Annette laughs. "Sorry! I should have warned you I played bartender."

"And what a generous bartender you are! God, what did you put in it? Motor oil?"

"Whiskey. It's got a little extra kick to it, though." She stands on her toes to whisper in his ear. "Alchemy—don't tell anyone."

Alchemized liquor is definitely not legal, mostly because prudish Katharist legislators think it's responsible for violent crime. Or maybe they just don't want anyone to have any fun. Nowadays, only those in the know can buy it at speakeasies or from home distilleries. But with so many alchemists packed into Wickdon, it's no wonder contraband liquor flows as free as water.

He's always wanted to try it, and having it now feels a little like the time Mad stole an expensive bottle of wine from her rich ex-girlfriend's pantry. They'd snuck onto the fire escape after Mam went to bed, and since they didn't own a corkscrew, they bashed it in on the stairs and fountained it into their mouths. His tongue bled and he probably still has shards in his liver, but it's one of the sweetest memories he has of Mad. It was the night she got her first job, the night he first tasted alcohol, the night he turned fourteen. His first taste of something bigger than himself.

"I wouldn't dream of it," he says. "Your secret's safe with me."

Already, a lazy, contented warmth spreads through him. Wes bites into his apple. It's crisp and so sweet it makes his head tingle—or maybe that's whatever Annette poisoned him with just now.

"So what do you think?" she asks.

For the first time, he notices the gold powder she's dusted on her eyelids. It shimmers beneath the lights strung above them, which seem to have gotten brighter in the last minute. He wonders if colors have always been so vibrant. "Of what?"

"The festival," she presses.

"Oh, um . . ." Have words always been so elusive? "I like it. Have you been before?"

"Once. My brother participated in the hunt a few years ago, and my whole family went to cheer him on. Rode out with the hunt and everything. It was quite a production."

"So you've seen it. The hala."

"Oh, I've seen it." Her voice grows more serious. "Have you?"

"Yeah." Wes drains the last of the spiked cider with a grimace. He's hardly had a chance to swallow before she pours him another round from a metal flask she's procured from somewhere on her person. "And what about the hunt? What's it like?"

"It's complete chaos. You can't really watch unless you follow on horseback. But you can hear it, and you can smell it. It's not something you'd ever forget. Like brimstone in a butcher's shop."

"Lord. Why does anyone do this?"

"God and country." She clinks the flask against his cup. "All men want to be divine."

He wrinkles his nose. "I don't know about that."

"No? So what about you and Maggie? Why are you doing it?"

"I can't pretend to know what goes on in her head."

"Then speak for yourself."

"This is my last chance to make my dream come true. It's the only chance I've got to help my family." And here he is again, mired in his feelings. Wes finishes his drink in a single gulp, desperate to escape them.

"Well, let's not think about that right now." He can't read her expression behind the firelight reflected in her eyes, but she's wearing the most peculiar smile. "What other mischief can we get up to tonight?"

The suggestive lilt to that question startles him. Before he can reply in kind, a horn echoes through the square. A few tourists—himself included—cringe, a baby cries, and the crowd whoops. People hem them in as they surge toward the beach.

"What's going on?" Wes shouts over the noise.

"The shooting competition."

Right, the shooting competition. The reason he's here in the first place. "Oh! We should go watch."

She presses closer to his side and makes a face. "Do we really have to?"

Of course they do. He has to see Margaret.

He can't understand her reticence, but before he can press her on the matter, they're yanked apart. Between the crush of people and the din of a thousand voices, he can't hear or focus on much of anything. Somewhere in the chaos, he loses his mug and, more tragically, his apple. At least the stupefying warmth of the alcohol dulls the brunt of his panic.

Wes follows the flow of traffic, bobbing along like a leaf on a river, until he's spit out onto the beach. Bonfires lick at the horizon, arching toward the moon. With only a week until the hunt, it watches him like a half-open eye. The darkness sways and wavers around him, but through the nauseating churn of his vision, he can make out the competitors lining up by the shore. Almost immediately, he finds her.

Margaret.

She stands off to the side, alone among all these people. The wind tangles in her hair and lifts it from the back of her neck, as if it's preparing to clasp a pendant at her throat. He imagines he can see the delicate patch of shorn-close hair at her nape, and then imagines how he might find it with his mouth. He wants to know what sounds she would make if he did. He wants to drag her down onto the sand right here and make her look at him the way she did in her mother's lab, wild and wanting. He wants to kiss the salt off her lips and slide his knee between hers and . . .

God, this stuff is way too potent.

Dimly, he registers that someone is glaring at him. When he turns his head, he sees Jaime Harrington looking at him with a startled fury in his eyes. Through the sparkly haze of the whiskey, everything goes red. Margaret warned him to stay away from Jaime, but tonight, he doesn't think he wants to.

"There you are!" Annette grabs him by the arm. "Do we really have to stay and watch this? It's so boring."

"Just for a little bit. I want to see Margaret shoot."

"She's good. Really good. What else is there to know? It's too dark to see much of anything."

The announcer says, "Jaime Harrington and Peter Evander."

"I want to watch Harrington, too." He shrugs her off and pushes his way to the front of the crowd. Annette's strangled noise of frustration pursues him.

With every step, the earth lurches under his feet, and the sparks hissing off the bonfire fill his vision with an orange glow. Yet as he watches Jaime swagger up to the range, everything comes into sharp focus. He fires his gun, and the air ripples with energy, as subtle as a heat shimmer. Realization strikes Wes like a sledgehammer.

He's cheating.

Wes looks around, but no one seems to pay it any mind. Did no one else see that? How can no one notice how obvious it is that his gun is enchanted? "I think he's cheating."

Annette stiffens beside him. "How do you figure?"

"The gun . . ." He gestures vaguely. "It's clearly been tampered with. It's cheating."

"How can you possibly know that?"

"I just do."

"You just do?" She lowers her voice pointedly, as if to tell him he's shouting. "You're completely zozzled, Wes."

"I'm *grand*."

"You're really not." She cups his cheek and guides his face back toward her. "Come on. Let's get out of here."

"And go where?"

"Somewhere else." Her free hand slides down his chest and presses flat against his ribs. She looks at him like she is trying to impart something very important to him. "I don't want to talk about Jaime or Maggie. I don't want to talk about anything at all."

He sucks in a breath. "You don't?"

"No, I don't. Please?"

Please. If a single word could kill him.

It would be so easy to succumb. With alcohol muddying his

thoughts, he can't bring himself to worry as much as he should about anything. Her unspoken promise makes it hard to think beyond the horizon of the next thirty minutes. Besides, she's right. No one will listen to him when he's this drunk. Jaime's cheating may not even impact him and Margaret.

Why didn't *he lie to you?* He remembers Mad snapping at their mother. *He's a selfish child who's never thought about anyone but himself a day in his life.*

Mad's right about him, too. Maybe this is all he will amount to. Maybe he hasn't smothered his feelings as much as he's deluded himself into believing he had any noble ones to begin with. After all, this is exactly what he wanted. Something uncomplicated, something to make him forget his own vulnerabilities. Winning the hunt is an abstract dream, one that will wreck him if he tries and fails to achieve it. But the feeling of Annette's body pressed against his is certain and comforting.

"So?" She tugs him closer by his tie until their foreheads touch. Her breath is warm and sweet with cinnamon.

"Jaime Harrington and Margaret Welty," the announcer calls.

Margaret.

The sound of her name turns his stomach with guilt, and there—there's a feeling about someone other than himself. God, Mad is so *wrong* about him. About everything. How could he let himself lose sight of that? He can't abandon Margaret now. Not only because it's his ambitions on the line, but because he cares—about his family, about his country, about *her.*

"I'm really sorry." He carefully removes Annette's hands from his tie and lowers them to her sides. "I have to go."

"Wait!"

He slips away from her and toward the shooting range. Someone hisses at him when he steps on their foot, but he hardly has time to apologize. Margaret and Jaime will be shooting soon, and he has no idea what to do. Jaime is a cheating son of a bitch, but unless he can figure out what he's done to modify the gun, he can't undo the enchantment. Unless, of course, he orchestrated some sort of wider-scale malfunction . . .

An idea strikes him. What is gunpowder, anyway, but potassium nitrate, charcoal, and sulfur? He just needs to get close enough to perform nigredo—and find something to draw with.

He's got a piece of chalk probably crushed halfway to dust in his pocket, but it won't stick to his skin well enough to work. He scans the crowd until he spots a young woman, a vision all in white save for the shock of red fur around her neck and the black slashes of face paint on her cheeks. That should do nicely.

"Whiskers." He can't remember how to formulate a coherent sentence at the moment, so he infuses the word with as much longing as he can muster.

She looks puzzled, then points to her own face. "What? You want some?"

He nods.

She reaches into her bag and hands him a pot of what he can only describe as goop. His vision doubles, and he almost drops the lid as he twists it off. He's never been so goddamn drunk in his life. As carefully as he can, he dips his fingertip in the paint and manages to scrawl a transmutation circle on the back of his hand. It goes on thick and cold as funeral sod.

"Thank you, ma'am." He hands the paint back to her. "I have to go now."

"Okay, honey. Good luck out there."

Jaime steps out of the crowd, his shoulders drawn back, and takes his place by the water. In another second, it'll all be for nothing.

"Hey, Harrington!" Wes shouts. It's nearly drowned out in all the noise, but Jaime hears him. He cocks his head and regards him, a malicious glee in his eyes.

Wes saunters toward him with all the self-assurance he can manage. It doesn't take much acting for him to convincingly lose his balance; as he stumbles forward, he claps one hand on Jaime's shoulder. The other, marked with a smudged formula for nigredo, catches on the body of his gun. And that's all he needs.

Muffled white light sparks beneath his palm, like an electrical socket shorting, and a thin wisp of sulfuric smoke curls between them. God, he hopes it worked.

"Maybe you ought to take it easy, Winters. You're making a goddamn fool of yourself."

"Sorry, sorry. I just needed to tell you to go fu— I mean, good luck."

Jaime's face flushes a murderous red. A few people jeer impatiently. From the water's edge, Margaret skewers him with those beautiful brown eyes of hers. She doesn't need to speak for him to know what she's saying. *What the hell are you doing?*

He winks at her, but before he can savor the prize of her reaction, someone drags him back into the crowd. It's Jaime's lackey, Mattis. He growls, "Get yourself together, man."

The same red-haired girl he saw at the Blind Fox, Jaime's alchemist, smirks at him and leans in to whisper, "Nice try."

Jaime approaches the ocean and unsteadily lifts his rifle. He pulls the trigger, and the gun wheezes out a pathetic *pop* like a sputtering engine. The bullet sails through the air in a languid arc and plops dully into the water.

Murmurs ripple through the crowd. Mattis's grip on his arm slackens. The girl's lips part in horror. And when Jaime turns over his shoulder to glare at him, Wes knows he knows. Maybe if he were sober, he'd feel an ounce of self-preservation. But right now, drunk out of his mind and high on his own brilliance, all he can think to do is remove one hand from his pocket and wave.

Margaret is disconcertingly quiet. She won, but she's not at all happy.

Through the dreamy fog over his vision, Wes watched her shoot with the same efficient precision she does everything else in her life. But even when the emcee declared her the victor, even when he read out their names on the list of the first flight, even as they broke free of the worst of the crowds, Margaret's stony expression didn't change.

Wes can only see her in profile now, her features traced delicately by lamplight, but he can tell that she's worried and watchful. He contains himself until they reach the edge of Wickdon, where the cobblestones give way to dirt and swaying brome.

"Margaret." When she ignores him, he drawls, "Maggie."

"What?"

"What's on your mind?" It's only now that he has her attention that he realizes how badly he wanted it. He wants so many things from her right now. More than anything, he wants to see her smile. "You did it. We got first flight. Shouldn't we be celebrating?"

Margaret finally condescends to look at him, but he almost wishes she didn't. She studies him with some mixture of frustration and confusion, as though it should be the most obvious thing in the world why she's upset. "Are you drunk?"

"No," he says defensively.

She opens her mouth, probably to scold him, but of all people to save him from her tongue-lashing, it's Jaime. "Hey, Winters."

If he were a better man, he'd keep walking. But his shoes scuff the cobblestones as he stops and turns around. There is ice in Jaime's eyes. They're a startling, cold blue.

"Oh," Wes says. "Hey."

They stare at each other in seething silence. He can hear the laughter of people making their way back from the beach. The distant beat of drums rattles his rib cage. But it's only the three of them here on this deserted street.

"Both of you have a way of sticking your noses where they don't belong," Jaime says.

"Wes." Margaret's voice is even, but he hears the strain in it. "We should go."

Wes rolls his shoulders back. "Stay out of this, Margaret."

"Oh, no. He's not going anywhere until we've had a little heart-to-heart." Jaime closes the gap between them. Craning his neck to meet Jaime's baleful stare makes Wes a little dizzy. "You shouldn't be in the first flight. What was that stunt you pulled back there?"

"I didn't pull any kind of stunt. You, on the other hand . . ."

Jaime laughs bitterly. "You're a fucking meddler."

"And you're a fucking coward!" Wes reaches into his pocket and brushes his fingers against a piece of chalk. When he pulls it out, Margaret and Jaime gawk at it like it's a switchblade in an alley fight. He revels in the rush of power. "You still want to try me? It was your gun earlier. What else do you want to lose tonight? How about I incinerate all the carbon in your skin?"

Decomposing something as simple as gunpowder is one thing. Setting an entire person ablaze requires a hell of a lot more expertise and sobriety than he currently has. Still, he can't help himself. He wants Jaime afraid, just as he's been afraid.

But then the fear on Jaime's face morphs into smug superiority. "You won't do it. You're no alchemist. You're just a drunk."

Wes drops the chalk with a brittle *plink* on the cobblestones.

"That's what I thought. Now go crawl home like a good dog. A dog of a filthy Yu'adir rat—"

His vision blackens. Jaime insulted him, but worse, he insulted Margaret. Maybe Annette is too much of a coward to stand up to him, but Wes has had enough. He swings his fist and cracks it into Jaime's sneering face.

It's going to hurt like hell as soon as the adrenaline wears off, but the sweet sound of Jaime's pained shout makes it all worth it. There's a heady thrill in seeing his astonished expression. His busted lip is as swollen and purple as an overripe fig. Why stop there? But right as he's about to land another blow, Margaret grabs Wes by the back of the collar so hard, he stumbles backward.

"That's *enough*." Wes has never seen her look as brilliant and fierce as she does now, her eyes sparkling beneath the golden light of the streetlamps. One hand rests on the gun strapped to her back.

Jaime glances back and forth between them, calculating. He spits a wad of bloody saliva on Wes's shoe. "Alright, Winters. Alright."

There is a threat somewhere in those inarticulate words.

"We're leaving," Margaret says.

"You're finished is what you are," Jaime says. "You hear me? Finished."

Finished. It echoes down the empty street.

Margaret hooks her hand in Wes's elbow and drags him away. As soon as they're out of sight and out of earshot, Margaret rounds on him. She smacks him on the shoulder, hard enough to startle him but not enough to actually hurt.

"Ow!" He rubs where she hit him. "What the hell was that for?"

"What were you *thinking*? That was incredibly reckless, interfering with his equipment like that. And if he tells anyone that you assaulted him, both of us could get disqualified! What am I going to have to say to make you understand? What can I do to convince you to stop? You have to choose your battles, and now you can't anymore."

It floors him. During his tenure as an older brother, he's fought more bullies than he can count on both hands. His sisters have always been grateful, but Margaret's acting like he punched a puppy in the snout. "What was there to think about? What else was I supposed to do? I wasn't going to let him cheat, and I sure as hell wasn't going to let him talk about you like that!"

"Oh, it was about me?" Her voice drips with dry condescension.

"Yeah! It was!"

"I'm not interested in being fuel for your ego. If I wanted Jaime to suffer for the bigoted things he says, I'd have punched him myself."

Wes doesn't have anything to say to that. Shame curdles in his stomach.

Margaret sighs heavily and pinches the bridge of her nose. The passion drains slowly from her face. "He probably won't say anything. He'll be too embarrassed to admit what happened. But you need to stay out of trouble until the hunt."

"Trouble finds me."

"No, you seek it out, and I can't be around to keep you in line all the time."

Wes laughs incredulously. "You don't need to."

"Clearly I do."

"That's not your job. You know that, don't you? It's not your job to babysit me or clean the house like a maid or make dinner for us both every night or—God, Margaret, it's not your job to take care of everyone but yourself."

She flinches from him like he struck her. "And it's not your job to protect everyone. Nor is it worthwhile to try and prove yourself to people who would think less of you anyway."

"What are you talking about?"

"You threatened to kill him."

"Oh, come on. I didn't mean it!"

"It doesn't matter if you meant it," she snaps. "Did that make you feel good?"

He can't deny it. It did. For that one glorious moment, he felt unstoppable.

"Is that really what you want to do with your life, your alchemy?" she continues. "You want to be just like Jaime—like the rest of them? You want to be a bully?"

It strikes him like a bullet in the center of his chest. Before he can say anything regrettable, he turns on his heel and stalks off toward the manor.

"Wes," Margaret calls after him impatiently. "Wes?"

He doesn't look back.

Margaret is wrong about him. This world is filled with bullies, but he's not one of them. They're the people who own his apartment building and raise the rent month after month. They're the people who own the factories and refuse to take any responsibility for his father's death or his mother's injury. They're kids like Jaime Harrington, who think they can walk all over everyone because they were born rich on New Albian soil.

As long as people like them exist—people who wield their size and their money and blood like a police bludgeon—Wes can't protect anyone. Because that *is* his job, his purpose, no matter what Margaret says. The fundamental tenet of alchemy is All is One and One is All. As above, so below. To protect one person is to protect all of them.

But he can't do that without alchemy. He can't do it without power.

20

When Margaret throws open the front door, the manor is, as always, deathly quiet. Of all things, it angers her. She's angry because she's afraid. Afraid of what she saw in Wes's eyes, afraid of what Jaime will do now, afraid because she *cares*.

"Wes?" she calls. "Are you home?"

Only silence answers her.

For years, she has kept this house. It has been her refuge, even in its disrepair. Every corner, every nook, and every warm, sunlit spot is filled with memories—reminders that this was once a home full of life and joy and happiness. But right now, its emptiness is a bitter reminder that she's the only one left. That if the shadows swallowed her whole, it wouldn't matter at all because there's no one here to mourn her. Where is her mother, demanding where she's been and who she's been with? To tell her not to associate with boys who pick fights with the son of the wealthiest, most powerful man in town?

What she would give for Evelyn to scold her.

Trouble pads out of her bedroom as she climbs the stairs. His tail droops sleepily but still wags for her. He yawns, a high-pitched sound that cracks the oppressive weight of her mood. Margaret drops to her knees beside him and pulls his ears through her hands. "You're a good boy, Trouble."

For once, he doesn't protest as she leans her forehead against his and whimpers. She can never hide her feelings from him, even if she wants to. Dogs always know.

The lock of the front door twists open, and the hinges creak like the death rattle of a wounded animal. Trouble jerks away from her and lets out a low, warning bark.

"Aw, shut up, Trouble," Wes says. "It's just me."

Margaret presses herself deeper into the shadows of the second-floor landing. From her perch, she watches him peel off his shoes without unlacing them and nearly trip as he tosses them into the foyer. Next, he fumbles with the buttons of his jacket. The rustle of fabric and several muttered *ow*s let her know he's having a hard time divesting himself of it.

With exaggerated care, Wes makes his way up the staircase. It groans beneath him, and when he eases his weight off each step, the nails give off an almost comical peep. The logical thing to do is to go into her room, lock the door, and shut off all the lights so he doesn't think she's awake. It's not productive to talk to him right now when he's sullen and stormy and *drunk*.

But when she sees him and the salt-stiff mess of his hair, the kernel of anger that has taken root within her kindles like a flash fire. It's irrational and inarticulate, which only makes her feel unmoored. She likes to file things away, to pin their skin back to understand them. To keep everything orderly, inside and out. But Wes has broken something within her.

She couldn't hold her feelings back anymore if she tried.

Margaret accosts him as he tiptoes into the hallway. In the dim blue light filtering through the window, his eyes are as round and shining as harvest moons. He has the distinct look of a dog caught sneaking scraps from the countertop.

"Margaret?" he stage-whispers.

She wants to ask him for whose benefit he's being quiet or who else it would possibly be, but she's too exasperated with him to get off track. Without answering, she closes the gap between them until they're nose to nose. The first question that comes to mind is "What are you doing?"

"Going to bed," he says defensively. "What are *you* doing?"

"Waiting for you."

"Why?"

"Because I was worried that Jaime would come back for you on your way home."

Some of the impertinence fades from him, but he's still got a haughty edge to his voice. "Well, you can rest easy now. I've returned in one piece and entirely alone."

He clearly means for his exit to be dramatic, but as he turns on his heel, he loses his balance and catches himself on the banister. Through the darkness, she can see the fingers of his right hand beginning to swell.

Margaret heaves a long sigh. "I'll bring you some water."

That's not your job, he told her. *It's not your job to take care of everyone but yourself.*

But it is. Once her father left, it became her job to take care of Evelyn, since she was so determined to self-destruct. Without her, how would the world hold together? How would *she* hold together if she couldn't occupy herself? And perhaps the most burning question of all: When did Wes get sucked into her contained orbit? She'd become such a sucker for his cheap words and showman's smile.

Without waiting for his response, she hurries downstairs to fetch a glass of water and a bag of frozen peas from the icebox. By the time she returns, his bedroom door is closed. Margaret knocks softly and waits. When she doesn't hear him inside, she nudges the door open with her hip and meets resistance. Did he barricade himself inside? She wouldn't put antics like that beyond him.

Grunting with the effort, she shoulders her way through and flicks on the light. There certainly *is* a barricade. She kicks aside the pile of clothes on the floor and scans the rest of the room in dismay. His things are strewn everywhere. Ties draped over the back of his desk chair. Books arranged in haphazard stacks on the ground like a small cityscape. Scraps of notebook paper littering every surface like snow. He's no better than her mother.

And he is gone.

She stands like a fool in the center of his empty room with her water and her peas, until the door swings open with such force, it slams against the wall. Wes appears in the threshold, looking at her with a great deal of consternation.

"What?" she asks.

"You can't just come into my room unannounced. What if I was naked?"

"What if, Wes?"

"Oho, were you trying to catch me out again?" He slurs his way through it admirably, the delivery landing somewhere between mock offense and flirtation. "Margaret, Margaret, Margaret . . ."

She rolls her eyes and gestures to the edge of his bed. "Sit."

He obeys. Margaret sits beside him and takes his hand in both of hers. His knuckles are already mottled blue and red. His breath catches when she runs her fingertips over the bruises. "Does it hurt?"

"No."

Of course not.

The moonlight streaming through the window is as delicate as lace. It paints his black hair with a coat of silver and softens the moody darkness of his eyes to the deep brown of coffee. A small part of her, the same part of her that sighed his name into her empty bedroom, wants to linger on the sight. She still hasn't finished grappling with whatever she feels toward him. But right now, he needs discipline, not fawning. Margaret clamps the bag over his swollen fist and ignores his muffled sound of protest.

"Treat me gently. I'm delicate."

"You'll live." She pins his hand in place on her lap. His palm is warm against her knee, a welcome contrast to the chill of the frozen peas between them. "This is your own fault, anyway."

"I guess." He falls silent for a moment. "I don't get it. Jaime made first flight, too, and it's not like he needs the prize money."

"It's not about money for most of them. It's not even about the safety of the town. It's about killing the hala, and more importantly, it's about who kills it." Margaret keeps her eyes downcast. "That's not an honor they'll hand over to people like us."

"What do you mean by 'people like us'?" He suddenly seems more sober.

"People who aren't like Jaime," she manages. "Whoever kills the hala is doing God's work, and that's the most patriotic thing there is. It's all symbolic. Defining what a hero is. Dominating nature. So what would it mean for someone like you to win? The soul of the nation is what's at stake for them."

"Then it'll be pretty heroic when we win. Admit it, Margaret. Slugging him was pretty heroic."

She won't. All she remembers is the panic she felt when she saw Jaime looming over him like a slavering hound and that hungry look in Wes's eyes as he drank in Jaime's bloodied face. Had she not interfered, who knows what might have happened? She still fears what will happen when Jaime decides to quit holding back. "Your intentions are noble, but your actions are reckless. You don't know what he's capable of."

"Yes, I do, Margaret." It's the first time she's heard him sound so exhausted. "You honestly think I haven't dealt with people like him before? They're everywhere in the city, and they run this country. They burn Sumic churches. They keep Yu'adir out of universities and shatter every window in their storefronts. They put immigration quotas on people fleeing starvation and massacres. They force us to live in slums and work jobs that'll kill us. They—" He cuts himself off and runs his free hand through his hair. "I'm so sick of it. I'm sick of enduring it. Aren't you?"

"What else can we do?"

"Fight back." Frustration edges into his voice. "Riot. Vote. Anything."

"It won't do me any good. I'm alone here."

"No, you're not."

She can't bear to keep the secret anymore—not when he's looking at her so earnestly. Not when she's so sick of holding him at a distance. "I'm Yu'adir."

In the wake of her confession, there's only the soft rustle of the curtains in the draft and the unsteadiness of her breath. Margaret braces herself for some kind of reaction, but Wes only frowns. "What does that matter? I'm with you."

She's filled with such relief it nearly bowls her over.

"I know you think I'm being reckless," he continues. "But I can't be any other way. I can't be quiet or make concessions if I'm going to change the way things are. By the time I'm through, it won't matter where our grandparents came from."

She can't envision a world like that. But then, she's never been able to see further than Wickdon's coastline. "I want nothing more than to see that dream made a reality, but you can't change the world if we don't win. You can't make it to the top if Jaime kills you first. You have to listen to me sometimes. You have to let me help you."

You can't let alchemy consume you.

But she doesn't say that. The words stick at the back of her throat.

Normally he's so expressive. But right now, she can't read him at all. "I thought you said you didn't have big dreams."

"I just want to survive this. I want to see my mother again. That's big enough for me." Margaret squeezes his hand between hers. "And I want to help you see yours through. Our dreams live and die together. Isn't that what you told me?"

Wes is drunk enough that she can taste it on his breath. It's sweet with liquor and candied apples. He smells like gunpowder and his aftershave and the sea. Like everything that makes her feel alive. "You want to help me? How?"

"For now? Let me counsel you. Let me protect you."

"And when we win? Then what?"

"I'll teach you to survive my mother."

He shakes his head. "After that."

There's nothing after that. "I don't know."

Wes lets out a frustrated, conflicted noise. "Don't you want to leave? See the world? Find people who won't judge you only by what god your dad worshiped?"

"I like it here. It's quiet."

"Then maybe I'll stay with you."

"No." She startles herself with how forcefully it comes out. Margaret's not sure where this is coming from or what's gotten into him. "You'd get bored of me. You'd be lonely."

"You'd never bore me," he says pleadingly. "Think about it. We could build a house right next to the train station. I'd go to the city a few days a week, and we'd go to the market on weekends and make pies or jams or whatever. There'd be a pasture for Shimmer, woods for you and Trouble, and all the sunny reading spots you could ask for."

When he describes this future for her, she can almost envision it. He has such beautiful dreams. "And for you?"

When he meets her eyes, she can't remember how to breathe. She has noticed the color of them before, a brown as rich as redwood, as dark as wet earth. This time, the noticing stirs her deeper than wanting.

It's true that Wes is a fool, and it's true that Wes is brilliant. Ambitious and lazy, giving and selfish, thoughtful and reckless—all of his opposites marrying together in a perfect whole like an alchemic reaction. At his heart, he's good and kind, and he's looking at her like she is something to be cherished. That scares her more than failure and more than death.

"Do you really need me to say it, Margaret?"

Margaret snatches her hands away from his.

He smiles at her slyly. "All the beautiful country girls who think I'm worldly."

Disappointment and relief both crash over her. "Shut up and drink your water."

"Yes, ma'am." He lifts the glass from the nightstand takes a half-hearted sip.

"All of it."

He scowls. "Anything else?"

"No. That's all."

Margaret lingers at his side, her hands folded tightly on her lap. It's only when his head lolls and the glass tips in his hand that she moves, grabbing it from him and replacing it on his nightstand. He's going to be terribly hungover in the morning, but there's nothing to be done for it now. He deserves it, anyway.

In sleep, he looks peaceful. No scheming, no temper, no fire.

Margaret turns over the future he offered her like an apple at market, weighing it against the bright, warm memory of her family. What kind of life would they actually have together? Would she remain a shade, haunting a new grand house? Would she continue her days only half-lived, braced for some inevitable tragedy to steal her happiness away?

No, she can't bear to lose something so precious again. She can't pine for him, and she can't give her heart to another alchemist.

The best outcome for her is the simplest one. They will win the hunt. Evelyn will return and remember how to love her again. Wes will earn his certification from her mother. And then he will leave, off to make his dreams a reality. Margaret brushes the hair from his forehead before she backs out of the room and closes the door on her desires.

21

The next morning, sunlight wakes Wes like a bludgeon to the head. The first thing he notices is that he's fully clothed on top of the sheets. The second, he's so nauseated that the very thought of sitting up makes him wish for death. When he finally rallies enough to peel open his eyes, he's staring down an untouched glass of water on the nightstand.

He's never hated himself more.

With the scuzzy film over his thoughts, it takes him a few blinks to register where he is. There are all his books butterflied on the desk. There are his crumpled shirts piled in the corner of the room. There's the note he hasn't been able to decipher for days, a shred of paper affixed to the bedpost which says *maype try addjust H?*

At least he made it home and to his own bed. Then, his hand throbs painfully, and he remembers where he was last night—and exactly what he did. Insulted Annette *again*. Punched Jaime and probably broke his goddamn hand in the process. Obliquely proposed marriage to Margaret. How much of his behavior can he blame on the drink?

The proposal, he decides, at the very least. That one isn't entirely on him.

Wes groans through the pounding in his temples and pulls a pillow over his head to block out the too-bright sunlight. Maybe it'd have been better to let Jaime kill him. At least then he'd know oblivion. He wouldn't be able to torture himself with images of Annette's wounded face or the sinking feeling that he's gotten himself in too deep with Margaret Welty.

The sound of gunfire ricochets through his skull.

He tries to tunnel deeper into the mattress to drown out the noise, but it's insistently deafening. Margaret has to be doing this to punish him. Throwing the blankets off, he staggers to the window and draws back the curtains. She stands on the edge of the yard, aiming her rifle at a target she's rigged at the tree line. Glass bottles, slivers of pottery, and cans hang from branches and sit on char-blackened redwood stumps. She shoots, and a bottle bursts into shards like a firework. Shoots again, and a plate shatters. Every shot rattles him to his bones. Still, he can't look away.

What am I even doing here?

What could someone like her possibly need from him? It's within the rules to enchant guns for the hunt, but when he looks at Margaret, he's not sure what he could possibly do to augment her shot. It's unlike anything he has seen, beautiful in its subtle imperfections. Her focus, her steadiness . . . It's magnetic.

She's magnetic.

Wes tears himself away from the window and decides to deal with the fuzzy, sour taste of his mouth. He scrubs his teeth twice over, then showers off the gritty feeling of sea air and alcohol on his skin. Condensation from the hot water mists the mirror. He smears it off so that he can examine his face. He looks as awful as he feels, with a sickly pallor and shadows beneath his eyes. As always, his jaw is rounder and smoother than he'd like, but if he tilts his chin to the light, he can see the faintest shadow of facial hair. It's the product of several days of hoping, but it's enough for him to feel satisfied—enough to lather on a layer of shaving cream and procure one of the ivory-handled razors from his father's kit.

When he finishes shaving and guzzling enough water to whittle the edges off his hangover, he goes to the lab. In the week since the exposition, he's worked on distilling an essence of buoyancy to enchant thread that he stitched into the horse's saddle blanket. It's probably got a few drops of his blood woven in it, too. Christine does most of the mending, so he's gotten rusty with a sewing needle. With another week until the hunt, he can start tinkering with something else.

But he still can't shake the worry that the bullet he made is insufficient. If alchemically enchanted weapons were enough to kill the hala, wouldn't someone have done it by now? Whether the demiurges are truly divine is arguable. That they're immortal is a fact, which means it's likely that they're fundamentally different from any other flesh-and-blood, carbon-based being on this planet. To destroy something alchemically, you must know what it's composed of. If they have any hope of killing the hala, he has to find out what it *is*.

Evelyn's strange alchemical texts lie on the desk, taunting him with their untranslatable secrets. *She knows,* Wes thinks. *She has to know.*

And whatever the truth is, it was dangerous enough to encode.

He picks up his pen and flips open one entitled *Mutus Liber.* It's another book like *The Chrysopoeia,* filled with strange illustrations. On each page is another disturbing oddity. The sun with the face of a man. Horrifying angels with eye-studded wings. People ascending ladders to nowhere. Dead demiurges staring out at him with their white, voidlike gazes. The pages are bordered with elaborate geometric patterns and alchemic runes. Unlike *The Chrysopoeia,* however, each illustration is inscribed with Evelyn's faint handwriting. She's written instructions, but only every third word is in Albian.

She must've cracked the original author's code—only to reinscribe it in her own. Alchemists are strange, secretive, and idiosyncratic people. They always encode their research to protect it from undeserving eyes and to tantalize fellow truth-seekers.

Wes squints down at the manuscript, his headache pulsing violently in his temples. Reading is an impossible enough task most of the time, but this is absurd. These instructions are nothing but a hodgepodge of numbers and words in foreign languages, including . . .

Banvish?

Finally, the shapes of words he knows. Wes taps each one with his pen. *Bás. Athbhreithe. Óir.* Wes doesn't understand much since his parents rarely spoke Banvish at home, but he's absorbed enough to know these are all common metaphors for the steps in the alchemical process. Farther down, there are names of runes and ingredients. Clever of Evelyn, to hide her research in a language few New Albians would know. He's never been a good reader, but he's good at patterns. Even with this small fragment of the code, he should be able to decipher it with enough time.

It's only when his bruised hand begins to ache that he sets down his pen. He blinks up at the clock, which claims two hours have passed. He lost track of time again, and all he has to show for it are pages full of abortive translations and a few doodles of eyes that look suspiciously like Margaret's.

Wes closes his notebook and massages the stiff muscles in his hand. A week isn't enough time to make sense of any of this, if there's any sense to be made of it at all. Maybe Evelyn never solved the puzzle, or maybe these manuscripts are nothing but an elaborate joke.

No, he has to crack the code. If he doesn't find a way to kill the hala, his apprenticeship and his family's security are forfeit. Which reminds him that he hasn't called home in a week. His mother is probably beside herself.

Wes drags himself into the hallway and peers through the double-hung window. Margaret isn't in the yard anymore, and he doesn't hear her puttering downstairs in the kitchen, either. But the bathroom door is ajar. A mist of shower-warm air drifts into the hall along with the scent of her lavender soap. He could slip out without saying anything, but surely she'd like to know if he's going out. Maybe she'll want something from town—or at least his gratitude for taking care of him last night. Wes cautiously approaches her bedroom door and knocks.

Rustling comes from the other side. A lock clicks. Then, her nose and one brown eye appear in the narrow space she's opened in the threshold. Her fingers curl around the edge of the door.

"Hi," he says.

"Hello."

The exact details of their conversation last night are admittedly a little hazy, but they're on good terms again, he thinks. The uncertainty makes his already-churning stomach twist up worse. Maybe it's the whole proposal thing that has her so cagey. God, he wishes he could keep his mouth shut sometimes.

"So," he says. "Are you going to talk to me like that, or . . . ?"

Margaret opens the door fully, and Wes tries his best not to balk. She's wearing a floral-patterned robe knotted shut at her waist. Her hair is darkened to the color of earth with water, and her skin is still flushed from the heat of the shower.

At this point in his life, Wes has largely forgotten what it means to be embarrassed by states of undress. His sisters traipse across the apartment in whatever they feel like: gingham skirts and unflattering aprons, silk slips and corselettes, loose pajamas, towels, the one sequined gown they share among them. But seeing Margaret as anything but perfectly composed stuns him into silence. She looks vulnerable—more unarmed than he's ever seen her. Her face is impassive but expectant, like she's gauging his reaction or waiting for him to say something smart. For once, he has nothing to offer.

With an exasperated look, she turns on her heel. She leaves the door open, which he decides to take as an invitation. And just like that, he's in Margaret Welty's room. A girl's room. A girl who isn't his sister. It frazzles him more than he cares to admit.

The room itself is horribly plain. She has fewer belongings than he does, which is saying something considering he's only got a wardrobe full of cheap catalog suits. Everything is clean and white. White lace curtains over the windows. White bookshelves above her white desk. A white four-poster bed, fastidiously made, of course. Wes has a sudden impulse to disturb her precious order. He wants to untuck those careful creases, to loosen the top sheet like a tie after a long day, if only to get a rise out of her. Then, he catches a glimpse of the polished row of guns mounted above her headboard and thinks better of it.

Margaret perches on the edge of her bed. "How are you feeling?"

Somehow, he doesn't think that's the question she wants to ask. He slumps into her desk chair. "Terrible, if it's any consolation. Thanks for taking care of me last night. I have to admit I don't remember it clearly, so I hope I didn't embarrass myself too much."

She makes a face, then begins braiding her hair over her shoulder. "No more than you usually do."

"What's that supposed to mean?" he asks sourly.

"Did you need something?"

"Do I have to need something to talk to you? You know what, don't answer that. I'm going to town to call my mom and wanted to know if you wanted anything while I'm out. Or if you wanted to come."

"Sure." She ties off the end of her braid. "We could take the horse."

"The horse," he repeats skeptically.

"You do need to learn how to stay upright in the next week."

"I know, I know." It takes everything in his power to resist taking the bait of "upright." Honestly, it's like she wants him to suffer. "I need to see if the enchantment on the saddlecloth works, so it's for the best. I like the bathrobe, by the way. You're going out like that?"

"No. You can borrow it if you'd like."

Did Margaret Welty just flirt with him?

While he tries to recover, she gives him one of her rare, secret smiles. A little self-satisfied curve of her lips that nearly undoes him. "I'll meet you downstairs."

Thoroughly chastened, Wes fetches the saddlecloth and trudges downstairs to wait for her. When she reemerges from her room, she looks like herself again, wearing a skirt down to her ankles, a sweater cuffed at the sleeves, and mud-caked boots.

She leads him outside and to the pasture fence, then calls for Shimmer. He comes galloping, eager as a dog, and scares Wes half to death when he doesn't slow down until the last possible second. The beast snorts and regards him with one giant brown eye, clearly as mistrustful of Wes as Wes is of him.

Margaret loops a halter over his head and fastens it to the fence post. She fusses over him for a while, knocking the dirt off his back and adjusting the buckles and straps on the saddle. When she finishes, she pats Shimmer on the neck and turns expectantly to Wes. "Ready?"

No. "Yeah. How do I get on?"

She offers Wes her hand. "Climb onto the fence and swing your leg over."

Her hand, warm and roughened from work, fits into his like a gramophone needle on the grooves of a record. Wes hoists himself onto the fence and clambers onto the horse's back. He's far higher up than he expected being—and far more unstable, especially with the subtle upward current of energy flowing from the alchemized saddle. His nausea comes back with a vengeance, but at least he knows the enchantment works.

"I'll lead him on foot so you can get a feel for riding." Margaret unties Shimmer and clips a lead line to his halter. "You're alright up there?"

He holds onto the reins with a white-knuckled grip. "Never been better."

With a skeptical look, she unlatches the gate and guides Shimmer down the road to Wickdon. Once Wes accustoms himself to the swaying rhythm of the horse's gait, it's surprisingly relaxing. The sunlit woods unfurl around them in patterned gold and brown. It reminds him of Margaret, autumn-bright and earthy. They make it halfway to town before she brings Shimmer to a halt. "Scoot back. I'm tired of walking."

"Alright, uh . . ." He's hardly shifted backward before she all but floats into her seat. As she settles against him, he's struck again by the scent of lavender and sea salt.

"Hold on."

"To *what*?"

"Me."

Wes circles his arms around her waist. She clucks quietly to Shimmer, who gives a resigned sigh before setting off again. With every step, Margaret sinks farther into him until they are flush and his breath stirs the hair coming loose around her ears. He can feel the ripple of her muscles and every torturous shift of her hips against his.

God, will being near her ever get easier?

She turns over her shoulder. In this golden light and the fond way she's looking at him, her eyes shine the color of browned butter and honey. "Do you want to go faster?"

"Okay," he says, feeling a little giddy.

She nudges Shimmer with her calves. As if they've spoken some secret language, Shimmer flicks his ear and transitions into a jerky trot. One stride, two, and Wes feels open air beneath him. He yelps and clings tighter to her to keep himself from falling off.

Margaret laughs as she steadies them, calling, "Woah, woah!"

It's the first time he has ever heard her laugh: a warm, soft sound that winds through his blood like wine. As Shimmer slows to a walk and gives them a reproachful look, Wes watches the sun glitter in Margaret's hair and spends the rest of the journey dreaming of how to make her to do it again.

Margaret hitches the horse in the town square and loosens his girth. Then, she fishes a carrot from her pocket—because of course, *of course* she would carry one—and offers it to Shimmer. Wes watches in horror at how close those teeth come to her skin, each one like a flat yellow tile.

"I'll meet you back here when you're finished." She scratches Shimmer's withers, then dusts her hands off on her jacket. "I'm going to take a walk."

"Alright. See you soon."

She leaves him alone with Shimmer, who eyes him resentfully. His tail lashes at invisible flies. Wes does not trust this thing, not for one second, after it nearly killed him. "You behave while I'm gone."

He considers going to the Wallaces' to borrow their phone, but he has a feeling Annette may not want to see him anytime soon. Or ever. It'll be a long while before he forgets the disappointment that flashed in her eyes when he left her alone on the beach. He can spare some change for the phone booth to avoid the awkwardness of that encounter.

He ducks down a narrow side street that branches off from Wickdon's square, which is as somber as an abandoned fairground. The entire town looks as though it's been ransacked. All the storefronts are darkened, and the cobblestones are littered with apple cores and crumpled paper cups. After dodging a few puddles of questionable mystery liquid, he finds the phone booth at the end of the road. Inside, it's like a confessional with its iron-gridded privacy. He fishes a few coins from his pocket and places them in the slot. They strike the bottom with a merry jangle.

The phone rings only once before someone answers. "Hello?"

"Well, well, well. If it isn't my favorite sister! What a pleasant surprise." It isn't, really. Mad is the last person he hoped to catch.

The line crackles. "Oh. What do you want?"

"I'm great, thanks for asking. What makes you think I want something?"

"You only call when you want something."

That's just patently untrue. Wes scowls but keeps his voice blithe. "I want only the gift of speaking to my beloved sister."

"You're full of shit." Then, after a beat: "When's the hunt?"

"Next week." He coils the telephone wire around his wrist. "You should come. It'll be fun, assuming no one dies."

"Christine and I have work, and Colleen has school. We can't take off to go traipsing around the countryside for you."

"It's a weekend, so Bean can come." He hesitates. "And if we win, you won't have to go back to work for a while if you don't want to."

"You really want to ask Mam to watch this?"

"She'll be fine. I already told her I'd go to confession. I figure saying a decade or two of the rosary should be penance enough." Mad snorts. He bites his lip to keep himself from pushing his luck. Joking with Mad is like boxing; you have to know when to get out of the ring. "Think about it, alright?"

"Fine. I'll think about it. Who do you want to talk to?"

You. The word catches in his throat, though, and even if she stayed on the line, what would he say? That he misses her? That he wants her to forgive him? It'd be the truth, but his intentions have never mattered much to her. Until he fills a bathtub full of gold for her or fixes Mam's hand himself, no amount of pleading will do him any good.

Instead, he says, "Could you put Mam on?"

"Sure."

He waits, twisting the phone cord around his fingers tight enough that the tips go red, then white. After a minute and another coin in the slot, his mother says, "Wes?"

"How are you, Mam?"

"I'm so happy to hear your voice. You haven't called in ages. I've been worried about you."

"Well, I've been a little tied up. I'm here now, though! Hale and whole."

"Are you really? Are you eating enough? Sleeping enough?"

Wes drags a hand down his face. "Yes, Mam—"

"Oh, don't give me that tone of voice. You sound tired. That's all."

"I'm just a little stressed. How are you feeling?"

"The wound's closing fine. I don't have much mobility, though. Don't worry about it, a thaisce. Nothing to be done for it right now. What's bothering you?"

He has to lie. But as soon as he opens his mouth to give her some evasive answer, his stomach lurches like it's trying to escape. "A lot, actually."

She goes silent for so long, he thinks she didn't hear him. Then, as if she's afraid of spooking him, she says, "Why don't you tell me about it?"

"Master Welty still hasn't come back to Wickdon. The other competitors are . . ." Telling her about Jaime will make her lose too much sleep; he can't burden her with that. "There are a lot of people who want to win. And if we lose, I'll never be an alchemist, and Margaret will be miserable forever, and we'll be homeless, and on top of all that, I think Mad hates me."

"Your sister does not hate you."

Wes wrinkles his nose.

"I heard that."

"I didn't say anything!"

"I heard what you were thinking," she chides. "Mad is angry about a lot of things, and you're an easy outlet. I'm not saying either of you is right. I'm just saying what is."

"I don't understand why it's *me*."

She sighs. "Madeline would take on anything for the people she loves. So would you. But her love is hard-won. Her heart only has room for a few people. And you. . . . You love everyone you meet."

"And yet she thinks I'm selfish."

"Maybe that's what she says. The reality is that you're too idealistic. She thinks you value strangers as much as your own family."

"But I *don't*—"

"I know that. But you don't make it easy for her to see. You don't make it easy for *anyone* to see. And you're too proud to recognize how she tears herself apart for you."

"I thought you loved me," he says sullenly.

"I do, which is why I'm telling you this. Focus on what you can control right now. Do your work and trust that God will provide the rest. We need you." She pauses. "Margaret needs you."

"More like I need her."

He doesn't like the heaviness of her ensuing silence. He doesn't trust it.

"She's a nice girl," she says.

"Are you serious?" He barks a laugh. "You know she's not Sumic, Mam."

"Well, as long as she'll get married in a church. Does she like children?"

"Lord," he mutters.

"Language, Weston."

"Sorry, sorry." He runs a hand through his hair. "I have to say, I don't think she's . . . I don't think I'm her type."

"Nonsense. I'm only teasing you, anyway. Just be good to her, will you? The poor thing could use a friend. Her mother really hasn't even written?"

Wes leans his head against the glass of the phone booth. "No. Nothing. It's like she disappeared."

"What kind of mother would do such a thing to her child? I don't care if she's old enough to take care of herself. Nobody should be alone like that."

He's thought the same thing countless times. He wonders what Margaret has endured if the very sight of her mother's office was enough to send her spiraling. But he doesn't know if he has the energy—or the money—to encourage his mother's outrage. "I know. Which is why she needs the whole Winters clan to show her some love. Are you coming to watch the hunt?"

"I don't know if I can bear watching, but I'll be there."

"Good." Wes hesitates. "I miss you, you know?"

"Oh, a thaisce. I'll see you so soon. Just do your best. Your sister will forgive you, no matter what happens. We'll survive it."

"I hope so. I . . . I don't want to hurt you anymore. I want you to be happy. I know it's been hard the last few years, and I know I haven't made it easier. I've been a bad son, but—"

He hears her sharp intake of breath. "Weston, don't you dare. You make me proud every day. It's only that I worry about you. It's been years since I've seen you smile like you used to before your father died. I don't know if I've ever gotten you to talk to me about what's on your mind since then, and I . . ."

And that's just the thing: she hasn't. He didn't want to worry her, but he never considered that closing himself off would hurt her worse. "Aw, Mam, please don't cry," he says hoarsely. "I can't take it."

"Sometimes you remind me so much of him. I know he'd be proud of you, too."

Would he? His eyes sting with tears. It's been two years, but it still amazes him what reopens the wound of his grief. He clears his throat to keep from making a sound. When at last he's steady enough, he chokes out, "Thanks. That means a lot."

"I love you. I'll see you at the end of the week, alright?"

"I love you, too. See you soon."

The line goes quiet. He's not sure when talking to her will feel less like tearing his own heart out. He's not sure when he'll begin feeling like he's doing the right thing, or if he'll ever be the kind of man who deserves his parents' pride. But for now, Mam is right—as right as Margaret was. Until they win, he can't do a damn thing for the people he loves, let alone an entire country.

So he will focus on the things he can control. Cracking Evelyn's research notes. Humiliating Jaime Harrington. Placing the hala's lifeless body in Margaret's hands.

After that, both he and Margaret will have what they want. Wes just wonders if it'll truly make them happy. Once Evelyn returns, they'll have to decide that much. If he's honest, he's not sure if he can bear learning from someone as cold as Evelyn—or if he can keep his tongue leashed once he's staring down the woman who ruined Margaret's life.

22

The sea is gray and restless beneath a darkening sky. Every now and again, a white-capped wave rears up, snarling, and breaks on the rocks—just enough bite to prove it's not a tamed creature. Margaret leaves her boots in the sand and walks the edge of the water, where foam traces the shoreline. It glimmers dully in the waning sunlight, a toothy half-smile.

A few yards into the surf, one of the wooden targets from last night's competition sways on its chains like a man on a gallows rope. Margaret finds a jagged piece of it knotted in a slick rope of seaweed that's heaved itself onto the beach. It's a grim reminder that after last night, neither she nor Wes is safe anymore.

"Maggie?"

She turns toward Mrs. Wreford's familiar voice—but her relief dies as soon as she sees Jaime standing beside her. His face looks even crueler than usual, with his lip gashed and dark bruises feathering his cheekbone. Wes will be pleased to see his handiwork.

Jaime keeps his mouth shut and his eyes averted, like he's embarrassed to be caught doing something as banal as walking on the beach. Mrs. Wreford cuts him a sharp look, and he mumbles a barely intelligible greeting.

Mrs. Wreford sighs. Her face is ruddy with cold, and with the sea spray beading on her flyaways, she is haloed with silver. "What are you doing down here? Storm's rolling in."

She jerks her chin toward the mountains, where thickening clouds creep down, as light-footed as a bobcat, and unfurl over the dark sprawl of the cypress groves. Mist pours into the cove and eddies around her ankles. Soon enough, they won't be able to tell the sea from the sky.

"I thought I might swim," Margaret says.

"Are you out of your mind? You'll freeze to death, or else drown."

She's about to tell her the cold water isn't so bad, but when she turns her face to the sea again, she gets a mouthful of salt. It churns restlessly, and although it's fearsome, Margaret likes it best when it's angry. There's something satisfying about it, the power of all that rage. She hikes up her skirt and ties it above her knees. "And what are you two doing out here?"

"Us? We're looking for Zach Mattis. His mother told me the damn fool never came home last night, and I told her I'd bet anything he's still passed out in that debauched cave you all think you're clever enough to hide in. As if I wasn't seventeen once and sneaking my parents' liquor in the same spot." She jabs a finger at Jaime. "I, how-ever, at least had friends with enough good sense to take me home at the end of the night. I suppose you were too busy brawling."

"I already told you I tripped," Jaime says, chastened.

Margaret ducks her head to conceal her smile.

"Right." Mrs. Wreford fixes Margaret with a probing look, as though she's expecting some confession. "Tripped. What do you make of that, Maggie?"

"I wouldn't know anything about it."

"No. I suppose you wouldn't." Mrs. Wreford sighs, and Jaime glowers at her. "Well, if you'd like to lend us a hand in looking, it'd be appreciated. I think the weather is about to turn for the worse."

Wind gusts around them, snatching at Margaret's skirt. The sound of the tide swells in her ears, louder, louder, until all she hears is the hissing of her name.

Margaret, Margaret, Margaret.

She clenches her fists against the fear that strikes her upon hearing that voice again, brittle as dry leaves, gritty as crushed shells in the sea. Sand crunches between her molars. The taste of salt and copper coats her tongue.

A terrible moan rises above the building noise of the storm.

Mrs. Wreford squints into the wind. "What in God's name was that?"

Margaret has heard a sound like that before. Last year, a deer slipped through the Halanans' pasture fence and got its head caught between the posts. While trying to thrash itself free, it broke its own neck. She found it there, sides heaving, eyes rolled back to the whites, legs twitching and splayed uselessly beneath it. It keened, again and again. Horrible, pleading sounds. Dying sounds. Margaret delivered it a merciful death, but it still suffered alone.

The moan comes again.

"That sounds like Mattis," Jaime says.

They run. The wind tears at them, lashing Margaret's hair against her face and stinging her eyes with salt. The sand is solid black and as glossy as a mirror, sucking hungrily at her bare feet, and her calves burn as they approach a small cave gashed into the side of a cliff. Carved into its stone walls is the secret, quieter history of Wickdon's youth: initials gouged into hearts, phallic drawings, and the odd confessional or snippet of a poem. Empty beer bottles clank together in the sand.

As soon as the tide rolls in, the entire cave will be submerged.

Margaret measures each step carefully on the unsteady floor. What little light there is refracts off the stagnant tide pools. Margaret can't see much through the gloom and marbled light—but she does see a dark shape crumpled in a heap a few feet in front of her.

Mattis.

"Oh my God," Mrs. Wreford whispers. "Kids, don't look."

But Jaime doesn't hesitate before splashing through the tide pools and dropping to his knees at his side. "Zach!"

Margaret carefully approaches them and crouches to examine the damage. Mattis's skin is pale as chalk, his lips the same sallow blue as fish scales, the bite wound on his shoulder a shockingly vivid red. He looks as though he's been rent open and soldered back together. Burned flesh bubbles over ragged strings of exposed muscle, and the edges of the wound are caked with a black paste of caput mortuum. Through the gore, Margaret can see all the way down to his shoulder capsule. He reeks of alchemy and the sea and death.

The hala must have found him here alone: the first human casualty of the season. It's nearing its full power now if it's grown bold enough to attack someone this close to town.

Then, the faintest breath whistles out of him.

"He's alive," Jaime calls. "Get help!"

"Don't move," Mrs. Wreford says. "Neither of you move."

Margaret does not.

As she watches the faint rise and fall of his chest, she listens to Mrs. Wreford's footsteps sloshing through the shallow water. To her shouts as they are snatched and tossed aside by the wind. To Jaime's muttering as he springs to his feet and paces like a beast in a cage. Still, the sea inches closer. Still, the waves hiss her name.

Margaret, Margaret, Margaret.

"Shut up," she whispers. "Shut up."

Water flows into the mouth of the cave and seeps into the fabric of her skirt. It's so cold, it steals her breath away. As the stench of salt and copper and brimstone sours the air, mist swirls through Margaret's vision. The memory of that awful night crystalizes over the real world.

She is here, and she is not. She is kneeling in the rising tide, and she is kneeling on the floor of her mother's lab. She cradles Evelyn's head while her golden hair paints the floorboards with blood. Her mother grabs her wrist. Her fingers are like bands of ice.

Maggie, she rasps.

"Maggie." She crashes back into her own body, gasping for breath. Her skin is slick with sweat and the sea. Mattis weakly clings to her as his eyes flutter open. "I don't want to die."

At the sound of his voice, Jaime stops his pacing. "Zach. Are you— Hang in there, alright? Help is coming. You're going to be fine, I promise."

Mattis's lip quivers. Her pallid, disoriented face is reflected in the glassy terror of his eyes. If he heard Jaime, he doesn't respond.

"He's in shock," Margaret says.

Jaime makes a broken, agonized sound she didn't think him capable of. He buries his face in his hands. "It was supposed to be a joke. It was a stupid fucking joke. I didn't think . . . I never should've . . . This is all my fault. God, this is all my fault."

"Maggie," Mattis whispers. "I'm sorry."

Jaime stiffens. His gaze darts back and forth between them.

"I'm sorry." Mattis chokes on every word as he begins to cry. "Can't you forgive me?"

If she were stronger, if she still weren't half-untethered from her body, she would ask him why. Why he's sorry. Why she should forgive him. Mattis has never been kind to her, but his cruelty was mild in comparison to Jaime's. It was rote and mindless, like a dog executing a trick to please its master. Easy to bear, easy to swallow.

Just survive, she has told herself for years. *Just endure.*

But she's tired of enduring it, just as Wes is. She can't bring herself to offer him any comfort, any absolution. In this state of eerie detachment, all she can think about is pushing her thumb into his wound to the knuckle, down to that yellow nub of bone beneath the shredded muscle. She wants to hurt him even a fraction of the amount he has hurt her. She wants Jaime to see what he has driven her to.

"Maggie," he whimpers. "Please."

Jaime rounds on her. "Say something!"

But what good would it do her, to turn the blade of her anger against him? Water drips from the ceiling, plopping as heavy as dropped stones into the rising tide. His hair and her skirts billow around them, blooming like blood in water.

"You're going to be alright," she says, and closes her free hand on top of his. "You're alright."

When the paramedics come, they find them with his hand going cold in hers.

Rain patters on the roof of Mrs. Wreford's apartment, a creaking set of rooms above the Blind Fox. Margaret sits at a rickety table that takes up half of the oven-hot kitchen, cradling her head in her hands as she listens to the faint laughter bubbling up through the floorboards.

She can't stop shivering, despite all the pains Mrs. Wreford has taken to warm her. As soon as she was all but dragged here, Mrs. Wreford coaxed her into a change of clothes and deposited her in front of the fire. Margaret said nothing as Mrs. Wreford toweled off and rebraided her hair, her throat aching from the simple tenderness. When she finished, tying it off with a thin strip of leather, Mrs. Wreford excused herself to ask the doctor for an update on Mattis.

A heavy fur-lined blanket hangs over her shoulders, and an untouched bowl of chowder goes cold in front of her. The brine of the clam and the slick, rubbery texture of it between her teeth reminds her too much of the exposed meat of Mattis's shoulder. Every time she closes her eyes, she sees the same image burned there. Mattis and her mother, one and the same, pale and bleeding out into the foam-laced water. Margaret scrubs her face and tries to forget.

The entire apartment smells of brewing beer and baking bread, yeasty and comforting. Bottles condition on the countertop, and what casks won't fit downstairs in the pub serve as a makeshift furniture here. Coffee tables full of stout, chairs brimming with porter.

From some hidden depth of the apartment, a radio crackles with static and the jaunty trill of a saxophone. The familiarity of this place isn't enough to calm her. Of all things, she wants Wes. She wants the steadiness of his gaze on her, the easiness of his laughter.

He's probably wondering where she is. She promised to meet him by the horse.

The door creaks open, and the floorboards whine under Mrs. Wreford's footsteps. She's carrying two frosted glasses of dark ale. Her coat is beaded with rainwater, and her hair is matted down with damp. She still smells like the cave they found Mattis in: sulfur and rotten seaweed. It fills her mouth with bile.

"Thirsty?" Mrs. Wreford asks.

She settles onto the chair across from Margaret and sets the glasses down. Margaret curls her hands around one, grateful for the sting of cold in her fingers. It's something she can feel. "Thank you."

"He's going to live."

Margaret's eyes flutter shut and her breath whooshes out of her. With no dread keeping her upright anymore, she's suddenly exhausted. "I'm glad to hear it."

Mrs. Wreford's gaze falls on the untouched bowl of chowder. "You didn't eat."

"I'm not hungry. Just tired."

"Then why don't you stay here tonight? I don't want you riding home in the dark and the rain, especially now that the hala's gotten its first taste of blood."

Margaret resents the idea of being scooped up like a stray cat. "I'll be fine. I make the trip often enough."

"When will you stop fighting me, Maggie?" The frustration in her voice startles her. "I don't have any children of my own, so you're as good as mine. For the sake of my nerves, stay. You'll be doing *me* a favor. It's one night."

"Fine," she says quietly. "But Wes—Mr. Winters is . . ."

She jerks her chin toward the window. "He nearly busted down my door when he heard you were here, but I told him you might want some space."

Margaret cranes her neck. Wes stands underneath an awning, looking half-drowned with his hair plastered to the sides of his face. He's gently pushing Shimmer's head away as he lips at the lapels of his oversized jacket. Just then, he glances up and meets her eyes. The smile he gives her is shockingly bright, tangled up with something else that makes her heart flop over like a dog showing its belly.

"He can stay, too, if he behaves." Mrs. Wreford gives her a meaningful look she doesn't much enjoy the implication of. "He's sunny."

Margaret takes a small sip of her ale. It tastes malty and dark, like oats and chocolate. She rolls it over her tongue before swallowing. "Yes. He tends to be."

"Do you like him?"

"Well enough."

"Why, that's about the most positive thing I've ever heard you say about someone."

Margaret prays the flush creeping across her collarbones doesn't reach her face. It's true enough. There are few people in her life she's ever gone as far as to entertain liking.

"He seems to care about you, too."

Now *that* is a thought she can't dwell on. She busies herself with tracing absentminded patterns in the condensation on her glass.

"Maggie." The gravity of Mrs. Wreford's voice stills her. "Why are you doing this?"

To make her mother stay. For love. That's always been the answer, without hesitation.

But in the weeks since Wes has wormed his way into her life, she's begun to question her own certainty. Love is not the sharp-edged thing she's always believed it to be. It's not like the sea, liable to slip through her fingers if she holds on too tight. It's not a currency, something to be earned or denied or bartered for. Love can be steadfast. It can be certain and safe, or as wild as an open flame. It's a slice of buttered bread at a dinner table. It's a grudge born of worry. It's broken skin pulled over swelling knuckles.

It's not enough anymore to do this for Evelyn. Maybe it's for Wes, too.

But caring for him might kill her. If she wins, he'll stay and become an alchemist. If she loses, he'll leave. No matter the outcome, she is sunk. No matter what she does, she'll forge the blade on which she will fall. Either he'll achieve his dreams and marry a beautiful, worldly woman, or he'll return to Dunway without her. She can't go with him. She couldn't stand it, its gray sprawl and its heaving crowds and all its horrible noise. She would live her days like a selkie wife, locked away in his home away from the sea.

There's no world in which they both can be happy.

"What's that look for?" Mrs. Wreford presses.

"It's nothing. I'm doing it because I have to."

"You do not have to do anything you don't want to."

"My mother—"

Mrs. Wreford slams her glass on the table. Thick foam sloshes over the lip of the glass and onto the table. "You almost saw a man die today. Forget your mother."

Margaret flinches.

"I'm sorry. That was out of line." Mrs. Wreford rubs her temples. "Listen to me, will you? I've lived a few years longer than you, which I like to think has given me some perspective. I'm wiser than you in some ways. Very few ways, mind you, but what I can tell you for certain is this. There are few people, if any, in this world worth chasing after. Even fewer worth making yourself miserable over. Do you understand me?"

Margaret nods.

This, apparently, is not a satisfactory answer. "When your mother comes back, what will you do?"

"I'll be happy, and Mr. Winters will have his apprenticeship."

"But what will you *do?*"

And when we win? Wes asked her last night. *Then what?*

She didn't know how to answer him then, and she doesn't know how to answer Mrs. Wreford now. What is there for her, beyond the looming wall of her mother's return? Who is she without the ache of her absence and the fear of losing her again?

"You're still convinced I'm a fool, aren't you?" Mrs. Wreford asks. "I know full well that she has no idea what you've been up to this month. What do you expect she'll do when she finds that boy in her house?"

Margaret has only considered it with her eyes half open. Evelyn is incredibly protective of her research. And of all the rules Evelyn instilled in her after her father left, these were cardinal: trust no one and depend on no one. Letting Wes into her life easily breaks both of them. "I expect she'll be angry. But if we have the hala, he'll have the leverage to win her over."

"Evelyn Welty is not the kind of woman to be bribed. I think you know that deep down."

"So what will you have me do? Quit?"

"It'd be far better for my nerves if you quit, but I won't hold my breath. What I'm asking you to do is think hard about what's best for *you*. Not for your mother. Not for Weston. For Margaret."

What if I don't know? she wants to ask. *How could I possibly know?*

"I know you love your mother, and I know she loves you in her way. But there are a lot of other people who love you, too." Mrs. Wreford reaches across the table and lays her hand over Margaret's clenched fist. "I hope you know that."

"I do," she lies.

Mrs. Wreford's eyes fill with a terrible sadness as she lets her go.

Outside the window, Margaret sees that Shimmer has successfully relieved Wes of his coat. He clenches the fabric between his teeth and tosses his head triumphantly. Wes shouts something she can't make out from here, imploringly reaching for the wet, limp mass of his jacket.

"That boy is . . . something else, isn't he?"

"Yes," Margaret says softly. "He is."

"I'll go let him inside."

Once Mrs. Wreford rescues Wes from the horse and lets him inside, she offers him a towel and a place on her couch for the night. He eats Margaret's cold chowder cheerfully, filling the silence with idle conversation until Mrs. Wreford's practiced skepticism breaks. He's cracked another one—only this time, Margaret feels pleased rather than annoyed that someone in her life has taken to him. Mrs. Wreford latches onto his arm and drills him with question after overly direct question until she's satisfied with his account of his family, his aspirations, and the merits of Wickdon over Dunway. After that, it's like they're old friends. Mrs. Wreford laughs until tears leak from her eyes, until she has to leave for her shift at the pub.

With her hand on the doorknob, she turns over her shoulder and gives them each a lingering look. "I'll be just downstairs, and I have ears everywhere. I'm talking to you, Weston."

"Don't worry. I'll take care of her."

Mrs. Wreford's eyes bulge, an unspoken warning. "I expect you will."

The door shuts behind her, leaving them alone.

Margaret settles onto the couch and draws her blanket up to her chin. The exhaustion of the past two days weighs her down, and she still feels as though she hasn't resurfaced from the depths of her episode in the cave. The cold hasn't lifted from her bones, nor the thick wall of fog that separates her from the rest of the world.

Her numb fingers are folded against her collarbones; it feels like a stranger's hand laid over her chest. She's not sure how anyone lives in Wickdon proper. Even the silence is not silent with the constant thundering of the breakers outside, the drum of the rain, the chatter of tourists in the streets.

"Margaret." Wes crouches beside her. He reaches for her, like he means to sweep the hair from her forehead or cradle the side of her face. In the end, he clamps his hand over his own knee. "Are you alright?"

"I'm fine."

"Do you want to talk about it?"

It. It's not about the hala. It's not even about what happened to Mattis. It's about her mother. It's about him. But how can she begin to tell him what she feels without frightening him away? How can she decide what's best for her when everything she wants will hurt her?

"No. I want to go to sleep."

"Sure, okay. I'll get the lights for you."

He crosses the room to flip off the switch. The lights flicker out, and Margaret nestles herself deeper into the cushions. Springs jab into her back and groan beneath her weight, but she's so weary she thinks she'll fall asleep the moment she closes her eyes.

Wes flops onto the couch kitty-corner to hers and turns onto his side. Even in the dark, she can see the catlike shine of his eyes. The light of the streetlamps bleeds gently into the room, limning everything in gold. They lie close enough that she could reach out and touch him if she wanted. As her eyes adjust, his worried expression comes into focus.

"The bullet isn't enough," he says.

"It was enough."

"It *was,* but it isn't. I don't think it'll kill the hala. In fact, I know it won't. And if you don't have the means to kill it, then all of this is for nothing."

Her heart leaps into her throat. No, he's wrong. His bullet has to work. There has to be another way. There *has* to be, or else what happened to Evelyn will happen again to Wes. She feels herself slipping into the cold waters of her fear again. "I can't talk about this. Not right now."

"That's fair. Sorry." He rolls onto his back and sighs. "I just can't stop thinking about if it was you who'd gotten hurt."

"It wasn't, though."

"That's hardly reassuring."

"It's not meant to be reassuring. It's what happened."

"I don't get you sometimes. Most of the time, really."

Margaret smiles, which seems to relieve him. "I'm sorry I worried you."

"Don't be. I guess you're right. That is what happened. But the fact of the matter is I still haven't finished my job. The only thing I can do is work harder, and I'm going to have a solution for you by the end of the week. I swear it." He extends his arm into the stretch of space between their makeshift beds as though he expects her to shake his hand.

"What's this?"

"A promise."

"You're ridiculous."

"I'm very serious, actually."

Margaret takes his hand. Compared to hers, it's smooth and unblemished by work. Neither of them pulls back. Although she can see his features bathed in soft, ambient light, she can't guess at what he is thinking. Wes loosens his grip enough to slide his thumb downward, sweeping it across the underside of her wrist. Her breath catches at the sensation, at how carefully he strokes her skin. She wonders if he's aware he's doing it. She wonders, more urgently, if he's aware of what it's doing to her.

"Mrs. Wreford said she has ears everywhere," she reminds him.

"And?" Once again, she sees his dark eyes gleaming. The weight of his gaze kindles a familiar tension in the pit of her stomach. "There's nothing going on for her to overhear."

He touches her with renewed intensity, every brush of his thumb featherlight, and she squirms at the shiver that ripples down her spine. As she listens to the sudden unevenness of his breathing, she can no longer convince herself that she's the only one imagining his fingers elsewhere. "No. I guess not."

"Do you want me to stop?" Despite the flirtatious lilt to his question, he does sound genuinely concerned.

If he stops, she'll have her wits back. But then he wouldn't be touching her anymore, and that'd be almost unbearable. She doesn't trust herself to speak, so she jerkily shakes her head.

His thumb presses in above the curve of her wrist bone. He guides her hand closer to him, until she can feel the heat of his breath fanning out against her palm. His lips hovering a bare inch from her pulse point feels like the moment before she pulls the trigger of her rifle. Blood rushing in her ears, heart thudding against her sternum, breath frozen at its highest point.

Pure anticipation.

But as soon as his mouth touches her skin, whatever this is between them will become concrete, impossible to ignore or dismiss
as folly. It's too terrifying to take that plunge. Margaret slips out of
his grasp. "I'll hold you to your promise, then."

Wes snatches his hand back and blinks as though he's been
snapped out of a spell. "Huh? Oh . . . Good. This time, I'll get it
right. It'll be perfect."

She wants to believe him.

As the minutes tick by, the silence around them softens. She en-
vies how quickly he falls asleep, but it gives her the opportunity to
admire him openly. He looks innocent with his mouth hanging
open and the crook of his elbow draped over the bridge of his nose.
His hair splays over the pillow like a rooster's comb.

Perfect.

Weston Winters is so far from perfect, but like this, he may as
well be. The warm glow of the streetlamps through the window and
the sparkling rhythm of the rain make everything feel somehow
unreal. Like she is dreaming with her eyes wide open.

23

The next two days pass like honey drizzled from the tip of a spoon.

Margaret spends her days in the woods, and Wes spends his in the lab, translating her mother's mysterious book. He's made some headway on the first step of her instructions, which seems to detail a particularly complicated transmutation circle. When he gets too frustrated with the code, he pores over records of demiurges' deaths for some hint or sign. All of them are the same: beneath the light of a full moon, some devout Katharist with a bow, a well-timed prayer, or a particularly sharp rock strikes it down in a fit of righteous fury. Wes doesn't think God'll be lending him a hand anytime soon, given the black state of his soul.

Margaret Welty has cast him into a state of mortal sin.

At night, when she comes home from training, he moves his work to the library and reads blearily while Margaret curls up with her pulpy paperbacks or finishes stitching the alchemized thread he made into her jacket. It's his favorite time of day because she lets down her hair, and it shines as gold as sunlight through water. He always knows exactly what she's reading by the rise in color on her cheeks.

It's horribly distracting.

Ever since he took her hand in Mrs. Wreford's flat, he feels as though she's bound him with some fey magic. He can't stop looking at her. He can't stop thinking about her. He can't stop noticing every soft *whisk* of the turning pages, or wishing he could make that passage he read a reality for her. He wants to tear the book from her hands and kiss his own name from her mouth and—

Alchemy. Back to alchemy.

God, she's not even here, and he's half sick with pining. She'd likely skin him alive if she knew the kinds of thoughts he has about her, but Wes has never been good at focusing on what he ought to. There's still more work he has to do before he can douse himself in cold water and pray for forgiveness. But if lust is so perverse, why would God make girls like Margaret?

He presses his pen into the paper and grasps at the tattered remains of his concentration. The work grounds him, against all odds. The *scritch* of his handwriting, symbols giving shape to his thoughts and guiding them soundly away from Margaret like a lighthouse through a storm.

He rubs at his eyes and gazes out the window, feeling too much like a dog waiting for its master to come home. Margaret took Trouble and Shimmer out a few hours ago, and he expects she'll be back soon. Late-afternoon sunlight spills over the fallen red leaves, gentle as a lover's touch. It's too hard to concentrate now, especially with this brewing tension headache. He's been working for hours, and he feels like he's going to rocket out of his skin if he stays still any longer.

In just a few days, all his problems will be solved. His family will be stable, and he will have the means to secure his apprenticeship. Assuming he can crack the secrets of this manuscript. Assuming Evelyn decides to return to Welty Manor at all.

Someone raps on the front door, startling him. Dread settles over him. Nobody comes here unless they're bearing bad news.

But when he opens the door, it's Annette.

"Oh," he croaks. "Good evening."

She stands on the porch in a loose dress patterned with blue paisley. The oversized lapels curl around her throat like a pair of hands, and a neat bow is fastened beneath her collarbones. Outside, past the front gate, her car's windows peer back at him, as solid white as the hala's gaze in the glaring sunlight.

"Hi." Annette tucks a loose curl behind her ear. "Do you mind if I come in?"

His family has given him many, many chances over the years. Annette, however, must be the most forgiving person on the planet if she still wants to see him. "No, not at all. Come in."

She brushes past him, close enough that he gets a whiff of her perfume. Cherries, he thinks—as sweetly red as her lipstick. Wes wonders if he ever looked so out of place in this house. As glossy and sharp-edged as a diamond, Annette is far too bright against the earthy browns and coppers of the manor. He's acutely aware of the dust motes dancing in the thick bars of sunlight.

"Can I get you anything?" he asks.

"No, I'm fine. Is Maggie home?"

"She's not." *Unfortunately.*

Annette glances at the front door. "Will she be home soon?"

"I expect so. Why?"

"I was hoping we could talk privately."

"We're alone now."

Annette lifts her brows. "*Alone* alone."

"Oh." His every coherent thought is replaced with the grainy static of dead air. He prays that the heat clawing its way up the back of his neck doesn't make it to his face. "Um, sure. Follow me."

As he leads her up the stairs, he can't quite convince himself that this is real. They haven't spoken since the night of the shooting competition. Although he's horribly confused, he's not exactly in a position to deny her. He still feels caged up in his own body, restless, like his skin is too tight. But with Annette in front of him, he finds he doesn't want to torment himself with thoughts of

Margaret. This one time, he can be decent enough to give her his full attention.

At the second-floor landing, he hesitates. The lab is too disorganized right now, with nowhere for her to sit, and he suspects it's beginning to smell awful, like stale air and sulfur and his own wallowing. "We could go to my room?"

"Perfect."

Wes opens the door to his bedroom and immediately regrets it. About five days' worth of empty mugs and half a library of books clutter every available surface. Wes snatches his jacket off the back of his desk chair and tosses it onto his unmade bed. "You can sit there if you'd like."

He perches on the edge of his bed as Annette closes the door behind her. It clicks shut with grim finality. She scans the room with amusement and judgment both before she pauses in front of the window. Warm, late sunlight cuts through the trees and paints the white walls with an orange glow.

She snaps the blinds shut. "Is there a key to this room?"

His throat goes dry. "Trying to lock me up? Trust me, there's nowhere else I want to be."

She looks startled, as though she's been caught doing something she oughtn't. Then she laughs. "Oh, you know. Just a habit to check. My dad comes prowling around the house every ten minutes whenever I have company."

He flings open the nightstand drawer with a little too much gusto. It shudders when it hits the end of its tracks. Fishing the key out, he places it on the nightstand. "To put your mind at ease."

"How kind." Annette surprises him by taking a seat beside him. The springs of his mattress groan beneath their weight.

It strikes him then just *how* alone they are. Five miles from civilization, on the purpling edge of dusk, behind his closed door, her knee brushing his. It's the exact situation a girl like her shouldn't be in. The exact scene her father would check her room for.

"You look nervous," she says.

"Do I?"

"Mm-hmm. I never took you for the prim and proper type. Could it be that all that bravado is an act?"

"No, no. You've just surprised me. I wasn't expecting you."

"I guess you wouldn't be." She leans back on her hands. "I'm sorry for coming here uninvited and going radio silent, and . . . Well, I'm sorry. That's what I've come to say."

"What? Why?"

"Because you did the right thing that night, standing up to Jaime. You were braver than I would've been. I shouldn't have tried to stop you."

"Oh. Thanks. I was just drunk, honestly."

The front door creaks open. Margaret must've come home, although he doesn't hear the telltale clack of Trouble's nails on the floorboards.

Annette swats his knee, pulling his attention back to her. "I guess I should apologize for that, too. I was the one who plied you with alcohol."

"So you were my coconspirator in bravery."

"Or the architect of my own misery."

"Misery? I hope you didn't lose any sleep over me."

She smiles thinly. "Some. Silly of me, really."

"I didn't mean to cause you any grief. It's not that I didn't *want* to spend time with you. It's just . . ." *Damn it.* Now he's thinking of Margaret again.

"I understand. I really do."

"Really? I mean . . . I'm glad. I'd hate to think I'd wronged you without having the chance to make up for it."

"There's nothing to make up for, honest. I'm happy we had the chance to talk." Annette pleats together the fabric of her skirt. "It's easy to talk to you. I feel like you understand me more than most people in Wickdon, and you certainly challenge me more than everyone else here. It's embarrassing to admit, but I was so upset that night because . . . Well, I guess it's because I like you. And I thought maybe I'd misread how you felt."

"No, you didn't. I like you, too." And he does mean it; Annette's a nice enough girl, even if she's sheltered. But as soon as it's out of his mouth, he's not sure if they mean it in the same way anymore.

Her eyes lock onto his, wide and hopeful. It makes him feel sick to his stomach. "You do?"

He's never had a problem with this before. He's no stranger to accepting confessions and vanishing when he's gotten what he wanted. Mad has yelled at him for it many times before, and while he's always known it's not his most becoming trait, this feels like a transgression in more ways than one. "I . . ."

Margaret's footsteps sound on the staircase, then plod softly toward her bedroom at the opposite end of the hall.

Wes runs a hand anxiously through his hair. "What do you mean by 'like' exactly?"

Annette squeezes his knee. "Do you want me to spell it out for you?"

The churning in his stomach fizzles out, then sharpens into a tug of desire as her hand drifts a fraction higher on his thigh.

He's been so pent-up these past few days, torturing himself with his own pathetic fantasies. It frightens him how badly he wants Margaret—how she consumes his every thought, how she makes him want to be vulnerable, how he's terrified of losing her. But two nights ago, she rejected him when she yanked her hand from his. Even if it was only nerves, it was for the best. He can't have her if he becomes her mother's apprentice, and he can't keep her if she won't leave Wickdon. But maybe if he has another outlet, he can endure this heartache. He can smother his feelings for Margaret just like every other emotion that's tried to drown him.

Easy, he thinks. All he has to do is let this happen. This time, it isn't entirely selfish to give in. It's self-preservation.

Annette shifts closer to him, and her lips find the curve of his jaw. He tips his head back, sighing. "It'll get dark soon."

"So? Are you going to kick me out?" she asks against his ear. It sends a shiver through him.

"Of course not. That would be ungentlemanly."

"I don't know that I want you to be *gentlemanly.*"

When her mouth slides over his, instinct takes over. His hand digs into the curve of her waist, and hers pulls at the hair at the nape of his neck. He feels boorish and clumsy, like his ink-stained fingers will ruin the delicate fabric of her dress, that he'll tear the sash around her waist as he unknots it. But she makes a soft, encouraging sound and parts her lips against his. She tastes as sweet as she sounds.

It feels good to kiss her, like slipping into a familiar sweater. But his heart wants something—someone—different. He wants solidity where she is soft. Golden hair, not brown, twined around his fingers. He doesn't know what it would be like to kiss Margaret, but he thinks there would be teeth and fire to it. Nothing like this, luxuriant and comfortable. He's been comfortable for too long. He doesn't want to hide anymore. He wants to be laid bare and consumed.

He wants Margaret.

Wes breaks away. "I'm sorry."

Annette's eyes flutter open. They glimmer with stunned hurt. "You're *sorry?*"

"Yes," he says miserably. "I'm sorry. I can't do this."

"Why not?"

He braces his elbows against his knees and cradles his head in his hands. "I don't know."

"You seemed perfectly capable a minute ago." He hears the sound of fabric shushing as she adjusts her mauled dress and reties the sash. Then, something bright and sharp, like metal sliding against wood.

"It's not you. It's me. My mind is all over the place right now, and my life is in shambles, and—"

"Is it Maggie?"

"No," he blurts out. Then, softer, he says, "No. It's not Margaret."

She looks at him skeptically, but what does she expect him to say?

Yes? Wes knows he's many things, not all of them good, but he's not cruel. What good would it do either of them to confess he'd imagined kissing Margaret instead? As horrible as he feels, ending this now is the kinder thing. The fairer thing.

"I don't know which of us is more a fool for not seeing it sooner. When are you going to tell her that you love her?"

"I don't love her." Every word sits heavy as a stone in his mouth.

Her expression is peculiar—her voice even more so, cold and composed, when she says, "Goodbye, Wes."

The door clicks shut behind her.

Groaning, he flops back onto his mattress and stares up at the ceiling with its sad collection of cobwebs and water stains. He's got half a mind to finish himself off, if only so he can get back to work, but he feels too miserable and ashamed of himself with the taste of Annette's cherry lipstick still lingering on his tongue.

When are you going to tell her you love her?

Wes scoffs. He doesn't love Margaret.

Does he?

Over the past month, he's acclimated to the idea that he's hopelessly attracted to her, as plain as he once believed her to be. It's never been difficult to admit that he admires her: her quiet strength and conviction, her surprising wit and tenderness, her devotion and tenacity. More than anything, Wes wants her to be happy, to protect her—the same as he would his family.

But is that *love*? Would he even know anymore, when he's so thoroughly deluded himself at every turn? Colleen once told him girls weren't as confusing as he made them out to be, and maybe she's right. Maybe it's people in general who are confusing. Himself most of all.

Distantly, he hears glass shatter and skitter across the floorboards. Muffled laughter echoes down the hallway. He recognizes that voice.

Jaime.

Wes throws himself out of bed and against the door, but it holds fast against him. It's locked from the other side. He turns to see the key has vanished from the nightstand. Annette must've taken it when she left.

"Goddamn it," he growls, pounding a fist against the door.

"What the hell are you doing?" Annette asks, clearly horrified. "You didn't say anything about—"

Glass bursts again, and cold spreads from the metal doorknob in his hand through his entire body. The only shot he has of getting out of here is beating down the door—or melting the lock. It takes only a minute for him to circle the doorknob in chalk and clumsily scrawl the chemical composition of bronze around it. Alchemical flame sputters weakly to life, but enough of the metal crumbles into caput mortuum that he can work the door open. The rest oozes onto the floor in thick, bubbling rivulets.

By the time he makes it into the hallway, it's too late. Through the windows above the front door, he can see Jaime, Annette, and Jaime's redheaded alchemist running to the car.

So it wasn't Margaret he heard come home at all.

Down the hall, the door to Evelyn's lab hangs ajar. He doesn't want to see what's inside. But he has to. He has to bear this. Wes feels as though he's moving through water as he approaches it and shoulders his way inside.

He stops dead at the gut punch of what he sees.

The alembics lie in shards on the floor. The unlocked drawers on the desk have been ripped out and cast aside. Shredded paper litters the ground, turning to paste in the silver liquid that spatters the floor like blood. The enchanted saddlecloth lies in tattered ribbons, and the spools of alchemized thread are gone. Everything he's worked on for the past two weeks, all the progress he made on deciphering Evelyn's book, all the equipment in the lab . . .

It's all ruined.

But worst of all is what's been written in chalk on the floorboards. One of the slurs is painfully familiar. It was cast after him and his sisters when they applied for jobs, or when he had trouble reading or focusing in his lessons. It echoed down the alleyways when he and his friends came home from the bars. The other is directed at Margaret and fills him with a rage he can't contain.

Jaime has gone too far now.

But who will care? No matter what paltry justice this town levies, it won't save their chances at winning, and it won't make them safe. The hala isn't the only monster in these woods. Humans are far worse. The hunt has never been for him and Margaret. It's never been about protecting this town or about money or safety or glory. It's not even about God. It's about the poison at the heart of this country.

The hunt is our oldest tradition. Our heritage as true-blooded New Albians, Jaime said on the night of registration.

Because what would it mean, really, for them—a Yu'adir girl and a Sumic city boy—to claim that heritage? People like Jaime would never accept it. And since he couldn't cheat or intimidate them out of the hunt, he sabotaged them.

And now he's going to pay for it. Wes will make him suffer.

He will devote his days to learning the exact composition of Jaime's life. It will be his obsession, his magnum opus, to destroy everything that matters to him. He will wither his orchards and tear down his mansion plank by plank. He will incinerate everything he owns until it's nothing but caput mortuum to scatter on the wind.

It feels so good to imagine it—more intoxicating than any wine, more tantalizing than any woman's touch. It feels like power. Jaime may be a true-blooded New Albian, but he's no alchemist. He's never touched the divine. He's never reached for anything beyond his limitations. He is painfully mortal and feebly unambitious.

And yet all Wes can see is Margaret's accusatory stare. *Is that really what you want to do with your life, your alchemy? You want to be just like Jaime—like the rest of them? You want to be a bully?*

"Fuck!" Wes finds a mostly intact hunk of an alembic and hurls it against the wall. It splinters and shimmers like rain as it falls. As much as he wants to, he can't stoop to Jaime's level. He can't bear to see Margaret disappointed in him again.

24

When Margaret returns from training, the first thing she notices is the horrible stillness of the house. Sunlight trickles in sluggishly from the high windows and patterns the floor. Nothing stirs save for the soft groan of the foundation in the wind and the dust that swirls around her as she shuts the front door.

She shrugs out of her coat and toes off her boots. "Wes?"

Almost immediately, he appears at the top of the stairs, backlit by the dimly burning sconces in the hallway. His sleeves are rolled to his elbows, the first few buttons of his rumpled shirt are undone, and his hair looks as though he's touched an electrical socket. It'd almost be endearing if not for the anger palpably radiating from him. She hasn't seen him like this since the night of the shooting competition, so unlike his usual carefree self.

"What's wrong?"

"Don't come upstairs."

As if that's an option now that she's seen him so rattled. "Why?"

He looks at her helplessly as she tosses her coat on the rack and begins to climb the staircase. She knows every crevice of this house. Where to place her feet on the tumbledown steps so they won't creak, exactly where the wood in the banister splinters so she won't cut her hand. But right now, it feels unfamiliar, like a wounded animal bristling at her touch. Wes intercepts her as soon as she reaches the second floor. Up close, he looks even angrier than he did before socking Jaime. Then, he was drunk and impulsive and righteous. Now, he's entirely sober, clear-eyed and quietly seething in a way that unsettles her.

"Margaret, seriously. Will you please go back downstairs?"

"You're being cryptic. Tell me what happened."

"I'm going to kill Jaime Harrington" is all he says.

She follows his brooding stare to the door of her mother's lab, which hangs open in grim invitation. "Is he tied up in there?"

"I wish." He extends an arm to block her path. "It's bad."

"There's nothing in there worse than what I've already seen." Margaret lowers his arm and nudges open the door. Her stomach bottoms out.

It *is* bad—worse than she was expecting.

Shards of glass alembics sparkle in a pool of red sunlight, and wickedly sharp pieces of the window gleam like sheets of ice on the sill. A grisly slurry of coincidentia oppositorum and caput mortuum spatters the floor, remnants from whatever transmutations Wes hadn't yet completed. It's far from the first time she has found this room torn apart, and she very much doubts it'll be the last. Equipment is replaceable. Even research is replaceable, considering nearly every alchemist can re-create their work from memory. But what stings the most are the words scrawled onto the floorboards with the same determined fervor as an alchemist drawing a transmutation circle.

Words she's heard whispered all her life but no one has dared say directly to her. Words she's sure Wes has endured many times before as well.

He appears at her shoulder. "I'm sorry."

"Why are you sorry?"

"Because you don't deserve to be treated this way."

"Neither do you."

Silent understanding passes between them. All her life, she's wanted to be small, to be unseen. But people like Jaime have never allowed it and they never will. *I'm so sick of it,* Wes told her the other night. *I'm sick of enduring it. Aren't you?*

She is. Jaime has circled her like a hungry dog for years, never biting hard enough to draw blood. A test of his power, a reminder of her powerlessness. But now that he's finally sunk his teeth in, she will not roll over for him so easily.

"How did this happen?" she asks, surprised by the steadiness of her voice.

"Well, um . . ." For the first time, she notices the faint smears of red on his lips and jaw—and just how ruffled his hair is. "Annette came over, and I guess I got a little distracted."

"I don't need to know the details." Margaret hates the hurt that creeps into her voice. A pang of jealousy drops into her stomach like a stone.

What should it matter to her what Wes does with his free time? It's not as though he's kept his interest in Annette a secret, even if she could have sworn . . . No, it doesn't matter now what she thought. She's pulled away from him too many times to expect that he would wait.

Margaret steels herself for him to make some joke or blithe remark, but he curls in on himself like a kicked dog. "I heard someone come in through the front door, but I assumed it was you. All of a sudden, she started acting strange—stranger than she was already acting, anyway—and stormed out of my room. She locked me inside, and by the time I melted the knob off the door, they were gone."

"You melted the knob off?"

"I'm sorry! I didn't know what else to do. I'll replace it."

Margaret heaves a thin sigh through her teeth. "I understand why Jaime would do something like this, but why Annette? She's never been openly cruel."

"No, I don't think she's cruel. Not on purpose, anyway." Wes frowns. "I've talked to her about Jaime before. She seems to think he'll ostracize her if she doesn't go along with whatever he says."

Over the years, Annette has never said anything overtly unkind to her. In fact, she's avoided saying much of anything to her at all. "That's probably true."

"I don't think she knew what he was planning. She sounded pretty upset when she saw the lab, but . . . God, maybe this is my fault. I ditched her on the beach the other night, and she didn't take it especially well."

"No," she says firmly. "This is not your fault. It's theirs."

He gives her a weak smile. "I guess so."

Margaret picks up a thick shard of glass, testing the weight of it. "Where does this leave us?"

Wes shoves his hands into his pockets and surveys the damage. "They destroyed everything I made. And all the equipment. *And* all the notes I was working on."

The edges of the broken glass press into her palm with a bright, throbbing ache. She drops it as blood beads on her skin. "So we're sunk."

"No." His mouth presses into a grim line. "We have four days, and I remember how to re-create everything. I can do it."

"Then I suppose we ought to get this cleaned up."

They work until night blankets the manor like a thick layer of snow. Once they sweep up the broken glass, they slosh a bucket of water onto the floor and scrub until there's no trace of the hateful message Jaime left behind. Margaret watches Wes's reflection ripple on the floorboards, both dreading and admiring the determination she sees in his eyes. She grips the key around her neck and squeezes. With only four days left, how much longer can she cling to her fantasy? No matter how skilled he is, no matter how hard he tries, he will fail. There is only one way to kill the hala.

And giving him that knowledge will destroy them both.

After two days, Wes emerges from the lab.

It happens when she least expects it, when she's leaving her room to take Shimmer out for a ride. They nearly bump into each other in the hallway, and for a moment, Margaret doesn't recognize him. He looks even more disheveled than usual. His hair stands up at impressive, stark angles, and—much to her shock—there's the faintest dusting of stubble on his chin. Ink and caput mortuum smudge his face, deepening the shadows beneath his eyes. He looks exhausted but somehow animated, as though some spirit has possessed him and leers out at her through the mask of his face. It almost frightens her.

"Oh!" He's apparently as shocked to see her as he would be a rare bird. "Margaret."

It's so inappropriate for the circumstances. So casual, as if he didn't disappear for two days and leave her alone with her dread. "Where have you been?"

"Working?"

She wishes that glib answer did not enrage her so much—and that her own anger didn't shame her. She wishes that she could make sense of the storm of emotions brewing within her and the sting of his sudden abandonment. "You smell like stale coffee, and you look like you haven't slept in days."

"Maybe I haven't," he says sourly. "You're in fine spirits today."

She shakes her head and swallows around the lump in her throat. "I'm going out."

Some of his irritation fizzles. "It's getting late."

"So?"

"I was hoping you could help me with something. I've remade everything, and I think I've almost figured out how to make something that will kill the hala."

Unease prickles along her spine. Can he truly have found another way? "Have you?"

"Yeah. Will you come look?"

"Of course." Her voice wavers.

As she follows him to the lab, Margaret once again feels like the scared little girl she is in all her nightmares. Her heart pounds as he pushes open the door. Inside, the air hangs as thick and still as fog. His notes paper the walls, each one frantically written and coffee-stained. A familiar manuscript lies open on the desk.

Margaret drinks in the scene with numb incomprehension. His lips are moving, but the meaning of his words fades into a hazy sound like the drone of bees. It's only when he furrows his brow and reaches out to her that she hears him say, "Margaret?"

She snaps back into herself. "Yes?"

"Well? What do you think?" His voice ripples as if they're underwater. It almost breaks her to see him looking at her with breathless anticipation, like a hound who has performed a particularly difficult trick. Does he truly want to please her?

"I'm sorry. What did you say?"

He looks put out. "I was saying I wanted to ask you about this problem I keep puzzling over. Why has no one been able to kill the last demiurge? If it was just a matter of making a strong enough bullet, someone should've done it by now, right? I figured there had to be some kind of lost art to it—something we'd forgotten in the last two hundred years. And since you said your mother was researching the hala, I figured she probably knew something about it. Maybe even uncovered what it was."

As Wes walks to the center of the room and kicks aside a precarious stack of books, the details of the room grow fuzzier. Her vision funnels tighter and tighter until all she can see is the transmutation circle at his feet, rendered with painstaking detail in chalk. A serpent consuming its own tail serves as the base of the array, surrounded by decisive dashes that look like the sun's rays.

Margaret would recognize that array anywhere.

It haunts her nightmares. It scars the floorboards of this very room. Its components fill all of her mother's encoded notebooks. The first step of the magnum opus, the formula that will decompose the physical body of a demiurge. With this, Wes could reduce the hala to ash and, if he deciphers the rest of her mother's research, purify its remains into the raw material of the philosopher's stone.

"I've been looking into this book for the past few weeks. It's full of these bizarre illustrations, but your mom wrote instructions. She must've spent years trying to extract the meaning from them."

How? How could he have found the only manuscript in her lab—perhaps the last one surviving in the world—that contains instructions on how to perform the magnum opus?

"She wrote everything in code, so it took me forever to figure it out. From what I pieced together, she explains how to draw three arrays—starting with this one. But she left the instructions unfinished, probably on purpose." He gestures at the empty innermost ring of the circle. "If only I knew what was missing, I think we'd be able to kill it. I was wondering if—"

"No," she says raggedly. "You can't do this. You can't look into this anymore!"

He looks utterly confused. "But . . ."

"Is this really what you've been doing all this time?"

"Partly, but I—"

Margaret drops to her knees beside the circle. She knows she must look unhinged by the wide-eyed way he's watching her, but she can't bring herself to care as she smears her palms through the array.

"Hey!" His voice lands somewhere between indignation and concern. Wes crouches beside her and catches her forearms. Her hands curl uselessly between them, white as bone and trembling. His gaze flickers from her chalk-caked palms to her face, and as her vision blurs with unshed tears, Wes speaks to her like she's an easily spooked pony. "Margaret, what is going *on*?"

"Destroy this. Now. Whatever you've found, burn it. Whatever you think you know, forget it. You have to. You have to promise me, Wes. Promise me!"

"This could be the only way for us to win."

"*Please*," she sobs.

"Okay, okay. I promise." Wes looks at her with helpless despair. Slowly, his grip on her slackens. "God. You're looking at me like I'm going to do something awful."

"You have no idea what kinds of things you're messing with. That book, this transmutation . . . It does things to people. It changes them."

"So you've seen someone attempt it before."

"Yes. My mother."

His lips part with surprise. Then, his eyes darken with anger. "What did she do?"

Margaret shakes her head. She feels her teeth chattering more than she hears them.

"You can tell me. Please, tell me."

"She didn't do anything. It was alchemy."

His expression morphs into skepticism, the same as it always does when she speaks ill of his precious science. How can she possibly make him understand? She *has* to make him understand, even if reopening this wound kills her. "About six years ago, my mother thought she completed the next phase of her research. The night she tested the second transmutation circle she deciphered from that book, I jolted awake because I heard this terrible sound. A scream."

At first, it was easy to believe she imagined it, that it was nothing but a fox screaming outside. But then it came again.

Maggie.

Even now, the memory of it makes shivers erupt all over her skin. It sounded like Evelyn had been rent open. Like she'd found David's body cold in his bed all over again.

"It was my mother, calling for me. She never called for me, and she never let me into her lab anymore, so I knew something had gone horribly wrong." Outside the safety of her bedroom, shadows made monsters of the furniture. There was the long and creeping one at the bottom of the staircase, the hunched one lurking on the porch, the one with gnarled fingers scraping on the windowpane. All of them seemed vicious and hungry that night. "When I opened the door to her lab, it was so hot, and it smelled awful. Like alchemy. Like blood."

It's been years since she has allowed herself to examine the details of the memory, and already, it feels as though she's scraping against the sun. Her chest constricts until she has to gasp for her next breath.

"I saw my mother lying there on the floor. For some reason, all I can remember clearly is her hair. She was always so composed, but it was everywhere and soaked in blood. I thought she was dead at first." The greasy shock of her hair was splayed around her like a halo. And beside her, the transmutation circle, carved in chalk and spattered with blood, glowed a sinister, lurid red. But worst of all was what smoked in the center of it.

Something blackened and misshapen, breathing as if through wracking sobs.

It wept a liquid as black as wet earth, as black as the sea at midnight. She can't remember the exact contours of it, no matter how hard she tries. She only remembers that it struck her with a terror that hollowed out her stomach, one that still makes her light-headed and panicky now.

"What did she make?" Wes asks hoarsely.

"I don't know. It was . . . this half-shaped *thing*. It wasn't anything at all. It felt evil. Like it wasn't meant to exist. Like she was being punished for even trying."

When she turned her mother over, her face was ashen, her eyes sunken and bruise-purple. *I was so close this time,* her mother rasped. *I could feel it. I could hear him.*

Come on, Mother, Margaret said, in a voice she had mastered over the last few months—a gentle, almost stern one her father often used before he left. *Let's get you to bed.*

She remembers how she dragged Evelyn to her feet, how she went limp against her like an overtired child clinging to their mother. "One moment, I was petrified. And then, suddenly, I didn't feel afraid anymore. I didn't feel anything anymore. Nothing felt real— not even me. I just did what I had to do. I got her out of the lab and into the bath. All she said, over and over again, was 'I'm sorry.'"

After that, Margaret went to the kitchen and filled a bucket with water. She climbed the rickety stairs and didn't look for any monsters in the dark. She went into the lab, still hazy with smoke, and emptied the whole bucket onto the floorboards. It sloshed over her bare feet and soaked into her nightgown when she knelt. She scrubbed and scrubbed until her hands and knees were raw and bleeding, until there wasn't a single trace of the alchemic reaction left.

"What did you do with . . . ?" Wes asks.

"I buried it in the woods."

His face pales.

"Do you understand now?" Margaret can't be sure if she sounds convincing or desperate. "Once, I believed all the lies. That alchemy is for the greater good. That it's the path to redemption or perfection or truth. But it isn't. It paves the road to hell. I saw it that night. It almost killed her."

"Margaret, what she did . . ." He hesitates. "I don't know *what* exactly she did, but whatever it was, it wasn't alchemy that possessed her to do it. It only enabled her. It was her choice to tamper with that transmutation, and if she knew it was that dangerous, she never should have exposed you to it or left you to deal with the aftermath."

But it wasn't her choice. Because if it was, if the woman her mother became crawled out from some rotten place within her, then Margaret doesn't know what to do. She doesn't know how to suck that poison out. Alchemy corrupted Evelyn. It had to have. Otherwise, what kind of person did that make her? What kind of mother?

She can't watch it happen again. Not to someone like Wes. "I need air."

Wes makes a strangled noise as she darts from the lab. She's drenched with cold sweat and her head swims and her rib cage pushes against her lungs like a corset. Even though the sun is beginning to set and the clouds are beginning to darken, she can't stay in this house for another minute. It will kill her; she knows it.

She grabs the gun mounted on her bedroom wall, pulls on her coat, and shoves open the front door. Margaret didn't call for him, but Trouble bounds to her side, his tail anxiously wagging. The sun languishes low on the horizon, oozing red light like a sliver of bloody meat. The wind hisses through the trees, calling her.

"Wait!" Wes shouts from the porch.

He's struggling with his shoes, only one sleeve of his trench coat on. The wind whips his hair against his face, then rips away his voice. She can only faintly hear him shout her name over the rattle of the dry, red leaves.

"Let's go," she whispers to Trouble.

He whines but follows close behind as the shadows in the tree line lengthen toward her and swallow her whole.

Margaret runs until she can't think of anything but the exhaustion in her limbs, until her entire body is buzzing with cold and adrenaline, until it feels like every breath shreds into her lungs like nettle. All that matters is that she is far, far away from that house and all the memories she wishes she could scrub away like a chalk circle on the floorboards.

When her legs threaten to give out, she collapses onto a rock. Trouble, panting hard, settles down beside her. Loyal and steadfast as ever, he's the only one who hasn't left her and the only one who won't. He lays his head in her lap and sighs out a warm, relieved breath against her hands. He didn't deserve to run so hard for her sake.

Margaret bends over and places a kiss on the top of his head. "I'm sorry. Are you okay?"

The trees stand sentinel around them, shivering in the wind. The light that filters through the canopy is thick and bloodred. On some level, she knows she made a mistake coming out here alone. She's seen what kind of damage the hala can inflict. But these woods were once her home—her sanctuary. While they haven't been hers for weeks, the manor feels as dangerous as any beast right now. She's glad of the miles she has put between them.

Margaret lifts her hair from the back of her neck and leans back until the cold of the stone beneath her seeps into her skin. She lets her hair fall and pool in the grass. Overhead, the brightest stars wink to life in the violet sky, each one shining cold and ruthless silver. Her eyes flutter closed.

And then the telltale smell of sulfur begins to rise around her.

Margaret, Margaret, Margaret.

She lurches upright.

The temperature plummets. When she shudders out a breath, it mists in front of her face and the world behind it shimmers like a mirage. With the smell of alchemy thickening around her and her worst memories picked raw, she's so addled she can hardly tell what's in her head or not.

Coming, coming, coming.

A growl rumbles in Trouble's throat, and his hackles rise. The fallen leaves hiss and rattle.

Here. The sound echoes all around her. *Here, here, here.*

A branch snaps like bone. Her vision shivers again. Somewhere in the thicket, a set of blank, marble-round eyes gleam in the darkness.

With only two days until the Cold Moon, its magic has never felt so potent—or so malevolent. It hums over her skin like electricity.

Hide, she thinks. She has to hide.

She flips the safety catch on her rifle and chokes up on Trouble's collar. A few meters off, there's a dip in the earth that leads down to a creek bed dammed with leaves. It's the only shelter they have out here, unless she wants to wedge herself into the flame-hollowed trunk of a redwood. If it finds her there, she'll have nowhere to run.

"Trouble, come," she whispers.

She slides down the embankment, wincing at the twist of her ankle. When she hits the bottom, cold earth seeps into her back, and her boots sink into the muddy creek. Black water burbles slowly around the soles like blood from a wound. Over the sound of its murmuring, all she can hear is the hammering of her heart and Trouble's labored breathing beside her. Margaret gently closes her hand around his muzzle. She tips her head back, if only to avoid his offended look.

Finally, there's complete silence.

She sighs shakily in relief—just as a creeping swath of decay curls around the embankment like long fingers. It dissolves the earth like fire licking across kindling, like rot fissuring an overripe fruit. Shining liquid puddles in the furrows until it dribbles down, down, and patters onto the top of her head.

Here.

Margaret bites down on her tongue to stifle a whimper. Another branch cracks in the clearing. Caput mortuum showers her like ash from a wildfire sky.

Please leave, she thinks. *Please, please, please.*

She dares to look up. It is staring directly at her. Margaret scrabbles backward, strangling a cry of fear. The hala stands perfectly still, but the trees seem to arch away from it, groaning and crackling like stiff joints. Its gaze, solid white and miles-deep, sucks her in until her thoughts sharpen into a horrible, metallic shrill.

Its black lips part to reveal a crooked grin of teeth. Trouble growls.

"Trouble, stay!"

She fumbles with her gun, but it may as well be a twig in her hands. What good will an unalchemized bullet do? It's not even the full moon. But if she does nothing, she will die, and where will that leave Wes? Swearing, she raises the scope of her rifle to her eye. Margaret fires, and the bullet shears through the fox's shoulder, just shy of a vital point. It doesn't scream or bleed, but a shudder wracks its body as if its bones are realigning themselves.

She staggers back a step and trips over a root. She strikes the ground, spattering herself with cold creek water. Before she can catch her breath, Trouble tears up the embankment, baying and snarling.

The hala doesn't seem to move at all. It is there, and then it is not. She only sees it again when its teeth sink into Trouble's shoulder. He yelps, thrashing as he goes down.

"Trouble!"

Her hands tremble, but she keeps the crosshairs trained on the hala. She doesn't think, just acts. She pulls the trigger again and again and again, until she empties the magazine.

By the time the smoke clears, the hala is gone. A few wisps of white fur float on the breeze. Over the ringing in her ears and the distant roll of the thunder, she isn't sure if the whimpering is hers or Trouble's.

Trouble.

He lies motionless, his copper fur like a smear of blood in the grass. She throws down her gun.

"No, no, no."

Margaret repeats it like a prayer as she crawls to him. God has never heard her before, no matter how much she begged. After what her mother failed to do in her lab, after everything she's endured in his name, she's not sure he's even out there or if he cares about them at all. If the Katharists are right, they are imperfect humans, reflections of an imperfect god. What interest could they hold to him? But if he has any kindness, any scrap of it, he'll let her keep Trouble. Just this one thing—the only thing that's truly hers.

Margaret lays her head on him and lets out a strangled sob as she feels his belly rise tremulously against her ear. Silver liquid and blood dribble from the ragged puncture wounds on his shoulder, but he is alive. Thank God, he's alive. The wound is deep enough that she'll need to give him stitches, but it's nothing she can't handle herself.

"Trouble," she whispers. "Are you alright?"

His tail gives a weak, answering thump against the earth. For the first time in what feels like years, she weeps. In guilt and fear and *relief.* The hala let him go.

Rain begins to fall, shearing through the bare branches overhead. In the distance, she hears something barreling through the woods. It's too clumsy to be the hala circling back. It sounds like an entire herd of deer trampling through the underbrush.

"Margaret!"

Wes.

"Margaret?"

She buries her nose in Trouble's scruff. Now that she's scraped raw, now that she's bared her soul to him, nothing remains but a feeble, stubborn anger. Anger that he dredged up her mother's work. Anger that she was too much of a coward to trust him or face his compassion. Anger at herself because she can't hold her feelings back anymore. With everything crumbling around her, how can she maintain her walls? She doesn't want them anymore.

She doesn't want to be alone.

"I'm here," she calls softly. "I'm here."

25

As Wes sprints toward the sound of Margaret's voice, all he can envision is that *thing* and its horrible eyes. Its teeth sinking into her neck. Her golden hair drenched in a spreading pool of blood. Fear and rage both sting the backs of his eyes. If anything happened to her . . .

No, he can't lose someone again.

Panting, he tears through the woods until he finds her kneeling in a clearing with her arms around Trouble and her rifle abandoned in the creek bed. He grabs it, then lays it down beside her.

"Margaret." He's never heard his own voice like this, ragged and desperate. "Thank God you're alright. I was so—"

When she turns to look at him, there's lightning crackling in her eyes. It takes him aback. "What are you doing out here? It's dangerous."

"Clearly!" Over the past three weeks, Wes has watched her withdraw time and time again. He's so sick of letting her push him away. He's so tired of watching her drown. "I heard you blasting something full of bullets. What the hell happened? And why did you run from me?"

Thunder rumbles in the distance. Margaret doesn't answer him. As he kneels beside her, shuddering at the mud squelching beneath him, he sees that her hands are covered in a pale liquid that sparkles like crushed diamonds. Coincidentia oppositorum. It oozes from a wound at Trouble's shoulder. His stomach bottoms out. "Is he going to be alright?"

"Yes." She strokes Trouble's ears restlessly. "The hala bit him."

It's made an alchemical reaction of her dog is what it's done, and they're lucky it didn't do worse. "We need to get you both home. I can make something to help him with the pain."

Margaret doesn't move, even as the rain falls harder. She looks so frail like this, the rainwater glistening on her skin and plastering her coat to her body. He wants to reach for her, to shake her loose of whatever spell has taken hold of her. He wants to scoop her up and carry her back, if only to feel her heart beating against his. But there's a whole ocean between them he cannot cross.

"Margaret," he says quietly. "We've already established that I'm thick, so you're going to need to explain this to me. You're angry with me. I want to do better, but I can't if you won't talk to me. So please, talk to me. Please don't shut me out again."

"You looked just like her. These past few days, you've acted just like her. You care about abstract things, your ideals and your ambitions. But do you see the people right in front of you?"

It stings, admittedly, because it sounds like a question Mad would ask him. That means it's probably got a core of truth to it. "Of course I do. I see you."

She flinches, and at last he knows he's hit on it. "I told you I would do anything in my power to help you achieve your dreams. Do you remember?"

The memory of that night is still hazy, as though it's trapped behind a rain-streaked window. But that much he remembers. "As well as I can."

"Then listen to me when I tell you that no good will ever come of what you've unearthed. You want to help people, and all that research can do is hurt."

"Then I'll burn it all the moment we're home if that's what you want. I don't care about the research. I only care about it if it'll help us win—if it'll help you, and well . . . I guess I've made a mess of that. I'm sorry. I've never been good at giving you what you need."

"That's not true, Wes." Margaret stares resolutely at Trouble. "But you're correct that the transmutation circle you drew, once it's complete, will be able to kill the hala. That manuscript is the only record of how to do it, as far as I know."

"Oh." Wes isn't sure he wants to know the answer, but he has to ask. "I know you said you didn't know what your mother made that night. But what was it supposed to be?"

"It was supposed to be the prima materia. She performed what she thought was the second step of the magnum opus. What you were attempting to do is the first."

The magnum opus: the great work. The creation of the philosopher's stone. With it, it's said an alchemist can live forever—and create matter from nothing like a god.

"And I take it you'd rather not let anyone see it through to its end," he says.

For a moment, he thinks she will shut the door on him again. She has that look in her eyes he knows all too well. There are times when a girl wants you to chase her and times when she wants you to leave. And as much as it'll gut him, he will walk away if she asks him. Her expression softens. "That's right. I would do anything to stop it.

"My mother wasn't always the way she is. But when I was about six years old, my brother fell ill and died in his sleep. After that, my mother threw herself into her work. She spent all her time acquiring and translating ancient apocryphal texts. Once she found *Mutus Liber,* she was able to piece together the process for the creation of the stone."

The philosopher's stone is a footnote in most textbooks, relegated to background reading or a bullet point on a list of alchemical taboos. Ancient alchemists devoted themselves to research on the prima materia—*the divine spark buried in the darkness of matter,* one of his teachers had intoned—with the same intensity of an ascetic saint. They believed distilling that divine substance and fashioning it into the philosopher's stone was the key to the prison of materiality.

No one had ever succeeded, though, and most who tried went mad. Eventually, the Katharist church decreed it a heretical pursuit, an offense against God himself.

Wes can almost understand how the quest for the stone would drive someone to single-minded self-destruction. Only the most desperate or power-hungry people would ever hope to achieve such a thing. "I would've expected your mother to be more pragmatic. Most people say it's a myth. Why would she devote her life to something like that?"

"Because she believes it can bring my brother back."

"What?"

If the stone can theoretically create anything, down to the very last atom, who's to say it couldn't bring somebody back from the dead—or more accurately, re-create them from nothing but memory? Disgust sours his stomach. Even God couldn't get humans right. Would whatever the stone made even *be* human, or would it be an empty vessel without a soul? A mass of carbon wearing her brother's face?

"It became her obsession. I think she blamed herself for what happened. She stopped eating and sleeping most days, and then she stopped coming out of her office for anything at all. My father tried to shield me from the worst of it, but I don't think he could bear it alone. He left, and he never came back for me. He never even wrote."

What kind of parent would leave his daughter alone with someone like that? "Margaret, you don't have to spend your life waiting for someone to come back. You don't have to stay anymore."

She hugs herself around the middle. With the water pearling on her eyelashes, he can't tell if she's crying. "But I do. I have to believe she isn't changed forever. I can get her back. I can't give up on my own mother. Would you?"

"No, I wouldn't. But not because I'm holding on to who she used to be."

"I'm doing it because I love her."

"I know," he says, even though he can't understand why. "But she hurt you."

"Not on purpose. Never on purpose." Her voice wavers. Although the rain has begun to slow, both of them are soaked through. Rainwater drips from the ends of her hair. Her lips are pale, and her eyes are feverishly bright. "I don't even know if she remembers the night she tried to perform the second step. But I can't stop remembering. Every time something reminds me of it, I feel like I'm in that room again. I feel like I stop existing except for how afraid I am. I'm sorry you keep having to see it happen."

"Don't. Please don't apologize, Margaret. *I'm* sorry." It makes a terrible kind of sense, and he wants to shake himself for not noticing the pattern sooner. Never has he felt so useless in all his life. Never has he so acutely felt the insufficiency of the word "sorry." He wants nothing more than to touch her, but he can't risk frightening her away again. "Your mother, she's—well, you know better than me how she is. But what happened to you, what happened to her . . . None of that was your fault, and it wasn't your job to keep her afloat. You were just a kid. You deserved to be taken care of, and someone should've done something. You deserve to be loved."

For a horrible moment, she looks at him as though he's uttered something unthinkable. "I'm not so sure. Some days, I thought I was invisible. Eventually, I learned how to convince myself that I was—that I didn't exist at all. I think that's the only reason I'm still here."

"You're weren't invisible, Margaret. And you're not now. You did what you had to do to survive." He lays his hand in the mud puddling between them, the tips of his fingers brushing hers. "I don't think alchemy is good or evil, just as much as I think people aren't good or evil. There's something within me—within all of us—that could turn. God, when my dad died, I would've done anything to get him back. Maybe if I'd known about the stone when it happened, I would've tried it, too. But I know he's gone, and all I have are the people still here. I swear to you, I won't abandon them."

He prays she hears what he is too much of a coward to say. *I won't abandon you.*

When she says nothing, he crosses the space between them to twine his fingers in hers. Margaret jerks away from him and snatches her gun from the ground. As she stands, Wes watches something within her give way, like a dam finally breaking.

And then she raises her gun, aiming it right between his eyes.

"H-hey, watch where you're pointing that thing."

"I am."

He raises his hands in surrender but doesn't move from where he kneels at her feet. "You're kind of scaring me."

"Good."

Wes opens his mouth to reply, but every word he knows escapes him the moment the clouds part. The sky is impossibly bright tonight. Beneath the near-full moon, the water droplets falling from the leaves and the ends of Margaret's hair shine a glistering silver. Just like that, she is dripping with starlight. She's more brilliant than he ever could've imagined.

It's then that he realizes she is crying. Margaret lifts her chin and smears away the tear tracks with the back of her free arm's sleeve. Mud streaks her cheek in thick, black lines. She's terrifying and wild, like one of the aos sí, and the sight of her punches a hole straight through his chest. He's left breathless and reeling, and this feeling . . .

It's not only that she's terrifying and wild. It's not that he wants her in spite of her plainness or that she's driven him mad or ensorcelled him. It is so much more than that. How could he have been so blind for so long? Margaret Welty is the most beautiful woman he has ever seen, and he is completely, hopelessly in love with her.

Lord, he is in so much trouble.

"You told me our dreams live and die together," Margaret says.

"So here is mine. There won't be any more alchemists like Evelyn Welty in the world."

"I'm not smart enough to be like her."

"I'm serious."

"I know it. I swear to you, if I ever even think of doing something like your mom did, I'll paint the target for you myself." Wes rises unsteadily to his feet, and although she keeps her rifle trained on his forehead, he grasps the barrel. He can feel her trembling down the length of it. Carefully, he lowers it from his face. "Okay?"

Margaret's shoulders slump. Her cold mask shatters, and her gun clatters to the earth between them. "Okay."

She flings her arms around his waist. Wes grunts in surprise as they collide, but it's the most natural thing in the world to enfold her. He slides one hand up the back of her jacket to pull her closer and cradles her head with the other, tangling his fingers into the hair at the nape of her neck. Through the cling of his sopping wet shirt, he feels how warm she is. He feels the beating of her heart against his. He presses his lips to her temple and breathes in the smell of rainwater and earth.

He has to tell her. Now that he's almost lost her, now that he's held her like this, he can't silently bear the weight of it much longer. He wants so much more than he has allowed himself to imagine. He wants *her,* desperately and entirely. But for now, with her safe and whole against him, it's enough.

26

By the time Margaret finishes cleaning and stitching Trouble's wound, Wes appears in the doorway of her mother's lab carrying two earthenware mugs of tea. Although he's toweled off his hair, it's still damp and as wild as it's ever been. It begs to be smoothed into place. He sits cross-legged on the floor beside her and presses a mug into her hands. The steam wafting from it smells richly of cinnamon and orange peel and brown sugar.

"Thank you."

"Sure thing." He blows out a breath through his lips like a horse. "Hey, Margaret?"

No one has ever said her name like that, slow and deliberate, like he wants to taste every syllable. She waits.

"Since we're clearing the air . . ." He trails off, tipping his head back as though he can find the words he needs written on the ceiling. "Me and Annette . . . I don't know what I was thinking."

Her stomach drops. "It's fine, Wes."

"No, it's not fine. I've given you both the runaround." He places his mug between them and clasps his hands on his knees. "When my dad died, it felt like the world shattered. All of a sudden, my mom had five kids to wrangle on top of her job. Christine was a complete wreck since she was closest to Dad, so after the funeral, Mad and I decided we were going to hold it down together. For me, I guess that meant shutting a part of myself off. It was too scary to confront how much I missed him, and I thought it would be better if I was the one who was fine—the one my mom didn't have to worry about."

Once, Wes told her, *I have to be cavalier, or I'll lose my mind.* Now she sees what exactly he's been running from.

"It kind of backfired on me, since now Mad doesn't think I take anything seriously and apparently my mom noticed what I was trying to do, but . . . They're my family, so I'm pretty good at ignoring the things they tell me that I don't want to hear. But ever since I've met you, you've never let me get away with a goddamn thing.

"You've chipped away at me, but when I saw you out there tonight, it was like everything I've ever tried to keep myself from feeling came back with a vengeance." Wes hesitates. "I've messed up so many times. I've thrown away almost every chance I had to be genuine with you. I've hurt you. But you still trust me. You still let me in. You still push me to be better."

Margaret feels strangely light-headed, like she has lost her grasp of language entirely.

He smiles at her, rueful and hopeful all at once. "I've been a fool, haven't I?"

No, she thinks. *But I have.*

Maybe she should have realized it before now. Maybe he's already told her a thousand times, in the way she catches him watching her, in the way he looked exultant at the end of her gun, in the way he has fought for her time and time again.

But she doesn't want his confession.

Would she even believe him? Would it change anything, when it comes time for him to leave Wickdon for good? She fears what will happen if she allows herself to take hold of this tentative happiness blooming within her. If she doesn't let him make it real, then she can't lose it. She can't lose him.

"Don't," she whispers.

Relief and despair cycle over his face so quickly, she can't pinpoint exactly where he lands. It stings more than she expected, but to comfort him would be as good as her own confession. But as he searches her gaze, he seems to find what he needs. His expression softens. "Right. The more pressing issue is that the hunt's in two days. We *are* sunk, aren't we?"

They are. Unless, of course, they take the most obvious path forward.

"No," she says. "We're not."

"What do you mean?"

Margaret carries her tea to her mother's desk and opens the topmost drawer, where a stack of papers conceals the lock to its false bottom. Her hands tremble as she slides the chain from around her neck and takes the key in hand. She twists the key in its lock and lifts the wood panel from the drawer.

Inside, there's a leather-bound journal—one that contains the missing piece of the transmutation circle, the last of her mother's secrets. Evelyn entrusted its location to her; should anything happen to her, she asked for it to be destroyed. It's just as well that her life's work will die with her. There are no alchemists in the world who are pure-intentioned enough to deserve the knowledge of the philosopher's stone.

But Wes is different.

Margaret brushes a layer of dust from the cover, which is stitched with gold and embossed with a bloodred image of an ouroboros. Wes watches her as she approaches, his expression foggy behind the steam curling from his mug.

"What is that?"

"You said you thought there was something missing from the transmutation circle you drew. You're right. These are my mother's complete research notes. You'll find what you need in here. It explains exactly how to perform the transmutation that will kill a demiurge."

He goes slack-jawed. "No. After everything you've told me, I can't take that."

"You have to."

"No, I don't."

"Then I *want* you to." She holds it out in the empty space between them. "I can't punish you for my own fears. I won't let your family suffer because I was too much of a coward to trust you. If there's any shot that we can win, then we have to take it."

"You'd really trust me with this?"

"Yes." Margaret presses the book against his chest. "I would."

Wes hesitantly cradles it against him. "You know that I can't just engrave a bullet with a transmutation circle, right? I can't activate the array from a distance."

Killing it in close quarters is far from ideal, but she'll manage. "That's fine. If you put it on a hunting knife, I can do it."

"Do you know how to perform a transmutation? Because if you don't . . ."

Then he will have to be the one who delivers the final blow. The very thought of Wes anywhere near that beast sends a bolt of panic through her. "You can't. The hala will kill you."

"I'll be fine." She can hear the fear tangled up in his usual breezy tone. "You'll just need to hold it down for me."

She lowers herself onto the floor beside him. They kneel in the center of the room, just above the scarred remains of her mother's failed transmutation circle. Margaret has always known what the hunt entailed. She's never been afraid to die. But tonight, with less than forty-eight hours before the starting gun goes off, every disastrous possibility feels too real.

Losing. And worse still, losing him.

"This is insanity."

"Maybe." He holds her gaze steadily. "Are you sure you really want to do this? What if your mom doesn't come back?"

"Then we'll find someone else who can teach—"

"I don't care about that," he says softly. "What does it mean for you?"

It's a fate too cruel to entertain. But it's been almost four months, far longer than Evelyn promised. Maybe whatever duty tethered her here has snapped at last. "If she doesn't come back, then she doesn't. I'm doing this for your family. For us."

His lips part, and his eyes go misty with the emotion she has forbidden him to name. It's there and gone before he turns away from her, scrubbing at his unshed tears with his knuckles. "Damn. Sweeping the other day really kicked up all the dust in here, huh?"

She lays a hand on his back. "So it did."

Wes sucks in a breath through his teeth, his shoulders slowly rising and falling as he composes himself. When he looks at her again, his dark eyelashes are matted and damp. "Well. Let's take a look at what your mom's left for us, shall we?"

He places her mother's journal on the floor and cracks it open with fearful reverence. Her mouth goes dry as she takes in her mother's familiar, frantic handwriting. Wes takes one look at it and laughs. It is a breathless, bitter sound. "I think your mother has a dark sense of humor."

"What do you mean?"

"It's all in code. This one's completely different from the other book. I'm sorry. I still don't think I can do anything with—where are you going?"

Margaret swipes a pen from the desk, then snatches the book from him. With careful, uncertain strokes, she inscribes a single Yu'adir word.

Wes runs his fingers over the page when she hands it back to him. "What is that?"

"The cipher. What God used to make the world."

Davar.

They spend the night holed up in the library, piecing together page after page of her mother's encrypted journal. They barely sleep, except for a few stolen moments when Margaret blinks out of unconsciousness and finds her head resting inches away from his on the table. She has to bite down on her urge to trace the soft line of his jaw and comb the hair back from his forehead. Especially when he jolts awake and smiles at her blearily. Especially when he still looks at her as though he wants to tell her the most beautiful secret she's ever heard.

It takes them until dawn to decode it, and when at last they finish, they're left with a codex of symbols—and the precise arrangement of them around a circle ringed by a serpent devouring its own tail.

"You should go to sleep," Wes tells her. He's begun carefully painting the transmutation circle onto the hilt of her hunting knife. "I can finish this on my own."

She doesn't want to leave him. It feels as though they've been bound together with some unbreakable thread overnight, but she does as he asks. Exhaustion has caught up to her, and with the hunt tomorrow, she needs all the rest she can get.

Hours later, she awakens to the steady patter of rain. The clouds are so thick, she can't tell what time it is. Downstairs, she finds Wes hunched over the card table in the sitting room, surrounded by haphazard piles of their notes. "What time is it?"

He startles, turning toward her blearily. "Almost four."

She can't remember the last time she slept so late. "Did you sleep at all?"

"Some." Wes turns the hunting knife in his hands over and over again. The blade flashes white, silver, white until she meets her own gaze in the steel. He offers it to her. "It's finished."

The detail on the hilt is breathtakingly intricate, every scale of the ouroboros painted red as blood. In her hands, it's a mean weapon. In his, it's almost divine. She can hardly believe that *this* will be what kills the hala. That these symbols inscribed here denote what a mythical beast is made of—what Wes's magic will incinerate into ash. She traces each one with a delicate touch.

"How are you feeling?" he asks.

"Fine." She places the knife back on the table. "And you?"

"I'm exhausted. A little nervous. But I'm ready." Both of them know it's more complicated than that, but Margaret supposes they're becoming adept at this game of meaning more than they say aloud. "Well. Shall we burn the evidence?"

While Wes gathers up their notes, Margaret stacks kindling in the hearth and coaxes the banked fire back to life. When at last it whooshes up the brick sides of the flue, she settles back onto her haunches and sighs at the sweet caress of its heat against her face.

Wes passes her the papers. "Care to do the honors?"

She hesitates for only a moment before she tosses them into the flames. As the fire sputters and hisses, the notes scatter like fallen leaves, then blister. He stands with his hands in his pockets, his expression unreadable in the flickering light. It's only when the last scrap of it has crumbled to ash that the tightness in her chest loosens, borne away by the smoke.

"What now?" she asks.

"We should celebrate."

"Celebrate?"

"Yeah, celebrate." Wes crosses the room to where her father's old record player is collecting dust. "You know. Unwind, relax, enjoy our last night on the material plane."

"That's not funny."

"It *is* funny." He rummages through a cardboard box until he finds a bright sleeve and slips out the vinyl inside. Setting it on the turntable, he adjusts the needle until crooning horns come crackling out of the bell. She recognizes the song—one of her father's favorites. "Do you even know how to relax?"

Margaret makes a face. He thinks he is so clever. "Of course I do. You make it very difficult, though."

"Then humor me. Why don't you make yourself comfortable?" Mischief glints like a blade in his eyes. "Or dance with me?"

Never in a million years will she dance. Margaret glowers as she perches on the edge of an armchair. "I'm very comfortable here."

"Good." Wes busies himself with extinguishing all the lights and raiding the bar cart tucked into the corner. With a self-satisfied *aha!*

he brandishes a bottle of scotch. It fills her with bitter nostalgia to be sitting in this room, listening to this music, while Wes uncorks the prize liquor her father never returned for. Wes beams at her in that goofy, boyish way she can't help smiling at. With affected pomp, he says, "Can I offer you a drink, madam?"

Some of her apprehension ebbs out of her. Maybe she can bear it if he's here to chase away the memories. "You may."

He pours them each a dram of scotch. It glitters like amber in the bottom of their crystal glasses, refracting the firelight, and when he presses the drink into her hand, she inhales the painfully familiar smell of it. Peat and woodsmoke.

"I haven't had this in years," she says.

"But you've had it. You're full of surprises."

"Once. Have you?"

He sinks into the armchair beside hers and kicks his feet up on the coffee table. "Please. This bottle is worth more than my life. I have to say, I'm glad I've projected the kind of image that makes you think I'd drink scotch and not cheap beer."

Margaret sighs with fond exasperation. As she swirls the scotch in her glass, it strikes her just how surreal this is. She feels as though she's peering through a window, watching another Margaret live the happy, domestic life she never envisioned for herself. It never occurred to her that she could exist outside her mother's shadow—or that she'd ever want to.

Yet here she is, drowning in firelight and the deep brown of Wes's eyes. It's almost romantic. Before she can let herself get maudlin, he leans over and says, "Shall we toast?"

"To what?"

"Winning."

"To winning," she echoes.

Their glasses clink together. As they drink, he watches her over the brim with an expression she cannot decipher. A knot of tension pulls pleasantly taut within her.

"What?" she asks.

"Nothing." His voice is as warm as the scotch in her belly.

"It's unlike you to hold your tongue."

"Only because you asked me to. And I'll do it because I don't want to push you, even though it's killing me a little whenever you look at me because I can *see* exactly what you'd say back, and—why?" He sets down his glass on the table emphatically, his brow pinched in consternation. "Why won't you let me say it?"

Margaret can't remember the last time anyone has told her they loved her. She can't bear the thought of those three words. They plunk into her gut like dropped stones, each one ringing hollower than the last. She doesn't want to see him hurt when the skepticism fills her eyes. She doesn't want to hear herself choke when she tries to say it back. It's for the best that they care for one another silently, that they remain in the safe realm of plausible deniability.

Love terrifies her. And yet, she doesn't want to dissuade him. Not when he's looking at her so desperately. Not when she doesn't want him to give up on her.

"Because I don't want to call you a liar."

"I don't have to speak," he says after a moment, "if that makes a difference."

A dull ache begins at the center of her chest, then unfurls like ink dropped into water. It's the drink making her face feel so hot. Even though it was barely a sip, it must be. "Yes. I think it does."

The arm's breadth of space between their chairs feels impossibly huge. Wes watches her like a coyote, hungry and skittish. He stands, and although she's not sure when she moved, she's on her feet, too. He closes the gap between them in a single stride, grabbing her by the waist. He walks her backward until she bumps into the writing desk that overlooks the window. As he helps lift her, Margaret swipes aside the books and papers in her way. They hit the floor with a *thud* she barely registers.

Once she's settled, Wes parts her knees and stands between them. His warmth rolls over her, and as he drinks her in, the ravenous intensity of his gaze melts into quiet reverence. The firelight paints his features in gold and washes his irises the same red as strong-steeped tea. She can read his every thought right now. He wears no pretense, no swagger, no gilt armor.

It's just him, earnest and hers.

Her stomach flutters with nerves as he removes the clip from her hair, letting it cascade over her shoulders. Wes twines his fingers into it and kisses her forehead, then her nose. Finally, his mouth brushes against hers with such tenderness, her breath hitches.

He is far gentler than he is in her fantasies. Worshipful, even, like she may shatter or bolt if he doesn't handle her with the utmost care. His hands set every inch of her ablaze as he trails them along her jaw and down her ribs until they settle on her knees. He traces restless circles against them, and every barely there caress is tantalizing, leaving her light-headed and mortifyingly eager. She has waited so long for this, and it is exactly as he said.

He doesn't need words to tell her how he feels.

"Wes," she whispers, her voice thick with emotion.

He takes the opportunity to slide his tongue past her lips. He tastes exactly as she imagined he would: like black coffee and scotch. Wes kisses her like he means to take his time with her, to torment and savor her. It's maddening how it deepens the ache building within her instead of easing it. Weeks of wanting him have consumed all her patience and rationality. Margaret grabs fistfuls of his hair, and his answering moan reverberates through her chest. It emboldens her, this strange new power she has over him.

She glides her hands lower, down his chest and along the plane of his stomach until she palms the cold metal of his belt buckle. She fiddles with it until it comes loose, clattering like ice in a tumbler glass, but her triumph is short-lived. Now that she has done it, she doesn't know what she plans to do next. Wes pulls back enough that she can see his widened eyes swallowing her up along with all the light. He looks both panicked and game.

"Um . . ." His voice is gravelly with desire, even as his face goes pink. "I should tell you I've never actually—"

"Me neither."

She yanks him in by his lapels and captures his lips with hers again. He rewards her with another low sound at the back of his throat and drags her closer. His palm is firm against the small of her back; his hips press insistently into hers. With his free hand, he finds the hem of her skirt and hikes it up until the chill of the room sighs across her bare skin. His fingers ghosting up the inside of her thigh draw a noise from her she didn't think herself capable of making. She feels him smirk against her mouth, the smug bastard.

And then Trouble bays.

Margaret startles. Their teeth clack together. The lock twists in the front door.

Wes jerks away as if she burned him, and the horror that lights his eyes is a mirror of her own. There's only one other person who has the house key.

Which means her mother has returned at last.

27

In her pressed suit, Evelyn Welty cuts a stark figure against the soft, warm light of the sitting room. Although she's narrow as a branch, her seething presence fills the entire room. Once Wes recovers from the initial shock, the first thing he notices about Evelyn is that she looks alarmingly like Margaret. She wears her golden hair pulled back at the nape of her neck, and behind her glasses, her eyes are as round as her daughter's. But where Margaret's are the color of whiskey, Evelyn's are the color of dark, strong rum. He watches her expression morph from surprise to disgust to anger in the span of a heartbeat.

Wes drinks in the scene through her eyes. Margaret, still balanced on the edge of the desk, her hair loose and wild. Him, equally debauched, fervently working to refasten his belt. A record jauntily spinning, a fire merrily crackling, and two crystal glasses sparkling with scotch.

He can't even say it isn't what it looks like.

He sputters, "Master Welty," at the same time Margaret chokes out, "Mother."

They've rendered Evelyn speechless, but her anger is a palpable thing, poised against the back of his neck like an executioner's blade. It's painfully obvious now where Margaret learned to stare a man down like she's skinning him alive.

Beside him, Margaret blanches. Her teeth chatter despite the heat from the fire. He should be mortified—and he is. But the sting of his embarrassment is swallowed up by the cold torrent of his anger, blacker than the ocean.

Where the hell have you been? he wants to shout. *Why weren't you here for her?*

At last, Evelyn finds her voice. "Get out. Now."

She speaks to him like a stray dog, but he swallows his pride. For Margaret's sake and his own, he has to maintain his composure. Wes rakes a hand through his hair, but there's no hope of smoothing over what Margaret has done to it. "Master Welty, please let me explain. My name is Weston Winters, and I'm—"

"I don't care if you're the goddamn president. I want you out of my house." Evelyn kicks the front door shut behind her. Trouble barks as he slinks around the edges of the room, his tail wagging anxiously.

Margaret collects herself enough to shush him, but as she eases back onto her feet, her voice is meek and far-off. "He's a prospective student. There's nowhere else for him to go in town, so he's been living here."

"He's been living here," Evelyn echoes. The detachment in her voice frightens him worse than the alternative. And then she laughs, a humorless, staccato burst of sound that sets his blood to ice. "You let a stranger live in the house without me here? How naive can you be?"

Margaret shrinks away from the scorn in her mother's voice. She's folding herself up smaller and smaller, disappearing before his eyes. She has none of her usual fire, none of the boldness of the girl he kissed or the ferocity of the girl who pointed her gun at him.

"As for you—enough, Trouble!"

Trouble rumbles again but obediently curls up by the fireplace, his eyes locked on Evelyn. She rubs her temples and hisses out a frustrated sigh.

"As for you, I'm not taking any students, which my daughter should've already told you. I expect you can find your way out. You've imposed on her hospitality enough already, don't you think?" Evelyn grabs her suitcases and stalks toward the staircase. "Margaret, come here. We need to talk."

When Margaret speaks, it's almost too quiet to hear. "No."

Evelyn looks at her daughter like she's never seen her before. "No?"

"You can't send him away."

"You're acting like a child. Come upstairs, and we'll discuss this like adults."

A memory resurfaces, and suddenly, he's six years old again, glued to the half-working radio in the living room. Almost every night, he would refuse to go to sleep, and his father would scoop him up and carry him to bed. Wes would cling onto everything in his path—the edge of the table, a doorjamb—while his father patiently and silently peeled each of his fingers off whatever he managed to grab.

That is what Evelyn will have to do to him.

He won't leave Margaret alone with her, and he won't surrender so easily when he still has their trump card. "I know you want the hala, and I know what you're working on. You can't get it without me. Margaret and I entered the hunt together."

Evelyn stops on the staircase and turns toward Margaret. "Is that true?"

"Yes," she whispers.

"When we win tomorrow, consider it my payment." Wes injects his voice with as much confidence as he can muster. "For both your hospitality and your instruction."

Evelyn drops her suitcases and walks toward him with the cold, slow precision of a predator. She is tall—far taller than him—and fixes him with a red-rimmed glare that could corrode metal. The smell of stale coffee and sulfur stings at the back of his throat. "What pretty words did you fill her head with to convince her to go along with this scheme of yours, you snake?"

"Mother—"

"Don't," she snaps at Margaret. "I can't bear to look at you right now."

"Don't you dare talk to her that way!"

Evelyn grins as though she's delighted by the outburst. "You have a hell of a lot of nerve, Mr. Winters, to take advantage of my daughter under my own roof and then tell me how to parent her. I know you think you can outfox me, but believe me, you don't want to play this game. Did you truly think you had any leverage here? That I don't have the means of getting what I want without you? That the scholarly world is so large that you can hide an insult like this? If you insist on meddling with me, my work, and my children, I will ensure you have no career, no future, and no hope. If you cross me, you will never perform another transmutation again. Do we understand each other?"

Wes cannot think of a single word to say. What *can* he say? He has nothing. Nothing but the rage boiling off him, and what's that against her influence? No matter what he does, he will always be powerless.

"That's what I thought. Now, unless you want a letter sent to every university, every political office, every seminary—hell, every household in the country, I expect your things gone within the hour." She turns on her heel. "Have a wonderful rest of your night, Mr. Winters."

The edges of the room go hazy as he listens to her footsteps strike the staircase, as forceful as the crack of a gun. Somewhere upstairs, a door slams. Margaret kneels by the fireplace and buries her face in Trouble's side. Even from here, he can see her trembling. All the warmth has drained from the manor. What once felt like home bristles around him, cold and desolate.

"It doesn't matter." He chokes on every word. "Let her do it. If she won't teach me, my career is already ruined. My family should've gotten into town already. I'll get my things, and then we can leave—"

"And do what?" Margaret turns her face to meet his gaze, and immediately, his breath escapes him. She's beautiful but so remote, like a distant star. The vacant look in her eyes convinces him that he must have dreamed their kiss entirely. "What kind of life would we have if we've both given up everything?"

His stomach sinks. "A good one. What are you saying?"

"Would we really?"

"Of course we would! It'd be better than this. Anything would be." But would he truly be satisfied if he could never be an alchemist? Would he feel like *this* for the rest of his life, defeated and utterly helpless? It's hardly a future at all.

"I can't leave her."

"What? *Why?* The way she treated you just now—"

"Don't. Don't presume to know anything about her."

"Sorry." Wes sits on the floor beside her. "I only know what I saw."

"She isn't always like this. She's just . . ." She digs the heels of her hands into her eyes. "Things might be different this time. And without me, I don't know what would happen to her. She's already lost everything. It would be cruel."

"She managed fine without you for almost four months. What happens to her isn't your responsibility." Although he doesn't mean it to, frustration creeps into every word. "Margaret, it's not your job to take care of her when she never gave you the same courtesy. This isn't how love is supposed to be. Can't you see that?"

"And how is it supposed to be?" Her voice trembles. "Following you without question?"

"No! God, no. That's not what I'm asking." He wishes he could touch her again, that he could take her by the shoulders and make her understand. "We could go anywhere you want. We'd figure it out together."

For one moment, he thinks he's gotten through to her. Hope fills her eyes and her lips quiver. But then she presses them into a firm line and shakes her head. "I can't. I can't trust that it would be better. I'm not like you, Wes. The only thing I've ever wanted is to be safe. This is my home, and it's the only safety I've ever known. I can't let that go any more than I can go through my life waiting for the other shoe to drop."

"But what if it never does?" He's begging now. He can hear it in the desperate edge to his words, but it's far too late to worry about his pride. "How can you possibly know?"

Her whole body tenses like she's braced for a blow. "I can't risk everything for what-ifs. Empty promises aren't enough."

It feels as though she's ripped him open. Empty promises? Is that still all she thinks he's good for? "So that's it, then?"

"Yes. That's it." Her expression freezes over. "I can't leave with you."

Something within him breaks. Just like that, he has nothing. No prospects. No money. No Margaret. Once again, he's nothing but a foolhardy kid from the Fifth Ward with a dream too big for the likes of him. Only this time, he's out of chances. Worst of all, he doesn't have a thing to say to her. Margaret has always been so good at rendering him speechless.

Wes goes upstairs to clear out his things. It's a familiar ritual by now, to pack up and leave. Later, as he walks to Wickdon in the last of the murky evening light, he doesn't remember doing it clearly—only that it took him no more than ten minutes to shove all his belongings into the single bag he brought back from Dunway. What he does remember was the look on Margaret's face when he said, "Take care."

Longing.

He thinks he'll spend the rest of his life trying to rid himself of this feeling. It fills him up from the inside like cold, dark water.

Margaret rejected him. That, he can live with. The fact that he saw the woman he loves for the last time nearly does him in, but he can endure it. What's worse is that she rejected *everything*. His vision, their dreams, their future.

He couldn't convince her. He failed.

For the first time, Wes understands what heartbreak truly feels like. Without alchemy, he's just a man. And without Margaret, he has no idea how to orient himself anymore.

Annette blanches as soon as she sees him walk through the door of the inn.

On another day, Wes may have relished the panicked shame on her face, but right now, he's too far past the point of emotional exhaustion to care much about preserving her feelings—or nursing his grudge. Seeing her there, pressed to the wall as if she could convince him she's part of the scenery, feels eerily like nothing. Underneath the bright crystal lights of the chandelier, everything here looks fake and sterile. He removes his cap and shoves it beneath his arm before dragging his suitcase to the check-in counter. "Hello."

"Wes," she sputters. "What're you doing here?"

"I'm looking for my family."

As if he said nothing at all, she blurts out, "I'm so sorry! If I knew what he was planning to do, I swear to God I never would've gone through with it."

"No?" He keeps his tone light, almost conversational. "And what did you think was going to happen?"

"I don't know! I just thought he was going to scare you, not actually—"

"And you were still up for it."

"I wasn't thinking. I was hurt, and Jaime can be very persuasive when he has a wound to pick at." She leans across the counter, her voice dropping to a near whisper. "That doesn't make it right, and I'm not proud of it. But that's the truth. We both know I'm a coward when it comes to him."

He's tempted to ask for his family's room number, bid her good night, and never speak to her again. But apparently he's not as emotionally boiled dry as he thought, because he feels flushed and shaky with a sudden rush of anger. All this time, he denied his feelings for Margaret. And for what? A girl just like him, trading in empty words painted over with gold. God, he is such a fool to not have seen through it sooner. "How much of it was fake?"

"Not all of it," she says quietly.

He's humiliated that his voice breaks when he asks, "How much?"

"The first time I saw you, I flirted with you because I knew you were from the city and that it would annoy Jaime. I wanted you to want me. I wanted to believe you could be my way out of this place. But I ended up having a good time, and even though I was angry with you at the exposition, it still wasn't like it was an imposition when Jaime asked me to keep you occupied during the shooting competition."

"So you knew he was going to cheat?"

"No! I swear, I didn't know." She lowers her eyes. "But I did like you, Wes. I do. That's why I was upset when I couldn't hold your attention. And I guess after you told me about your parents . . ."

"I didn't seem as good of a prospect?" he asks wryly.

"No," she admits.

"Then you never liked me. You liked the idea of me."

"It sounds awful when you say it like that." Her eyes brim with tears. Four sisters have inoculated him well against this. The kind of tears that come from wanting to be absolved, not from wanting to make amends.

"If you want to leave, then leave. You never needed me to whisk you away, and you sure as hell don't need Jaime and the rest of them. They bring out the worst in you." An edge creeps into his voice, which he does regret. It's part of his code to refrain from yelling at women who aren't his sisters, and he doesn't want to violate it now in a moment of weakness. Wes draws a steadying breath and rakes a hand through his hair. "What you did was cruel, but it doesn't matter now. Jaime's gotten what he wants, no thanks to his own antics. I quit."

"You *did*? Why?"

"Evelyn wanted me gone, so I'm gone. I'll be back in Dunway tomorrow."

"But what about Maggie?"

Even her name is enough to stab through his heart with hopeless longing. It nearly undoes him. "What about her?"

The silence is filled with the chatter of people in the bar, the clinking of glasses over the glittery swell of music. It makes him feel unbearably, wretchedly lonely.

"I'm sorry, Wes," Annette says. "For everything. If nothing else, I know now that Jaime isn't harmless. I wish I could take it back or find some way to make it up to you."

He wants to laugh. How could anybody possibly make it up to him? If she could pull out the rotten core of New Albion that births sons of bitches like Jaime Harrington, maybe she could make it up to him. But she's just one girl who will never face consequences for what she's done to him and Margaret.

All the same, he's softhearted, and this time, she seems sincere.

"I forgive you." He sighs. "Mostly because I just want to go to sleep. Have you seen four women and a little girl come through recently? Loud? Kind of look like me?"

"Yes, actually . . . Wait. That's your family?"

Wes manages a real smile at the alarmed look on her face. "It is."

Annette flings open a drawer and begins rummaging. "Then you have to let me comp the room. Please. It's the least I can do."

"Won't you get in trouble for that?"

"I ought to get in trouble for something, don't you think?" She thrusts a handful of bills at him. It's more money than he's seen in quite some time. Mad must've used a solid portion of her savings to get them here, which makes his stomach knot itself up with guilt and gratitude both.

"Thanks. This means more than you know."

"Sure." She smiles uncertainly. "They're on the second floor, room two hundred."

Wes ducks through the lobby and up a flight of stairs, and almost immediately, he hears them. God, he pities their neighbors. Colleen's speaking voice carries at least a mile, and Christine's cackling threatens to shake the gold-framed mirror at the end of the hall from its perch. Wes tears his gaze away from his own reflection. He's already feeling sorry for himself and doesn't need the visual reminder of how rumpled and hollowed-out he looks to make it worse. His footsteps echo gravely against the glossy parquet floor as he approaches room two hundred. He knocks, and barely a second later, the door swings open.

"Wes!" Colleen throws her arms around his neck, nearly toppling him over. When she relinquishes her stranglehold to peer up at him, she frowns. "Oh. You look awful."

Before he can muster some sort of limply barbed reply, four other dark-haired heads appear in the doorway. His mother looks practically radiant with joy, but as soon as she takes stock of him, her expression dulls with worry. "Oh, a thaisce. What happened?"

"Why are you sad?" Edie chimes in.

"What's wrong?" Christine asks.

Mad stares at him silently, which he appreciates, considering he doesn't know where to begin with any of those questions. All he can think of is how desperately he wants to lie down. He drops his suitcase and flops onto the nearest bed, which is strewn with a truly astonishing number of colorful and unnecessary decorative pillows. The springs groan in weak protest as his sisters and his mother pile onto the mattress beside him.

"Well, I'm out of the hunt," he says as cheerfully as he can. "But the good news is I got your money back, Mad."

As quick as a strike of lightning, his eyes start burning and his vision goes blurry, and—damn it all, he's crying like a goddamn fool in front of his entire family. They'll never let him forget it for as long as he lives.

Christine says, "aww," in a way that somehow manages to be both comforting and condescending. Colleen leaps from the bed to fetch him a tissue from the bathroom, while Edie curls herself tighter against him.

Stiffly, Mad lays her hand against his forehead and pushes

the hair out of his face. Her tenderness surprises him. "Where's Margaret?"

The story pours out, everything from Jaime's sabotage to Evelyn's research to Margaret's refusal to leave with him. By the time he finishes, they've all gone silent. He can't interpret their puzzled expressions. Even the creepy painting of the fox above the headboard regards him with judgment.

"So, let me attempt to understand this," Christine says. "You're telling me you just left her there?"

"What else was I supposed to do? Throw myself on my knees and beg her?"

"Yes!" Colleen blushes when everyone turns to look at her. "I mean, *I* think that would have been romantic."

His anger and grief return with a vengeance—and along with them, all his self-pity. He scrubs the tears from his cheeks. "There's nothing romantic about it. Even if she came with me, I don't have anything to offer her. No money, no job, no prospects. Nothing. I'm worthless."

All he has is a dream of a better world where they could be happy together. But that's all it is. A stupid dream. An empty promise, just like she said. Once, he believed that the sheer force of his will was enough to carry him through. But now he sees that Mad and Margaret have always been right. He was naive to believe he could make something out of nothing, a worldview based on an alchemical impossibility.

"Weston Winters," his mother says. "You will not talk about yourself that way."

"Cut the bullshit, Mam! Margaret told me as much herself, and it's true. I couldn't help you. I couldn't help any of you, and I sure as hell couldn't help Margaret. What good am I if I can't do a single concrete thing for the people I love?"

"Your father and I had nothing but each other and a dream when we left Banva. You have more than enough to give her." She jabs him in the center of his chest. "This."

Wes squeezes his eyes shut, desperate to hold himself together. "She doesn't want it."

She doesn't want me.

"Oh, shut up," Mad snaps. "When has that ever stopped you before?"

Christine rounds on her. "Can you two not fight, just for one night? I'm so sick of this. You've been at each other's throats for years, and—"

"I'm not picking a fight." Mad smooths her hands primly over her skirt. "I want him to answer my question. When has a rejection ever deterred you? When have you ever decided that you've run out of options? When has anyone's opinions of your naive, selfish decisions ever stopped you from making them?"

Wes scowls. "Never."

"Exactly. Now explain to me what makes this situation any different."

"Because she told me to leave."

"And? So has every alchemy teacher in Dunway. Not to say she didn't have a good reason to tell you to get lost, mind you. I love you, Weston, but I won't disagree with you when you say you're not the most promising of matches. You're a hotheaded idealist with no money, and she's a practical girl who's shut herself away in that house to hide from the world. It makes sense that she was gun-shy."

Not all of us have big dreams, she told him once.

Wes thought her so small-minded back then, and now he wants to kick himself for being such a fool. Of course she had no big dreams when she couldn't see much past surviving another week. She can't hold them like a gun, or eat them, or burn them to keep the house warm.

"Have you told her how you feel?" Christine asks.

"No, but—"

All of them, save Mad, shout something inarticulate and outraged.

"But why would that be enough to sway her?" Wes groans.

"Because you're not just offering her your love," Mad says. "You're offering her hope."

I can't risk everything for what-ifs, Wes. Empty promises aren't enough.

Then he will give her something solid to hold on to. If he can convince her of one thing in his life, let it be this: A life beyond that house, beyond all the ghosts that haunt it, is a dream worth believing in. One worth trying for.

"Mad . . . Thank y—"

"Thank me later." She squeezes his shoulder. "Now go get your girl."

28

Now that her mother's laboratory door has locked and the silence of the manor has settled like a chill into her bones, Margaret doesn't know what to do with herself. She doesn't know how to rest with her mother's anger filling up the house like smoke.

Soon enough, everything will return to normal. They will resume the comfortable rhythm of their lives, a planet and its orbiting sister moon. That prospect should be a comfort. The sliver of light knifing out from beneath the crack in the door should be a relief. Evelyn is at last home, all hers.

And yet she's still alone.

The sound of the door closing behind Wes still echoes through the halls, and she swears the strained formality of his farewell and the hurt in his eyes will haunt her for the rest of her life. Watching him go was almost more than she could handle, and now all her oldest wounds are aching. If she lets herself think about him any longer, she'll crumble. So she cleans the house. She scours every surface until it gleams, until her mind begins to disconnect from reality, until her pain feels distant. But when she begins to wash the dishes, she's yanked back into her body at the sight of the coffee-stained mugs Wes hoarded in his room for days on end. He's tainted even this routine. There's no one to annoy her or distract her or fill the silence with incessant chatter and humming and laughter. By all accounts, it should be a blessing.

But it's not. It's stifling.

There's nothing left in this place untouched by him. Margaret wants to throw the rack he hung his tattered coat on through the window. She wants to snap every one of her father's records in half. She wants to smash all the crystal glasses and burn every alchemy book collecting dust on the shelf. She wants to scream until what comes echoing back isn't her, just her, only her. As she fills a bucket in the sink, she watches her reflection shatter over and over again, pale and already half-dead. Her mother has always contented herself with ghosts, but Margaret is alive for the first time in years. She isn't ready to go back to haunting this place, silent and unseen.

"Margaret." Evelyn's tall silhouette stands at the top of the stairs. "We need to have a talk."

Her hands are trembling so hard, she nearly tips over the bucket. Numbly, she sets it down. Water sloshes out over her feet, and she tracks wet footprints through the house as she follows her mother upstairs and into her lab.

Over the past several weeks, she and Wes have replaced almost every painful memory of this room with something joyful and new. But when her mother takes a seat behind her desk and folds her hands, it once again feels oppressive and too dark for the evening light. The sleeves of Evelyn's jacket ride up enough to expose her wrists. It shouldn't surprise Margaret how frail they are, but it does every time.

"The window is broken," Evelyn says, "and it seems my alembics and several of my manuscripts have vanished."

Her mother is a brilliant hunter, in her way. She has laid her trap with simple observations and an airy tone. Now it's only a matter of waiting until Margaret steps into it. But of all the places she could have started her interrogation, this is by the far the easiest. She has nothing to hide. "That was Jaime Harrington. He destroyed the lab."

"And why would he do something like that?"

"You know why."

"I suppose I do." Evelyn removes her glasses and rubs the bridge of her nose. "Has his father been informed of this?"

"No."

The first fine crack in her composure appears. "And why is that?"

"He wouldn't have done anything. Wes and I—"

"Wes." She sneers through his name like it's sour on her tongue. "Yes, let's discuss him. I think you understand why I'm frustrated, Margaret. Had you two not gone behind my back to register for the hunt, I very much doubt Jaime would have paid you any mind. I doubt I would be out tens of dollars for replacing my equipment, and I doubt we would be having this unpleasant conversation at all. But here we are."

Her mother's leather-bound journal plops onto the desk between them. Fog swirls through the edges of Margaret's vision until she can see nothing but the gilt on the ouroboros stamp gleaming red as sunset. It shivers like a coin dropped to the bottom of a well.

"Now, would you care to explain to me why you took this out of my desk?"

Margaret had replaced it in the drawer exactly as she'd found it. She'd erased any marks they'd made in it. How could she have *known*?

"Well?" Evelyn still does not raise her voice. She's never had to resort to that to get her point across. Her anger is like the slow simmer of water. Confronting it is like taking the first, tentative step onto thin pond ice.

"I'm sorry" is all Margaret manages through the chattering of her teeth.

"As I suspected," she hisses.

She'd fallen right into this. The snare tightens around her throat. "I'm sorry."

"Why are you cowering like a kicked dog? I haven't done a thing to you." Evelyn sounds muffled, as though thick wool has been pulled over Margaret's ears. It's getting harder to cling to details when she so desperately wants to flee. "You expect me to come home to my lab destroyed and ransacked, my daughter cavorting with some up-start, and be glad of it? To overlook it? No. I will not be disrespected like this. Now answer me. Did you show this to him?"

"Yes."

"Does he have a copy?"

"No." Margaret curls around herself tighter. "No, I swear."

"But he's seen it. God, Margaret, what were you thinking?"

Margaret feels as if she's been thrown back into that inlet, crouch-ing beside Mattis as the tide churned his blood to pink froth around her. She'll drown if she doesn't move, but she can't. All she can do is shiver as the waters of her own fear rise around her and fill her ears, her mouth, her eyes. Her mother has never raised a hand to her, but when Margaret thinks of what will happen if she disappoints her beyond forgiveness, it's a void as vast and terrifying as her memory of that thing that smoked at the center of Evelyn's transmutation cir-cle. For so long, Evelyn has been her entire world and the god of it, too. There are punishments far worse than being struck. To be forsaken and unloved—that is the worst fate of all.

Wes was always so outraged for her. *Someone should've done some-thing,* he told her once. But what would they have done? What would they have intervened in? Evelyn has never hurt her in a way anyone can see.

"Do you understand what the ramifications would be if that de-coded transmutation were widely circulated? Do you have any idea what could happen if this research falls into the wrong hands?"

"Yes, I do." Margaret freezes as soon as the words slip out. She can't be certain if it was actually her who said that—and clearly nei-ther is her mother, because she blinks, astonished, as if she's been slapped.

"Be careful of what you're implying."

"I've seen firsthand what this research does in the wrong hands."

Her voice trembles as badly as she does, but she forces herself to go on. "I showed him because there's no other way to kill the hala. I showed him because I trust him, and he's my friend."

"That was friendship I saw, was it?" Evelyn rises from her seat. Her shadow cuts across the floor. "Honestly. Are you so starved for attention that you'll let any smooth-talking boy poison your mind—"

"Yes! Because you left me here alone. For so long, I've lived like I don't even exist. I thought it was the magnum opus that consumes people. I thought it was alchemy. But all along, it was you. You *let* it consume you. How can you act like a mother to me now when you haven't in years?"

Saying it aloud cracks open something within her, and now, she can see with perfect clarity. The worst has already happened to her a thousand times over, and she has survived it. Evelyn has already forsaken her.

This isn't how love is supposed to be.

Margaret cannot believe she just denied herself the chance to learn that firsthand. She cannot believe she all but shoved Wes out the front door.

"What has gotten into you?" Evelyn's eyes shine with hurt. "You can criticize me all you like, but everything I do, I do for our family. I'm sorry I can't be like all the good Katharist women in town and devote my entire life to you. After your father left, I had to support you alone, and I wouldn't have left you here if you weren't mature enough to handle it."

"Maybe I'm not mature enough."

Evelyn draws in a deep breath, as though she is gathering the very last of her patience. "No. Maybe you're not. But I'm home now, and I thought of you every day. I've been as patient with you as I could given the circumstances. Isn't that enough for you? The least you could do is treat me with some decency, instead of being cruel."

No, she wants to say. *It's not enough.*

Evelyn is here, but she's not present and hasn't been for years. Part of her walked out the door on the day David died and never came back. Hot tears stream down her face, and Margaret tastes salt on her lips. She is so humiliated to be crying—so humiliated to prove her mother right. Maybe she isn't mature enough to handle any of this, but she's so tired of trying to be. She's so tired of waiting for things to change.

She's so tired of being alone.

"First thing in the morning," Evelyn says, "we'll go to town and have him replaced with me as your alchemist. It certainly wasn't what I had in mind, but as long as you've presented me with this opportunity, it'd be foolish not to take it."

"No," Margaret says softly. "I can't do this anymore. I won't."

Evelyn laughs incredulously. "Do you want to try extorting me, too? It turned out so well for your friend. Be my guest."

"No. This isn't an extortion. This isn't a negotiation. I'm leaving. Tomorrow morning, Wes and I will win the hunt, and you can do as you like. By all means, continue working yourself to the bone for your family of one."

Before she can lose her nerve, Margaret escapes into the hallway. She hears her mother's half-hearted pursuit. The exasperated scrape of her chair against the floorboards, the condescendingly slow clack of her heels. "Who the hell do you think you are to talk to me like that?"

Margaret flings open her bedroom door and pulls her suitcase from beneath her bed. All she can hear is the wild beat of her heart against her eardrums, the panicked rhythm of her breathing. *Pull yourself together.* Her hands are shaking so hard, it's all she can do to not tear every cardigan she owns as she rips them from the hangers in her closet and shoves them into her bag.

Surely there must be something else she is forgetting, something else that's hers. But apart from her clothes and her gun, nothing in this house holds any sentimental value to her. Nothing but her books, but the age-worn pages will crumble to dust if she tries to cart them down the mountain. She'll have to leave them.

Evelyn waits for her in front of the landing, her arms crossed impatiently. "And where do you plan to go now? Have you thought any of this through?"

Away from you. Anywhere. To Wes.

"Move."

"I'm not letting you walk away from this conversation."

She shoulders her way past Evelyn and hurries down the stairs. "Trouble!"

He springs to his feet as Margaret snatches the painted hunting knife from the sitting room. She slips it into her skirt pocket as discreetly as she can.

"Don't." The roughness of her mother's voice nearly sinks her. "You can't do this. You can't leave me, too. I love you, Maggie. Doesn't that mean anything to you?"

I love you. How long has it been since Evelyn told her that?

Once, she said it every day in a thousand different ways. When she reaches into that bright pocket in her mind, full of all her happiest, safest memories, she finds one as golden as rye and sunlight. In the spring, they'd walk the hilltops, where poppies bloomed riotous for miles and hawks winged overhead. Evelyn would pick every wildflower they passed and tell her their names like they were a precious secret: yarrow and morning glory and skullcap. They'd lie side by side in the grass as her mother wove them carefully into a crown. *Queen Maggie,* she'd say reverently as she placed it on her head.

Margaret chokes back a sob as she clutches the doorknob.

How can she cut her own mother loose? How can she repay her love with abandonment? How can she force herself to forget all the small kindnesses, the tenderness, that she has shown her? But that's never been the whole of her—of them—no matter how desperately Margaret wishes it could be. She has built herself a mother out of those precious memories and kept herself alive on them. But she can't subsist on crumbs anymore.

As she opens the door, she makes the mistake of looking back.

Although Evelyn is backlit by the eerie, yellow light emanating from the sconces, Margaret watches her change like quicksilver. Her crumpled face smooths over into a mask so calm and collected it's as though she'd never broken at all.

"Fine. Go, then. You're your father's daughter through and through."

Margaret slams the door shut behind her.

She walks with grim determination to the paddock and fetches Shimmer. Then, with hound and horse in tow, she heads down the path and into the woods. As long as she keeps moving, she won't crumble. Mrs. Wreford once told her there's more to life beyond preserving that manor, that there are people who love her. People like her—and Wes. They have thrown her lifeline after lifeline, and she's finally ready to take hold of them. Somewhere on the other side of these redwoods, there's a world waiting for her.

Bit by bit, the towering trees give way to rolling, rye-covered hills. The Halfmoon Sea sprawls out lazily against the beach tonight, glimmering beneath the light of the waxing moon. And there, in the distance, she sees the faint outline of a person.

Her heart lurches with anticipation. It's unusual for someone to come out this far from Wickdon, especially on foot and at this hour. Margaret trots along the path until she can see the figure more clearly, bathed in the silver glow of the moon. From here, she can make out the whip of coattails and a tangle of disheveled black hair.

"Wes?" she calls. The wind snatches her voice away.

But she can tell he hears her by the sudden slackening of his shoulders. She's never tasted anything sweeter than this relief. She doubted him. She rejected him. And still, he came back for her. He's as stubborn as ever.

Margaret lets go of Shimmer's bridle and her suitcase and runs toward him. As soon as she's within reach, he enfolds her in a hug that squeezes the breath out of her. She could lose herself in this. The heat of his body against hers; the heady, ridiculous scent of his aftershave and the wild, bright salt of the sea; the way he holds her as though she's something precious.

"I never should have left you," he says against her ear.

"I never should have let you go."

Wes draws back enough to look into her eyes, but he still holds her by the shoulders. He's wearing a very serious expression, one that makes her stomach swoop low. "Margaret, I know I don't have much to offer you, and I know it's hard to imagine anything going right after the hunt, and I know you could probably think of at least a hundred better men than me to marry, but I meant it when I said there's a life for us—a good one. A country where we don't have to be afraid. A house in the countryside. A whole library full of smutty books and a huge kitchen and seven kids—or no kids—and five hounds just like Trouble. Whatever you want, I swear I'll make it happen. I swear I'll make you happy."

It knocks the wind from her. Once, when he was very drunk, he described this exact scene to her, and it was the most beautiful thing she'd ever heard. She never could envision a thing beyond Wickdon or the walls of her mother's house. But in Wes's eyes, she can see a thousand possibilities, all of them bright and vivid as pearls.

How can he truly believe he has nothing to offer her? She's never had the gift of imagination, or a dream or a future to believe in, but he's giving it to her. She wants it—wants *him*—more than anything she's ever wanted, and that terrifies her. She feels as though she's stepped from the edge of a cliff. But maybe just this once, she can let herself believe that someone will catch her.

"Did you just propose to me?"

"What? No! God, no." He blanches as he processes what he said. "Not because I don't want to, but . . . I don't even have a ring, and I still haven't told you—"

"I know." Margaret cups his cheek.

"I just want to do it right. And I will someday, if you'll let me." He looks at her like she's the brightest thing here, brighter even than the Cold Moon and all the stars above them. "How are you doing?"

She laughs softly. "I don't know, honestly. I've never been so miserable or so happy."

"I can work with that." He rubs his hands against her bare arms. They're stippled with gooseflesh. "Where's your coat?"

"I must have forgotten it. I left in a hurry."

"Well, we can't have you freezing to death." He shrugs his jacket off and drapes it over her shoulders like a cape, the same way he always wears it. It smells like him, and the fabric is soft with wear. He has a peculiar expression on his face as he smooths the sleeves out, like he's examining a very strange work of art.

"That bad?"

"No, not at all. It suits you. I like it when you let me do this."

"Do what?"

"Take care of you." He rubs the back of his neck. "My family's all waiting for you. They're excited to see you."

"Really?"

"Really. But I can fend them off if you're tired."

Strangely enough, the thought of spending time with all five Winters women sounds . . . nice. "No, that's alright. I'm excited to see them, too."

He takes her hand and presses a kiss to her knuckles. "Famous last words, Margaret."

Jacket or not, as long as he turns that smile of his on her, she'll be warm.

The two adjoining suites in the Wallace Inn look as though a storm has torn through them. With six suitcases, all the sheets, and throw pillows scattered across the floor, there is only a small corridor of open space. It makes for treacherous footing as she is wrested from Wes's grasp and passed from person to person. Margaret isn't sure she's ever been hugged so much in her life. It's a strange, giddy feeling, and when at last she's allowed to sit, a cup of tea is pressed into her hands. She's beginning to understand that the Winters family can make a home anyplace they land.

"We missed you, dear," Aoife says. "And we're so glad you're here."

Margaret smiles, lowering her gaze. "Thank you. Trouble is, too, I think."

He's quickly found a favorite in Edie, who crouches on the floor beside him and scratches behind his ears.

"I'm going to go out to pick something up for dinner. Can I get you anything?"

"No, that's alright. Thank you, Mrs. Winters."

Aoife sighs, clearly aggrieved. "Alright, then. I'll be back in a few."

Once the door shuts behind her, Christine says, "I hope you know you're going to be force-fed anyway. It's pointless to refuse."

"Well, we'll cross that bridge when we get there." Wes makes a grand show of yawning and stretching, then stoops to collect her suitcase. "It's been a long day for the both of us, so I'm going to put our stuff in the other room."

"Oh, no you don't." Christine grabs it from him. "You are *not* treating that room like some honeymoon suite while the rest of us are right here."

Colleen covers her ears. "Seriously? Can you not?"

"Margaret and I will share it." All of their heads whip toward Mad, who leans against the window overlooking the ocean. She taps her long, lacquered cigarette holder on the casement, showering ash onto the ground below. "I've been wanting to get to know her better anyway."

Wes's face falls.

"Don't look so gutted. Christine, Margaret, come with me," Mad says. "We're going to get ready."

"For what?" Christine asks.

"To go out."

"With what money?" Wes scoffs.

"If I recall, you seemed to have worked your magic on the girl downstairs."

"Right." Wes rubs the back of his neck. "Hey, was that finally a recognition of my contribution to this family?"

Colleen claps her hands. "Can I come, too?"

"No," Christine says pleasantly. "Be annoying by yourself. Or play with your sister."

"I don't want to play with her!" Edie throws her arms around Trouble, who grunts as he startles from sleep. He blinks blearily at her. "I have Trouble."

"Then I guess you're stuck talking to Wes. Too bad. Bye!"

"Hey!" Wes protests.

It's all Margaret can do to keep her composure as Christine and Mad whisk her into the spare room. They seat her in front of the vanity, which is cluttered with more cosmetics than she's ever seen in one place. A mirror bordered by too-bright lights reflects her weary face back at her. The two oldest Winters siblings study her, dark-eyed and assessing.

Christine breaks the silence first. "If you're tired, you don't have to come, even though Mad says things like you don't have a choice."

"I want to," Margaret says, although she doesn't know exactly what she's agreeing to. She has never been "out" before.

Her easy acquiescence, however, seems to please Mad. She lifts a strand of Margaret's hair. "May I?"

She nods. Mad carefully gathers up her hair and tosses it so that it spills down her back. It's knotted from the rough ocean wind, but Mad diligently works her fingers through it until it lies flat. Her eyes burn, and Margaret wants to shake herself for being so easily moved by any small tenderness. Margaret doesn't want to cry in front of Wes's sisters—not when they're being so kind to her.

"Hey." Christine squeezes her shoulders. "We've got you. It's going to be alright."

"It will be," Mad says absently. "So, what are your intentions with my brother?"

Christine groans. "Is now really the time?"

"I'm making conversation."

"No, you're gearing up to conduct an interrogation. Honestly, Margaret, ignore her. She's like a steamroller."

"I'm simply doing my due diligence. Besides, she ought to know what she's getting into." Mad meets Margaret's eyes in the mirror. "He likes you, which I doubt he's said to you in as many words because he's allergic to being honest half the time. He talks a big game, but he clams up when he has to follow through. But when he does, he's not capable of doing anything halfway if he has the option to do it extravagantly. I understand if you don't think you can tolerate it. I just don't want to see him hurt. He's very annoying when he's upset."

Nothing Mad has said surprises or scares her, but she wants to ensure she gives her the right answer. Mad, undeterred by her silence, rummages through a bag on the vanity. She procures a small dish of eyeshadow and dips a brush into it. She angles Margaret's chin up with the crook of her finger and begins to paint her lash line. Her eyes water in protest, but she doesn't dare move or breathe until Mad withdraws and grunts her approval.

"You're right," Margaret says. "He is all of those things, but he's also kindhearted and good. Tomorrow, I intend to protect him with my life. And after that, I intend to do everything I can to help him see his dreams through."

And someday, she will be brave enough to let herself love him as she wants to—as he deserves.

Mad caps the dish with an emphatic *click*. "Then you have my blessing. Now let's go."

Christine sighs in relief, and Margaret's heart swells with hope.

Tomorrow morning, the hunt will begin. The dream she and Wes share hangs in the balance—as does the fate of his entire family. But right now, surrounded by people who've accepted her, it isn't so difficult to believe that everything really will be alright.

29

With less than twenty-four hours before the hunt, Wickdon is lively and wild.

In the Blind Fox, a band plays on a makeshift stage, and a fine haze of tobacco smoke swirls through the bar like mist off the harbor. People dance in short, swishing dresses and rolled shirtsleeves. Tonight, everything glitters. Sequins and crystal glasses and Margaret's eyes as she drinks it all in. Wes can't keep his gaze from her.

Near the back, they find a miraculously empty table. Christine sprawls herself across the bench to stake her claim. Margaret perches across from her, entirely overwhelmed by the ordeal judging by how stiffly she carries herself. He still can't reconcile his Margaret—fierce, mud-streaked Margaret—with this Margaret and her black-lined eyes.

"Wes." Christine bats her eyelashes. "I'm parched. Be a dear, won't you?"

He sighs. "What do you want? I'll get you both a drink."

"Anything is fine," Margaret says.

"Gin!"

Mad rests a hand on his shoulder. "I'll come."

"Sure." It's a miracle his voice didn't crack with surprise—and fear. They weave through swing dancers and whipping tasseled skirts until they reach the bar. Down on the other end, he spies Mrs. Wreford pouring a pint with lacy foam that dribbles down the sides of a frosted glass. Eventually, a harried bartender takes their order, which leaves him and Mad alone—truly alone—for the first time in weeks. She props her chin up on her fist as she leans against the bar, scanning the room as though she's waiting for someone—or something.

"You said I could thank you later. So I'm thanking you now." Wes leans in so he doesn't have to shout over the noise. "And I'm sorry."

"For what?"

"What, you want a whole list?"

"Yes, grovel," she says, although it has little bite. Still, he wishes she would smile or at least stop looking so unimpressed. "I'm waiting."

"I'm sorry for making your life miserable."

"Not good enough."

The bartender drops off their drinks. Even after they've settled up, she doesn't make a move to head back to the table. She swirls her whiskey neat with grave focus. It casts a watery, amber shadow across the bar.

"I let you down. We promised to hold it down together, but I left you to handle a lot more than you should've handled alone when I started taking off all the time for my apprenticeships."

"I never wanted you to put your life on hold for my sake, you know."

"I know. But I still could've consulted you more. I'm sorry for thinking you were out to get me and that you didn't want what's best for me, and for expecting you to agree with everything I did, and—"

"Alright, alright. That's enough."

"I miss him," he says after a moment. "I miss him every day."

Her expression softens. "Me, too."

"I miss *you*."

"I miss you, too." Mad slings one arm around his neck and pulls him down into a hug. He has to bend over a little to accommodate her, but once he does, she kisses the top of his head. "And I'm sorry, too, for assuming the worst of you."

"You had reasons to. But I promise I'm going to make everything right."

"You better not die. If you do, I swear to God . . ."

Wes grins in a way he knows would irritate her if she could see it. "Aw, Madeline, are you getting weepy?"

"Ugh." She shoves him away. "You're impossible."

"You love me."

"Yes, I do." Wes doesn't much care for the scheming look she's giving him. It's somewhere between mischievous and calculating. She opens the purse slung around her shoulder, an oversized beaded number she got for her birthday last year. "Close your eyes and hold out your hand."

His childhood has taught him better than to oblige. Mad herself has placed a variety of upsetting things in his hands with a trick like this. An ice cube. One of their sisters' baby teeth. A dead roach. But she's got that glint in her eyes that leaves no room for argument, so he does what he's told. Something crinkles between their palms, and when he looks down, he nearly hurls it back at her.

"Seriously?" he sputters.

A condom wrapper glints like metal in the light.

Mad feigns innocence as she fishes a pack of cigarettes from her bag and lights one. "Mam won't give it to you, and she'll burst into hellfire before she even utters the word 'sex,' so you're overdue for this talk. If you two need to stay with us until you get your footing, Lord knows we don't need any more kids in the house."

He wants to combust. Or melt. Anything to escape this hell. "Great. Thanks. Anything else you want to tell me? Any other advice?"

"Advice? Sure. Don't be selfish, ask what she likes, and for God's sake, don't stare at her like she's going to suck your soul out through your mouth all night. It's like you've never seen a woman before."

ALLISON SAFT

Wes shoves the condom in his pocket, praying no one else saw it. Even though he has a pretty solid idea of what would've happened had Evelyn not interrupted him and Margaret, the very fact of having this makes him feel a whole mess of things, mainly presumptuous. And terrified. Maybe mostly terrified. "I was being sarcastic. God. Can we *please* not talk about this now? Or ideally ever again?"

"One day, you will appreciate me. Now let's go before Christine scares Margaret away."

They take their drinks, and as they begin wading through the crowd, someone jostles him. Some of Margaret's beer spills onto his hands, and he lets out a slow, irritated breath through his teeth.

"Winters."

Wes's stomach drops at the sound of that baleful voice. Jaime Harrington stands not an arm's length away, swaying slightly, his face flushed with drink and cold. Hatred burns solidly within him, but at least the bruises daubed on Jaime's cheekbone make it easier to keep his voice jovial. "Harrington. A pleasure as always."

Mad stops beside him and rakes her gaze across Jaime's face. "Who's this?"

Jaime opens his mouth, probably to say something caustic and inane, but when he looks at Mad, his jaw hinges open. His eyes ping-pong between them, like he can't quite make sense of either their likeness or Mad's appearance. Wes has learned his lesson now, but God, what he wouldn't give to have another shot at him. The bastard has some nerve to look at his sister like that.

"This is Jaime Harrington," he says. "And this is my sister, Madeline."

"Sister?" he echoes.

"Ah, yes, I recognize the name." Mad smiles, sweeter than he's ever seen her smile in her life. It petrifies him. "I like your jacket. That's an expensive brand."

"Oh." Jaime looks down, clearly still off-kilter. "Thanks?"

Before he even finishes speaking, Mad dumps the entirety of her drink down the front of his jacket. As she strides past him, she clips him on the shoulder. "Oops."

Jaime swears, and Wes is left floundering, half-stunned and waffling between dread and delight. Before he recovers enough to make his exit, Jaime grabs him by the collar and pulls. They're close enough that Wes can smell the stale beer on his breath and the whiskey drying on his jacket. "Annette's not talking to me anymore. I know you're behind it."

"Maybe you ought to take it easy. You're making a fool of yourself." Wes watches the rage ignite in his eyes the exact moment Jaime recognizes his own words. "I've been there, but I find women tend to like you better if you recognize they make their own decisions."

Jaime bares his teeth. "Wipe that smug look off your face. You've always got a plan and a joke for everything, don't you? But I'm done playing with you, Winters. You better hope I don't see you alone during the hunt because if I do, I'll have my hound tear you apart like the vermin you are."

Wes wants to laugh, but any retort he can think of dies as soon as he meets Jaime's gaze. There's a sharp, overeager look in his eyes he hasn't seen before. It runs deeper than frustration, deeper even than hatred. It's pure desperation.

He really means it.

Jaime lets go of his collar but doesn't break eye contact. Unsettled, Wes takes a step backward, then two, before turning and hurrying back to the table. He hates that Jaime rattled him, but he can't deny it felt more like an omen than a threat. In his mother's legends, the goddess of war always appears just before a battle, spelling portents of doom for hapless men. It's as though she spoke through Jaime's mouth to foretell his grisly fate. Wes imagines himself dragged to the earth like a fleeing hind.

He slides into the seat beside Margaret and drapes his arm over the back of her chair. Immediately, she pins him with that too-perceptive stare of hers. "Is everything alright?"

"Yeah." He tosses back his drink in a single gulp. "Completely fine."

"Someone's ready to dance," Christine singsongs.

"I certainly am," Mad says.

"Let's go, then."

Christine drags her into the crowds, which have risen to a near fever pitch as the band strikes up a jaunty, breathlessly fast song. As Wes watches them spin and twirl, he's struck by how different his sisters look in this light. Carefree, like they're the kind of city kids who sneak into speakeasies every weekend. Like they're not on the brink of ruin.

For their sake, they have to win tomorrow.

When he glances at Margaret again, she's still watching him. He sighs. There's no point in hiding it from her. "I ran into Harrington again. He was happy to see me."

"I'm sure he was."

"He said if he sees me alone tomorrow, he'll kill me."

"I won't give him the chance." Margaret presses her knee against his, which he realizes now is bouncing a mile a minute. "I promised Mad that I'd protect you with my life. I intend to keep that promise."

"What would I do without you?" He swirls the dregs of his drink. Ice clinks in the glass, the sound as brittle as his nerves. "You know, until now, it's always been easy to say I had the courage to do this. Now look at me. Afraid of Jaime and afraid of myself. What if I can't bring myself to do it?"

"What do you mean?"

"I can't do the things I need to do without power. But if I kill it, how am I any better than the rest of the alchemists in this country? If I'm willing to sacrifice my roots, if I'm willing to play by the rules of their game . . ."

"But you aren't like them. You're playing their game; that's a fact. But the moment you joined the hunt, you broke their rules. And if we win, you're on your way to changing the game entirely."

What *would* it mean for a Sumic kid from the Fifth Ward and a Yu'adir girl from the countryside to win? It would mean nothing, and it would mean everything. It would—at least for one night, at least in this one nowhere town—force New Albion to reconsider what its heroes look like. To acknowledge its heritage, its identity, is not and was never homogenous.

He only wishes there was a way to do it without committing a mortal sin.

"It that what you tell yourself?" he asks.

"No." Margaret smiles at him gently, almost sadly. "I don't know that I have the right to claim I'm betraying anything or anyone the way you do. I tell myself that I'm doing what needs to be done. And so are you."

"Yeah. I guess so." He rests his head on the table.

"You're a good man, Wes." The weight of her hand settles on his back, and he straightens up to meet her gaze. "Your mother will forgive you. And if God put the hala on this earth for our sake, then he can't be too angry with you for using it. Try to take your mind off it for tonight. You should join your sisters."

"*We* should join them."

"No, I couldn't."

"Oh, come on," he cajoles. "Dance with me."

"I don't know how."

Wes extends his hand to her. "I promise it's not hard."

Very reluctantly, she accepts it. As she lets him sweep her to the edges of the crowd, where it's thinnest, he feels some of his trepidation melt away. The song changes tempo just as he gets his arms around her, and he can't help feeling fizzy, even happy because she is here with him, letting him hold her, when he almost lost her tonight.

I've never been so miserable or so happy, Margaret told him.

He thinks he understands that well enough now. As the singer croons and the drums crescendo, the bar goes soft and hazy and twinkling, and the magic he feels among all these people finally makes its way into her eyes. They are warm and intoxicating as whiskey, and if he doesn't kiss her now, he thinks he may die.

As if she can read his thoughts, Margaret catches him by the lapels. But before he can even think about closing the gap between them, he goes cold at what he sees over her shoulder.

Jaime Harrington watching them with the look of a man who knows he's already won.

On the morning of the Halfmoon Hunt, Wes wakes before the sun.

Christine snores next to him, still fully dressed in what she wore the night before. He makes a mental note to tease her for it later as he slides out of bed. His mother and Edie haven't stirred, and in the adjacent suite, Mad and Colleen lie on opposite sides of a wall made of pillows. Margaret's bed is empty, the sheets pristinely tucked and folded as if no one slept there at all.

Judging by the dull exhaustion buzzing in his skull and the darkness of the sky, it can't be later than three or four in the morning, which worries him a little. Maybe she couldn't sleep and went downstairs to read. Lord knows he can't, now that the jittery realization that the hunt will begin in a matter of hours has set in.

He brushes his teeth, swills a mug full of water, and gets dressed in the dark before creeping downstairs to find her. It's deathly quiet in the lobby. Only Annette remains, drowsing with her chin on her fists at the check-in counter.

"Have you seen Margaret?" he asks.

Annette jumps. "Oh, Wes! Good morning. Yes, actually. I saw her leave about fifteen minutes ago. I think she said she was going for a swim?"

It sounds just ridiculous enough to be true. "Thanks."

She smiles at him knowingly. "Good luck."

Wes pulls on his coat and follows the rocky trail to the cliffs that overlook the water. A driftwood fire flickers near an inlet, its flames sparkling purple as the salt and metals burn off. The reflection of the full moon shimmers on the waves, a bridge of light he swears he could step onto and follow to the horizon. And there, out in the surf, is a dark shape.

Margaret.

He sees that she's left her clothes folded neatly in the sand, just out of the tide's reach. There's a timid, God-fearing part of him that says, *Turn around and go back inside.* But there's a far stronger part of him that says, *Tell her now, you coward, before it's too late.*

Today, one of them could die. There's nothing for them to tell each other that they don't already know. He sees it in her eyes. He's tasted it on her lips. She writes it on his skin every time she touches him. But in all his mother's legends, there is binding power in words, and Wes doesn't want to die without his soul entwined with hers.

He clambers down the path, swearing as the rocks loosen beneath his shoes. It is a still night. Only the barest breeze ruffles his hair and paints his lips with salt. He's afraid he might shatter this glass-like peace if he so much as speaks. He walks to the edge of the water until he can see Margaret clearly. The moon is enormous tonight, bright as a streetlamp, and its silver light dusts her shoulders. Her hair is sleek and wet, fanning out around her where it meets the sea. Right now, she strikes him as entirely otherworldly. A siren—or one of the aos sí liable to drag him to a watery grave. Fey magic as ancient and wild as the hala, wearing a girl's skin.

She is so beautiful.

Over the past few weeks, he has memorized everything about her. Every shift of light in her honeyed eyes. The way she smiles at him when she's about to laugh or can't quite pretend he's as annoying as she'd like him to believe. The way she looks when she's about to crumble. But this is uncharted. He doesn't know what will happen if he confesses without dancing around it or offering her hypotheticals. Their future is bright in its infinite possibilities, but the present frightens him as much as it exhilarates him.

He doesn't know what he will do if she wants to finish what they started. But there's nothing for him to hide behind anymore—and no one here but the two of them.

This time, he decides, it will be perfect.

Wes clears his throat loudly, and Margaret whips her head around. She sinks deeper into the water and gasps, "Wes?"

He tries to smirk at her, but it feels wobbly. "Hello, Margaret."

"What are you doing here?"

"Well, it seemed like a nice morning for a walk on the beach," he says as casually as he can. "Looks like I wasn't the only one who thought that."

"There's a lot of beach to walk."

"I like this spot in particular." He finds his footing here, in the obsequious tone of voice that has irritated her so many times before. "I think I'll stay right here if it's all the same to you."

She glowers at him like she might really crawl onto the shore and drown him. He doesn't think he'd mind it much, to die by her hand. "Suit yourself."

"In all seriousness, I wanted to talk to you. We have unfinished business."

Her expression softens as she begins to put the pieces together. "So come here."

"The thing is, I can't swim."

She smiles at him. Fond and exasperated, as all his favorites of her smiles are. "It's shallow enough to stand."

"I'll be right there."

Somewhere between tossing his coat in the sand and unbuttoning his shirt, it occurs to him that they are very much in public and anyone could stumble upon them here. But it's still hours before dawn, and the thrill of it—of her—burns away his reservations like salt in a bonfire.

He yanks off his shoes, then his belt, and when he's thrown the last of his clothing onto the shore, he takes a step into the water and goes rigid. It's fucking *freezing,* which isn't exactly doing him any favors, but at least she's turned her face partly away to preserve his dignity.

Steeling his nerve, he wades deeper into the sea. The cold snatches away his breath as soon as the water rises above his waist, but he perseveres. Here, with only inches of space between them, he is paralyzed. He thinks of the condom in his pocket on the shore. He thinks of what it'd be like to touch her now, to trace the line of the water rolling down her neck with his tongue.

"So, what is it you wanted?"

He did come here to talk. He wanted to tell her something. It all eludes him now, especially now that she's worrying her lip with her teeth and watching him with anticipation. He lifts his hand to the curve of her neck and leans closer, until he can feel her breath warm against his lips. "I don't remember."

Margaret presses her hands to his chest, putting some distance between them. "And what if someone else decides it's a nice morning for a walk?"

"I don't care. Let them see. I know you told me not to, but I can't not tell you that—"

"I already know, Wes."

He groans. "You're killing me."

"Then tell me *why*."

"How can I say it in a way that at all covers it? Nothing is ever going to sound sufficient." He rests his forehead against hers. "Because you're loyal and kind, even though the world was determined to make you otherwise. Because you make me laugh and ground me and challenge me. Because you could probably kill me if you wanted."

"Oh" is all she says before she wraps her arms around his middle.

Somehow, she feels feverish through the cold embrace of the ocean. Wes lets out a helpless sigh as he slides his hands down the slick ridge of her spine, her waist, the swell of her hips. It's addictive, the way her breath hitches when he kisses the tender stretch of skin below her jaw. Her pulse flutters against his teeth, and God, that sound she makes is enough to sustain him. He could live on nothing but that.

When he at last brushes his lips against hers, a fire ignites within him, hotter than an alchemical reaction. If she won't hear him, he will tell her he loves her in the only way he knows how. He tangles his fingers into her hair at the nape of her neck and drinks the salt from her mouth. The day he met her, streaked in dirt and despising him, he never imagined she could do this to him. How could Margaret ever think he'd lose himself to alchemy when he has already hopelessly lost himself to her?

Margaret draws back, just barely. "It's cold."

"Oh, really?" he asks hazily. "I hadn't noticed."

"Really."

He tries not to be too disappointed as she takes him by the hand and leads him to a small cove. It mercifully shelters them from prying eyes and the wind. They huddle close to the fire, which spits embers that swirl like dust motes into the night. By some miracle, she doesn't protest as he openly watches her towel off, greedily memorizing every inch of her. When she finishes, she tosses it at him. It hits his chest with a wet *slap*.

"Thanks," he says dryly.

With a self-satisfied smile, Margaret pulls her dress on and wrings out her hair like a dishrag. The towel is as good as useless at this point. The sand caked onto it rubs his skin raw, but it gets the job done well enough for him to shimmy back into his damp trousers.

He lays his jacket out by the fire and sprawls onto it. His head swims lazily as he basks in heat—and in her, lustrous as a saint in the blue flames. "What are you doing out here, anyway?"

"I couldn't sleep, so I came out here to clear my head." She pulls her knees into her chest. "The ocean always soothes me."

"Did it work?"

"Mostly."

He crosses an arm behind his head and flashes his most obnoxious smile. "Mm. Still thinking of me, Maggie?"

She rolls her eyes. "Don't flatter yourself."

"Well, I'm still thinking of you." He does his best to sound wounded. "Will you come here?"

Margaret sighs and comes to sit beside him. Unable to resist, he snakes an arm around her waist and flips her so that she's lying flat beneath him. She lets out a soft *oof* of surprise. Her hair spills off his jacket and onto the sand like liquid gold, and her eyes darken to the color of warm molasses. She gazes up at him like she's considering shoving him off just to spite him, but the hunger in her eyes convinces him that he'll get to keep all his appendages if he stays put.

He draws absent patterns along her rib cage, and when he slides his knee between hers, she shifts her hips at the exact right angle to make him nearly unhinged with wanting her. Against her, he is powerless. *Useless.* He buries his nose in her hair and inhales the briny scent of it.

"You're insistent," she tells him, although there's no venom in it.

"I'm weak," he mumbles. "And you're ravishing. But I'll keep my hands to myself if you want."

"No. Please don't." Margaret brushes the wet hair from his eyes. Her palms, still coarse with sand, rasp his skin. And then she guides his face to hers and kisses him until his entire world and his every thought is her.

He draws back and continues downward slowly, along her throat and collarbones; then, after he gathers up her skirt, to her stomach and each of her hip bones. His mouth is gritty with salt and sand, but he doesn't much care—not when she weaves her fingers into his hair and practically drags him where she wants him. He considers teasing her for being impatient but decides it's best not to press his luck when it'd be so easy to toss him into the bonfire. He lifts his gaze to hers, admiring the way the cool light pools in all the curves of her body, and presses a kiss to her inner thigh. Margaret's breath catches.

"Do you know how often I've thought about doing this?" He relishes the way her entire face goes red, how she squirms with every word he speaks against her skin. It's more endearing than it has any right being. "Ever since I saw that scene in your book, it's been torture watching you read it."

Sweet as candy, she says, "Then why don't you stop talking and put us both out of our misery?"

He can't argue with that, so he does. When he finds the exact rhythm she likes, the distant thought occurs to him that maybe he ought to be more self-conscious that nothing but the pressure of her fingers against his scalp and the taste of her reduces him to this, overeager and moaning softly against her. But he doesn't think he's ever experienced anything more exquisite than the satisfaction of hearing her whimper his name like that when he pushes her over the edge.

He's hardly had a chance to catch his breath when she rolls him onto his back and straddles his waist. Her chest heaves, and her simple cotton dress, which he has thoroughly rumpled, is maddening in how it conceals her from him.

When she looks like this, flushed and hazy and haloed by the moon, he truly can believe God exists, and her name is Margaret Welty.

As she leans over him, her hair slips over her shoulders and curtains them. "I want you."

"God, yes," he says, which encompasses his entire faculty of language at the moment. Then, in a sudden burst of clarity, he stammers, "I . . . just have to . . . Uh. Hold on."

His heart threatens to burst out of his chest from nerves, and his fingers don't quite work right as he rummages through his pockets for the condom. When he's at last found what he's looking for, he works down his trousers and tears into the foil. Margaret watches him roll it on with rapt attention. Never in his life has he felt so out of sorts, so insecure, so *much*.

Her eyes are warm and puzzled as she traces his lower lip with her thumb. "Are you nervous?"

"Of course I am. I want this to be . . ."

Margaret stares at him expectantly. He should have known she wouldn't let him get away with it. She will extract every last truth from him.

"I want this to be perfect," he says.

She blesses him with another of her rare, secret smiles. "It already is."

It already is. The three sweetest words he's ever heard.

She settles onto him, slow and agonizing and so good he fears he will never come down from the high of it. In her eyes are the very words he wants so desperately to say. But this is close to a confession. He could spend an eternity learning to love her this way and still want for more. But it's over far sooner than he hopes. When he pulls her down against his chest, he mutters "sorry" against her ear.

She laughs and nestles her head beneath his chin. "Don't be. Please."

Together, they listen to the sea crash against the shore. His ragged breaths even out until they keep time with the roll of the tide, a steady whisper of *Margaret, Margaret, Margaret.* In a matter of minutes, she dozes off, and he lets her sleep until sky goes lavender with dawn.

30

In just three hours, the hunt will begin.

After Margaret and Wes returned to the inn, they crept back into the room as quietly as they could to get ready. She's plaited her hair and armored herself in her formal hunting attire: a white turtleneck, tan britches, and brown paddock boots. Her black jacket hangs over the back of the chair she's claimed in the inn's dining room. She sits at a small breakfast table, anxiously tearing apart the biscuit Annette insisted on bringing her, and waits for Wes to come downstairs.

The window at her shoulder offers a view of the water, slate gray and marbled with restless whitecaps. It feels like a different ocean entirely than the one she lay beside this morning, listening to Wes's heart beat steadily against her ear. Even now, she thinks she is half-dreaming. She fears that this pleasant ache within her will wash away with the encroaching storm—that this impossibly bright happiness will be taken from her before the day is done.

The sound of footsteps echoes in the silence. *Wes,* says the giddy leap of her heart.

But it's not Wes approaching her table. It's Evelyn.

"Mother."

Evelyn wears a tweed suit and her golden hair in a loose queue that's draped across her shoulder like a serpent. Without the haze of despair or exhaustion in her eyes, she looks far more lucid than she has in years. She looks almost as Margaret remembers her before tragedy tore their family apart. "I need to talk to you."

"I only have a minute."

"I only need a minute." Margaret's heart climbs higher in her throat as Evelyn takes the seat across from her. The air thickens around her, harder to breathe. "You didn't have to leave, Margaret. How long do you plan to hide from me?"

Margaret keeps her gaze trained on her mother's cuff links, not trusting herself to speak.

"I'm worried about you. What good can possibly come of running off with him?"

"He's a good man."

"No better than the rest of them. They come and they go as soon as they get what they want. Perhaps I've kept you too sheltered if you don't understand that. Your father—"

You're your father's daughter through and through. "I don't want to hear about my father. And I don't want to hear what you have to say about Wes."

"Why won't you listen to reason? You're a well-educated girl. Even if we've fallen on hard times, the Welty name means something. As for Winters, he's . . ." Evelyn gestures vaguely. "He's a ruffian. The only thing he can offer you is trouble. He'll ruin you, assuming he hasn't already."

Anger sparks hot within her. "What I do is none of your business."

"I'm your mother. Of course it's my business."

"And you've shown me what that means to you."

Evelyn looks genuinely wounded—enough that Margaret wishes she hadn't said it at all. She leans across the table, as if she means to reach out and take her hand. "It means the world to me. Everything I do and everything I have done is for my children."

Children. Not child.

"I love you, Margaret. I've tried to take care of you the best I know how, and I suppose that wasn't enough for you. But believe me when I say I know men like Weston Winters. I've taught them. I've loved them. He will leave you as soon as he's finished with you. Whether that's after the hunt or after he marries you for my estate."

"You're wrong."

"He is *using* you," she pleads. "Can't you see that? What interest could you hold to him? What has he given you besides promises and pretty words? Maybe he loves you now, but what about in a year when he grows bored and restless? I saw it the moment I laid eyes on him. He looks at the world like he wants to swallow it whole."

Her mother speaks her worst fears into existence, the ones she has locked away since she watched him fall in love with her at the end of her gun. But now, she can't shake the fear of what lies beyond the shroud of today. They could have a life together—a life as good as he dreams. But they could have a terrible life, too. Wes, hungry for what he denied himself for her sake. Her, his selkie wife in the pitiless sprawl of Dunway. Both of them, poor and resentful and trapped.

He will grow bored. He will lie. He will leave you.

He has shown her both sides of himself: loving and spiteful, ambitious and selfless, untethered and hopelessly devoted. They are both him. They will both always be him. She cannot make the same mistake again; she cannot make a whole of only one half of him. If there is one alchemical law she believes in, it's that one.

"I see myself in him. The type who's more interested in the way things could be than the way things are. But that's not you, Maggie. His ambitions will exhaust you."

"He doesn't want to be an alchemist for the research. He wants to be a politician—to help people."

"Listen to yourself." Evelyn clutches her forearm. "If you showed him my notes, then he knows how to distill the prima materia. If you win, you'll have the hala. And as long as you have it, that temptation will always exist for him. Politics is nothing but bureaucratic drudgery. But what do you think will happen when he realizes what potential the stone has? What idealist can deny the power to make any dream a reality? There's no man alive who has the power of a god within his reach and turns away from it."

Her hands tremble. "And what would you have me do?"

"Give the fox to me." Through the thick fabric of her sweater, Evelyn's fingers dig in hard enough to hurt. Her eyes burn. "I'll get it right this time. We'll be a family again."

A family. It fills her with a longing so intense, she feels sick with it. For so long, she's languished as if in a desert, chained just outside the oasis of her mother's affection. Hearing those words is like the first sweet drink of water in years. If her mother fails, then her suffering will end. The hala is the last demiurge—the last opportunity to create the stone. Once it's gone from this world, Evelyn's quest will be over. They really could be a family again.

But would it ever really be the same, as easy as turning back the hands on a clock? After everything Wes has promised her, would she truly be content with the safety of that quiet, recovered life?

"Think about it. Good luck today." With that, Evelyn releases her. She rises from her seat and straightens the lapels of her jacket.

As soon as Evelyn steps into the lobby, Wes descends the staircase. The two of them stop dead as their eyes meet. Wes's fist tightens. The world freezes. The air crystalizes in Margaret's lungs.

His expression, however, doesn't change. He shoves his hands into his pockets and continues walking toward Margaret as though he didn't see Evelyn at all.

Margaret lets out a shaky breath, resting her face in her palms.

The chair legs whine against the tiled floor as he pulls it out. The sound is too loud and garbled in her ringing ears. "What did she say to you?" he asks.

"Nothing really."

"Margaret . . ." The concern in his voice and the way he glances at her mangled, uneaten food is almost more than she can bear. Her heart will rend itself in two before the day is done.

"I'm fine. Please don't worry about me."

She feels as though she's been threaded through with an electrical wire, jittery and wild with dread. Nothing can be fine when nothing is certain. The only thing certain in her life has been the same core truth. Survival means clinging to what she knows. It means fighting tooth and nail for what she has, not for what she wants. But right now, she doesn't know what she has any more than she knows what she wants.

Wes takes her hands and presses them to his lips. They're soft and warm against her knuckles. His hair is smoothed back into submission and shining like lacquer. A few stubborn strands, however, slip free and fall into his eyes. Sometimes, he is adorable. She's such a fool, she thinks, to love him.

I love him. It doesn't surprise her to finally admit it to herself. It feels nothing like a revelation, nothing like falling—only like the punchline of some cruel, predictable joke. She has only given the universe more ammunition to wound her.

"Are you ready?" he asks.

"Yes." Margaret smiles in spite of herself. "Are you?"

"As ready as I can be." He hesitates. "Are you afraid?"

"I'm terrified." But it's not the hala she's afraid of.

She is terrified that when the times comes, she will make the wrong decision.

It's too cold for midautumn, colder than it's been in weeks.

By the time they register their alchemized items with the hunt officials, it's late afternoon and the sky is gashed with thick, dark storm clouds. Somewhere in the distance, Margaret hears the rumble of thunder like a dog's warning growl. Anticipation crackles in the air like static. They stand in the waist-high rye, which stretches out before them for nearly a mile. It's cut up by pasture fences and fades into groves of cypress and maple, whose branches are gnarled and crooked like beckoning fingers.

All around them are kennels full of dogs snarling at the bars and horses snorting their restless, cloudy breaths into the bitter cold day.

Hunters dressed in scarlet regalia chatter among themselves, while children too young to join the hunt pass out glasses of sherry from silver trays. Closer to Wickdon, the hilltoppers, eager to watch the spectacle, tack up their horses. The wind tugs greedily at their solid black cloaks; fabric unfurls like a dark wave against the golden fields.

There's more of them than Margaret expected. Most tourists follow the hunt for the pomp and not the bloodshed. They'll sleep off their hangovers until tonight, when the hala is dismembered in the town square and they anoint the first-timers with its blood. Everything the victors won't keep will go to the hounds, assuming there will be a victor this year.

There will be. There has to be.

But the prospect of winning, once so uncomplicated, fills her only with a horrible dread. If she surrenders the hala to Wes, her mother will never speak to her again. If she gives it to her mother, she risks losing her to the stone. If she throws the competition, his family will be sunk. No matter what she does, she will hurt the people she loves.

A phlegmy voice crackles over a microphone. "I will now begin the blessing of the hounds."

Pastor Morris stands with his back to the woods, dressed in a solemn black pulpit gown and a stole of black velvet. He squints into the invisible sunlight, out at the wall of kennels. Somewhere among all those hounds rattling their cages is Trouble. Margaret can hardly bear the thought of letting him loose. The hala's magic weaves through the air, calling to the hounds, and with all of them slavering for the kill, she fears he'll be torn apart.

When Pastor Morris begins to speak, she can barely hear him over the eager howl of the wind and the hiss of the rye. It ripples like a storm-churned sea around them. "Father above, creator of all things, who is all things, we are gathered here today to uphold the most enduring and most sacred of this country's traditions.

"We ask your blessing for all of the hunters before me and that one of them may at long last kill the hala, the last of the false gods. We offer you our praise and thanksgiving for our spirited hounds, for our sure-footed horses, for the woods and the sea, and for all the creatures in our free land of New Albion. Keep us safe, lead us true, and bless all those here to celebrate this hallowed sport and all those who have died in your name. Guide their souls to your holy light, free at last from the shackles of this material plane. Amen."

A muttered chorus of "amen" follows. As soon as silence descends again, the master of the hunt kicks her horse into a gallop and tears off toward the woods.

"Somber," Wes mutters. "What's happening now?"

"She's going to search the covert for quarry. It's tradition for the master of the hunt to flush the fox out and put some distance between it and the hounds. It's not a proper hunt if it's over too quickly."

"How long will that be?"

"A couple minutes. A couple hours."

"A couple *hours*?"

"I don't know." Shimmer drapes his head over her shoulder, and she absently rubs his cheek. This morning, Aoife braided his mane in a complicated pattern she assured them would bring them luck.

They don't have to wait longer than a few minutes today. The blare of a horn swells across the fields beneath a roll of thunder. Then, distantly, someone shouts, "Tallyho!"

Whoops rise up from the crowd, and a group of volunteers rushes forward to slide open the doors of the kennels. Hundreds of dogs come pouring out, baying and snapping at each other. Like a copper-and-black river, they slip into the rustling tall grass. The noise is awful, unlike anything she has ever heard.

"First flight! First flight to the starting line!"

Margaret's stomach sours. It's all happening too fast. Just as she feels herself coming loose from her body, Wes twines his fingers through hers. She snaps back into herself.

"That's us," he says.

"Right." Keeping ahold of Wes, Margaret clutches the bridle tighter and begins to lead them toward the starting line. People press close—too close—and suddenly those few yards feel like they stretch on for miles. Someone's elbow lands in her ribs, and as they push deeper into the crowd, she hears them hissing through their teeth.

Banvishman. Yu'adir.

Word must've spread, and she'd be shocked if it wasn't Jaime who started it. Someone sloshes beer onto Wes's boots. Another tosses a handful of coins in their path that wink in the frost like droplets of spilled blood.

Shimmer shies, whickering anxiously beside her. Her face burns with anger and humiliation, but she keeps her chin lifted. Beside her, Wes looks tense and more unhappy than she's ever seen him beneath the spotlight of a group's attention.

They break through the crowd, where the rest of the first flight gathers. They fan out in formation behind the field master, all wearing jackets in shades as brilliant as gemstones. But she cannot let herself be cowed. Not by anything, not even by Jaime.

Margaret finds him in the crowd immediately, sitting high atop his mare. She's as stormy black as the sky roiling overhead, a shocking contrast to his scarlet coat. He turns away from her and mutters something to his alchemist, the auburn-haired woman beside him. She glances over and meets Margaret's gaze with a smirk. Her lips are painted for war in a venomous shade of bloodred.

All she can think of is what Wes told her last night. *He said if he sees me alone tomorrow, he'll kill me.*

She'll just have to lose them as quickly as possible, then. Tearing herself away, Margaret helps Wes onto Shimmer's back, then hoists herself up. Shimmer is restless beneath them, for once eager to run. She gathers up the reins as Wes locks his arms around her. Out on the horizon, the sun glows red behind a break in the seething clouds. It's the red of an ember beneath ashes. The red of the philosopher's stone.

Her heart pounds in her ears. The wind hisses her name. A horn blasts.

And with that, the hunt begins.

31

They race beneath clouds as dark as caput mortuum. In the clawing wind, Wes's hair comes loose from the layers of gel, Margaret's from her clip. They tangle together, blond into black, and lash his face until his eyes water. Over Margaret's shoulder, he can clearly see the chaos of the field stretching out before them. The grass is charred in the hala's wake and dewed with coincidentia oppositorum. More horses than he can count gallop past them, their hoofbeats echoing the roll of approaching thunder.

Margaret's knuckles are white against the reins. His every muscle is wound tight as he clings to her waist, his feet grounded in the stirrups of their double saddle. Bit by bit, they gain on the hounds, all of them in full cry. Out in the middle of the pack, he spies a familiar copper coat—and Trouble's ears flopping behind him as he runs. He's lumbering in comparison to the small, lean beagles and foxhounds, but he keeps pace with them. Farther ahead of them is a streak of white slicing through the grass like a razor.

The hala.

It slips beneath a pasture fence, pursued by a rising cloud of smoke. The hounds scrabble under the cross braces, snapping at one another. The hunters in the lead leap over the fence to follow the pack, but if they even try to jump, Wes will be flung off or else break his tailbone. It'll cost them precious time to go the long way around the pasture, but they don't have another choice.

Margaret urges Shimmer around the bend, hugging close to the fence. A few of the weaker riders press in around them. His leg nearly gets crushed between two horses and he feels dizzy with the thickening stench of sulfur, but crowded in like this, there's nowhere to go. Gritting his teeth, he glances over—only to see someone matching them stride for stride.

Jaime's alchemist.

Her red hair streams behind her like a flame as she reaches toward Shimmer's shoulder. A transmutation circle embroidered in fine blue thread glows on her leather gloves. It takes Wes only a second to recognize the symbols for decomposing carbon. The moment she touches Shimmer's bare skin, it'll singe him. Wes has to do something, but like this, he's a sitting duck. He can't loosen his grip without losing his seat.

"Margaret, to your left!"

She jerks her head to look just as another rider's hunting knife flashes and nicks the alchemist's horse. It bolts sideways, throwing her off. Wes doesn't dare look back when he hears her strangled shout of pain.

"We need to get out of here," Margaret says. "Hold on."

His arms are already sore from holding on, but he finds it in himself to press more firmly against her. They pull ahead from the squabbling pack, eating up the rye beneath them as they close the gap between them and the leaders. He keeps his stinging eyes trained on the gleam of white fur until it disappears into the coiling underbrush. The hounds slip through the other side of the pasture fence and careen headlong into the woods. The trees loom, waiting for them.

Over the baying of the hounds, someone shouts, "Lieu in!"

Wes's stomach sinks as he counts down the seconds until the woods swallow them whole.

Here, beneath the pines, there's no light. His breath comes harder, misting in the air. Somehow, it's louder than the clamor of the hounds, than Shimmer's exerted snorting, than the branches snapping beneath them. They're close enough to the leaders now that he can see Jaime in his scarlet coat, a bloodstain against the inky black of his mount. What the hell does he think he's doing without his alchemist?

A gust of wind buffets them, sending a tremor through him. It's the same rush he gets when channeling alchemy—and the same horrible dread he felt before he saw the hala alone in the woods.

Wes blinks, and the hounds scatter like struck billiards in every direction. Their determined cries break into confused, desperate yelps. It must be the fox's doing—some subtle pull it has on that divine spark within all of them. Margaret veers hard to the left, following Trouble. The wind that whistles past his ears speaks with that eerily familiar, whispering voice.

Come.

He swears. "Did you hear that?"

"Yes," Margaret says grimly.

The horse in front of them shies and stumbles; the rider lands in a heap, slamming his head against the edge of a stump. Wes only catches a glimpse of him as they gallop past, but the image is burned behind his eyelids. By the angle of his neck and the blood trickling from his ears, he knows that he won't be getting up again. Wes's stomach lurches. Death has touched his life profoundly. But he's never watched it happen, the plain and awful fact of it. Someone there and gone. He's never seen the moment someone's soul comes untethered from their body.

What kind of person does this every year? It's been no more than thirty minutes, and he's already seen enough to last a lifetime. He buries his forehead between Margaret's shoulder blades and desperately tries to remember a prayer—any prayer.

God, he thinks. *Just let Margaret live through this.*

When he turns his cheek against her spine, he finds the world has grown hazier, as if frost has bloomed over his vision. Silver fog weaves through the thick redwood trunks like a slinking cat. The whole forest hisses like the ocean, furious and wild, and although he can see little more than dark, indistinct shapes around them, he swears white eyes keep blinking open in the shadows. It's impossible to know just how many people are around them—if there are any at all anymore.

It's like the hala is trying to isolate them. It's flushing them out like they're *its* quarry.

Shimmer's hooves kick up the sooty caput mortuum dusting the undergrowth. The smell of sulfur hangs in the air, wafting up from the blackened swathes of decay the hala has left like a trail of bread crumbs. The bone-dry rattle of the leaves grows louder, harsher, and from that horrible swirl of noise, the sound of their names rises out of the mist.

And then: the distinct, four-count drumbeat of a galloping horse closing in on them.

"We've got company." Wes turns to look over his shoulder just in time to watch a sleek foxhound dart by them.

Gunfire bursts.

Shotgun spray whizzes overhead. A tree branch explodes into a thousand pieces and batters them like hail. Shimmer tosses his head against the reins, his eyes white all around, but Margaret holds him fast.

"What the hell was that?" she snaps.

Wes chances another look behind them. And there is Jaime Harrington, emerging like a wraith from the fog and gun smoke. He has a fistful of his horse's mane in one hand, a shotgun dangling from the other. No wonder his aim was so piss-poor.

"Are you insane?" Wes shouts. "You're going to kill someone!"

"I told you if I found you alone, Winters, you're dead!"

"I can't shake him," Margaret says, an edge of panic creeping into her voice. "He's too fast."

"It's fine. I'll figure something out." But his thoughts are churning so quickly, he can't hold on to a single one of them. His mouth sours with the taste of fear. Their only blessing is that Jaime can't reload another round while he's moving.

Jaime gains on them quickly, until they're riding side by side over the treacherous path. They duck beneath the eager grasp of low-hanging branches. Jaime could easily overtake them, could easily follow their hounds to where the chase would end, could easily make his move to win. But he's not playing to win, Wes realizes.

He's playing for them to lose.

As they skirt close to a ravine, Jaime forces them closer and closer to the edge. Pebbles clatter down the side of it with every strike of Shimmer's hooves. They're shoulder to shoulder now. Near enough that Wes can see Jaime's eyes burning with pure, determined malice.

Time slows to a crawl as Jaime throws out his arm to shove him. If he loses his balance now, he'll drag Margaret down with him. He doesn't think. He unhooks his feet from the stirrups and lets go of her. He grabs Jaime's wrist.

Then, there is nothing but open air.

"Wes!"

He strikes the ground hard enough that the breath is knocked from his lungs—hard enough that he hears something pop. Together, he and Jaime tumble over the ridge, snarling and tangled like fighting dogs. Exposed roots and rocks tear at them all the way down. When they land in a heap, Jaime crawls over him. His knees dig into Wes's arms, pinning him beneath his weight. He couldn't feel whatever snapped earlier through the sudden rush of adrenaline, but now his shoulder throbs with a pain so sharp, the world flickers black. He shouts into the pulsating dark.

Jaime's scarlet coat is spattered with mud, and his eyes are veined with red like a cracked slab of concrete. The curl of his fist and his vicious smile are the last things Wes sees before his vision bursts with stars. The agony comes a split second later, licking into his skull like a flashfire. By the time he comes to a second later, he feels blood streaming down his face, hot and wet.

"I've been waiting a long time to do that."

Wes tastes copper and spits out a wad of blood. A quick sweep of his tongue over his teeth, at least, lets him know that they're all still intact. "Got it out of your system, Harrington? You threw the whole damn hunt for this chance?"

"Better to let it go than let it fall to you."

"Even after what happened to your friend? You want that thing to come back next year for another shot at him?"

"This is the last thing we have! The last New Albian tradition that's *ours*."

Jaime shrugs off his backpack, rummaging until he finds a shell glinting dull and gray. He hauls himself to his feet, then reloads his shotgun.

"I'm not an idiot, Winters." He pumps his gun. "There's no stemming the tide of people like you, no matter how many quotas are put in place. Soon enough, even places like Wickdon will be overrun. But I'll be damned if I don't protect our way of life for as long as I can."

"And you've done a fine—"

He levels the shotgun at him. "I don't want to hear one more smart-ass comment from you. I'm serious."

"So am I. You've made your stand, so why don't we call it even? You're not a murderer."

"And I won't be by anyone's estimation, even if I kill you. Do you think anyone will think twice about it if you don't come back? Do you think they'll miss you? It'll be two less vermin in this country."

Two less.

"Leave her out of this, you son of a bitch! If you lay a single hand on her—" Before Wes can clamber to his feet, Jaime kicks him in the ribs. He curls in on himself, wheezing.

"Jaime."

"Margaret," Wes rasps. She stands a few yards away, her rifle trained steadily on Jaime and her golden hair billowing in the wind. "Get out of here."

"Put the gun down, Maggie," Jaime says.

She doesn't move. Her eyes blaze with quiet fury.

"Now! I swear to God, I'll shoot him before you can even blink."

Tension ticks in her jaw. Every second stretches into an eternity. *Please,* Wes thinks. *Get out of here. Just go.*

His heart drops when she sets her rifle down and raises her palms in surrender. "What do you think you're doing?"

Jaime turns the barrel of his shotgun at her. "I'm going to make him watch the life drain from your eyes. And when I've done to him what he's done to me, I'm going to kill him."

No. It can't end like this. He can't fail to protect someone—not the one time it truly matters. Wes jolts upright but collapses again at the sharp pain in his ribs. Every drawn breath feels like a twist of a knife in his lungs. "Don't you dare. Don't you fucking dare! Haven't you done enough already?"

"Do you really think we can ever be even? My parents were driven from the city by her people. I lost Annette because of you. You! A Banvishman with nothing. You take and take what you don't deserve, and you'll leave this country a shell by the time you're done with it. Nothing but a puppet for your pope and your sham of a religion. This is just as much a service to this country as killing that monster is."

Jaime lifts the gun to his shoulder. Draws in a steadying breath. Margaret doesn't say a word, but Wes knows her well enough by now to see the wild spark of fear in her eyes. She squeezes them shut and rolls her shoulders back.

"Don't. I'll kill you." Wes can hardly recognize his own voice, raw and furious. "I'll kill you! I swear to God, I'll—"

A gust of wind tears through the clearing. It hisses over the fallen leaves and clatters the bare branches. Salt coats his tongue, and the stench of sulfur scrapes down his throat.

And then, in the corner of his eye, he sees it.

As though yanked on marionette strings, all three of them turn toward it. The hala sits barely an arm's length away, luminous in the fog. Those horrible, empty eyes are flung wide open—wide enough to fall into. It stares directly at Jaime, perfectly still and perfectly silent. Even when he saw it alone, it didn't feel like this.

The aura it's radiating is malevolent.

"What the hell is it doing?" Jaime mutters.

Its lips part slowly in a grin, each tooth locked together like a zipper.

Jaime turns his gun on it, but before he can pull the trigger, it lunges. Its teeth sink into Jaime's calf with a sickening crunch.

He screams as his skin chars and bubbles. His gun clatters at his feet, and the mud drinks his blood, the earth running silver and red and black. As soon as he crumples, the fox releases him and clamps down on his shoulder. His flesh yields easily, exposing a stringy mess of red gore. Wes can only watch in stunned horror as he scrabbles to his feet.

Margaret unsheathes the knife at her hip. Its blade reflects the glowing white of the beast's fur. She drives it into the fox's back.

It screeches, a sound that rattles all his bones and curdles his blood. It's *awful,* like a thousand human screams layered beneath a fox's shrill, eerie cry. The hala thrashes until it finds its footing, then darts into the trees with the engraved hilt still notched beside its spine.

"Go!" Wes says.

"I can't kill it without you."

"I'll find you in a minute." His gaze flickers to Jaime. "I need to take care of him."

Margaret hesitates but nods. Once she disappears into the underbrush, Wes turns his attention to Jaime. He lies at the toe of his blood- and mud-caked boots. He clasps a hand to the gaping wound on his shoulder, as though he can push the ruined muscle back inside. There's a small part of Wes that admires him for holding it together as well as he is. No tears. No begging. He only glares at Wes, his eyes full of spiteful pride.

"Do it, then," Jaime says.

"What are you talking about?"

"Don't play dumb. Isn't that what you're staying for? Revenge?"

Wes can't deny the prospect fills him with a strange sort of fascination. Maybe Margaret has always been right to doubt and fear him. There is something dark within him that enjoys this heady rush of power. It's intoxicating to at last hold all the cards—to cradle a life in his hands. The divinity of God lives within each of them, but only an alchemist can harness that spark. Jaime's is just a pale, insignificant glimmer against his.

This is what he wanted to be an alchemist for. To protect people from those like Jaime Harrington. For everything he put them through—for everything he would continue to do to the vulnerable populations of New Albion—it'd be just to put him out of his misery now, or at least to turn his back and let him bleed to death. No one would question it was the fox's handiwork if he finished the job with alchemy. Ninety-nine percent of the human body is composed of six simple components. Carbon, hydrogen, oxygen, nitrogen, calcium, and phosphorus. He wonders if it hurts or if the body goes up in flames all at once. He wonders if it would be as easy to dissolve a human as it would be to dissolve a stone. If All is One and One is All, what's the difference, really?

Jaime clearly sees what's on his mind. His throat bobs.

But Wes can't do it.

He can't solve a systemic problem like this. And it's not enough to believe in a better future, as though it's something as inevitable as God himself. He has to demand it. He has to work for it. And even though Jaime deserves to suffer, even though he will never change, even though he hates him, Wes can't bring himself to wield this stolen moment of superiority like a club. If he wants to change the world and kill the hala with a clear conscience, he has to do this on his own terms.

"Come on, then," Wes says. "Get up."

As best he can, considering Jaime is twice his size and unwieldy as anything, Wes slings Jaime's good arm over his shoulders. The ache in his ribs worsens with every step, but he manages to drag him to a tree. After propping him upright against the trunk, Wes shrugs out of his jacket.

"What're you doing?" Jaime groans.

"Stripping," he snaps. "Do you want to die or not?"

Jaime keeps silent, even though Wes can still feel the anger radiating palpably from him. He winces as Wes knots the sleeves just above the wound on his shoulder, tight enough to stanch the blood flow. "Why?"

"I'd sooner let you die, but I think Margaret would kill me for it, and I can't let that happen yet." He claps him on his good shoulder. "And now you're in a Banvishman's debt. Remember that."

As much as he wants to stay to relish the bitterness and confusion twisting Jaime's face, he has a girl to find—and a fox to kill.

32

Margaret's lungs burn like they're full of seawater, but she doesn't slow down. If she lets up even for a moment, the hala will go to ground. Everything they've suffered, everything they've fought for, will be for nothing.

The branches overhead tear the feeble wash of moonlight to shreds, but it's enough to cast an oily, iridescent shimmer on the trail of the hala's blood. Out in front of her, Trouble and Jaime's hound are streaks of copper and black in the fog. They disappear through a thicket, and Margaret breaks into a clearing only moments behind them, shaking off leaves and trails of spiderweb. She's just in time to watch the hala scrabble up the thick trunk of a redwood. Trouble bays triumphantly as he circles it.

Finally, it's cornered.

Margaret unstraps the rifle from her back and takes aim. It's almost pathetic to have something as majestic as the hala wounded and fearful in her crosshairs. It brings her no joy to end its long life—not when she feels a strange kinship with it. It's more than her Yu'adir blood, more than the fact that it saved her life. It's that, for hundreds of years, it has evaded everyone who hoped to kill it. It's survived. Just like her, maybe that's all it's ever wanted.

Drawing in a shaky breath, she fires.

The thin branch it's made a refuge of collapses beneath it, and although it desperately seeks purchase with its claws, it goes down, twisting through the open air before landing with a broken *thud* on its side.

The hounds spring immediately. Trouble seizes it by its scruff, Jaime's hound by its leg. The hala snaps at them, writhing and screaming. It feels like a terribly cruel thing to let it suffer like this, but until Wes finds them, they're both pinned.

She's done it, but it feels nothing like triumph. She's nauseated with guilt and indecision. The last demiurge will fall by her hand. A Yu'adir girl will be remembered by this country. Wes's family will be safe. And Wes . . .

If he wants it, he will have the power to bend the universe to his will.

Her mother's words torment her, even now. *What idealist can deny the power to make any dream a reality? There's no man alive who has the power of a god within his reach and turns away from it.*

She trusted him with the magnum opus, but that was before there was anything tangible for him to claim. Now, staring down the reality of the hala, either the instrument of her downfall or salvation, she doesn't know how to do what Mrs. Wreford implored her to: decide what's best for her. Survival or hope. The pain she knows or a life beyond Wickdon, infinite in both disastrous and wondrous possibilities. Evelyn or Wes. Even now the two of them tear at her heart like hounds.

Leaves rustle behind her, and Wes stumbles through the underbrush, breathing hard and clutching at his side. His right eye is swollen shut, but the other is wide and shining with awe. Bruises, mottled purple like the band of a galaxy, rake down the side of his face. Even like this, he's the most breathtaking thing she has ever seen. More than anything, she wants to keep him.

But she can't.

Yesterday, she thought she was strong enough to leave her mother. For a night, she believed his love was enough to save her. But if she's let herself doubt him again so easily, she doesn't know if she will ever be more than this core of fear within her—than this cold, feral will to survive.

There's a break in the clouds, and the cold light of the moon washes over the clearing. It looks as though they're standing in the center of a giant transmutation circle. Magic shimmers in the air and prickles along her arms.

"Did we do it?" His voice is full of wonder.

"Almost." All there's left to do is for him to activate the array painted on the hilt of the knife. As he takes a step closer to the hala, Margaret lifts her rifle and aims it at him. "Don't move."

When the safety clicks, he turns slowly toward her, his hands lifted and his expression entirely unreadable.

"I told you I would shoot you if you gave me reason to," she says.

"You did. And have I given you reason to?"

"No." She searches his face. "That's the problem."

Confusion softens his features. "I don't understand."

"You've promised me everything." Her hands tremble. "And yet, I still can't . . . I don't know what I'm supposed to do. I don't know how I'm supposed to trust that you won't break your promises. I don't know how I'm supposed to believe that you won't leave the moment I close my eyes tonight, or that you won't create the stone, or that we can be happy. That *I* can be happy. How can I know?"

"You can't. Margaret, please . . . What do you want me to say? What do you want me to do?"

"Nothing! There's nothing you can do and nothing you can say. I'm never going to get better. I'm always going to be broken. This is all I am."

The wind gusts through the trees, hissing and seething.

"You're *not* broken. You're incredible. You've come such a long way since I met you, even if you're still afraid. Even if you have doubts. When I look at you, I don't see someone broken. I see someone hurting—someone healing. It'll take time, but that doesn't matter to me." Wes tentatively closes the gap between them, until the barrel of her gun is nestled against his chest, right above his heart. "I love you. Please, let me."

She rears back at the sound of those words, but he curls his fingers around the barrel and holds it in place. His expression is unbearably earnest, his eyes as warm and rich as coffee.

"I said it, and I'll say it again. I love you, Margaret Welty. I think I've loved you since I first saw you. I love you now, and I will love you when we walk back into Wickdon with all the world hating us, and I will love you whatever happens tomorrow. Look me in the eyes and call me a liar."

She can't.

"As soon as it's dead, it's yours. You can give it to your mother if you want. Hell, tonight, we can burn it all to caput mortuum and scatter it in the sea, if that's what it takes. No more words. No more promises. No more chances for alchemists like your mother to exist. And if that's not enough, I . . ." His voice breaks. "We could throw the competition."

He can't mean that, the romantic fool. What a stupid, self-destructive thing to promise her. If her mother won't teach him and he doesn't have the hala's corpse as proof of his skill, then he has no recourse to become an alchemist at all. "If we don't win, you won't become an alchemist. You won't become a politician."

"I know."

"You won't be able to pay for your mother's surgery."

This time, he hesitates. "I know."

Margaret squeezes her eyes shut. "No. That's not acceptable, Wes. I can't ask that of you. I can't ask you to give up everything for me."

"That's the only guarantee I can give you."

"Then I don't want it."

As soon as the words leave her mouth, her vision blurs with tears. She doesn't want to live in a world where he suffers because of her. She couldn't bear it if she was the one to smother his dreams. A guarantee against something he's already sworn not to do isn't worth that. Nothing is worth that, especially when her peace of mind can never truly be guaranteed. She's lived her whole life braced for another blow, but no amount of preparation or precaution has stopped them from landing.

All her life, love has been a scarce and precious resource, something earned or denied, something she starved for every day. But with Wes, love is different. It is reckless and inexhaustible. It is freely given. It simply *is*. Time and time again, he's stayed beside her through her doubt. He's shown her that she is enough, lovable despite her fears and her walls. That she is more than what happened to her and the pains she's taken to avoid it happening again. And now, he's given her the chance to prove it to herself.

For so long, she has survived. Now, she wants to live.

"All I want is for you to be happy. So I have to trust you. I *do* trust you."

"I'm easy to please," he says quietly. "Just let me take care of you. I swear I won't let you down. I won't leave you until you ask me to go."

"Then don't go." Margaret drops her rifle and winds her arms around his neck. "I love you, too."

Wes looks stunned, red zipping up his face. Then, he smiles at her so radiantly it hurts. "I wish I could lay you down right here, but we have a hunt to win."

He is incorrigible, and she is so in love.

The fizziness in her chest dissipates when her gaze lands on the hala, puddled in the moonlight. Its sides heave laboriously, but it's gone still and slack against the jaws of the hounds. This is the beast half of the hunters here today would've killed them for. The last demiurge: the last of the Katharists' false gods, the last of the Sumic god's children, the last of the Yu'adir god's gifts.

Nearly all the fight has drained from it, but the trees still rattle and shiver as they approach. Margaret kneels beside it, and it's almost a comfort when the voice of the wind sighs her name. It recognizes her.

Once, she asked her father how anything so terrible and destructive could possibly be a gift, even if God did place the secret of the making of the world in its heart. This is what he told her: *There is a Yu'adir word for wisdom, chokhmah. Scripture tells us that chokhmah is the unspotted mirror of the power of God, the image of his goodness. Fear of the Lord is the foundation of understanding. We must always seek chokhmah, even at a great cost to ourselves.*

Wes grips the hilt of the knife still embedded in the hala's back. Between his fingers, she can still see the brightly painted transmutation circle. He looks up at her through the tangle of his hair, as though he's asking her permission.

She nods.

He draws in his breath. The blade glows, as blinding white as lightning, as white as the hala's eyes. It lets out a strangled, mournful yelp. It shudders, crumples, and does not move again. The hounds release their grip on it. The wind quivers, as tremulous as a long-held breath.

And there is less magic in the world.

Wes whimpers softly. Margaret crouches beside him to smear away the tears streaking his cheeks. He pulls the blade out and lets it drop between them. It's coated in black caput mortuum that flakes off like rust.

"It spoke to me."

"What did it say?"

"I don't know exactly." He smiles ruefully. "I know it had to be done, but it still feels wrong."

"My father told me that God gave the demiurges to humanity so that we could learn from them. He believed that an alchemist's purpose is to always seek chokhmah, the truth." She takes his hand in hers. "He said true understanding of the world doesn't come without hurt and sacrifice. There's a psalm he would quote. *Chokhmah can do all things and make all things new.* If there's anyone who can do that—make the world a better place—it's you."

"Margaret . . ." His voice wobbles.

"Besides, your family will be safe. No one else will die because of it. And you believed it had dignity. Those are noble things."

"Thank you." He offers her a small, uncertain smile and squeezes her hand. "What do we do now?"

"We have to sound the call."

He pauses. "What call?"

"The death halloa."

"Excuse me? The death halloa? You made that up."

"I did not. You do this, three times."

She cups her hands over her mouth and lets out a *whoop*. It begins low and swells, like the rise of the tide. A three-part cry that Trouble takes up with an excited bay.

Wes blinks at her, perplexed, like he can't believe such a sound came out of her. Then, he throws back his head and echoes her. By the third call, they're both delirious, collapsing halfway through into breathless laughter. It hums in the stillness of the air. Before the silence smothers the woods again, the bright, clear sound of a horn swells in the distance.

It's finally over.

Wes gives her a sly, silly grin that makes her heartbeat stutter. Despite his bruised face, despite the blood drying on their skin, he pulls her against him and kisses her until there is nothing in the world but the two of them.

Without Shimmer—the coward is probably off grazing in someone's garden by now—it takes them the better part of two hours to make it out of the woods. Overhead, the night sky is impossibly clear and bright, the solid jewel blue of the ocean at dusk. The full moon is nestled in the clouds like a pearl in the mouth of a clam.

On the earth, however, grim reminders of the hunt remain. Ash swirls listlessly in the breeze. Blood beads on the leaves like dew. Bodies lie draped in white sheets.

Wes keeps Margaret tucked close into his side as they emerge into a wide-open expanse of field. A cavalcade rides toward them, little but charcoal smudges against the golden rye. Jaime must've done a good job spreading gossip. Margaret can tell by the look on their faces they share the same concern that chafes at the back of her mind. What will the crowds do when they realize who exactly has won?

As they approach, Wes whispers against her ear, "Do you think they're going to feed us to the hounds?"

Margaret fixes him with a deadpan glare. "Probably."

The hunt officials come to a stop in front of them. They sit astride a row of imposing black horses, their snorted breaths pluming in the air. The master of the hunt gives them a long, assessing look. "You kids wait here a minute while we figure out what to do with you."

They return almost an hour later with Mrs. Wreford and a paramedic in tow. Her horse has barely slowed to a walk when she slides off its back and storms toward them, looking like a fluffed-up cat in her thick fur jacket.

"You two," she growls, "had me scared half to death."

She crushes both of them into a hug. Wes whimpers in protest. It lasts only a moment before she draws back and gestures toward the hunt officials. One shuffles over to take Trouble's leash from Margaret while Mrs. Wreford gazes almost wistfully at the hala.

"May I?" When Margaret nods, she takes it from her and wraps it in cloth like cheese from the market.

"As you can imagine, we're concerned about what a mob of people may do if we drag the fanfare out, so we're going to make this quick and efficient. First, we're going to do something about your face"— Wes flushes as she jabs a finger at him—"and then we're going into town to present you two *briefly*. You will not say a word, and you will not wander from my sight until we get you home, or so help me. Do we understand?"

They nod.

"Good." Mrs. Wreford sighs. "Since I won't get to do this later,

I may as well do it now. It's tradition to anoint all first-timers with the blood of the kill."

She cradles the hala in one arm and runs a finger along the seam of the wound in its back. Setting it down, she grabs Wes by the chin. He grimaces as she paints his forehead and cheeks with lines of glittering silver. Its blood illuminates the planes of his face with a soft, pulsing glow.

"Don't give me that face, Weston. It's disrespectful," Mrs. Wreford hisses under her breath, although Margaret can tell she's only pretending to be annoyed. "Now go get your wounds looked at."

She turns her attention to Margaret next. Cupping her face, she brushes the hala's blood onto her cheekbones. It goes on warm. As it dries on her skin, as Mrs. Wreford meets her gaze with quiet reverence and the world softens with a haze of silvery light, it sinks in that this is real. Even if the whole town despises them for it, even if it's only six people and the Cold Moon as their witness, here in the quiet of the night, what happened tonight is undeniable.

A Yu'adir girl and a Banvishman have won the Halfmoon Hunt, and all of their dreams are within reach.

"Well? Did you figure it out—what you're going to do?"

Margaret glances at Wes, who's already begun animatedly chatting with the harried paramedic shining a flashlight into his eyes. She can't fight the smile tugging at her lips.

"Yes. I think I have."

Mrs. Wreford's eyes brim with tears, and she kisses her forehead. "I'm happy for you, Maggie. Come visit sometimes, won't you?"

The rest of the night passes in a blur.

As hoof-churned dirt gives way to cobblestone and the golden light of lanterns washes softly over them, the noise of the crowds reaches a fever pitch. They're paraded through the packed streets, beneath strings of red flags and the wide-open eye of the moon, and toward a makeshift stage that's been erected in the main square. Every single person in Wickdon is watching them.

In their jackets, they are a mass of color, brown and blue and black like the swirl of a tide pool at night. Not all of their gazes are unkind—she catches a glimpse of Annette Wallace and Halanan enthusiastically waving at them as they pass—but the ones that are steal her breath away with dread.

The ceremony is as brisk as Mrs. Wreford promised. They are presented, and Pastor Morris gives his closing remarks, a droning speech about the goodness of God and the wickedness of materiality. There are pictures—more pictures than she ever could have imagined. While she wants nothing more than to sleep for a thousand years, Wes basks in the attention. The paramedics did their best with his face; they managed to bring down the swelling, although his one eye is still bloodshot and a bruise snakes alongside his nose like the bend of a river. He spends the majority of their photoshoots turning his head this way and that to make sure it's always out of sight.

By the time they're released, most of the participants have gone to ground at the pub or to their rooms. Margaret, however, has one last thing to do before she can rest.

When the worst of the traffic clears out, they hire a cab to take them to Welty Manor. As soon as she sees it, forlorn and curled up like a sleeping dog in a hollow, she wishes she could turn back. Her breath quickens with fear, but Wes's hand in hers keeps her grounded as they pull into the driveway. A single light burns in the second story, bleeding out from the jagged pieces of her mother's broken window.

"I'll be right there with you," Wes says as they climb out of the car. "I've got your back."

The driver leans out the window. "I'm only waiting ten minutes, got it?"

"Thank you, sir." He sounds convincingly gracious. "That's all we need."

Margaret breathes steadily through her fear as they climb the rickety porch stairs and open the front door. Cold sweat trickles down the back of her collar. Inside, dust swirls through columns of watery blue moonlight. It's like walking into a tomb. Still and oppressively silent.

There's no movement upstairs, even as they shut the door behind them, even as they trudge to her room to load the last of her things into her suitcase. Evelyn will let her go without a word, and somehow, that's worse than any alternative.

It's only when they make it back into the foyer that she appears at the stop of the stairs. Her gaze is trained on their joined hands, then lands on the suitcase Wes carries for Margaret. Behind the white light glancing off her glasses, Margaret can't read her expression.

"I see you've made your decision."

"I have."

"Very well." Evelyn sounds exhausted. "Then I'll direct my appeal to you, Mr. Winters. Maybe you'll be more reasonable or can talk some sense into her."

"You'll be disappointed. I'm not really in the business of telling your daughter what to do. She's kind of stubborn."

"A trait you share, then. Since you don't respond to threats, then I'll compromise. Have her. Take the house, too, if you insist, when you inevitably spirit her away to the courthouse and wait for me to die. All I'm asking is that you give me the hala. I'll give you anything. You want an apprenticeship? I can do you one better. I'll graduate you now and write you a recommendation for the University of Dunway—or anywhere you'd like that I have connections. You name it. Whatever is in my power to give you is yours."

"No. I don't think so."

Her face draws taut with anger, but as the silence lingers, it crumbles into defeat. Evelyn curls her fingers around the banister with a white-knuckled grip. "Margaret, please. Don't do this to me. I'll have nothing."

Margaret at last sees her for what she is: a frail woman clinging to her last scrap of power. She feels sorry for her. It's wrong, to see a woman like her mother reduced to this. Once, she was vibrant and passionate and doting. But Wes was right in saying that there is a darkness in everyone. Maybe all of them have another self, one that waits unseen like the far side of the moon. David's death sparked something within her, and passion festered into obsession.

"Is the stone truly what you want?" Margaret asks. "It won't make any of this right. It won't bring him back, and even if it does, will it even matter after everything you've thrown away? Or did you always love the memory of him more than you loved the reality of me?"

There it is. The small, horrible fear she has kept locked away for so long.

"I've always been right here. Growing up with you—it felt like starving. For everything. Your affection, your protection, your interest. I thought if I never needed anything, if I never bothered you, if I took care of us until you finished your work, you'd love me. But it didn't work. You never saw me. You never cared."

"It goes both ways, Margaret. If that's how you want to paint me, then I suppose you've never seen me, either." Those words are like a shock of cold water.

She will never change, then.

"Why did my father never write?" Of all the things she expects herself to say, it isn't that. "Why did he never come back for me?"

Evelyn seems equally surprised. She sighs, a defeated sound. "He wanted to take you with him. But I couldn't bear to lose you, too. I told him he'd regret the day he came near you again."

It feels like a knife in her gut, and it feels like absolution. He didn't forget her. He didn't abandon her. Her memories didn't deceive her about what kind of man he was. The thought of what kind of life she could've had fills her with a longing and rage that tears through her like wildfire. But Margaret still cannot bring herself to hate her. When her anger cools, all that remains is grim certainty.

This will be the last time she steps foot in Welty Manor.

"Thank you," she says softly. "Goodbye, Mother."

Margaret doesn't wait for her response before pushing open the front door. Their driver honks the horn impatiently as soon as they step into the headlights, but she can't bear to sit in that stifling car when she feels like she wants to peel off her skin. Like she'll crumble to dust if she so much as draws a breath. Margaret slumps over and sits on the porch. Wes lowers himself beside her. The horn blares again, and he waves at the cab with a strained smile.

"Asshole," he mutters. Then, to Margaret: "That was brave of you."

"It didn't feel like it. It felt cruel and unfair."

"It wasn't." Wes wraps an arm around her. Margaret wishes she could drown in the comforting heat of his body, in his familiar bay-and-sulfur scent. "She's the one who's been cruel and unfair to you. You don't owe her anything, Margaret. You're doing what's best for you."

"You really think so?"

"I like to think so." Wes offers her a small, shy smile. It's nothing like his usual catlike grins or flirtatious smirks. This is one of the few he saves just for her. "But I wouldn't presume."

She leans her head against his shoulder. "You can."

"Come on." He brushes a soft kiss against her temple. "Let's go home."

33

The town of Wickdon writes him a very, very large check.

When the bank teller hands it to him, there's a delicious sort of satisfaction in seeing Walter Harrington's name in thin, jagged letters, as if the very act of signing it was an intolerable imposition. The number on it boggles his mind. Seventy-five dollars is more money than Wes has ever seen in his entire life—more than he expects to see ever again. Enough to cover his mother's surgery. Enough to put toward moving with Margaret somewhere, anywhere, other than here.

Enough, he hopes, to make up for everything he's put his family through.

The town has emptied out since the hunt ended yesterday. Only the gulls crying and squabbling over pieces of stale bread disturb the midmorning quiet. From here, he can see the waves lapping gently at the shore, docile as a kitten. The crisp breeze that wends its way through the streets cards its fingers gently through his hair. It carries no voices. No secret to the universe he feels like he'll spend the rest of his life trying to remember. It smells like the sea, full of promise.

He finds his family with Margaret at a café. They're seated at an outdoor table surrounded by a pile of suitcases that looks like the beginnings of a small city. His family is being his family, which is to say far too loud. Margaret sips her tea out of a dainty ceramic cup, clearly trying to decide whether she's amused or embarrassed by them all.

Wes approaches as silently as he can, then covers Colleen's eyes. "Guess—"

She jerks back in her chair, flailing, and clocks him in the ribs. All the air rushes out of him, and a hot burst of pain lights up his entire body. The paramedics told him his floating rib was broken, and although they were able to speed up the healing with alchemy, it'll be a while before he's fully recovered. Even longer now.

Colleen claps her hands to her mouth. "Oh my God, I'm so sorry, Wes!"

"You deserved it." Christine sets her teacup down on its saucer with a prim *clink*.

"I ought to withhold both your cuts for that," he says, "but luckily, I'm feeling generous."

He lays the check on the table in front of his mother. She gasps—actually gasps, which makes his stomach twist into knots. "Wes. That's too much. I can't accept it."

Mad takes a long drink of her coffee. "I can."

Christine snatches it off the table. "No way."

"Let me see, let me see!" Colleen reaches for it.

"If you rip it, I'll murder you both," Mad says.

"Everyone needs to share," Edie says serenely.

While his sisters bicker, his mother stands up and enfolds him in a hug. "I don't know what to say except thank you."

He rests his chin on top of her head. "Don't thank me. Thank Margaret."

Margaret flushes but hides it quickly behind the gilded lip of her cup. "It's nothing."

"It's everything." His mother carefully takes his hand in her bandaged one and ensnares Margaret's with the other. "I'm so grateful to you both. And I'm so glad you've found each other. I've always wanted a fifth daughter, you know. And Weston needs to settle down."

"Mam!" he protests. "Enough, okay? You'll scare her off."

"Alright, alright." She smiles knowingly. "We'll have a room set up for you when you get home tonight. I think that's our cab coming now."

Wes kisses her on the cheek. "See you soon. Be safe, alright?"

A sleek black cab rattles down the cobblestones and rolls to a stop in front of them. He peers through the window, catching a glimpse of a curled blond mustache, and groans. By his luck, of course, it's Hohn. Wes sees the exact moment he regrets taking their call. His face goes deathly pale, but he rolls down the window and smiles uncertainly. "Oh, Mr. Winters! And . . . the Misses Winters?"

"That's right!" Colleen says brightly.

While his family piles inside, Wes unlatches the trunk and loads all their things inside. "Take care of them, Hohn. And good luck to you!"

Lord knows he'll need it.

Wes waves goodbye, and as the cab trundles away, he swears he can hear his sisters shrieking and laughing all the way down the block.

The sea breeze caresses his face and sweeps the hair from the back of Margaret's neck. She gazes up at him pensively, the sunlight warm in her whiskey eyes. They have the whole afternoon to while away as she makes her peace with leaving. And then from there . . .

Well, he supposes the possibilities are endless.

"Alone at last," he says as deviously as he can.

"So we are." Her words are clipped, but he can hear the smile behind it.

He snags her by the waist, pulling her close enough that he can nearly taste the sweetness of the tea on her breath. Mint and honey and something uniquely Margaret. "And how ever shall we pass the time?"

Margaret bites her lip to keep from laughing. Before she can reply, a voice cuts in. "Sorry to interrupt. Weston Winters, right?"

"Yeah, that's me." Wes slackens his hold on Margaret and glances up begrudgingly. It takes a moment to recognize the young woman standing there, considering she's dressed much plainer than she was when he first met her at the alchemy exposition. But he wouldn't forget someone with such a guileless smile—or someone who helped him for nothing in return. "Miss Harlan?"

"You remembered! Call me Judith. Well, I think congratulations are in order. I thought I saw a spark in you, but I'll be damned. Who would've thought an unlicensed alchemist would be the one to finally pull it off?"

Margaret stiffens beside him. They exchange a look. He still hasn't quite figured out what to say if someone asks him how he did it.

"Not me," he says with a nervous laugh. "Thanks, though. I appreciate it."

"Of course. I'm glad I ran into you. I have a proposition for you, actually."

"What kind of proposition?"

"How about we take a walk?"

He glances at Margaret, who nods. He sees the warning in her eyes—*tread carefully*—but her voice is pleasant when she says, "I'll wait here."

"Alright, then." Wes tucks his hands into his pockets. "Let's walk."

They stroll past a row of colorful storefronts, where the vendors are desperately trying to get rid of the last of their hunt-themed knickknacks—fox-fur stoles and bugles carved from cow's horns and cupcakes iced with white-masked foxes. They hardly make it a block before he's ready to burst out of his skin with anticipation.

"I'm not going to ask you how you managed to kill it," Judith begins, "and somehow I doubt you'd tell me anyway. That doesn't matter to me. I was recently licensed myself, and I'm a little short on funding right now. You know how it goes. I live in Bardover, a few towns north of here, and was hoping to take on a student to get some government support and build a reputation."

"And you're asking *me*? Why?"

"Us Fifth Ward kids have to stick together. Besides, you can't teach talent, and you've clearly got talent. It'd be a shame to let that go to waste." Judith slows down to inspect another market stall, which is laid out with glazed cinnamon twists. "Tell me, what do you want to do with yourself?"

Wes hesitates. "I want to be a politician."

"Well, I happen to have graduated from the University of Dunway, so maybe we could help each other out." She rummages through her purse until she procures her card. He takes it from her gingerly. "Give me a call if you're in the area and want to get that letter of rec squared away. Bring your girl, too. Voters love a good rags-to-riches story, you know. Especially if there's romance."

Wes turns her card over in his hands. Her name is embossed in gold; it catches the light like a pendant. He feels like a shaken-up champagne bottle. The pressure building in his chest makes it hard to find the exact words. His girl. A letter of rec. Another shot at his dreams.

It's everything he's ever wanted.

"What do you say?"

"Let me talk to my family first and, uh . . . my girl." Wes clears his throat, searching for his most mature, even-keeled voice. "We'll be in touch soon."

"So we will."

It takes every ounce of strength he has to walk, not run, back to Margaret, wearing his widest, stupidest grin. The future is finally as rosy as he always dreamed.

34

That night, they go to the sea.

Margaret sits on a piece of driftwood as smooth and pale as marble, watching Trouble run laps at the waterline. He snaps up the salt water that splashes up from his paws with every joyous leap. Farther down the shore, Wes traces a transmutation circle in the sand with a stick. His shoes are discarded beside her, and his slacks are cuffed above his ankles.

When he finishes, he places a wooden box at the center. In it are the remains of the hala, drenched in waning moonlight. Like an icicle winking in sunlight, its fur sparkles coldly against the velvet lining of its makeshift coffin. Wes crouches beside it and lays his hands over the array.

It's no wonder people think of alchemy as magic. There's no effort in it, it seems. There is Wes kneeling in the sand. The next moment, there is Wes lifting his arm against a gust of hot air that arcs off the flames he's created. They leap into the night, brighter than a felled star.

Once the fire exhausts itself, crackling down to embers, all that remains in the box is a pile of black caput mortuum. With one more transmutation, he could purify it into the prima materia—and from there, forge the philosopher's stone.

After tonight, no one will ever get the chance.

Margaret rises from her perch and approaches Wes. Even now, she can feel the heat of the alchemical reaction. It washes over her, the smell of sulfur twining with the rich brine of the sea. Wes picks up the box and presses it into her arms. It is warm against her skin, and its contents are black as the sea. All her pain, all the tradition and hatred and fanfare, for just this pile of ash.

The tide rolls over their ankles. Her toes curl into the sand at the sudden sting of cold. Out on the horizon, the reflection of the moon sparkles on the waves, like God has scattered a handful of diamonds across the water. Wes shoves his hand into his pockets, his eyes fixed on some far-off point she cannot follow. The wind tangles in his hair and whips the tails of his coat.

Like this, Wes looks very serious—almost mature. There's a small part of her that's ashamed to be throwing away the opportunity to achieve the magnum opus. To so callously discard all her mother's fruitless ambitions.

"Are you sure?" she asks.

"What use do I have for a pile of ashes, Margaret?"

There is no smile in his words. He treats this with the reverence of a funeral, which she's glad of. It's relieving that he doesn't find this makeshift ceremony ridiculous. Mad was right about him. When it comes to dramatics, he will never do a thing halfway.

Her heart squeezes with longing. Someday, when he achieves what he sets out to do, there will be radio broadcasts and newspaper articles written about him. Ones about a man who loves a country that never loved him back. A man who changed it for the better. She knows they will capture many things about him. His grit and bullheadedness, and his temper and his hunger for justice. But she hopes, more than anything, that the world will see what she does when she looks at him. His compassion and gentleness. His willingness to walk into hell beside her.

She says, "If anyone could finish it, you could."

"No, I don't think so. I'm still trying to figure out what it told me, what I was supposed to learn. But I think the magnum opus is a trap or a test or a fool's errand. I don't know. All I know for sure is that if God or the truth or whatever you want to call it is out there and we can reach it, we're not going to find it in that box. We'll find it in other people."

Margaret considers this.

"Or maybe just in you," he amends.

She lowers her head, if only to keep him from seeing her smile. "How sacrilegious."

Wes winks. "Maybe you should've found a nice Katharist man instead."

"I think I'll manage with you."

She doesn't know what exactly lies ahead. All their belongings are crammed into the suitcases stacked on the beach behind them. But when she stands beside him, the rippling band of the horizon doesn't feel as much like the end of the world as the beginning of it. Wes meets her gaze, and what she sees there fills her to bursting with a sparkling, giddy happiness.

It's safety. It's love.

As Trouble turns merry circles in the sea and Wes slides his hand into hers, the wind tenderly lifts her hair from the back of her neck and whispers its secrets in her ear. With her eyes fixed on the horizon, she lets the ashes go.

ACKNOWLEDGMENTS

Everyone warns you about the sophomore novel. By some miracle, however, this book fought me only intermittently and without much bite. In many ways, writing it felt like coming home. It felt like letting light into a room that's been locked for a long time. I'm incredibly grateful to all the people who made *A Far Wilder Magic* possible and supported me every step of the way.

First, thank you to my editor, Jennie Conway. It's truly an honor and a joy to work with you, and I'm so proud of what we've shaped this book into together! Thank you, as always, for your incredible notes, for all your support of me and my work, and for loving Margaret most.

To my agents, Jess Mileo and Claire Friedman. Where would I be without y'all? Thank you for having my back and always steering me true. Although I initially despaired when you asked me to scrap the entire second half of the outline for this book, you were right, as usual.

To the Wednesday Books team, who have given my books the perfect home. A special thank-you to Mary Moates for all your hard work—and for always brightening my inbox! I also want to thank Rivka Holler, Brant Janeway, Natalie Figueroa, Sara Goodman, Eileen Rothschild, Melanie Sanders, Lena Shekhter, and NaNá Stoelzle. Thank you to Kerri Resnick for designing the jacket of my dreams, to Em Allen for the absolutely gorgeous illustration, to

Devan Norman for once again knocking the interior design out of the park, and to Rhys Davies for the incredible map. This book doubles as an art object thanks to all of you.

To the people who shaped this book. Alex Huffman, you gave me both the fuel and the spark that made this book possible. Christine Herman, you let me get away with nothing; I'm so grateful for suffering at your hands. Ava Reid, you encouraged me to write about and embrace the most vulnerable parts of myself, which made me realize what this story was meant to be about.

To the rest of the Mighty Five—Audrey Coulthurst, Elisha Walker, Helen Wiley, and Rebecca Leach—for moral support in life and in writing. You all got me through this year. Extra thanks to Audrey for the lovely blurb and to Elisha for your consultation on animal behavior. While I still may have taken a few liberties, rest assured that no horse will ever fear-neigh on my watch.

To Lex Duncan and Skyla Ardnt. Your talent and incredible work ethic inspire me every day. To Zoulfa Katouh, Meryn Lobb, and Kelly Andrew. Thank you for the early reads and your support (for me, of course, but mostly for Wes). To Courtney Gould and Rachel Morris, whom I would be genuinely lost without. I'm so fortunate to know such bighearted and talented people.

It wasn't easy to debut in 2021; however, so many in the book community were staggeringly generous with their time, energy, and love. Thank you, Joss Diaz, for being an all-around incredible person and for all your hard work on my preorder campaign. Thank you, Cody Roecker, for your Indie Next blurb and, more important, your friendship. You're going to take publishing by storm. Thank you to Cossette at teatimelit and Taylor (taylorreads), who were tireless champions of *Down Comes the Night*. I don't know what I did to deserve you two! From the bottom of my heart, thank you to DJ DeSmyter, Cristina Russell, Kalie Barnes-Young, Rachel Strolle, Mike Lasagna, Maddie at Books Inc. Palo Alto, Lori and Glen at Books Inc. Mountain View, Chloe (theelvenwarrior), Skye at the Quiet Pond, Charlotte at Reads Rainbow, Michelle at Magical

Reads, Allie Williams, Cheyenne (cheykspeare), Emily at Adaptation Brain, Cait Jacobs, and every member of the Queen's Guard. Your support has meant the world and made all the difference.

To Aziz, Fudge, Brandon, and Ryan—the final boss of BYB—for keeping me caffeinated and humble. Thanks for getting me out of the house and into the sunshine (and sometimes wildfire smoke).

To Mitch Therieau. Thank you for loving me. Thank you for helping me dream.

Lastly, to every reader who has picked up this book. Thank you, thank you, thank you. You are the reason I do what I do, the spark without which my writing is cold. If you need it, I hope you find comfort in these pages.

PHOTO © LISA DENEFFE PHOTOGRAPHY

ALLISON SAFT

is the author of acclaimed romantic fantasy, *Down Comes the Night*. *A Far Wilder Magic* is her second novel. After receiving her MA in English Literature from Tulane University, Louisiana, she moved from the Gulf Coast to the West Coast, where she spends her time hiking the redwoods of California and practising aerial silks.